Kipner's Boon

By Boz

Copyright © 2023 John Pettit
All rights reserved.

DEDICATION

To my parents who patiently allowed me to spill out countless made-up stories and flat-out lies as a kid but knew I was full of shit.

ACKNOWLEDGMENTS

This book is not too bad.

Book One

CHAPTER I

England, 1926

He felt the cold steel of the pistol's barrel against his chin, the sharp edges of the trigger against his finger, and the comforting leather from the gun's grip.

He had hoped to have the strength to go through with it, but his eyes kept wandering around his office with a peculiar distraction. There was the small, white clock on the wall to his left, which had a habit of stopping at exactly 11:17, the same time he had been notified by the hospital of his passing mother.

Three fingers of amber whiskey looked tempting in a crystal glass nearby, which had been a gift from an old college roommate. There was a small round of jokes on the irony he had graduated by slipping through the cracks as it had a tiny fracture at its base. Still, smiles vanished after hearing an escaping droplet's slow, eerie wail. Over the years, he had tried patching it, but the horrible sound continued through the same fracture with each drop. Something distracted him each time he thought of tossing it into the bin.

A suit he had bought at a secondhand store was draped over the chair in front of his desk. A matchbook from a laundromat had been inside one of the pockets with his name hastily scribbled across it. The address and phone number had come up empty without any records of it ever existing.

He had plenty of odd and downright spooky things lying around both in his office and at home that had come into his possession at one point or another. Each somehow felt supernatural, and he wondered if life had secrets. Despite old relics delaying him on past memories, they didn't prevent him from blowing himself away.

The pistol began to shake in his grip as he contemplated his next move, although he knew he lacked the willpower to do it. No matter how hard he tried, he had to find out what he had seen – what it had been. After what he had witnessed earlier, a seed had been planted in his mind that empowered his curiosity more than his fear and foreboding.

*

He allowed the haunting memory to be recalled even though it caused him to shudder. The rain had been falling for most of the morning in London earlier that week. If there had been a break in the weather, he didn't notice. He was cooped up in his office, wearing out a pair of binoculars while gazing onto the street below. It hadn't mattered to him he had lost track of time. He knew he had seen it before among the people as they went about their busy day, and he stayed confident it would reappear.

It had been repulsive.

Entirely unnoticeable by the pedestrians on the sidewalk, the source of nightmares crawled among them. Over them. On top of them. Long projections of tendrils jutted from its center portion, each coated with dozens of moist, swollen lesions that puckered and sucked as the arms slithered across each person. He froze in catatonic horror as he witnessed them wrap around people's bodies, using them as locomotion to weave through, and how the lesions tugged at their skin like a bottom feeder fish. Yet everyone was oblivious to its touch.

It had been only for a moment, but he was sure as the nearly empty bottle of booze on his desk that it had surfaced from a gutter and slithered into a crack between two buildings.

But there had been no further sightings of the creature since then; he had been locked to his binoculars for days at the narrow alley. By now, he was familiar enough with the area to know the two buildings that formed the passage met in the back at a tall brick shed that prevented progress. He had been waiting for days for it to retreat back out and barely sleeping or eating to avoid missing sight of it again.

*

Hours before he drew his pistol to his chin, he failed to notice his secretary enter his office. She was a young lady, barely in her twenties, with bundled blonde hair and soft blue eyes. Before she had worked for him, her only job had been helping her mother clean houses. While lacking in many secretarial skills like proper filing and efficient typing, she excelled at keeping him alive by making sure he ate and slept occasionally. He often neglected to show appreciation.

"Mr. Kipner? Are you okay?" she asked. He thought he heard her soft voice from far away. He didn't bother turning around to look at her after she tried again for his attention. It wasn't until she gently touched his shoulder that his eyes finally left the window.

"What is it, Natasha!?" he said more harshly than he intended, but it could return at any moment. He tried to retract the tone of his voice with a soft expression, but it went unnoticed by the young woman.

She quickly retracted her hand from his shoulder and took a step back. He was shocked to hear his own. He had never lashed out at her before.

"Natasha, I'm...I'm sorry. You didn't deserve that. My mind was on something else that caused it," he said.

She partially regained herself, but her voice was still shaken. She stammered before composing herself and said, "Mr. Kipner, Sir, I am heading home for the evening. Is there anything else you need me to do?" He answered with a hasty shake and abruptly turned back to his binoculars.

"Oh, there is a letter from a Mr. Delven Montgomery out of Cairo," she added. "I left it here on your desk this morning. The postman informed me it was urgent from the triple postpaid." She paused and waited for an indication he was listening. She received none.

"Goodnight, Sir. Have a great weekend."

He never heard the door close with a pleasant bang from an unappreciated lady. Deep in the night, he did not discover the letter until hours later.

*

Frustrated from a week of disappointment, he pushed his chair away from the window. Finally, he saw the letter from his old mentor. It read October 13, 1926, a week ago.

The letter was brief, devoid of small talk, cutting right to the chase. He wanted Robert to lead an expedition into the Belgian Congo to investigate a medical clinic whose communication had gone suddenly silent. Montgomery had financed the construction of a field hospital deep in the jungle to aid natives against diseases from European explorers. The letter mentioned an initial expedition, but they were long overdue.

A folded piece of paper fell out in the letter's envelope with Delven's handwriting on the back. "Native scribbling – familiar to you." The front side had harsh, random charcoal strokes from the likes of a madman. To Robert, however, it was the same creature he had witnessed. There was no mistaking it from the black puckered tendrils. It was no octopus. This was a creature of unknown origin.

*

In the early spring of 1868, a young Delven Theodore Montgomery III was walking along the boardwalk of what would later become Lower Manhattan. For several blocks, his ears perked up to an unidentifiable sound. Each time he investigated the sound, perhaps it came from an alley or behind a napping horse tied to a post, and there had been nothing. He felt uneasy as the day ended, although he was in a safe part of town.

As he picked up his pace, the sound grew closer in every direction. Turning down an alley to shorten his walk, he saw a man quivering and shaking while a dark, shapeless mass feasted on his body. It had numerous arm-like extensions wrapped around him, each pulsating, ripping his skin. It created clicking sounds while it ate its meal that struck Delven as either joy or pleasure from the tone and rapidness. It was as if numerous people were rattling noise makers. All the poor man could do was gasp for air in silent shock until the creature finished, dropping him lifelessly onto the cold, wet concrete.

Delven was frozen with fear as he stared. There were no visible eyes on the beast, but it motioned toward him. Delven thought he was following for a moment. Yet the creature slithered off like a spider to a nearby drain and, unbelievably, squeezed through.

It wasn't the only phenomenon Delven witnessed. Several years later, he saw it again when he traveled south to Maryland with his parents. They were riding a carriage through the country when Delven heard the same clicking noise again. His parents could neither see nor listen to it.

It was the same creature as before. Like a spilled pool of oil, it lay motionless at the base of a tall oak tree.

When it suddenly moved, its method of locomotion made Delven's skin crawl. It lurched up, forming the loose shape of a person devoid of appendages. The crest listed forward like a wave toppling onto the beach. A split second before it crashed down, numerous tendrils sprouted with such quickness they appeared out of thin air.

These tendrils, he guessed a dozen, reached out to nearby foliage and pulled themselves through every branch, leaf, and stem like water flowing over smooth river rock. The eloquence of motion was hypnotic yet terrifying. While he was no zoologist, he was confident it wasn't terrestrial.

As an adult, Montgomery was eccentric to most of his close colleagues. His estate was a museum of antiquities and oddities that would give anyone a reason to pause. To the general public, his interests were quirky. To the uneducated, his collection appeared to have no connection or theme. It was sporadic from different eras and geographical places. It wasn't uncommon for a mastodon's skull from northern Russia to be displayed beside a blood-stained, sacrificial dagger from Peru. However, he passionately believed there was a connection to every piece. To Delven, they related to something that was not originally from this world.

So there was no doubt or confusion from Delven decades later, in 1926, when he received scribbles from a madman from the Congo jungle. He had seen it before. It was still roaming the world.

He needed help beyond those he had sent on the original expedition to the hospital. It required people like him who had experienced the strange. Experts of the occult, the supernatural, and forbidden secrets were the type he needed. Experts like Robert Kipner.

*

The private detective finished the last booze as he leaned back in his chair and tossed the revolver back in the drawer. His head rang from drinking too much that day, but the liquor helped him cope with the anxiety. The office was illuminated by the full moon shining through the blinds. He craned his neck to peek outside without binoculars and watched the evening traffic move up and down the street. Seeing such sights rattled his consciousness, challenging it not to collapse and make him point a gun at his head. There had been times he felt it would, especially in the earlier years of his career when he hadn't seen quite as much.

The moon's brightness reminded him of the first time his eyes saw cosmic terror. He had still been an investigator, but his cases were what anyone would expect from his profession: missing women, blackmailed businessmen, cheating souls.

His living had been good back then as those jobs paid well.

One evening, he had been following a gentleman across several blocks, expecting the man to lead him to the brothel his wife suspected him of disappearing to every Tuesday between 9 and 10. Kipner was confident the man hadn't detected his presence despite the deserted street save for a few passed-out drunks.

Half a block from the brothel, the man suddenly disappeared into an alley.

Robert crept up slowly to the alley, carefully avoiding crunching gravel on the sidewalk. It was a particularly narrow gap between the buildings, just wide enough for a man to walk through without turning sideways. He didn't have a light source with him.

No sound came from the alley. Noise from the city elsewhere was far off, leaving only the cry from a stray cat and the rustling of littered paper.

He suspected the man was not far inside, so Robert stood motionless for hours. Finally, his ears heard faint movement that caused his hair to stand on end. Bone on bone crackled. His mind filled with terrible visions of fractured limbs and necks as the sharp, distinct sound ricocheted off the walls. It came from more than ten feet away, but Robert found it challenging to enter the darkness. He wasn't worried about being jumped by muggers. His confidence in a fight had kept him in business and gotten him out of sticky situations. But this was no mugger. The sound was grotesque and bizarre. Fear spread quickly in his mind.

The crunching continued for several minutes, rattling downward like a relieved spine at a chiropractor.

Before he mustered enough courage to investigate further, a long, scraping sound escalated from within the darkness against the brick walls. The movement was slow and steady with a high pitch as each scraping sound became closer than the last.

Robert backed slowly from the opening, stumbling off the curb's edge. He clung to the bathing light of the streetlamp like a child to a blanket.

Not bringing his revolver was an immediate regret, but the case had indicated a nonviolent solution. He wasn't sure what would emerge, but he would have felt more relieved and better protected.

Nothing prepared him for what he saw that night. It changed his lifestyle, his profession, and his philosophies. It wrecked the truths he held that led him down the paths he chose daily.

The first bone-like finger that pierced the thick, black darkness sent chills down his spine, and he found his mouth open in shock. Each extended piece of bone that reached out and curled around the lip of the building pushed Robert back another step before realizing he had left the comfort of the street's light.

A monstrosity of bone and black, ooze-like tissue pulled itself out from the alley. Numerous appendages arched from its body, encased in a thick, oily membrane with exposed, protruding white cartilage. Its movement, toppling over itself with sudden, jerking motions, was unnatural and unpredictable.

Sheer terror planted Robert's feet to the ground while his instincts screamed to flee. He could only stare at the behemoth as it crackled from the alley onto the sidewalk. It quickly made for a nearby gutter drain and, despite its proportion, promptly slipped through the grate bars and into the sewer below.

Suddenly Robert felt alone. The sound of absolute silence kept him frozen in fear until his mind finally broke through. He fell to his knees, shaking and sobbing uncontrollably as a soft, warm mist began to fall. It left no evidence of its existence, but Robert could not erase the vision from his mind. He tried to dissuade himself from it, blaming it on a few swigs of whiskey earlier, but he was still terrorized by morning.

Later the next day, he contacted his client, dropped the case, and leased a small apartment above the street where he had witnessed it.

He knew he was crazy to be so close. Even so, a second look was necessary to understand what he saw wasn't his imagination. By the end of the week, he had a truck bring his office furniture to the new location where he planned on staying for quite some time.

Although he would spend weeks staring out of the window in hopes of seeing the creature again, it wouldn't be until years later when he saw it the second time, this time a mass of black, oily tentacles and orifices emerging from the sewers and enveloping the people on the sidewalk as it slithered into the same alley it had once came from. It never occurred to him it might not be the same creature. He didn't want to think there might be more.

By then, he had given up traditional cases and focused more on strange macabre, and supernatural mysteries. During his findings, he had seen more horrific, forbidden sights, but his mind had grown a thick skin. Whether he was suppressing the fear or truly unafraid anymore, he could withstand the experiences better, or so he thought after a stiff drink.

There had been a moment when his fear of the creature mixed with the curiosity of seeing it a second time, which resulted in a stand-off between his revolver and him. Fortunately, his stubborn mind won the battle, needing to know how he and it shared the same world.

*

He tilted his head back and held the glass of ice-chilled whiskey to his forehead to soothe his aching head, but he knew it wouldn't help. The pistol wouldn't help. Even seeing the creature a third time wouldn't help either, but he had no other ideas. His fear had turned him into a walking obsession of morbid fascination.

For a moment, his mind traced over the words on the back of the etching. "Familiar to you," he thought as he gazed back out the window and into the night. Old Delven had been his academic advisor in college. Throughout his education and into Robert's professional years, Delven was one step ahead of everything he did. He even went so far as to use young Robert as a pawn to do his dirty work.

Back then, Robert had taken an interest in other careers besides private investigation. Foreign languages, theology, and ancient studies were just some of the classes he dabbled in between his major. He even earned a minor in historical architecture.

Studying abroad in Prague during Robert's fourth semester had been Delven's suggestion. It came after the young student's remarkable paper on a linear pottery settlement in Czechoslovakia's central Bohemian region. The report was filled with solid evidence of its specific location, all discovered after spending countless nights delving through forgotten books and ancient manuscripts to piece the puzzle together.

Delven arranged for a site to be formed and invited Robert to be his lead student on the dig with the promise of academic credit upon validating his paper's research. The entire gesture was highly unusual, but the college had approved with growing interest what Delven could find.

Robert was the first person at the site to uncover 7,000-year-old Neolithic tools. In spite of that, Delven quickly removed him from the project soon after. He was sent back to England to learn all records of his involvement before leaving had been erased. Soon, articles in several credited academic journals were published, with Delven's discovery showcasing photographs of him holding the same artifact Robert had dug up. As for the missing records, Delven regularly claimed he would look into it until the subject was forgotten. However, his naiveté and Delven's silver tongue convinced him it was standard practice.

Several years after receiving his Master's in Archaeology, Kipner was on a risky expedition he funded in southern China, hoping to uncover a lost palace built during Shang Dynasty. He had kept the trip quiet with only a few trusted colleagues to prevent the Chinese government from interfering. He had become desperate from so many of his expeditions thwarted by Montgomery already being there.

He ran into Montgomery, despite the secrecy, less than half a mile from Robert's target location. His old mentor told him he was "tardy to class," referring back to his days at the university, and that a great fortress had already been found and excavated. The discovery had awarded Montgomery considerable government grant money, private funding, and worldwide recognition.

Each time they crossed paths, Robert's plans were already known by Montgomery. Eventually, Montgomery would simply call Kipner before he had left on his trips, informing him with bravado not to bother leaving the house.

Robert was suspicious Montgomery had people spying on him, but he never discovered any truth to the theory. With little money left, Robert threw in the towel and chose the other profession he enjoyed private investigation.

*

He wondered why Montgomery had considered him for this expedition. His mentor had endlessly mocked and patronized him during his studies with condescending tones during his lectures. While Delven was never one to praise his students, he was the only one to never receive any positive feedback. It was as if Montgomery thought of him as only a puppet, and looking back now, it made sense.

The creature still hadn't shown itself from the alley it had entered earlier that week, and Robert suspected it wasn't about to. The wall clock still read 11:17, but he knew the night was growing old, which made his eyelids suddenly feel heavy, and he wasn't sure if he could make the walk home. He decided to hunker down for the night beside his desk with his suit jacket tucked under his head.

In the morning, he awoke to the sound of his secretary bending over him with hot coffee and some aspirin.

"Good morning, Mr. Kipner. From the looks of things, you need a doctor, if you don't mind me saying so, Sir," her voice was gentle, caring like a mother to her child.

Robert tried sitting up, but last night's whiskey told him otherwise. He laid back on the floor with a grunt. His secretary's delicate hand deposited pills in his hand and managed to help him swallow before he passed out again for several hours.

The sun was hanging low in the afternoon sky when he finally recovered enough to rise and sit in his chair.

Natasha, whom he had recently hired to replace the last eight, sat in his guest chair, his suit jacket neatly hanging on a hanger nearby.

He mumbled a thank you and tried explaining that her services would not be needed until the morning. Still, she rebutted to stay by pointing to the aspirin bottle.

He closed his eyes, giving up, and returned his attention to Monty and the sketch. The last time he had talked to him was before he had become a private investigator several years ago. All the same, somehow Robert knew Montgomery was well aware of the creature he had seen. He knew the sketch would rattle Robert's curiosity until he accepted his invitation.

He hated the thought of seeing Delven again, especially on his terms. Robert suspected it would be his demise one day. Yet he knew his insatiable appetite for discovering the unknown could never be satisfied.

"Natasha, I need travel arrangements to Cairo at the earliest available date," he told his secretary as she nodded. It would be a shame he couldn't bring her along. She had been the sharpest and most attractive of his hired help. He had never hired a bad girl to work for him; it was a lack of tolerance towards him they each had in common - except for Natasha.

"Mr. Kipner, arrangements have already been taken care of through Mr. Montgomery. That was part of the urgency behind the fast parcel delivery. I have the information right here for you, Sir." He was handed a piece of paper with dates and times listed chronologically. Scanning them briefly, he would be in Cairo by next week by way of the Orient Express. Something struck him as he reviewed the list of destinations the train's route included. Why such a roundabout, elaborate method to get to Cairo? Robert despised flying for lack of trust in human assurance, but even traveling by sea would have been quicker. Why had the postage been urgent to have him travel a slow route?

He would make the trip across the channel to Calais, France, where he would board a train that led through Strasbourg, Vienna, and Budapest. Once the Orient Express arrived in Constantinople, a combined collection of ferries and motor cars would eventually lead him down the Suez Canal to the port of Cairo.

It would seem Delven hadn't lost his touch to be eccentrically extravagant, Robert thought as he asked Natasha to keep an eye on the office. His only worry was he had retained his acquisitiveness.

CHAPTER II

France, 1926

Preparation had been brief due to the short notice, but he preferred traveling light. Dragging a couple of suitcases across two continents didn't appeal to him. Along with the suit from the secondhand store, he brought a large satchel containing his binoculars, a travel-size excavating kit from college along with a pocketbook of notes, a few pocket-sized foreign language dictionaries, a can of mosquito repellent, a few hygiene essentials, and his .38 pistol which was familiar with the contour of his chin. He decided to buy a few articles of clothing along the way to fit in with the varying styles. He realized after packing he was a little rusty from traveling as an archaeologist, be he didn't know what Montgomery had in store for him. He knew this expedition wasn't some archaeological dig, but it's what Montgomery knew him for. Asking to lead such a bizarre trip made Robert believe there was significance to his former career. He was better at adjusting to the situation at hand than preparing. While it had been several years since he was abroad, he felt right at home when traveling. It was in his nature to adapt to unexpected, sometimes unpleasant, situations, and he had good intuition when he trusted himself over others.

A motor car had been arranged to take him to Tobacco dock in East London where a fully laden cargo ship, christened the Jack Whistle, would sail to France.

The Jack Whistle was a tramp freighter constructed to haul anything but passengers. It had no fixed schedule like a freight liner, trading on the spot at whichever port they happened to be anchored. Robert went to the gangplank, immediately noticing he was not welcomed. The crew, carrying all shapes and sizes of crates, deliberately pushed him as they walked by. They made it clear he was in the way.

"It seems strange for your crew to be so resentful towards a paying passenger," Robert said as he patiently waited for the quartermaster to find his name on the manifest. Robert heard a dissatisfied grunt after he spotted his name and gestured for him to board. The quartermaster said nothing to him along with the crew. In fact, no one spoke at all, even to each other.

There was neither a reception by the captain nor anyone to greet him when he reached the main deck. He was unsure where his quarters were, so he tried the first door he came to with a knock and entered when there was no answer. Someone had tied a hammock to the walls, and a fountain pen with ink rested on a desk. He made himself at home, expecting the cabin's owner to return at some point. He took advantage of the opportunity to look over his pocketbook notes.

Among the numerous journals and records he maintained in his life, he had chosen the notebook he kept during his second year as a private detective. It included the first experience of the strange entity that had crawled into the sewers. He had notes scribbled hastily across dozens of pages in wild, chaotic order to get down precisely what he saw on paper.

One page brought his casual flipping to a sudden halt. He quickly located Delven's envelope and withdrew the charcoal image. In the upper right corner, surrounded by his chicken scratch handwriting, was his best effort at a sketch to replicate the oddity from London. There wasn't just a similarity or likeness. They were identical down to the individual strokes. He layered them on top of each other to double-check and held them up to see the two. There was no doubt - they lined up perfectly.

He felt uneasy while his fingers touched Delven's paper. It was coarse, made with primitive methods, unlike the pages of his journal. "Native scribblings," Robert read again on the backside. He couldn't come up with an explanation for the astonishing coincidence.

His attention was taken away when a small piece of paper fell out of the pocketbook. On it was written "umewindwa." The word was unfamiliar to him, although it vaguely resembled some East African languages that he remembered during his studies in college. He stared in confusion as he rapidly felt drowsy, sliding onto the hammock.

It wasn't the unfamiliar language of the word that puzzled him but that it wasn't his handwriting. As he dozed off, he couldn't recall ever allowing another access to the pocketbook.

*

The strident shrill of the ship's whistle woke him with a start. Night had fallen as he gathered his belongings, stepped out of his cabin, and into the fresh air. The twinkling town lights of Calais sprinkled the coast in front of him as the Jack Whistle had already docked. Robert neither heard nor saw anyone on board, which he found unsettling. He was no expert with merchant ship protocols, but he didn't believe an entire crew would be granted shore leave.

The gangplank was down, but the quartermaster was not at his post. Robert strolled down clumsily from the awkward steepness of the ramp. He wasn't sure what time it was, but he felt well-rested.

Down the length of the wharf, other ships were anchored with cargo. All were unattended. Something was off and didn't feel quite right. He glanced up at his ship's bridge, but there was no one there either.

Someone had to be up there to have blown the docking whistle. He had several questions, but no one was around to answer them.

The numerous lights that once sparkled from the city were now only a few, as if he was unwelcome. Heavy shadows hid the streets while he strolled, hoping to find the station. While an itinerary was given, specific directions were not. He wasn't too worried, though. Calais was small, so he was confident he'd eventually stumble upon it.

Half a block ahead, a stone-like, still, dark figure stood under an awning. It was facing away, preventing him from details, silhouetted in front of the lone streetlight.

Robert was eager to see someone since he left the ship and called out to the mysterious figure. Like liquid over ice, it flowed over itself in response to his voice, echoing off the buildings.

It collapsed briefly to the ground, then immediately rose closer to him. The motion was sickeningly quick. Robert wasn't sure what he had called out to, but he was sure it wasn't human. It had vague resemblances to the creature from his office, yet unique enough to itself.

His thoughts were interrupted by a sound elsewhere.

He could barely hear a voice crying out to him, but it was too far from understanding. It could be coming from inside Robert's mind; he wasn't sure.

Robert stood within feet of the abomination, having slipped into a dreamlike haze, hypnotically watching it approach. It towered over him, forcing him to tilt his head to its limits as it slowly bent over him. Although it possessed no eyes, Robert felt it gazing at him intensely and piercing into his brain. The creature was petrifying, and Robert found himself unable to move. While he had seen horrific sights before, this thing frightened him useless. His mouth gaped open to scream, but barely a whimper escaped.

The distant voice returned, much louder and close enough to hear. The investigator was so confused between sight and sound he struggled to differentiate where it came from. It sounded like his name repeating.

His thoughts were surreal, swirling through a kaleidoscopic vision, lingering on nothing more than a second. He couldn't focus on anything and struggled to make out the voice while fighting his fear of the looming threat before him.

Robert tried to prevent his mind from envisioning it attacking, but like a dream, he couldn't help himself. As if his thoughts commanded the creature, it matched the exact motion of what Robert had imagined. The black mucus glob was poised to pounce, and the two froze in silence for an eternity.

He became instantly engulfed like a cocoon, surrounded by a black membrane. He wasn't able to breathe from the tissue sliding down his throat.

His suffocation was unbearable as he slowly slipped unconscious. Somewhere far off, he heard his name again with more clarity. When his last senses nearly failed, he listened to his name, "Robert! Robert! Robert!"

The creature shook him violently, yet his vision shifted from pitch black to light gray. His blurred vision cleared, and he saw a man in a dark shirt and cap shaking him. He realized with a start he was lying in the hammock aboard the Jack Whistle. A black man stood over him with a firm grip on his shoulders. At his side was an older gentleman, holding a set of metal tongs and a crumpled sock in the other. He had a bewildered look while staring down at Robert.

"Mr. Kipner, it was just a nightmare. Everything is going to be okay. Just try and relax," the man said, releasing his grip.

Robert gathered his surroundings and felt the grogginess from a deep sleep. Although the experience felt real, he now understood he had been dreaming.

The man waking him wore a French naval uniform though Robert was unsure of what rank he held from his insignia. He was decorated considerably, as most of the left breast of his uniform was covered in medals.

Robert looked up at the man. "I suppose it was just a bad dream. Have we docked yet?" he asked the man.

"Negative, Sir," the man spoke English with a French accent. "But the tugs are bringing her around to port as we speak."

"You were making quite a fuss in your sleep. One of my crew members heard you, but none of us could wake you up. You must have been dreaming something fierce. You had lodged your own sock so far into your mouth we were worried the ship's doctor wouldn't be able to cut it loose."

Robert peered past the man and looked at the gentleman holding the sock. He vividly remembered every detail of exiting the boat and the creature approaching him. The way the sticky membrane felt as it latched onto him was still etched in his memory...as if it had happened. His suffocating episode had been a subconscious reaction from the lodging of his sock. That had been some powerful dream indeed! He had once fallen out of bed from a violent nightmare but never this severe.

It had been nothing more than a nightmare, no matter how real the sensation and fear had been. Kipner could feel his heart beating slow down, and he nodded to the uniformed man.

It wasn't as challenging to rise from the hammock as he had anticipated feeling no soreness or pain. However, he swore he felt the effects immediately after he awoke.

Helping Robert out of bed, the captain smiled. "My name is Harold Tee. I'm captain of the Jack Whistle. My sincere apologies, Sir, for not being available when you boarded yesterday. We had a particularly delicate piece of cargo that required my undivided attention. My ship's quartermaster and several of my crew members have been reprimanded for treating you poorly."

Shaking his head, Robert dismissed the necessity, but Harold insisted and informed him it had already been done. Robert raised an eyebrow at the gesture. Harold seemed to keep it strict on board. While rude, they hadn't treated him that badly. At least they allowed him on board.

Cheerfully the captain walked him to the gangplank while the Jack Whistle was gently tethered to the dock. He talked briefly about the ship's owners and how the name of the owners' son is painted on the hull, but Robert paid little attention to him. He noticed how difficult it was to ignore his nightmare. Momentary visions were flashing in his mind as he unintentionally retraced his steps. It was as if he hadn't woken and was still in some semi-conscious dreaming state. It troubled him that his mind hadn't forgotten the dream like all the others.

The tug boats had positioned the ship properly against one of the docks, and a gangplank had been extended to bridge the gap. Here, Captain Tee stopped and bid Robert farewell and good luck on his journey. Subconsciously Robert shook the man's hand and departed for the town's train station. He stepped off the gangplank and passed by a man he recognized as the quartermaster from the day before. Robert made a double take at the odd expression on his face. It was completely neutral, showing no emotion and looking through Robert as he walked by.

"It was a pleasure serving you. My apologies for my behavior. I have been reprimanded," said the quartermaster in a monotone voice. It certainly wasn't the same voice he had heard the day before.

He stopped and looked at the quartermaster. "Everything okay?" he tried to peer into his eyes as he asked the man the question. There was no eye movement.

"Everything is fine. I am sorry for yesterday's performance. I have been reprimanded," he said again.

From behind him on the ship, Captain Tee called down to Robert. "Don't worry about Mr. Thomas, Sir. He needs to tend to his duties now. Safe travels to Cairo!"

He felt an odd mood change as he walked away from the ship. It felt unsettling of the quartermaster's behavior and the sudden cheerfulness from the captain. Upon stepping off the dock, Robert suddenly spun around to the ship as a thought occurred. The captain and quartermaster were gone. How did Harold know he was headed to Cairo?

*

Calais was a charming northern town in France offering a large ferry port for locals and tourists. Its position was closest to England, overlooking the Strait of Dover, where the English Channel was narrowest.

Robert gazed back out on the water from the viewpoint. The skies were favorable for once, providing a magnificent view of the white cliffs.

The Orient Express hadn't arrived yet and wasn't due for a few hours, so Robert felt a stiff drink was in order to calm his nerves and rid him of his memory. It did the trick, and he soon forgot what he had witnessed. Now that he had a level-headed mind, he wasn't surprised that seeing the strange entity back home had influenced his dreams.

After buying literature and a newspaper, he returned to the train station and awaited its arrival.

*

The setting sun started to descend under the western horizon, enriching the area with a deep, golden hue. Six men, each wearing crisp, clean green uniforms bearing no emblems, heaved a tall wooden crate onto a train. It was improperly marked with odd symbols along one side, but no one working on the Orient Express seemed to care. A quick X was scribbled onto the manifest, and Captain Tee nodded to the train's crew and then led his sailors back to the ship.

A few cargo staff cautiously shoved it into a dark corner of the car, and the shadows gathered heavily around it. Something within softly stirred.

*

The ride on the Orient Express was a pleasure to anyone fortunate enough to garnish a ticket. It was a long train ride that led passengers through numerous countries known for their breathtaking scenery. Although the Orient Express was merely an international train at its heart, there was a sense of bravado and luxury behind it that drew people to hop on board just for the experience. Several routes now traveled from west to east, bearing the same name. Robert's private sleeping car was a part of the original train built in the late 1800s and stretched from Paris, France, to Constantinople in Turkey.

Once aboard the train, he learned his ticket gave him considerably more luxuries to enjoy. Montgomery had purchased the First Class option that granted him free alcohol and meals at any time. His room was accompanied by a private butler waiting outside his cabin.

After finding a comfortable seat in an observation car, Robert wasted no time ordering a libation and a long cigar.

Taking in the passing French countryside, Robert enjoyed himself feeling like a millionaire aboard the train. People treated him differently here, catering to his every whim and appreciating his thoughts during conversations. It barely occurred to him that it was an illusion created by Delven Montgomery's money. The fact it wasn't his own money was all that mattered to Robert.

While the accommodations were beautiful, the experience of the trip itself could have been better during the first leg. After a few hours, the train arrived in Paris, which was considered the true origin of the journey. He had hoped to get out and stretch his legs to see some of the city's sights, but the conductor only granted a short leave before they were headed off again. There was not enough time to leave the train station, let alone go sightseeing. The other passengers didn't care much, but he assumed most were locals. Even so, he regretted not having an opportunity to see some of the magnificent architecture of Paris.

In college, his primary focus was archaeology. It had been his passion since childhood, wishing to discover ancient secrets. There was a romantic idea he carried that learning something important in the past might shed light on a better future. Because of his founding love for old relics and sites, he also studied historical architecture as a minor. The two went hand in hand, and he excelled at both.

He reminded himself this was not a pleasure cruise and remained focused on the real reason he was there. He took advantage of stretching his legs at least, strolling around the grand station Gare de l'Est, which alone was a feast for the eyes. It stretched for as far as he could see in either direction, with abundant light coming in from all forms of glass windows that brilliantly illuminated the incoming trains. Even in a train station, there was a rich culture around him.

Only a few minutes had passed before he heard the first warning whistle, so he strolled back to the platform. Following a few turns, he was fed into a vast open chamber and froze in his steps. Numerous people clammed across a marble thoroughfare that joined both station wings, and all stood in place. Like statues of flesh, each held emotionless faces staring blankly in various directions. Silence vacuumed Kipner's ears it was so unnaturally still. The void of noise brought out the mad pounding sound of his blood pumping.

While he found it eerie, it didn't bother him as dreadfully as his accounts in England. He cautiously approached the nearest person, snapping his fingers in front. Puzzled, Robert gingerly touched their wrist and searched for a pulse. He found none, nor could he detect any breathing. He slowly withdrew his trembling hand and stepped back, staring. There was no reaction.

His back collided with another person, giving him a start as he whirled to face the newcomer. Like the first, it was solid like stone.

Robert's perspective was playing tricks on his eyes. Every gap between people seemed tighter than a moment ago. With every startled glance around, the avenues between them diminished.

Trying to avoid contact, he stepped through the grand hall back to the train as nimbly as possible. The strange phenomenon didn't mean his train wasn't still leaving, but when he reached the platform, the locomotion was silent and still. He wasn't sure if the people or silence unnerved him more.

His butler, Andre, was standing just outside the door to his cabin, rigid as death. There was no life in him.

It was bizarre, and although time wasn't passing by, his patience was. Seating himself beside the cabin window, he lifted the curtain.

Pressed tightly against the glass, a crowd gazed hypnotically at Robert. Their mouths gaped open and smacked shut chaotically. The sporadic, harmonious pucker sounds hastened into a unified word Robert thought was "umewindwa." He stumbled back, letting the curtain fall, feeling his heart jolt. His eyes fixed on the curtain as his curiosity eventually drew him back to it. Hesitantly he reached for the curtain and lifted it up. People were moving about as they usually would.

A solid knock at the door sent Robert over his edge. Andre leaned in with confusion and concern.

"Is everything alright, Master Kipner?" the butler asked, raising both eyebrows.

Robert gulped deeply, caught his breath, and nodded. "I'm fine, Andre. Thanks, I'm fine." Robert ordered a Scotch neat when asked if he wished for anything.

The Orient Express lurched forward on its long journey to Turkey. Robert took a loving sip of his beverage and opened the curtain as he watched the sun set behind him.

The peculiar word umewindwa remained in his memory after dismissing Andre for the evening. He stretched his legs on one of the divans and removed his shoes. The nonsense word was puzzling until he remembered the piece of paper from his notebook. It must have influenced his imagination, he thought. He had experienced a strange episode of delusion caused by the stress of his trip. But he had touched them! How far could a misconception go?

While sifting through his satchel for his toothbrush, he paused after spotting a Swahili dictionary. He never owned a Swahili dictionary. He vividly remembered what he had brought along.

The toothbrush was long forgotten. He lifted the book out of the bag and thumbed toward the back. Through the series of strange coincidences, somehow he knew umewindwa was in there. He had guessed the phonics to be an East African tribal language, but that had been a rough guess.

Reaching the U's, his finger began sliding down the page with trepidation. The words were listed alphabetically along a left column, then scanning across the page to a column on the right gave the English term or phrase.

The word was there, and he began tracing his finger to the right, where the English version was listed. "It's a window" was the translation.

"It's a window?" Robert said out loud. The people had been beside a window, but that didn't make sense. He looked back at the book and realized his shaky finger had shifted to "umewind." Feeling foolish, he quickly scrolled his finger over to the proper translation.

"You are hunted."

CHAPTER III

Germany, Austria, & Hungary, 1926

The stop in Munich was as equally short-lived as Paris. News of the leader of a rebellious organization being released from Landsberg prison gave caution to everyone. The conductor placed a restriction to remain within eyesight of the train at all times. Boarding was brief as possible.

Only a year earlier, Munich had faced an attempted coup. The man who had led the few thousand armed men sent to Landsberg for treason had suddenly been released far ahead of his five-year sentence.

Robert's mind was focused on the next stop after he checked his itinerary – Vienna. A cold, solemn stare filled his eyes as he leaned back and thought of his missed opportunity to visit Vienna during his senior year.

An evening downpour had caught him during his walk home from a demonstration. The night air was heavy with a thick mist and pungent ozone.

He ducked into a small bus stop that barely fit two people, but it kept him dry. Another had already taken a small, wooden bench; she was huddled against her coat while the rain fell on her shoes. Most of the light from the streetlamp was shielded by the shelter's roof, making it difficult to get a clear view until her head turned to face him. He wished that night he had picked another bus stop.

She was a featureless black mass. It was a sitting blob of black substance. With a smooth motion, two glowing soft yellow eyes appeared as they peered up at Robert. They were narrow and piercing like a vengeful judge full of prejudice.

"Uh, hi. I'm not looking for any trouble, whatever you are. Just needing some shelter from the rain," Robert said disturbingly, too casually. He was still determining where his confidence had come from and if he was fooling himself.

There was a violent vibration inside of him. Perhaps too abrupt to be coincidental, his head surged with a sudden migraine headache. He grabbed his head, holding it tightly as he doubled in agony. He tried to yell at the figure, but his voice failed him.

The frequency of the vibration changed like the twist of a radio knob. It became more focused and less obtrusive, and he could just make out words formed by the humming.

"Bousche Rose" was all he could make out from the chaos raging in his head.

Abruptly it terminated with a shriek from a scared girl. "What's wrong with you?" she asked. The migraine vanished with the sound of her voice. He opened his eyes to see a student sitting on the bench. There was no sight of the creature anywhere.

He sheepishly apologized and darted back into the rain, leaving the overwrought girl behind. Later that night, he shrugged off the experience from a lack of sleep.

"Bousche Rose" played a part in missing the opportunity to visit Vienna. In late October of his final year, his university began accepting applications to study in Austria. By then, he had forgotten the strange episode at the bus stop.

On the day the names were announced, he was invited to a meeting to be introduced to the other students. The name Rose Bousche on the list jarred his memory, and the same girl was present among the others. It was clear by her expression she remembered him, and her eyes flickered. It wasn't the light's sparkle but a self-illumination that mimicked the same yellow glow from before. There was the faint trace of a smirk, then her head shook from side to side in a wild blur like a horrific seizure. It abruptly ended with her attention directed casually to the faculty members as if nothing had happened. He quickly excused himself from the trip when he realized no one else had witnessed it.

Looking back at the experience, he wondered if he had been hunted all of his life by something. He sometimes kept passing off these occurrences as delusions that felt too real. There were moments of doubt he could shrug off the memory. While he had experienced difficult or impossible phenomena, he often told himself it was a figment of his imagination, juxtaposed over reality like mistaking a detail in a photograph for something else.

*

There was a considerable delay when they reached Austria on their way to Budapest. A vigilante had dislodged the rails outside of town. The train's chief operator announced after arriving in Vienna to expect a full day before repairs could be made. Robert was the only delighted passenger and quickly stepped off the train.

He began his tour wandering, taking in the sights, the sounds, and the beautiful smells that wafted in the air around him. He avoided tourist areas and tried blending in with the locals as he did his business. Perhaps subconsciously, he walked by Burgtheater, the Austrian National Theater, that afternoon.

Grand Neo-Baroque archways, leaping above the street, captured Robert's excitement and pulled him inside. Lavishly long, red velvet-lined stairs took guests from the entrance to the theater beyond.

A new film by Greta Garbo, "The Joyless Street," was premiering. The theater pamphlet he picked up briefly described the film portraying poverty in Austria after the Great War, among greed and corruption. Soon Robert had a ticket in hand and acquired a comfortable chair toward the back of the great theater among a crowded audience. He cherished the stage's history while recalling Mozart had performed there centuries ago.

Midway through the film, out of the corner of Robert's eye, half a row of people had turned their heads and looked directly at him. He quickly snapped his attention to them, but they watched the film as if their heads had never moved. This repeated several times as the movie continued, but they turned their heads each time Robert tried looking. He felt his eyes were playing tricks on him from the projection's reflection and tried disregarding the occurrence. Yet when he chose not to turn his head, he was confident he could see numerous people staring at him from the corner of his eye. It tarnished his experience.

When the movie concluded, and the lights were brightened, no one in the busy theater glanced at him. By then, he felt it was undoubtedly his imagination or an optical illusion.

Outside, the sun was already setting lazily over St. Michael's Church. He thought about dinner and locating a soft bed for the evening.

Up to this point, he could get by without understanding the Austrian language. Still, he soon struggled to ask simple questions. When he tried hand gestures, people scoffed and hurried down the street.

The sun had long since set, and streetlights were reflecting off the cobblestone avenues when Robert found himself upon the steps of St. Stephen's Cathedral. His legs had slowed considerably from the unusual walking he had experienced that day, and his mind was becoming hazy from being overwhelmed by the sights. Just behind the magnificent structure was the Hotel Konig von Ungarn, where he longed for his bed.

As he passed the cathedral's front doors, something caught his eye yet again. Unlike the theater, however, the vision remained. Melted with the shadows was a hooded robe figure. Robert made a double take. Although the figure's face was obscured by the low draping hood, Robert could feel them watching him.

"You're following down a path that will lead you astray," came a hushed, raspy voice from under the hood.

"I beg your pardon?" Robert replied, stepping toward the figure, but the figure melded further into the shadows.

"You are beginning to draw attention. Do not meddle in his affairs as he lures you into a pit." The voice was harsh and masculine.

Robert's eyes had been glued to the figure, trying in vain to make out features, but for a brief moment, he peeled them away to scan his surroundings for others. What had been a reasonably crowded street moments ago was now deserted.

He consciously thought of the nightmare he had days ago on the Jack Whistle and wondered if he were dreaming in some hotel. Despite the phenomenon of the missing people nearby, he felt conscious and in control of his actions. His senses were working, which was a sure sign of being awake, as nearly any dream dampens at least one of them.

"Are you talking about Montgomery?" Robert asked as he turned his eyes to the figure, but he was talking to no one. Among him, people walked down the sidewalks on either side of the street as if they had always been there.

A puzzled look crossed Robert's face as he cautiously approached the doors to the cathedral where the man once stood, but the doors were closed and locked. There was nowhere the person could have gone.

He felt perspiration drip down his forehead as his heartbeat spiked momentarily. He knew what a hallucination was. Although it had been years ago when he was much younger, he had been introduced to nitrous oxide when he befriended a chemistry graduate. During that time, the reaction to the chemical was still new, undetermined of the effects and consequences. Yet, there was no doubt that he had witnessed the encounter this time.

He closed his eyes, rubbed his face, and took a slow, deep breath as he headed toward the hotel. A hot bath, a stiff drink, and perhaps a cigar were what he needed after the long day. He wasn't going to let the disturbing occurrences ruin it.

*

By the time the train reached Budapest and neared the end of its line, Robert had contemplated his strange experiences. If taken by itself, the nightmare he had experienced on the Jack Whistle could be passed off as just a nightmare, albeit severe. However, a tiny seed of doubt would grow if the events from Paris and Vienna were included. It was becoming difficult to find excuses and justifications. Some of his old cases had pertained to the unusual and unexplained. He had witnessed strange sightings of inhuman people that he disregarded as freaks of nature. A mind eventually runs out of logical reasons to explain extraordinary occurrences. A bipedal caveman spotted roaming the forest is nothing more than a large bear on its hind legs, and these were only misinterpretations of reality, Robert thought to himself. He never actually saw them in the theater while they watched him. He only felt they were out of the corner of his eye. He couldn't make out any details of the figure at the cathedral because the shadows were so thick near the door. There were explanations for each encounter, but Robert's problem was that he needed these explanations to calm his mind.

Bad luck was also following him. Apart from the vandalism in Vienna and short stays in Paris and Munich, the train had yet another delay in Budapest.

This was so severe he worried he might have to seek a motor car for transportation the rest of the way to Cairo.

Robert had arrived in Hungary sitting in the seat he had grown accustomed to on the long voyage. It comfortably reclined and was padded with velvet upholstery. While he couldn't nap in it, his body fatigue from sitting all day had been minimal.

Outside the train, several armed Hungarian officers gestured for the passengers to remain on board. Robert heard a woman ask in English what was going on, but she was somewhat sternly answered in Hungarian. The officers had little patience with passengers and refused to answer any questions. There were a few words Robert thumbed through his Hungarian dictionary to understand. All of it pointed to demanding obedience to their commands.

The officers were searching for someone, but they were doing so through the windows from outside. The more adamant passengers were promptly escorted off the boardwalk into a large unmarked shed.

This peculiar behavior lasted longer than Robert would have liked. He was about to pick up a nearby newspaper when the conductor addressed the passengers, making his way through the cars.

"Ladies and Gentlemen, we have been ordered by the Hungarian police to vacate the train immediately. I am unsure of the reasoning as no one wished to explain. All I can recommend is to gather your belongings as quickly as possible and follow whatever instructions the police give you," his worried voice broke as he gestured to passengers off the train.

A similar uproar came from the train car ahead. None of their questions was answered, so Robert got his bag and stepped back off the train, walking by a police officer.

With great nimbleness, the officer violently shoved Robert and sent him tumbling toward the station entrance. He barely kept from planting against the door.

There was little time to be irate while being hastily corralled through the train station doors. Two rapid gunshots came from back on the train, but he couldn't determine who fired or at what.

The train had stopped at Keleti Station, Budapest's central depot, for international and inter-city transportation. It was an impressive structure with high-reaching glass windows along the front facade that allowed tremendous light during the day, along with the numerous windows that ran on either side of the 600-foot-long platform. Four tracks entered the station, with additional ways parallel outside, typically reserved for cargo transportation.

Anxiety began gnawing at him from the inside as his situation became more and more peculiar. It suddenly dawned on him the Orient Express had parked outside rather than entering the station correctly. He hadn't planned to get off the train in Budapest since he wasn't fluent in Hungarian, but he had no choice but to follow the masses and oblige to the police requests.

Numerous officers herded the crowd of passengers into a large storing chamber at one corner of the station. It was typically used as a storage facility for awaiting crates to be loaded onto trains, but it was currently nearly empty, which was fortunate for the people as they needed almost every inch to fit everyone.

Several of the officers were referring to clipboards. Around him, Robert heard various languages, and he could safely guess they were all about their predicament. Once the officers were satisfied with whatever they were discussing, one addressed the crowd. He began speaking in Hungarian, then repeated in several languages.

"Ladies and Gentlemen, we apologize for the harsh conditions and treatment. We have assured no injuries were experienced by those who complied with our requests. It is for your safety you continue to comply with our instructions so that you may board your train quicker and be on your way," he said upon reading from his clipboard in English.

After a considerable long time of repeating himself in, what Robert counted, 8 languages, the officer shouted only in English. "Is there a Mr. Robert Kipner in attendance, please? Robert Kipner, if you are here, please step forward."

Robert's blood ran cold from hearing his name called, but what made it turn into ice was the people's reaction to hearing it. Suddenly every set of eyes turned to stare straight at him. He was surrounded by strangers, but unlike the theater in Vienna, his eyes didn't deceive him. Everyone, some of whom he had never seen, gaped at him with morbid curiosity like a mortician to their first cadaver. With slackened jaws, their mouths dangled wildly, swaying side to side. Their eyeballs rapidly filled with blood and then curled into their sockets.

Robert knew he was hallucinating like before. The shock of hearing his name called out by the officer had triggered some fear mechanic in his brain to create the illusion.

His name was repeated in English both times. He couldn't see the police officer very well, but it felt like he, too, was staring straight at Robert through the crowd.

His natural ability to remain calm in complex situations drained away. Panic-struck, he knew he couldn't stay in the crowded room. He might not know what the police wanted of him, but he decided not to wait and find out. Glancing around the room, I saw a large sliding door in the back for loading. He began pushing through the tightly packed crowd, but it was slow going. Some people refused to move, and as he progressed, they began to suspect he was the wanted man. Shouts in various languages rose above the crowd as he could hear them calling out. He pushed harder, trying to slice through and get behind the crates to hide.

He felt his arms held frequently and thrashed each time to free them. When he finally broke through and dashed around the crates, He saw some of the police had cut through, and a few were running from outside. Eyeing the large metal door, he doubted he could wrench it open before they arrived.

With all his weight thrown against it, the rusty iron door began moving inch by inch. The door just needed to open a few inches more to weasel through. He heard the voices of the officers approaching behind him though he dared not look.

A hand reached through the door, followed by another who had vice grip strength. His shoulder and forearm were restrained.

He was not lightly handled. His body was shoved to the ground with tremendous force and then handcuffed. Robert didn't put up a fight, but they threw punches against his kidneys before hitting the back of his knees with a blunt object and dragging him outside, his shoes scraping against the dirt.

Suddenly his vision went black.

CHAPTER IV

Hungary, 1926

Little was spoken and always in Hungarian. Robert was shoved into a vehicle and drove what felt like for hours. Two men sat tightly against him on either side, one of whom had a strong cologne. The car began its journey along a smooth paved road, but at some point, the vehicle turned onto gravel, and the speed reduced to a crawl.

When they came to a stop, he was dragged onto and across the rough gravel that scratched at his clothes. Being kidnapped triggered the memory of a case he had never solved several years ago. It involved a young boy kidnapped by what police had suspected were common criminals. After finding no solid leads on the case, Robert was hired by the child's family to investigate further. It was a lengthy case, and it took several months before he landed a lead. Finally, an anonymous tip led him to an abandoned cottage several miles outside the town of Bath. The information proved truthful, but the tip had been a setup. The same criminal who had kidnapped the boy had placed a trap on Robert. Before he had reached the door, he was grabbed from behind and restrained with thin, strong cordage, and a bag was pulled over his head. Robert's feet stumbled, and they dragged him inside. His struggles to keep up were rewarded by a rigid metal object striking the back of his knees, sending him to the ground and shrieking in pain.

The case had been a disaster to Robert financially, mentally, and physically. He had only been promised payment with the boy's safe return; Robert barely escaped with his life, unable to save anyone. It took weeks before his legs healed, and his mind never fully recovered from the cannibalistic sights he witnessed. He hoped he wouldn't experience more than déjà vu with those he now faced.

Strong hands gripped his shoulders and snapped his nightmare to a quick close. Abruptly the mask was pulled off, and Robert squinted his eyes at the afternoon sun. He was unbound, but his escape was denied by the numerous armed men surrounding him.

They had brought him inside a large house, nearly a mansion in volume, and sat in a brightly sun-lit room. The decor was plain and simple, with a sizeable desk and one ornately carved, high-back chair. Through bay windows beyond, three bronze animal statues rose above properly trimmed hedges.

Kipner didn't recognize the person seated in the chair but felt like he should. She was an attractive woman in her early 40s with jet-black hair tied tightly into a ponytail and piercing bright green eyes that demanded attention. Modestly dressed, her dark plum suit gave authority in high class.

Her attention was undivided on him. There was a brief, nearly undetectable smirk of appraisal at the corner of her mouth.

"It would have been simpler for both of us had you raised your hand, Mr. Kipner," she said as she leaned back and crossed her arms. On the desk, Robert noticed several papers fanned out and a dossier envelope over to one side. His eyes lingered too long, and she perked up.

"Don't worry. All of our information on you shows great interest," she said, casually sifting through the pages. "Master's degrees in archaeology, six years employment under Dr. Delven Montgomery, including twenty-seven site discoveries, twenty-three of them renowned, thirteen journal publications, and a knack for being ahead of your field." She leaned back again, tossing the pages back onto the desk. "That's one hell of a resume for six years in the field, but you only worked independently for a few years. Why quit so soon?"

He wasn't sure who she was and wouldn't start trusting a kidnapper. Her eyes were sharp and cunning, and he suspected she was several moves ahead of him.

"I wanted to take up knitting," he said with a deadpan face, but she took the sarcasm with a patronizing grin.

"I can see your sense of humor is on par with your naivety." She paused at Robert's raised eyebrows. "Dr. Montgomery, Mr. Kipner, is a fraud. His methods are sloppy and unprofessional, and he slings his money around to cover up the mess he makes."

He couldn't help but sense the irony in her words, thinking back to how much must have been spent to buy the police to escort everyone off a train just for one person. She had wealth and, from the sound of it, was closed-minded to the thought she was just like all the rest.

To look uninterested, Robert occasionally glanced through the window behind her, watching a gardener trim the hedges.

"What has he got you involved with?" she asked with raised eyebrows.

The question threw him off. If only she knew the truth about how he felt about him. Perhaps she already knew and wanted to test Kipner's loyalty to Montgomery.

"I really am not sure, to be honest, Miss...?" he asked to gain her name.

"Mr. Kipner," she said, ignoring the gesture. "He has been meddling in my affairs for several years. I have approached him countless times to keep him out of my business. There have been... unfortunate accidents, shall we say, that he suffered, yet he continues to insist on being confrontational."

The gardener continued trimming the hedges, but Robert's trained senses could tell he was deliberately close enough to eavesdrop on their conversation. He had cut the same area for several minutes.

Robert returned his eyes to her. "He is a bit of a pest, isn't he?"

The look she gave showed she agreed perhaps too much. She opened a drawer in her desk and withdrew a stack of bills, but Robert didn't recognize the currency.

"Mr. Kipner, I want Montgomery. I don't care how – tied up, in a cage, or in a coffin. I know you have done some cold jobs you weren't too proud of in the past, so I know you have it in you."

She was right about her information. He had been in a fair share of gunfights, surviving by avoiding being fatally shot and savvy with a revolver.

He remembered his last gunfight, which involved himself back at his office. It continued to plague the back of his mind whether he would pull the trigger someday.

Pointing the gun at someone other than himself had always been more straightforward. In one case, Robert uncovered a madman hiding in a ransacked, forgotten home. He knew there would be no negotiations with the crazed man's gun when Robert arrived, so Kipner sneaked quietly into a small closet hoping to jump him, but when Robert closed the distance enough to knock him out from behind, he shot the man instead before realizing what he had done. There had been great suspicion from the coroner's report Robert had been point-blank behind the lunatic when he unloaded his revolver.

Robert's attorney never would come clean, saying who the stranger was, only to keep his mouth shut. By the end of the trial, he was acquitted by an unknown eyewitness giving a statement they had been present and were threatened at the time had Robert not killed the man.

"My gun is really just to light my cigarettes," Robert said, returning his attention to the lady while smirking at himself. She was not amused by his wit this time.

"I won't ask this again," she said as she slid the stack of bills over. "What do you say? You would be free to return to your true passion of digging in the dirt."

The thought was unsettling. While a gun in hand was not foreign, no one had ever offered him a case that involved murder. He was a private investigator, not a hitman.

"After such a warm welcome from your happy helpers, I would be inclined to accommodate any request you ask," he said as he glanced around the room. None of the goons had a shred of emotion on their face, as if they were stone.

"I don't even know who you are, lady. Before I can commit murder for you, I'm going..."

His voice trailed off as his eyes returned to the gardener outside. He had stopped pretending to trim the hedges and was staring directly at him. At first, Robert thought the man had mascara running down his face. A dark hue surrounded both eyes; rich, black streaks ran from them to his jawline. His lips, ashen and horribly chapped, curled back, revealing unnaturally cracked teeth with dark residue along the gum line.

However, his eyes, or lack thereof, locked his attention and filled him with fear. Bright, blood-red stitching harshly sealed his eyelids. His sockets were void of eyes.

Robert was pulled forward against his will and crashed through the window within inches of his face. Like thunder, the gardener's voice resonated around Robert, shaking him to his teeth. It boomed in his ears, and he could feel warm liquid ooze out from them, pulsing with each word spoken.

"She will use you as her tool, then discard your carcass. You are being hunted by creatures of a world your mind cannot conceive. Nothing can be done to avoid the inevitability of them feasting upon your savory flesh, sipping your blood from chalices of obsidian, and imprisoning your soul to an eternity of ultimate pain and torture. Your fate shall only be a boon with his guidance. Do not betray him, or you will die from what hunts you."

Robert recoiled back, screaming out. His hands struck out before him, frantically pushing the abomination away.

His wrists were gripped by a vice. Both arms became restrained, and he was fixed on the spot no matter how much he tugged back.

"Mr. Kipner! What has gotten into you?" came a voice far off as if at the end of a tunnel. It was vaguely familiar as he struggled to focus on the sound. There was a moment where he questioned himself, wondering who he was. He rushed through his memories, trying to find an anchor for stability, but they were scattered everywhere.

The voice returned a second time, this time closer and more irritated. "Mr. Kipner! Get a hold of yourself!"

Mr. Kipner? Where had he heard that name before? It was close to him like a forgotten childhood toy discovered decades later. He began to cling to it, frightened he would lose it.

Suddenly with a loud snap, he felt a surge of an avalanche pummel his mind as his psyche returned to him. His consciousness came back into focus, and he remembered who he was.

Around him were men with weapons drawn, two holding him by the wrists. Before him was an attractive woman with a ponytail, irately yelling at him.

Realizing he had been struggling against the men, he relaxed, trying to catch his breath and calm down as he looked at her.

"I'm... I'm sorry. I have no idea what came over me. I'm fine. I'm okay now," Robert said as he felt the vice grip ease off his arms.

The woman peered closely into his eyes, like searching a room for a hidden item. She reached out and firmly held his chin, turning his face. Apparently satisfied with what she saw, she let go and stepped back.

"You have seen things you were not meant to witness, Mr. Kipner. That is not how a common lunatic reacts to a psychotic episode. What did you see?"

He wasn't sure if he wanted to reveal how delusional he was to her. With each encounter he had experienced since he left home, he struggled to understand what was causing these visions. There had been bizarre occurrences while he had been a private investigator, but nothing like this.

He recalled a case he had taken several years ago for an elderly man. The gentleman claimed a wild dog chased him each time he walked by the wharf. Both pest control and the police investigated the area. Yet, they couldn't find any signs of an animal besides the street rats. The man was insistent on his attacks. Robert had tried to suggest altering his route, but he was determined to stay with tradition. Enough money was offered to entice Robert to at least search the area.

Unlike the authorities, he had come across the beast. It had been scrounging around a pile of trash as he approached. Its head suddenly perked up to look at him, but a second head from the animal raised up just below the other. Robert immediately froze, thinking he had come across a pack of strays and didn't want to have to put them all down.

A soft red hue reflected from their eyes as they peered with demoniac intensity and illuminated as they gazed at him. The beast turned toward him, and two heads were fused to one body, one of a hyena and the other resembling an ordinary dog. Taking steps slowly backward, Robert hoped he would feel the comfort of a doorknob or the handle of his car as he reached behind him, unable to take his eyes off the approaching creature, but his fingers touched only air.

Something told him his pistol would be ineffective towards the two-headed dog. Even so, his revolver came out of its holster in a shaking hand. A few blasts from his gun, mere warning shots around the dog, went unnoticed. The creature didn't flinch at the noise. He knew he was in over his head, and his mind began scrambling for an idea.

His feet crossed over a manhole cover, and he imagined enough time to lift it and dive in before being mauled to death. Risking a quick look around, he couldn't find any other options nearby. He holstered his revolver in preparation for the crazy plan.

When he lunged at the manhole cover, it hadn't crossed his mind how heavy it might be to lift it. The creature paused momentarily, both heads slowly wavering next to the other like a cobra. Robert couldn't force his fingers around for a good grip; he could only wedge two fingers into the lift hole used by the poker. He strained with all his might while hearing the creature rumbling low growls in a warning.

The cover moved just enough for Robert to desperately dive into the darkness below. He heard the uniformed scream from the dog's heads and felt the unbelievable pressure of their jaws biting down on his shoes. For a moment, he was dangling a lure to a fish, suspended in utter darkness by the beast's jaws wishing nothing more than to devour him. His free foot kicked wildly against the dog's face, but the other head nipped quickly, lashing with its teeth and holding it firmly.

His head rapidly filled with blood, and his focus became dizzy. He feared he would lose consciousness soon if he didn't free himself. Far below in the darkness, flowing water echoed off the stone walls. At this point, he cared little if it was clean as long as he could reach it.

The pain intensified as the creature slowly pierced its teeth through the shoe's leather and bored into his flesh. His arms hung helplessly as he reached for his revolver, but the gun had slipped out while dangling upside down.

The dogs slowly pulled him back up, inch by inch, scraping his body against the rough edge of the open hole. The dog's size was immense. No amount of effort from Robert could free him.

He recalled the moment his fate was doomed had it not been for the old man. Just as his hips reached the lip of the hole, several gunshots boomed nearby. They sounded louder than his revolver, gaining the dog's attention. It immediately dropped Robert's feet and glanced toward the noise. The sight of the man holding a shotgun made them flee into the night.

Robert didn't bother looking up as he lay panting. His eyes were still blurry, but they soon recognized his client standing over him.

"I thought, for sure, I had it that time," said the old man, holding a smoking sawed-off shotgun. He was dressed for a hunting trip with a flat cap cresting his bald head.

"You weren't lying about the strange dog," Robert said, thanking him. "I wasn't expecting you down here, but I owe you my life."

The old man shook his head. "No, you owe me nothing. I have never had a chance to get close enough to shoot the mangy beast until now, thanks to you. That two-headed critter won't return soon since I skinned its nose with buckshot. Still would like to have that shot again."

Robert stood up and shook the man's hand. He said he wasn't prepared to face such a creature, not knowing what the beast was.

"Creatures from Leng," the old man said as he looked in the direction the creature vanished. "Rotten beasts sometimes find their way to this world. The problem is, no one seems to believe me, so no one helps."

Robert looked like he had stared directly into the sun too long. His face was raw from the rough dive, his feet ached from puncture wounds, and he was trying to understand what he had just encountered.

"Leng, some hellish place in the Dreamlands filled with damnable hoofed things that worship beasts from the moon and other impossible monstrosities your mind wouldn't understand."

It was far too much for him to take in at once. Robert's knees buckled, and he slumped to the cold, damp street and rested a hand against his head. He had been foolish to take on a client who was so blatantly crazy... and yet he saw a dog with two heads.

There was a battle inside him between logic and imagination. His psyche regulated the fight, hoping the damage wouldn't be too severe. He could have been influenced to see differently. Perhaps it really had been two dogs, and the old man's ranting of what hunted him every night on his walk altered his vision.

The memory flashed through his mind in a fraction of a second. It brought him back to the lady awaiting an answer with impatience in her eyes.

"I saw my imagination getting the best of me," he told her.

She stared at him for a moment longer. Her expression clearly showed doubt, but she let it go.

"Mr. Kipner, I am beginning to wonder if I have the right person for the job." She grabbed the stack of money and flipped the bills against her fingertip. "This is more than you make in several years. I'll even consider a bonus if you're quick about it. And it's Genevieve Mitzkowitz "

At this point, Robert just wanted a stiff drink and to sleep. He couldn't trust whoever this woman was, but she didn't like Montgomery any more than he did. If the situation came up, could he kill him in cold blood? He had ruined much of Robert's career and life. Being a private investigator had been enjoyable, but he wished to be among his old colleagues, digging and discovering ancient knowledge every day. It had been his passion from childhood, and Delven Montgomery ripped that away from him with his incessant and peculiar luck of always knowing what Robert was about to do. It infuriated him as he stood there watching this unknown woman hold more cash than he had ever seen.

He took a swipe at the money in her hand, but she quickly pulled it away from him and wiggled her index finger.

"We can't just let you leave with the reward, now could we? There is a necessity to complete your job first. Run along, would you? You'll be escorted back to the station, as I'm sure your train will be leaving any minute."

His desire for a stiff drink weighed heavier than noticing how curious the Orient Express had remained waiting for him to board. He needed an hour or two of peace and quiet, and a few dollars given to the manager guaranteed that. He found an empty car and closed his eyes with the glass to his forehead.

There was dread on his mind as he tried to relax with visions of a tropical beach or breathtaking view of the mountains. Nothing could distract his attention from what kept following him during his travels. "You are being hunted." Delusions were becoming more sinister and felt real, especially the gardener. A person's face could not distort in such a way, but he struggled to find a suitable, logical explanation. It was like hallucinating from opium. There was no way of understanding what he was seeing other than mental projections carried out by his imagination. Yet when he reflected back on them, they were vivid and detailed. None of his memories had voids or haziness behind them.

Each one was as rich and clear as the next. He hardly believed hallucinations would linger as long.

He regretted he hadn't asked the man more questions, but he was adamant his mind was exaggerating reality. Deep inside his mind was the seed of an idea that itched to grow. Could things like a two-headed dog come from a place called the Dreamlands? What if they were not hallucinations?

His sore legs stretched out on the bench, and his back leaned against the wall beside the window. Outside there was more sand and fewer trees. To capture and organize his thoughts and experiences so far, he retraced them step by step in his mind.

As the train slowly approached its destination, his mind felt uneasy with each recollection.

CHAPTER V

Turkey, 1926

Eyelids began to droop as the train slowed to a stop in Constantinople. The conductor had opened his cabin door and gently shook Robert before he awoke. A groggy mind managed enough to focus on disembarking from the train. A few people held signs with names written on them, but none matched his. He withdrew the itinerary from his satchel and carefully reread it for the hundredth time. All it said was to wait outside the station.

Hours passed, and the sun began to set. The hard floorboards of the station battled a war against his pacing feet the longer he waited. It was as if a mystical power interfered with his arrival in Cairo. Each destination had yielded some delay and, chained together, played it hard to discard as coincidence. It was approaching nine o'clock, but foot traffic was still prevalent outside Sirkeci station. The thought of a hotel crossed Robert's mind, but Turkish wasn't his strong language. He doubted his ability, and perhaps his trust, to acquire directions from the locals.

The earlier nap kept him wide awake as the station emptied out. The next train was expected at dawn, and Robert found himself quickly alone. At first, there was a peaceful calm from the sudden silence after the day's commotion, but it quickly gave way to a jarring presence. It crept slowly across the boardwalk towards him like a shadow from a stranger. The void of sound reached a vacuum, and the distant sounds of the city were muted.

Robert's nerves were jittery, but he chalked it to a lack of drink. Deep down, it was more than that. He was losing the battle against his delusional mind and that these visions might hold some truth. He felt entirely sane other than when strange phenomena occurred. There was nothing wrong with him as far as he could tell. He recalled reading somewhere that an insane victim doesn't know he is insane, but he was so sure of himself!

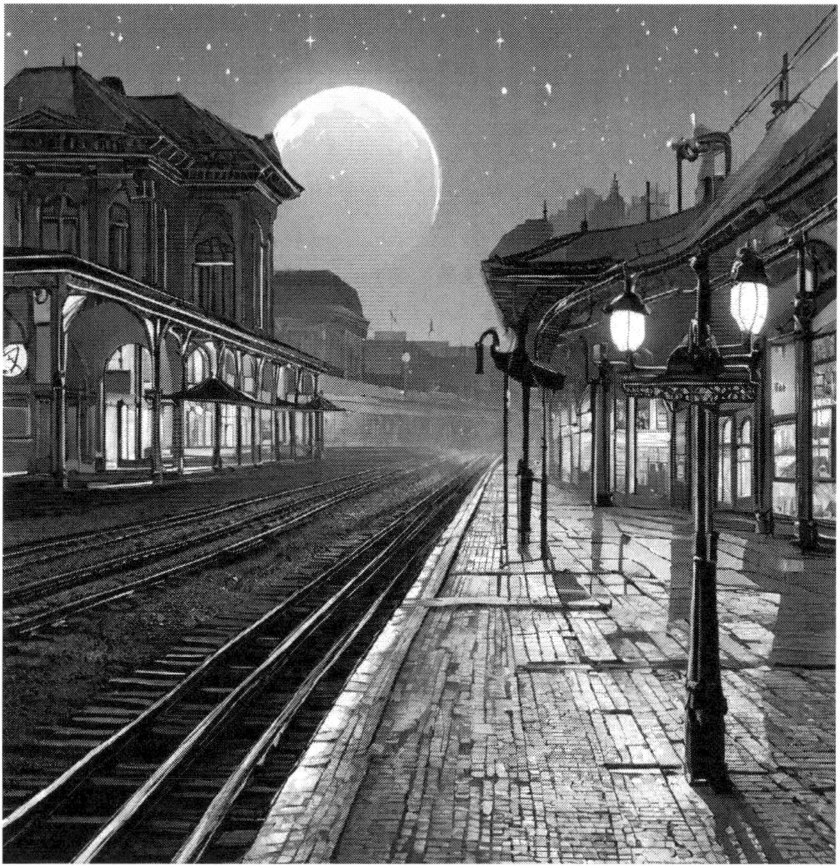

So that led to the possibility that all of it was real. Suddenly the shadows around the boardwalk gathered closer to his epiphany. Instinctively he drew his jacket tighter, despite the mild night air.

Desert trees swung hypnotically and unison, pushing the shadows nearer like an imminent tide. The soft breeze shifted the shadows towards him further. He drew his legs to his body to avoid being touched.

The hair on his neck perked up, realizing the breeze was all in his mind. The trees around him were still and silent, yet the shadows continued to move as if rustled by the wind. The corner of his eyes kept seeing figures at the end of the boardwalk.

He longed for the morning sun to crest over the distant hills and rid him of this curse! He dared not look at his pocket watch for fear that time had stopped to toy with him.

A whisper, raspy and dry, came over his shoulder from behind. "You can't be alone when you're hunted."

Robert shrieked with fright and leaped from his bench, drawing his revolver towards the voice behind him. He was entirely alone. Only the wall of the station was there. No one was within sight in any direction.

"Are you so sure?" came the voice again from behind. He whirled around with such haste and toppled from buckling knees. He gripped the gun tightly as he pointed into the darkness.

No other voices were heard that night, nor did the shadows move in the moon's reflection. Robert did not sleep. His eyes were bloodshot like a night with the bottle, and his vision was hazy.

He staggered up from the iron bench for something wet to soothe his sore throat. Against the instructions, no one arrived that morning either. He made due by finding outdoor seating at a nearby cafe so he could keep an eye on the station.

Usually, he detested the taste of water, no matter how clear it was. No one served alcohol, and he was too thirsty for coffee. He surprised himself with the soothing feeling against his palette. A lack of sleep began tormenting his mind, so he dared close his eyes briefly, but rest didn't come.

The hot sun shifted slowly and rotated the shadow of his glass across the table. What little patience he had remaining was gone. He was getting further behind schedule.

After paying his bill, his wallet held only a few pounds. It wasn't supposed to be a survival trip. He had waited at the station long enough. It would be easy to follow his own path to Egypt assuming he found suitable transportation.

There were only so many options other than camels. Motor cars were unreliable in the hot desert and cost too much. A large map of the region at the station greatly tempted him to attempt reaching Antalya and shipping across the sea to Cairo. It had only been a few years since Turkey won independence, and bandits on the trade route drew concern. However, the memory of the short trip across the English Channel suddenly made him wish to remain on land regardless of danger. At least he knew he could protect himself with a gun.

Camels were abundant from numerous herdsmen bringing them in to be bought and sold. Acquiring one would be simple, but Robert also desired a guide.

An open market had been built, and caravans nearby prepared to travel. His ears were plagued with dozens of languages spoken at once, but he soon deciphered an English-speaking merchant. He was standing near a makeshift shelf clustered with clay pottery painted by an amateur's hand.

"I'm looking for a guide to Cairo," he began but was quickly pushed aside by others seeking the merchant's attention or needing to get by. The crowd tightened in the area, and Robert clung to his satchel.

He tried speaking like the others, screaming as loudly as possible. "I SAID I NEED TO GET TO CAIRO!"

A quick shake of the merchant's head was all he got for an answer as his attention turned back to the customers.

His arm was suddenly gripped by numerous merchants wishing to sell him things of no interest. He had feared Genevieve's goons had caught up with him, but the merchant's handling was less severe. With great effort, he freed himself from all but one person with dark skin and round, wired glasses. The man's eyes were not cheerful but determined. With a brief nod to one side, he was off in the crowd with Robert still in hand.

There was little effort needed to spot Robert in the market. He was slightly taller than the natives and much paler. His suit was in better condition, and he wasn't wearing silk. He thought his transportation had finally arrived, so he followed the stranger.

He was drawn out of the meddling crowd and close enough to speak without being overheard.

"Do not waste your time with him. He is a trickster of poor pottery." His breath could physically be felt and tasted in Robert's mouth.

"Who are you?" Robert asked the man, trying to turn his head to one side to avoid the ghastly smell. It only made the man pull him to within an inch.

"That doesn't matter right now. I'm your only way out of the city because you look like you're in trouble. You shouldn't shout so loudly that you're lost. It's how you wind up missing."

The rancid breath was not growing tolerable to Robert, so he tried to end the conversation quickly.

"Good tip. I don't suppose you can take me to Cairo?" He looked into the eyes of the stranger, noticing his peculiar bright blue eyes as if for the first time. There was only one blue-eyed Turk within 50 miles. This man wasn't a native, either.

The grip on his arm loosened to where Robert could shake it free. The stranger wore silks across his Western European face. He carried several satchels over his shoulders and numerous pouches tied to his belt. Robert could feel a large hunting knife strapped to his leg.

With a flash, the man darted away, glancing back to see if Robert was following. He led Robert through the streets of Constantinople with the ease of a veteran guide to the city. At no point did he slow or wait for him. It was everything Robert could do to not lose sight of him.

Their expedition through narrow alleys ended close to the ancient stone walls of the city. A sudden sidestep by the stranger brought them into a private courtyard surrounded by buildings. A poorly constructed stable had been put together in one corner, where he heard the grunts of several camels. The camels had not have been treated well if they had been kept there long. The ground was dirt with the pungent smell of dung.

"You wish to go to Cairo?" the stranger asked rhetorically. "You will never make it. The roads are riddled with devilishly-minded men who want nothing but to rob you of your wealth and life. I cannot guarantee your safety, but I can ensure you don't stray too far into the harsher regions. But I don't come cheap." He leaned against the stable, which listed dangerously to one side and caused the camels inside to stammer their feet.

Robert was in over his head and felt like declining was not an option. At this point, he thought he was too deep to back out.

"I only have a few English pounds left, I'm afraid. Do you trade? Perhaps I have something in my satchel," as he began rummaging through his case.

He was interrupted by a quick raise of the stranger's hand. "I'm not interested. What I want is your service for one simple task if you should survive the trip."

Robert raised two eyebrows and inquired about elaborating.

"I'm looking for an individual in Cairo. Someone has hired me to return him, dead or alive. You will help me locate him and kill him for me if the need arises."

The bluntness didn't faze Robert as he had heard it before. It was beginning to seem everyone wanted him to kill someone. No part of being an investigator meant killing people, yet that truth eluded many clients who felt otherwise.

The notion of being indebted to this man, whom he knew nothing about, was the last thing Robert wanted, but his eyes moved down to the large knife. Robert could shoot him if he drew it. Was it the only weapon he carried?

"I'm looking for someone in Cairo as well, so I wouldn't be able to spend any time searching for your bounty," replied Robert, looking over his shoulder to the sound of a gate closing. The gate hadn't been closed when they entered.

A thin, tight smile appeared on the stranger's face. "Perhaps the two are one and the same, thus, providing a quick solution to that dilemma." He stared at Robert, his smile fading.

A small goatee was on his chin, mostly concealed by the silks. His fingers were covered with a gold ring and decorated with various gemstones. His motions were cat-like, smooth, and calculated as he navigated his way there, and he bore a look of a man who doesn't enjoy hearing the word "no."

Kipner caught something in the man's voice that gave him a sudden start.

This stranger knew Montgomery. Kipner could read the facial expression clearly enough, after spending years observing people's faces as a detective.

With a tap of his knife, the stranger gestured towards the stable with a tilt of his head. "Get on a camel." Robert's revolver was in his satchel, so he complied.

There was no hesitation from the camels. They seemed docile, but no one attempted to climb on them. Each had correctly been saddled and bags attached in preparation for a long journey. It had been years since he was on the back of an animal, and they all had been pack mules. The beast showed signs of aggression as it was being mounted. A snap from a whip the stranger produced yielded the animal to submission.

A jovial expression crossed the stranger as he gracefully leaped on the other camel. Leaning over, he patted Robert on his shoulder, perhaps a little too firmly.

"Don't worry. Our paths crossed at perfect times as we both are in need of the other's assistance. It wasn't fortuitous that we chance met but alignments of two destinies. My task will be brief and you will be on your way before you realize it."

Their camels needed little encouragement to leave their stalls and exit the courtyard through the same gate that had closed. Robert turned back to see it had closed once again and latched.

"Something the matter?" Robert was asked as they turned and headed toward a city gate. If visions followed him, he had better embrace them or shut his eyes indefinitely.

Being in the stranger's company proved better than he had feared. While the man had yet to reveal his name, he wasn't lacking in conversation. From his accent, Robert could only guess Greece or Italy. He never had much of an ear for nationalities. When he spoke, which was often, it was with a worldly flair of current news and historical recollections but seldom paused for conversation. Whether he was exaggerating or making it up, it didn't matter to Robert. He had been occupied with the dread of traveling the desert on the back of a camel. His body already ached from the awkwardness of the saddle, and the rhythmic movement of the animal's walk continuously sent ripples up his spine.

At the end of the fifth day, Robert was told they were over halfway to Israel. He tried calculating the length of this trip, which was longer than intended. Perhaps it was the reason his actual transportation never arrived. By now, Robert feared Delven had replaced him and sent the expedition.

With a day's ride left to the northern border of Israel, they had picked a quiet spot with an outcropping that had provided shade during the day. Conversations had run their course, and the two had spent much of the last two days in silence.

"There is a gentleman named Robert Kipner," the stranger said that night as he stared into the fire's flames. A look of disgust filled his face as he told Robert about him. Robert tried to conceal his surprise the best he could but feared he would give himself away.

"The person who hired me said he would be heading into Cairo. Lanky fellow with long hair and round glasses. Told me I should expect a fight out of him. So far, you've been the only person I've seen running that direction, but you sure aren't lanky."

He finally looked up with a serious expression. They locked eyes for several seconds.

"Come to think of it," he trickled out his words. "Your hair is kind of long."

Kipner stared him down, feeling perspiration build on his scalp. Robert had once been lanky, but his age had won the war on his gut.

The stranger was suddenly crouched to lunge, but at the last moment, he feinted and laughed.

"I had you worried for a second, didn't I? You have been so serious the entire trip, barely saying a word." He leaned back, still laughing at his sense of humor, which Robert was not sharing. Robert's gut said the stranger did know who he was and only toyed with him.

"Is he a criminal of some sort?" Robert asked.

The man shook his head as he returned to staring into the fire. His eyes were glazed and moist from the flame.

"No, no criminal. I was told very little about the guy except to keep him from reaching Cairo. I have a feeling he slipped past me. That's where you come in."

"You still want me to do your dirty work for you?" He was dancing on eggshells, deeply concerned that he needed to sleep soon.

The man shot him a glance that told him he had been too bold.

"You're paying for my services." His voice was cold as steel. "Besides, you're a bit of an observer. I saw you sitting at Sultanahmet. You stuck out like a tourist, but you had the confidence of a seasoned traveler looking for someone in a sea of people.

"I was only having afternoon tea. There had been no one to wait for. Perhaps you misread me," retorted Robert.

"So the man had been spying on me for who knows how long," Robert thought. His eyes wanted to go to his satchel and draw his gun to end this before it got out of hand, but he dared not agitate the stranger. The hunting knife was always closer than Robert's gun.

The man gritted his teeth in frustration. "Do not toy with me. It was clear as the sun you were scanning the crowds for someone."

"That doesn't make me more of an observer than the next person."

The knife suddenly appeared in the stranger's hand and flung into the sand; it was nearly buried. His motion was sickeningly quick.

"Enough of this!" he spat. "I've spent long enough track, and I'm not making any money until he's brought in. So you're going to help me, understand?"

There was a moment Robert wanted to continue his sarcasm to see if he could cause the stranger to explode with frustration and make a mistake, but he didn't wish to push his luck.

A brief nod eventually calmed the man down. "You had better get some sleep. I'll keep first watch. We have a long trek tomorrow."

Although he was aware of the cold nights, Robert had little understanding of surviving the desert. For the trip, the stranger had brought blankets that provided warmth while he slept and kept desert crawlers from stinging. The nights had been comfortable, but he slept very little, fearing an attack. The stranger kept his eyes towards the darkness all night instead.

CHAPTER VI

Return to the Dreamlands, 1926

Troubling dreams were tainted by his experiences on the trip. He later recalled sitting on the Orient Express looking out. Outside, the stranger squatted near a campfire made of blue flame. His legs, longer than the average human, were bent sharply at the knees and towered over his head. He radiated an unquenchable desire with outstretched arms, equally as long, if not longer, as his legs. His back bent so tightly his spine should have shattered. He held this position with a devilish grin, staring intensely at Robert through the window.

From behind the train station, which was in the simple form of a large trapezoid, the horrific creature from Robert's office shambled into view. Its body emitted a wet puckering audible from deep lesions covering its membrane. Each sore smacked loudly with kiss-like desire.

It drifted past the stranger, heading towards the train with the same motion as before: numerous tendrils jutting out and retracting with sickening speed.

Other figures, ghost-like apparitions, manifested aboard the train, but Robert barely noticed. They formed a line like waiting to buy a ticket to a freak show, and the beast guided smoothly over their bodies. Their flesh was stripped away effortlessly by the black arms like jelly from its mold. They were caught in a trance, mindlessly walking off the train toward the creature.

The beast wrapped around him, sending the odd sensation of cool water trickling over the skin. It caused a ripple of goosebumps down Robert's arms, which rapidly enlarged to welts from the intense suction of the lesions. Filling with puss, they grew to the size of golf balls while pulsing with life, individually rising and falling in chaotic patterns.

Kipner was torn out of the car through the window, slicing violently against the broken glass as it shattered. His body was dragged across the coarse ground covered in hot sand where the creature engulfed his body.

Suddenly the memory from Jack Whistle came to mind, and his dream shifted worse. As if his thoughts controlled his environment, his experiences tarnished his subconscious mind.

As the tendrils slid around his face towards his mouth, it dawned on Robert he was conscious of his surroundings. He was having a lucid dream, a phenomenon where the dreamer knew they were dreaming.

With a start, the creature released its grip around him and backed away with such speed that it disappeared instantly. The skin on his arms and legs was smooth again.

The moonlight illuminated the train from above, sending the cabin into heavy shadow. A lone passenger remained on the train with a fedora hat. It was a man in his early 60s with graying dark hair. His stature was small, adorned with a tailored three-piece suit that matched the white hat. Braced with his resting hands was a snake handle cane, its crystal eyes shining through the shadows. Clean-shaven, the man had a handsome smile, bookmarked with wrinkles, that was suspiciously welcoming.

Delven Montgomery. He had aged since Robert last saw him with a leaner look around his waist and a replaced, discolored tooth beside his left canine. His smile hinted he was about to sell snake oil.

Shadowed by the car's roof, he exited and approached Kipner with a quick tip of his hat. He addressed the detective with sheer joy in his voice.

"There you are, Mr. Kipner, there you are! I had hoped we would have a chance to visit before you arrived in Cairo."

Kipner answered with confusing silence and a raised eyebrow.

"Don't worry. Rest assured, you are still very much asleep," Montgomery said, maintaining his elaborate smile.

With the dramatic flair of a circus ringleader, Delven removed his hat and extended his arms out in either direction.

"Welcome to the Dreamlands, my dear son!" He paused in awkward silence, expecting more reaction from Kipner. He received none. Kipner glanced around, unimpressed. While there once was a campfire of blue flame nearby a moment ago, now it looked just like any ordinary train station. The only difference was the unnerving vacuum-like silence. He could hear his heart pumping blood through his veins.

Realizing Robert wouldn't react as he had hoped, Delven lowered his arms and continued, "You're clever enough to know you're lucid dreaming. Very well done, indeed! I knew I chose the right person for this expedition."

His confusion passed, and Robert quickly adjusted. "It sounds to me like you're communicating from somewhere else. Or are you just from my subconscious? How would I know the difference?"

"How would you, indeed?" Delven answered with a question. His overuse of the word, indeed, was already annoying Kipner. "Nothing I can say would give you assurance to believe me, so let's drop the silly talk and discuss the matter of why I am here."

He turned back to the train with a casual gesture. Shortly Delven was in his original chair in the dark shadows of the car. Robert was a few steps behind him.

Settling in, Delven rested both hands on his cane and let his snake smile return.

"Mr. Kipner, it has been a very long time. Since you are here, we can assume you have disregarded animosity towards me all those years ago. It was just how our field worked. First one there," Delven said with a wink at the end.

Kipner refused to return any gestures or smiles as he recalled the many times Delven had been one step ahead of him as if he could read Robert's thoughts.

"Sure, Monty. What brings you to this part of the train tonight?" Robert said with a cynical smirk.

The flashy smile instantly disappeared on Montgomery's face upon hearing the nickname. He loathed it even before he knew Robert at the university. Its origin came from his mother. The childhood name lingered too long with her, and he was often mocked in school. He discovered the secret late in Robert's short-lived career with him. His only regret was that he didn't get to use it more.

"Enough of this," Montgomery said, gritting his teeth. "I thought we were past our differences, but I was obviously wrong. So listen closely. Despite our history, it is imperative you reach me in Cairo safely. The expedition I am forming will require you for reasons I have no time to explain here.

"The companion you travel with is Ronan, who is not working for me. Genevieve Mitzkowitz, the lady who kidnapped you in Budapest, is doing everything in her power to keep me from safely completing this expedition."

Montgomery showed genuine concern, though Robert knew better. He had lied to him many times in the past.

Robert was unsure how he knew about the kidnapping or who he had traveled with. The phenomenon where two people could converse in the same dream was changing his theory on spy involvement. Perhaps after all this time, he had a unique secret that allowed him to closely watch Robert.

"What does she have against you?" Robert asked. He had never heard her name mentioned during his time working for Montgomery. While a man of mystery, there was no doubt of the attention he drew from his eccentric behavior and lavish lifestyle. Eventually, someone would feel bitter about things he had gotten away with. There had been plenty of reasons that Robert had witnessed.

By Robert's third year of college, he had become star-struck by Delven, who had become his faculty advisor after he changed his major from law to archaeology, which had been a considerable task at the time.

After the spring semester, he was invited to shadow Montgomery's crew in Egypt to study the Great Sphinx. It was a dubious honor, and many declined the offer, but after his success in Prague, Monty especially handpicked him. The sting from the previous trip had long since healed and was forgotten through rose-colored glasses.

The trip took most of June, and Robert had hoped it would result in a position after he graduated. But the trip went differently than he had expected.

The bad luck began when a terrible sandstorm nearly obliterated them shortly after setting up camp. It lashed their tent and buried almost all their equipment under the coarse, hot sand. Some of Montgomery's crew tried fleeing in fear the fabric would fail, only to become lost forever in the storm. The trip was forfeited, but Montgomery remained cheerful and optimistic. Their luck changed on the third day when the storm blew itself out. The storm had eroded enough sand near the Great Sphinx to reveal an undiscovered hidden passage. Montgomery took the small crew and journeyed down the dark path through thick dust clouds. Remarkably they came across a discovery that shook the foundations of Egyptology. Drawings and hieroglyphics clearly described terrible aquatic beasts surging from the sea, enslaving many Egyptians and dragging others back into the depths of the dark waters that covered countless walls. They led to a room of mummified oddities with the likeness of the painted walls.

Robert was too awestruck at the findings to notice one of the crew had sprung a trap. Everyone felt vibrations that intensified as they dashed through the labyrinth of passages.

Along the sprint back, other traps that had been cleverly set thousands of years ago sprung up before them. The result was terrifyingly catastrophic as stone slabs began to descend rapidly in their way.

One of the crew members slipped and fell in a panic. A stone slab descended so quickly hesitation would have meant certain death.

Looking back years later, Robert knew there had been time to help her, but Montgomery said it would be their deaths, too, and urged them to leave her behind. Her screams were brief, echoing off the walls, and suddenly silenced.

His crew abandoned the job once back at camp. He regretfully reassured them remaining would have jeopardized everyone, but only Robert bought his lies. One crew member was the lady's brother, and he had to be physically held back. His eyes were filled with so much hate and vengeance he would have killed Montgomery if not restrained.

Robert had often heard her screams in his nightmares and wondered how far Montgomery would go for his own gain. Montgomery had created a monster from his selfish greed and heartlessness. How many others had he made in the same manner?

Sitting in the train car, their eyes locked in the moonlight. Delven's eyes reflected a silver sheen against the black silhouette outline, giving them a demonic glow. His equally devilish smile returned.

"Genevieve and I have a long history together that I need not get into details now. If I know her well, I know she has several tricks. I can take no chances as this trip is absolutely critical."

A lingering sensation of impending doom lurked just out of the corner of Robert's eye. Much like his experience in Vienna, nothing was seen when he turned to look outside. It was as if he was stalked by something that knew precisely when to hide from sight. It was coming from both sides of the car. Some evil wanted to rend him. The feeling was something he couldn't fight – a gathering of impenetrable entities that would soon overwhelm him. Panic set in, and he felt his heart race. He wasn't used to panicking; he hated the feeling.

Montgomery nodded and gazed out the window. "Yes, our time draws short, dear Mr. Kipner. We are trespassers in a world not meant for mortals. Linger too long, and the horrors will devour our flesh, which reflects back on Earth. So listen to me very carefully."

He leaned mere inches away from Robert's face. A strange, pungent aroma drifting from Montgomery's shirt reminded Robert of a wild animal's musk.

"Do not aid Genevieve in any way, lose Ronan as soon as possible, and find me in Cairo. I'll wait for you in ---"

A shriek came from just outside the car. The sense of doom appeared abruptly and threw them both off guard. It was kneeling just under their window out of sight, but with sudden fervor, it launched itself up and over the rim of the window, seizing them both with wicked, clawed hands. Its elongated fingers quickly wrapped around their necks, collapsing their windpipes.

Even Montgomery, who, up to that moment, had been at ease in the sinister world, was now terrified. His eyes bulged while being ripped through the window. The horrors hinted at their disdain for the train as Robert was pulled out for a second time. Kipner had little time to reflect on how Delven had wished to converse with him on board.

It was barely humanoid, with a face lined with short, stubby horns along its jawline. Its eyes were only thin slits giving off a soft yellow glow. Four gnarly, twisted horns curled from the top of its cranium. The flesh of the bestial creature was caked in ash that flaked with every move. It was an inhuman species of unworldly sights no man was meant to see.

Although he never saw the creature approach the train, Robert had braced himself, expecting an attack. His muscles were tense, and the monster's vice grip didn't completely close his windpipe. Struggling in harsh gasps, he reached for his revolver, which was in his hand. It was as if he compelled the gun to materialize in his mind.

Three rounds were fired before the creature reacted. It let go of Montgomery, who keeled over, gasping. The extra arm went for Robert's revolver and, with incredible speed, ripped the weapon from his hand. It gave a gurgling chuckle that was wet and sputtered thick mucus. The holes from the gunshot closed as if they had never been shot.

By then, Montgomery had recovered and caught his breath. Through coughing spasms, he forced himself to speak.

"I'll be waiting in Tahrir Square. Find me, Mr. Kipner, as soon as possible." He rose, tipped his hat as Robert struggled for his life, and boarded the train.

The locomotive vanished in wispy, dark purple smoke and green flash, leaving Robert to his fate.

His vision was beginning to darken. Hopelessness crept over him, giving him little reason to fight and allow the creature to finish him off.

With but a pinprick of eyesight left, Robert thought of his revolver and how he had conjured it by thought alone. Montgomery had called this place Dreamland since everything appeared dreamlike. His mind was blank, brought on by fear, but he forced himself to focus on the finger-like tendrils gripping his neck. Pointing his mind to nothing but the pain, he thought of the fingers loosening and letting go. He thought his imagination made him feel the effect, but he could breathe again as the fingers were repelled slowly.

Robert dove out of arm's reach of the creature. The adrenaline pumped loosely in his veins, and the odd sensation of awakening from a dream began. He could feel the disconnection of the Dreamlands, and the lack of contact infuriated the horror as it tore the train station to pieces.

Kipner faded away from the Dreamlands as a chuckling voice off in the distance reminded him of Montgomery.

"I chose the right person after all," it said.

CHAPTER VII

Egypt, 1926

Despite the harsh, sweltering conditions for the past week, Ronan had been very talkative, while Robert preferred to be silent.

The last night the two were together, however, Ronan was unusually quiet. There was a foreboding in his eyes while staring listlessly into the small campfire. They were close enough to Cairo that he had insisted on keeping the fire hardly more than embers to attract less attention. City thieves were bolder than desert raiders as they had a safe place to retreat if a robbery got out of hand. Caravans were more frequent here before taking different routes, which gave brigands more opportunities.

Robert enjoyed the silent conversation compared to the endless rantings and intensely embellished stories Ronan was fond of spouting. It troubled him, however, that something was clearly on Ronan's mind.

He prodded at the hot coals, letting a few flames lick up in the air, then broke the silence with a confession.

"Luck did not bring us together," Ronan began, letting each sentence linger into silence. "Genevieve has her doubts after meeting you. Your little daydreaming episode troubled her, and you lost her confidence. She sent me to make sure the job was done right."

Ronan's eyes, watery and red from staring into the fire, slowly drew up to focus on Robert. There was no hiding the tense animosity he possessed. What he had against Robert beyond her assignment was anyone's guess, though. Ronan was nothing more than a mercenary to the highest bidder. For a better price, Robert was sure he would have worked for Montgomery instead.

"We are meeting someone tomorrow morning who has been closely monitoring Montgomery. Genevieve has paid well for the information, and I'm here to ensure you don't waste it. Once we know where your little school teacher can be found, I'll tell you precisely how her wishes will be carried out."

"To ensure you take this seriously, I'll let you in on a secret. Genevieve ordered me to kill you both if you try and double-cross her. That's why I will be intimately close to you during your meeting. Honestly, it would make this miserable trip worthwhile if I could draw blood on a few souls before heading home." Ronan drew his knife and slowly scraped it across a nearby rock with a crazed look, making the camels shudder restlessly.

The private investigator drew up his best poker face. Increased pressure to take out Montgomery was putting a sour taste on Kipner's trip. Monty might be horrible, but Robert wasn't a ruthless murderer. The eagerness, once felt back home, of the expedition had all but left him. He wasn't wild about siding with Montgomery. Still, Genevieve now put him in a difficult spot to make a decision that suited him.

An especially cool, crisp night had greeted them, and the moon had risen brightly above. He drew a leather blanket tightly against the chill and decided his next move. They exchanged nods without speaking another word, and Ronan quietly snored himself to sleep, leaving Robert to devise his plan.

*

A dull roar could be heard well outside the great walls of Cairo, caused by a mixture of merchants and shoppers making vaguely peaceful negotiations and creating a permanent dust cloud above the city, which could be spotted from miles away. It was swarming with business, no matter the day of the week, with throngs of people moving about the vast intricacies of its streets from dawn until dusk.

"Stay close, or the crowd will consume you," Ronan warned as they passed the giant city gates. "Keep your hands in your pockets at all times, and grip your valuables tightly."

Fifty-foot tall gates opened into a broad avenue lined with brick shops and colorful, gaudy merchant tents.

Traffic became an issue immediately. Hundreds of silk-covered people pushed and shoved their way to their destinations. At the same time, fantastic beasts of burden narrowly avoided trampling them. Numerous pack animals were being loaded up for caravan journeys into the desert.

Ronan said something at the top of his lungs that snapped Robert's attention back, but the roar of the people around muted him.

It had been wise to hold his possessions tightly. Wandering hands, nimble and skilled, occasionally searched against his pockets. He elbowed a stranger across the forehead who had gotten too frisky, and the mob swallowed the thief.

The crowd finally thinned after several turns that felt aimless, allowing the two to walk side by side casually. Rich smells were thick in the air of hot spices and elaborate herbs, and each block offered at least three or four cafes with open-air seating in front.

Ronan sidestepped to his right in a casual effort to appear interested in one of the cafes but smoothly slipped into the alley at the last minute. It was uncomfortably narrow for Kipner, but twisting his body gave him enough room to keep up.

Ronan stopped at a small door only waist-high midway through and drew his index finger across its surface in a slow diagonal motion. The door opened to a low-lit room.

The bold, delectable smells of cinnamon and aloe from the cafes were overwhelmed by the stench of opium. A humid, nearly invisible cloud of heat poured from within.

Little light illuminated the low-ceiling opium den. Throughout the room were motionless bodies, essentially void of life, attached to long hoses. Their skeletal frames were all that remained, loosely wrapped in tattered rugs that were infested with bugs. The echoing sound of an Egyptian flute came from the back corner where Ronan headed.

There was nothing more than a large pile of silk rags loosely shaped into an obese sitting figure in the rear of the place. Robert was fooled into believing some wondrous, self-orchestrating machine was responsible for the music, as no one was nearby. However, the music ceased as they approached, and the rags shifted.

Somewhere deep inside, spotted through a thin gap among the rags, a pair of yellow eyes gazed at them. No noticeable illumination made them so prominent within the shadows of silk. Yet, Robert could see them glaring vividly with piercing red blood vessels framing the perimeter.

Ronan squatted to address whatever was inside the rags. "Feng, let's not waste any time. She sends her best," Ronan spoke in a hushed whisper. The piercing eyes shot a look of warning when Robert leaned in too closely to hear better.

The silk rags said nothing, yet a short, thin envelope, was withdrawn from Ronan's jacket and shoved between the many silks. It quickly disappeared, and a high-tone voice finally spoke.

"He is waiting for him." The beady, yellow eyes turned to Robert as it spoke, and a blood vessel ruptured, filling it with dark red blood. "He knows he has arrived and is not alone."

Ronan shot a quick glance back at Robert with a look of frustration. "So where is he then?" he asked, turning back to the yellow eyes.

There was a long pause in the den while they waited impatiently for an answer. Ronan swayed with anxiety from squatting, then shifted his feet to lean in closer. His lips moved slightly, but no sound came out. Whatever was said was brief and silent.

He rose and gestured for Robert to follow as he exited the den. A few times, Robert turned back to look at the silks in the corner, half expecting someone to follow behind. Only the low sounds of the flute were heard.

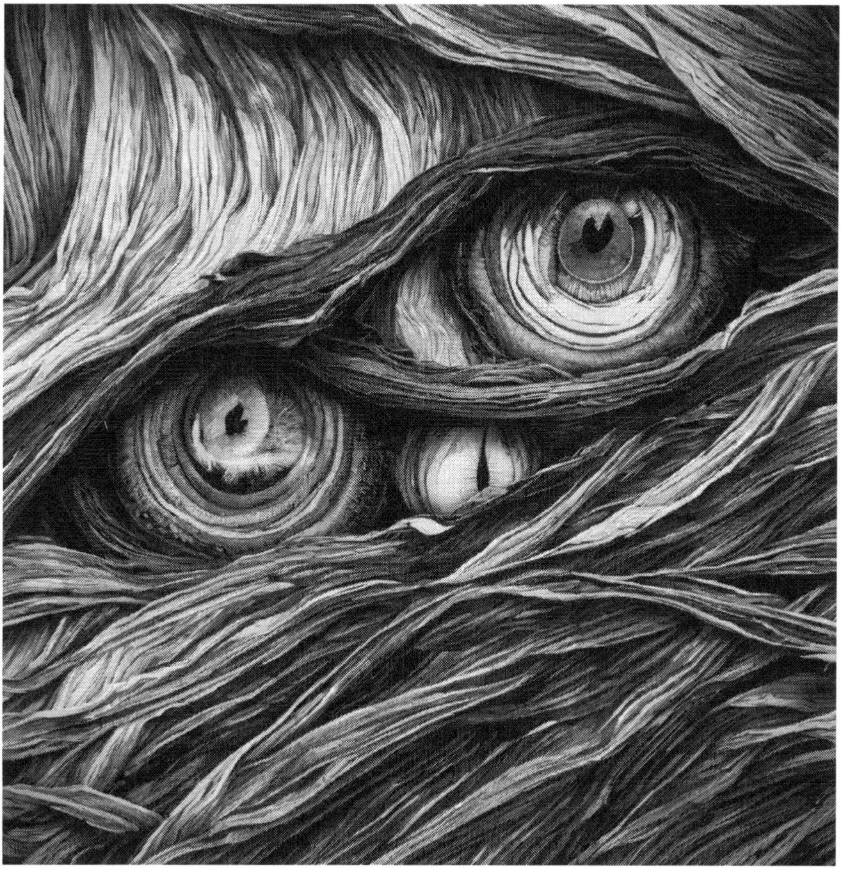

He was guided to a local restaurant for lunch that offered thin slices of lamb and camel meat, steaming hot, laid over darkly burnt toast. The only thing Robert found edible was the robust coffee served with it.

"Your friend frequents an underground cabaret in Azbakeya," Ronan said between slow, slurping sips of his coffee. "Downtown. It may be too crowded for your task, but you'll meet him there and then go to a more secluded place. It seems he's taken to liking one of the singers working the seedy nightlife establishments - Miss al-Mahdiya.

"He knows I'm with you. I've heard this guy is sharp, so while you chat, I'll be within earshot but out of sight. So don't expect to get away with warning him. Make conversation short and sweet, then tell him you'd rather talk somewhere quieter. Offer to buy a drink at the Alhambra Casino over on Bab al-Bahri Street. There's an isolated bar in the back that will offer a more private place. Do the deed, then I don't care what you do. Just make sure he's dead."

The last of Robert's coffee had long been finished, but he continued to draw it to his lips to control his nerves. He had slept terribly the night before after creating his plan, which made him feel weak and uncertain.

He had thought of various options to avoid Ronan's assault if it came to that. Many were riddled with so many variables none could be counted on. He knew he couldn't tip off anyone to interfere without drawing attention, so he was counting on sitting in a more crowded part of the club. With enough patrons nearby, he was confident Ronan would remain passive. He hoped an undetected escape could be made through the crowd if it was exceptionally crowded. Otherwise, Robert figured he would flip over their table and start firing at him.

When Ronan was done reciting his orders, he questioned Robert with a look of suspicion. "You don't look like a killer to me. Have you ever killed a man?"

Staring at Ronan, he held his cup to his lips. "My career involves investigating dangerous circumstances," he said, dodging the question. "It comes with the job."

Ronan ordered another round of coffee with a grunt. "Your cup has been dry for quite some time, Robert. The dusty dry air is bad for the throat."

It had occurred to Robert that Ronan might be toying with him and had every intention of murdering him and Montgomery anyway. The overcrowded streets would provide an easy escape.

Several cups of strong coffee later, they had made their way across town to investigate the cabaret. The area downtown, which the locals called Azbakeya, was littered with venues that offered theaters, dance halls, cinemas, and gambling. The facades were adorned with bright hues and elaborate carvings depicting frivolous designs. By day, bankers and lawyers hurried past the deserted district, hypocritically condoning the sinful area only to venture there after sunset each night.

They wandered throughout the area until they reached Badia Masabni's famous cabaret, Sala Badia Masabni, on Emad el-Din Street. Robert tried peering through the dust-covered windows, but the curtains were drawn.

Ronan stepped behind a giant papyrus that grew in front of a window. Obscured well from the street, a series of narrow steps led down between the storefront and the plant. At the bottom was a green door badly in need of paint.

Bab al-Bahri Street ended at a t-intersection within sight of the nightclub. "You'll see Alhambra Casino the moment you turn onto the street. Work your way into the back, and you'll be at the bar through glass doors," Ronan said, pointing down the road.

Nightfall came too soon, in Robert's opinion, and he found himself taking the partially hidden steps down to Sala Badia Masabni's basement entrance. There had been barely enough time to purchase a gray suit that was tight under the arms and long in the inseam.

Montgomery was known to arrive late just before the lovely Mounira al-Mahdiya glided onto the stage. Robert's nerves had been begging for a drink all day, so he found a thatched wicker chair towards the back, forgetting for the moment of his initial plan, and studied the room.

The ceiling was low for a room this wide, supported by two rows of four-inch pipes and painted black to reduce its height. There were enough chairs to accommodate over a hundred guests. An open kitchen roasted lamb over vertical skewers along one wall while the other wall hosted back rooms for unknown purposes.

The grand stage centered the room in the back, bridging both walls and providing ample space for entertainment. A score of semicircle tables lined the front of the stage with elegant steel tops that produced a satisfying sound when glasses were set on them.

A scattering of night goers huddled around the tables waiting for the evening festivities to begin. Montgomery had not arrived yet, and with each passing minute, Robert became compulsive to check his watch. Drink offers from the waitress were frequent, and he knew to refrain from too many cocktails and keep a level head. However, his anxiety got the best of him, and soon a collection of whiskey glasses accumulated on the table. The liquor took the edge off until he spotted Delven come through the entrance.

It had been almost two decades since they had spoken in person. There had been noticeable aging around his eyes and mouth, and the hand gripping a walking cane of ivory suffered from spots and enlarged veins. The man now dressed in tight, tailor-fit black pinstripes and wingtip Oxford shoes looked identical to Robert's vision at Constantinople's train station. There was no mistaking it - it was the same aged Delven he had met in his dream.

Montgomery quickly recognized Robert sitting in the back, and he weaved his way between the polished tables to join him. An unmistakable smile spread across his face like garnished parsley on a dish. While it looked lovely, it was unwanted and in the way.

The waitress was signaled by a casual flick of Delven's finger as he took one of the empty chairs, and she smiled and walked to the bar without taking his order. It was apparent he had been there many times.

"My, my, my, Mr. Kipner, you look like hell. A lot worse than when we last visited. A cheap suit cannot hide the toll the desert has taken on you," Delven said with a look of concern on his face.

"It has been an exhausting trip," he continued. "I understand you missed my valet, who sent word you walked right by without even saying hello. Tsk, tsk. Very rude of you, but I suspect the yearning for desert adventure was too tempting. The long ones take half a life out of us when it's all said and done, they say. I bet you met some interesting characters along the way, though!"

His voice was filled with mockery, while his delivery was charismatic. Each sentence ended with a caregiving smile or a cane tap to emphasize his point. When the waitress returned with his drink, barley-enriched beer, he tipped embarrassingly well with a wink.

"It has been a long trip, Monty. You're bound to meet people along the way." Robert enjoyed the twitch in Montgomery's eye at the sound of his nickname. "You're right, though. I'm exhausted from the road. Perhaps we can get down to business?"

In the short time he had arrived, the cabaret had quickly filled up. Robert tried to be nonchalant when he saw Ronan sitting at a table behind Delven. He pretended to be interested in the upcoming performer, but he continued to glance toward the two of them. So much for remaining out of sight.

"I see you are still as juvenile in your behavior as you were at the uni," Delven said with a harsh, cold voice. "Very well."

Delven shifted in his chair, crossing his legs, and leaned back comfortably. He paused long enough to take a draft from his beer.

"My life revolves around antiquities and rare artifacts," he began. "It has been my passion for over forty years to seek history in order to learn and improve ourselves. At the same time, I recognize my predecessors were foolish and careless in their techniques, leaving behind significant damage. You know the kind - digging holes in forbidden lands, destroying priceless relics for greed, or rushing work from political pressure.

"It is why philanthropy is my secondary duty to my field of work. Acts of generosity to society. Among these are hospitals I have financed to be erected in areas generally inhospitable and remote. These provide healthy means to local inhabitants who may become infected by the exploration of outside civilizations. As civilization journeys further into the unknown to learn and improve, we must take care of our discoveries."

Ronan lit a cigar and drew deeply, letting the thick, dark smoke weave into the air. Kipner tried not to let his eyes waver too much, but having two pairs of eyes boring down on him was becoming unnerving. He was unsure why Ronan was so bold; he wasn't supposed to be within eyesight.

The philanthropist work Delven bragged about was filled with controversy from what Robert had read in the papers. Many physicians recruited for the remote clinics had little knowledge of the indigenous tribes. Frequently the clinics were nothing more than tents with basic medical supplies. Reports of violent reactions to the medicine had returned, often resulting in severe illness or death. Delven tried to ensure the messages were doctored or disappeared, but a few had fallen into Kipner's hands. It helped to be an investigator.

Delven finished his glass of beer and dabbed his mouth with a cloth napkin. "Naturally," he continued, "being so far out in the bush creates safety concerns. I provide several means of communication at every hospital to use for requesting supply restock and status updates. From time to time, equipment becomes faulty, and so I arrange for small relay towers to be constructed at various intervals. Morse code is used with signal mirrors by day or lanterns by night should an emergency occur, but this method takes time to reach any city."

Robert leaned back and crossed his arms as he listened to Delven gloat about his significant operation. He suspected something had gone wrong at one of the clinics, which wouldn't surprise him of Montgomery's negligence.

"Just how far are we talking into the middle of nowhere?"

To answer, Montgomery withdrew a small map folded twice and spread it flat on the table. It took a moment for Robert to recognize the borders of the Congo and Uganda. It was well-detailed, displaying waterfalls, caves, and tribe locations. Delven pointed along the eastern edge of the Belgian Congo that led into Uganda.

"This marks the first relay tower to Marconi Station," Delven said, tracing his index finger slowly across the map in a westward direction. "The map shows each tower's location before reaching the hospital. Marconi Station is located thirty-five miles into the Belgian Congo. With flat, clear terrain, it can be reached on horseback in a few days, but not through this part of the country. You will be lucky to get there in a week."

Kipner's curiosity lingered on the map too long. When his eyes glanced at Ronan's table, it was empty.

It had barely crossed Robert's mind that he was expected to relocate with Delven to the casino. He knew his years as a private investigator was not why he was asked to come along on this expedition, so he had assumed the hospital, while operating in the dense jungle, had made a discovery of some ancient relics or even a significant structure left behind by an extinct and unknown civilization.

"Recently the transmitter broke at the station, and they had resorted to using the relay towers to let my office know they had equipment malfunction and requested assistance. According to the office manager, they followed protocol and arranged to hire a local militia to escort a sizable group to deliver the new equipment."

Keeping his finger on the map, Delven looked up at Robert. "That expedition failed to return, and all communication through the towers has gone silent as well. I was notified of the situation and financed a full investigation regalia. I paid them extraordinarily to ensure their loyalty, as I suspected the local tribes were retaliating.

"When this group failed to return, I believed I had something far worse on my hands and immediately began arrangements to reposition the clinic considerably further south. Then this arrived at the Uganda office," Delven took out his bi-fold wallet made of shark skin and removed a piece of paper crumpled at one point. Despite having been in his wallet, he handed it to Robert with delicate sincerity.

It was the original sketch he had received in the post back home in London. There was no mistaking the figure as the monstrosity he had witnessed numerous times since his days at the office. It made his hands tremble to hold the paper, and Delven quickly removed it from his hands as gingerly as he handed it to him.

"How did this come into your possession?" Robert asked as he watched the page be reinserted into Delven's wallet. "If no one has returned from the expedition or the site."

Another dark beer was placed on the table by the waitress. Delven didn't address her but waited before she left to speak. "Shouldn't we make our way to Alhambra Casino, Robert? Or perhaps you have changed your mind?"

The daze Robert had found himself falling into after seeing the actual sketch vanish with Montgomery's words. It was absurd to think that he had somehow overheard them talk about Ronan's plan earlier that day. Robert guessed they had been picked up at the city gates and followed in the sea of people. Keeping up with anyone without practically holding onto them through the crowd would be very challenging.

What was Montgomery's secret? Robert refused to believe in dumb luck, primarily when it occurred so frequently by one person. A network of spies large enough to cover his range would be unfathomable in size. The information he acquired constantly was impossible to obtain.

Their previous meeting had been surreal at the time. This so-called Dreamlands was difficult to believe while simultaneously challenging to disregard how real it felt. Robert had been unable to breathe while the creature wrapped itself around his neck. Montgomery had spoken to him consciously; he had heard his voice.

Robert quickly scanned the room with too much eagerness in his behavior.

"You don't have to worry about Ronan anymore, Mr. Kipner. He has chosen a different task this evening that won't be interfering with our conversation. You, on the other hand, still have a decision to make. I will not defend myself."

Several moments passed in silence between them while the roar of the audience cheered for Mounira al-Mahdiya to begin her evening concert. The

Sultana of Tarab stepped delicately across the stage. She started her first song like a nightingale warming up to an evening serenade.

"It's time you stop these pathetic attempts at passing your experiences off as delusional nightmares. There is no point in getting a grip on reality because there is no reality. Not in the sense you believe in. We are the very few who have come to this truth and exposed ourselves to the dangers. We are among the elite with this knowledge, and it is high time you took advantage of it."

It was evident Montgomery was in no rush as Robert watched a cigar appear from his inner coat pocket and be lit by a match on the table. Several drags were taken with a soft pop of the lips, then Delven leaned back and slowly let out the thick smoke. It made Robert realize it had been days since he had his last cigarette, and he suddenly needed one.

Montgomery gave him time to join before continuing. "Mr. Kipner, you are certainly welcome to follow through with Genevieve's request and try to collect your reward. It would please many people in the world." He reached over to the table Ronan had been sitting at and removed an ashtray.

"On the other hand, you could be on tomorrow morning's southbound train, destination the Belgian Congo. As far as I'm concerned, you'll lead this expedition with six other like-minded individuals to explore the unknown reaches and discover what mystery is plaguing my employees. Whichever you decide, you have until the stub of this cigar before I return to my hotel for the evening." To dramatize, Delven widened his eyes as he quickly drew in a significant amount of tobacco, pulling the ring of embers quickly towards his mouth.

Robert felt a horrible stinging pain in his shoulder and instinctively reached toward it. His fingers ran across the hardness of a knife's handle buried deeply into his flesh. He leaned over from the pain as Delven, cane and all, slid to Robert's side of the table, flipping it on its side along the way. All Robert could do was pull the knife out and grit his teeth.

"It would seem your traveling companion was wittier than I anticipated," Delven commented as he withdrew a Browning and peered over the table. The crowd, pushing towards the stage, hadn't noticed the odd behavior.

Robert looked over the table with his .38 drawn by his left hand. He hadn't shot with his offhand in a long time, but he could feel his right arm was out of commission.

Few tables were this far from the stage, and they could see most of the area except for four support poles. Across from them was a coat check counter with a hallway. Robert thought he saw movement beyond the counter but needed a better viewpoint. Delven signaled him to make his way around toward the hallway using the tables along the way. Robert considered how thoughtful Delven suggested he charge into the darkness while Delven remained behind cover. Still, he had seen how little mobility Delven had in his older years. Between the two, the one who was winged was the more agile.

He knew his shoulder was in more trouble than it currently felt. Keeping low and avoiding arm movement, Robert shuffled over to the first table and quickly shoved it over. There was no sound of knives being thrown from the dark room ahead. He glanced quickly over his right shoulder toward the stage and was perplexed how no one seemed to notice the small fight in the back of the room. Waitresses were weaving through the tables, but they didn't seem to mind or look in his direction.

Taking a deep breath, Robert ran in a squatting position to the following table, and the sound of an object whistling through the air passed his left ear. To his surprise, Delven was watching him, although he had yet to fire any shots. He didn't dare look over the table. It took a moment to ensure Delven was covering him with his Browning or if he had abandoned him.

It looked like the hallway was only a few feet ahead of him. For a moment, Robert felt like ignoring the other tables and risking diving into the darkness. He was running on borrowed time with his knife wound as his skin felt a quick bleed at the puncture.

He quickly made up his mind, burst out from his hiding spot, and began zig-zagging to make himself a difficult target. With each step, his mind played convincing tricks of being besieged by knives and other sharp projectiles. Finally, he planted a foot just inside the hallway entrance and halted as quickly as his momentum would allow.

The door to the coat check was open, although it was difficult to see in the dim ambient light. The music from the stage was buffeting any sound he could make out from inside, and he used that to his advantage. He squatted back down and used the wall as support while crawling to its edge.

He whirled around the corner, hoping his eyes had adjusted enough to spot who he presumed was Ronan. In a brief moment, he scanned the room. It was empty except for the hanging coats, hats, and canes. A split second too late, he realized the person had escaped further into the hallway.

There was a sudden new sharpness of pain coming in his back. The blade was longer than the first and sank deeply. Robert's knees gave out from under him from the shock. In the dim and smoky room, it was difficult to tell his vision was failing. He felt himself drifting away slowly as if on a raft navigating a slow river. The charming melody of Mounira al-Mahdiya's voice and the crowd's murmur faded in the opposite direction. He almost thought he heard a single gunshot.

CHAPTER VIII

The Ritual

He had the strangest feeling he had never been there before, yet it all felt familiar. Lying on a highly uncomfortable slab of rock, his arms and legs were restrained with rough hemp rope that rubbed his skin raw. All around him were different pitches of humming originating from odd, inhuman beings.

Each one was different than the last. Curved horns were on one head, and numerous tails extended from the front and back of another. Yet an altogether different creature had extended projected long arms that reached the floor.

They were all chanting through monotone humming, which combined for a hauntingly eerie sensation in Robert's ears and his entire body. The noise made him anxious and fidget.

The slab he was tied was positioned midway up a tall stairway lined with torches. A large platform had been built to interrupt the stair's ascension and provide a ritual area. Above was an angry, starless sky filled with dark purple clouds. Through brief moments of relief from the clouds, the shade of an enormous figure towering over the land swelled.

One of the creatures, decorated by dozens of runes deeply burned and sliced into his flesh, hungrily approached him. Its eyes were human but filled with a deep yellow surrounded by thick red veins. They gave him a fleeting, vague memory of a past experience. The eyes were from someone he had met before, but his past life was a mystery to him without any idea of who he was or where he had come from.

From what little the beast was wearing, its garb looked less of a necessity and more of a formality. A wide sash of rough leather angled across its gory chest while dark liquid oozed from the gashes and smeared when it moved. It withdrew a wickedly curved blade from behind the leather strap, causing shrieking surges of victory from the rest of Robert's audience.

Its eyes widened excitedly as the weapon's tip reached Robert's chest. The sensation was odd to him while the sharp point tore away his shirt and pierced his skin. He felt the pressure of the cut but not the wound itself. It was a struggle to tilt his head down enough. He couldn't resist watching with fascination as the creature dragged the blade down his sternum and saw the exposed bone beneath. The crowd's screams turned into shrieks of delight. The blade wielder's eyes grew bulbous with intensity as it continued making a bloody trail down Robert's body.

For a moment, Robert's attention was pulled away from the grotesque sight of being mutilated alive to the monstrous vision in the sky. A mighty figure, a shadow against the black sky, wreathed a slender, stalk shape head like a branch in a slow breeze. It covered most of the sky by its sheer size, its motion a slow and steady sway. The movement was hypnotic, but none seemed too out of the ordinary to Robert, as if this had happened before.

By now, the creature beside him had made its way down to Robert's genitals, and many others crowded around close to where he could feel their clammy skin. Claw-shaped stones tied to ropes were buried into his flesh, and they heaved on the ropes to peel him open.

With the inside of his chest exposed, his organs still working as they should, he watched with morbid curiosity as the creatures began shoving and biting each other to vie for position and get the first choice of his innards. His blood was splattered on them all, and they licked it off one another.

Higher up the stairs came an echoing shout of an unfamiliar language. Each word, a smattering of caws and high-pitched buzzing, was followed by a ferocious roar that sent the inhuman fleeing in panic.

Whatever made the noise couldn't be seen from Robert's predicament at first. Soon a figure dressed in white with an inverted triangle surrounded by several symbols stood before him. It was the mysterious woman Genevieve Mitzkowitz. The sight of her pulled at his memories instantly, reminding him of his uncertainty about being here and not in the cabaret.

She still held the attractive vision he had fondly remembered. Her hair was held back by a circle on her head decorated with a green leaf.

Genevieve was not in a pleasant mood from her dark expression. Her eyes were calm, like a predator patiently awaiting their prey to come closer.

"Blind curiosity has always been your greatest weakness. Even the promise of wealth could not divert your desire," she spoke with tension in her voice like a mother having lost her patience with her child.

The gaping wound on his chest continued to go unabated and entirely unnoticed by Robert. "If your puppet hadn't attacked me before I made my choice, I might have followed your request." He lowered his head back to the hard slab and looked up at the menacing figure dancing slowly among the clouds above.

One of her hands moved to rest on Robert's exposed sternum, and he suddenly felt the shock of pain. His strained eyes watched her slender hand melt through his bone, grabbing the heart beating beneath.

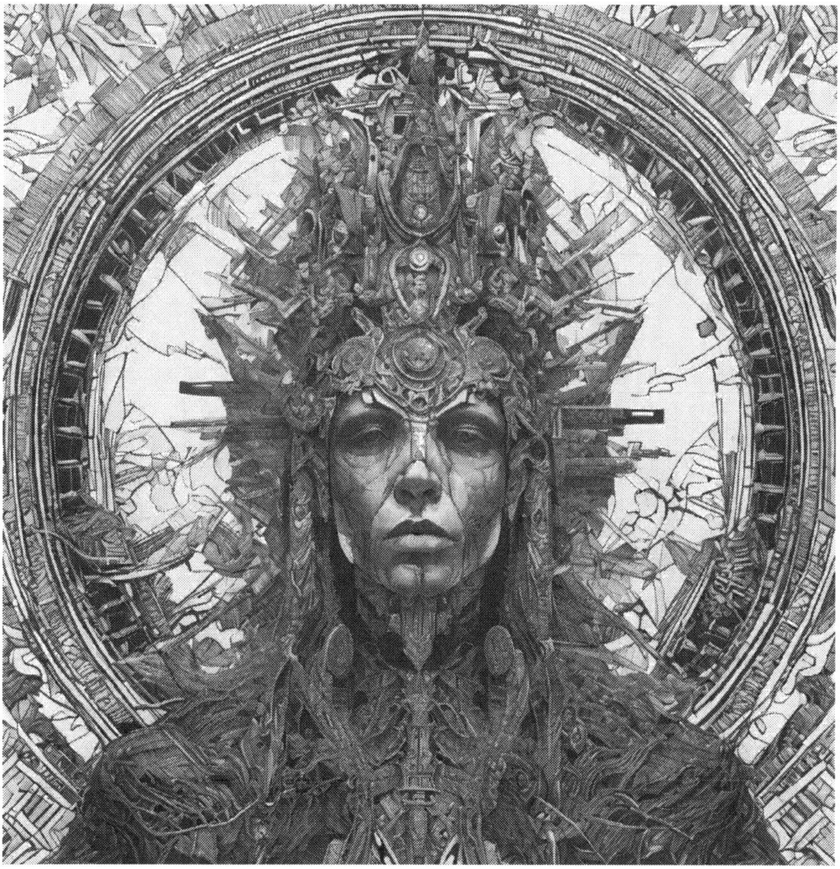

His body surged with adrenaline, bursting down his arms and legs, followed by complete numbness. The overwhelming pain was replaced by a hollow, empty sensation in his chest. The stillness of his heart from her tight grip amplified in his head, and he began to suffocate. There was a devilish, satisfied look in her eyes as she tortured him, squeezing his heart as his arteries turned white and empty.

"Lessons are taught to those who are stubborn, Mr. Kipner," she said, bending down to whisper in his ear. "You failed. Do you deserve a second attempt?"

His body was entirely numb and paralyzed. Try as he might, the sensation of cement bricks baring down prevented him from moving, but he tried nodding.

The grip from his heart loosened, and breathing along with circulation returned.

"So eager to agree when facing pain," Genevieve purred as she ran her fingertips across Robert's palm. "This next lesson shall have consequences if not learned."

As her fingers dragged along his skin, thin wisps of smoke trailed up from his hand, leaving behind a dark burnt emblem of an inverted triangle on his hand. His palm seared with pain, but her fingers quickly pinned his fingers down as they tried to clench.

"Pay close attention to your new teacher, Mr. Kipner, as it guides you."

Robert gasped for breath while the pain subsided until he could speak again. "Cryptic riddles don't bode well for my thick head. What is it you want me to do?"

Light from the flickering torches illuminated her disappointment and frustration. She crossed her arms and tucked them into the sleeves.

"It will be painfully obvious," she said. Her continued vague speech caused Robert to roll his eyes.

Before anything could be said, she spoke similar words earlier, and Robert lost consciousness.

CHAPTER IX

Egypt, 1926

"There's no sense in going back now. He's coming with us either way," came a woman's voice nearby. It was sharp and pointed with copious amounts of impatience.

Robert's eyes had remained closed after a few unsuccessful attempts to open them. Each try gave him a splitting headache.

Disorientation clogged his mind as he grasped at his environment through other senses. There was a cradling motion, up and down, which matched the rhythmic sound of train wheels rolling along rails. A wooden door slid open long enough to hear people casually visiting as they passed by.

His lungs took a deep breath, and his eyes slowly opened to take in the room. To his relief, his head gave him a break. It was a sleeper car, made of several private rooms along a row available only to those with considerable coin. His room had a hideaway in which he laid upon, a wash bin beneath a mirror, and a small table and chair. It was uncomfortably small, which explained the woman's close proximity.

She resembled Natasha strikingly, except she had reddish hair pinned with a pencil. Her clothes were durable and mostly made of denim, but her soft, smooth hands said she was a stranger to the outdoors.

No trace of a warm greeting could be found on her face when she stood up. They were alone, but Robert had heard her speak to another.

"You're Delven's little pet? I've never heard of you. I'm still trying to understand his logic for you leading this expedition. You look more like a cop than an archaeologist," she said with annoyance. Robert banged his head on the bed above while trying to sit up.

"Ah, clumsiness should come in handy in the jungle."

Rubbing the top of his head, he said, "It didn't come in handy as a ballerina either. Had to quit." She scoffed a chuckle and moved over to the lone chair by the door. Crossing her legs, she took out a cigarette and lit it without offering him one.

"Clumsy and a comedian. When it gets dangerous deep in the Congo, we can rely on you to keep the morale up with bad jokes. Now I get Delven's decision." Her lips popped from each quick cigarette drag. One final, long drag and the butt was flicked out the window. She paused a moment, then blew the smoke at Robert. He smiled and inhaled deeply.

"Just wait 'til I warm up to my main act, lady," he said now that the sting from his head had subsided. "Who are you supposed to be beside my plus one to the jungle party?"

The lady sat there staring at him for a few seconds taking him in, then rose and offered her hand. "Patricia Lee. Just call me Trish, and we won't get into many fights."

Her grip was firm and aggressive. Robert returned the gesture in kind. She was bitter about the decision by Delven, but he couldn't blame her. She thought this would be an archaeological journey. Delven must have told her whatever she needed to hear.

Then again, Robert didn't trust Delven, and this trip could be anything. He couldn't offer much support if they were ambushed by some incongruous creature. He doubted she knew about the sketch or saw what he had. Delven was obsessed with discovering more about these strange inhabitants like Robert but with exceedingly more money to support it. Now it looked like another set of pawns he bought off was to do his dirty work, but he remembered six were coming along.

"What do you know of our destination, Robert?" she asked.

The door opened to a tall, lanky man who looked like he had spent his entire life spewing over calculations by candlelight. He craned his neck forward in an awkward stance to stand fully upright. A pair of thick, black-rimmed glasses drooped heavily on a long nose. The man was clean-cut but bad at shaving from his neck's numerous nicks and scars.

Trish smiled the second he walked in with an alarming glow of happiness that was void a moment before.

"This is Sinclair," she introduced. "Quentin Sinclair."

"Just Sinclair will do, Robert," he said, extending his hand. Along with his long nose were two equally long ears completing the Ichabod Crane impersonation. Sinclair's smile felt genuine, and they looked happy to be alive.

"Pleasure to meet you, Sinclair. I was just about to tell Trish here what Delven has suckered us into if you'd like to hear," Robert said as he returned to the bed. Sinclair shifted weight in his feet and appeared satisfied to remain hunched over for the time being.

"To be honest, Delven hasn't told me much of the details, but it would seem either natives or some wild animals have given trouble to a makeshift field hospital he ponied up to run." He paused and took a deep breath watching for any expressions that might indicate they had been told otherwise.

"We aren't the first to investigate either," he continued. "He already sent a militia who are long overdue."

Trish began to swing her leg and gripped both sides of her chair firmly. Sinclair nodded with fascination.

"Now, here comes the part that's difficult to swallow," Robert took another deep breath and let it out slowly while looking outside the window. The cabin had been quite warm, but the sight of the desert made him sweat. A mixture of desert sand and xerophyte plants was all he could see against a glaring sun.

Up to now, he had fought back the temptation to believe his absurd visions. However, witnessing odd creations and bizarre manifestations gave strong evidence of the inevitability of accepting fantasy as reality.

"I don't know what old Monty has told you, and I'm not sure if you are ready to hear my thoughts on the matter. This isn't some archaeological excursion, and I certainly don't anticipate finding ancient souvenirs along the way.

"Monty has conned you all into endangering yourselves for his private obsession." Robert had noticed his belongings had been graciously kept with him when he was carried on board the train. He leaned down and sifted through the contents until he had what he wanted to pull out.

"This isn't much to go on, but I have witnessed something similar. Delven thinks it's what caused the hospital to go silent," he said as he handed the copy of the sketch to Trish. Sinclair glanced down at it, and they exchanged looks, but neither acted surprised by the image.

That gave pause to Robert. It had not occurred to him that he and Delven had been the only people who had seen it. In his self-absorbed world, the thought of others knowing his secret put him off. It took away some of the mystique that drove him.

"He didn't give me much to go on save for a glance at a map showing where the hospital generally was. I got caught up in a tight spot and lost a fight before I could ask questions," he said leaning back and rubbing his thighs.

"That's all I know, so now it's your turn. Let's start with how I wound up here," Robert glanced at them both. He was uncomfortable about his situation and felt suspicious after their subdue reaction to the drawing. Both held poker faces so well it was impossible to make out any hints.

Trish looked at Sinclair to see who would talk first, and she nodded. "We were already in Cairo with Delven when you arrived. We've been here a few weeks planning the expedition and arranging travel plans. You were carried into the cabin by two men neither of us recognized, with Delven close behind. He overpaid well for a doctor to make an overnight house call to stitch you up. Our window to leave was closing quickly since you took your time getting here, so Delven made the call for us to depart and look after you until you recovered."

Her reminder of stitches brought his attention to his shoulder. There had been no feeling where the two knives had been jammed into him, but his fingers ran across dozens of tiny stitches on both sides.

"Laudanum," Sinclair spoke up. "You were cut up pretty badly. There was little choice. Delven said you could handle it."

Tracing a finger across the stitches, Robert thought back to the opium den and the two yellow bloodshot eyes staring back. He had enough addictions, he thought to himself. Realizing now his body was filled with opioids, he worked to focus his attention on Trish as she explained the plan. He heard every word but wondered how much he would retain after the drugs wore off.

The rumbling rhythm he felt below since he awoke was part of the Egyptian National Railways currently following the Nile in a southerly direction. The rail line meandered towards Anglo-Egyptian Sudan, a unique agreement between the United Kingdom and Egypt where the former had complete control while Egypt maintained local influence.

Trish had learned that the tracks ended in El Obeid, where a steam liner would pick up further transportation south. Robert listened patiently as she continued her well-rehearsed speech leading to her most significant concern, the final leg.

"Close to the Nile's birth," she said, her eyebrows pressed together, "the waters are at their roughest. The boat can only make it part of the way upriver. It's swarming with crocs and hippos, too."

"We'll need to buy horses in Khartoum or El Obeid if any are for sale," Sinclair added, finishing Trish's thought, "along with a guide who knows the northeastern region of the Congo." Sinclair crossed his arms when he finished with a look of satisfaction.

The room went silent for several minutes. The two strangers looked at each other, anxiously wondering what he was thinking. Robert stared beyond them with unfocused eyes, letting them stew.

"So? What do you think, Mr. Leader?" She emphasized the nickname dramatically.

In answer, the bed creaked as Robert shifted his weight, laid back down, and closed his eyes. He let them sit longer in silence, enjoying the thought Trish's impatience was driving her angry.

Robert already knew he was going to like her. She lacked experience in the field, which was obvious. Robert couldn't make a guess as to what either of them did for a living. He doubted they were archaeologists from their behavior alone. He had no idea what she or Sinclair were doing on this trip.

His breathing slowed down as he felt the drugs reclaim him. At last, he asked, "Which one thought traveling by land was a good idea? I mean, I hate flying, but there are other ways."

There was no need to look; he could tell they exchanged glances again with silent conversations. Robert wondered what their history was and Delven's fascination with recruiting them. They were younger by at least ten years. Perhaps they had been Delven's students as well. His ear had picked up the Yorkshire dialect in Sinclair's voice, and he was confident Trish was from Liverpool.

It was alarming to Robert how he allowed himself to get this deep without understanding the situation entirely. Suddenly he was sharing a cabin with two strangers without much finance, heading through harsh terrain and missing four other travelers.

He was curious to know if either of them had survival training. But then again, neither did he. There had been plenty of planned trips, but few came to fruition because Montgomery stuck his nose into his business.

His immediate thought was suddenly cut off by Trish's voice answering his question.

"Going this way was not our original plan," she said, and Robert opened his eyes to look at her. "Delven was more adamant about us reaching our target than travel details and left it to us.

"Plenty of ships were heading into the Red Sea, but none were going beyond. We were curious why, but none of the Chief Officers felt like telling us. We couldn't find anyone willing to talk. Even Sinclair thought of embellishing a few sailors with alcohol."

Sinclair immediately chimed in, "At the time, it sounded like a good idea. I thought someone might have a loose tongue after a few drinks. The closest I came to finding an answer was a low-ranking sailor on one of Her Majesty's fleets who thought his wages were a bit low.

"Sailing around the horn has become too dangerous for commercial ships. The best way he could explain was frequent attacks at night when most of the crew were asleep. Crewmates vanished, and no others witnessed how. By morning, a team of 20 would be halved.

"Buying a ride on Her Majesty's ships was out of the question, so we had no choice but to go by train as far as possible," Trish finished after Sinclair paused.

That sounded wrong to Robert. He hadn't heard about strange attacks on vessels. Most of the ship's traffic along the East Coast of Africa was protected by the Imperial colonization of Britain. Why hadn't any military ships been deployed to the troubled area? Most likely, pirates were to blame. Any convoy with minimal protection would be sufficient, but finding available naval vessels might prove difficult.

Outside, the cream-white sun was setting casually against the dunes of Egypt. The train puddled on, working past fishing villages and abandoned hut communities and making less than desired time. Robert could already feel the journey taking a turn for the worse. It could be weeks before they reached the Congo with any delays.

Behind Sinclair came a knock at the door, followed by a brief announcement that dinner was being served in car number four. Many passengers were making their way down the narrow corridor, their gossiping voices carrying on along the way.

The awkward shuffling between the three took a moment before they exited the tiny, cramped cabin. There was a second bunk above Robert's, but he hoped Delven had sprung for separate cabins. The thought of good smoke and enough drinks to forget he agreed to the trip was too tempting.

Two cars up were intended for dining, but it was more of an afterthought. The chairs were nothing more than wood poles hammered into rough cuts of driftwood that had barely been leveled. Repurposed wood planks, possibly from former wagons, had been used to make the tables.

Scanning the room, Robert found a table and balanced himself on a one-peg stool. It had been formed into an inverted "V" to appear as a saddle. The staff clearly wished for passengers to only last for a short time.

No menus were provided to the three. A lamb dish was the only entree offered, and to drink was water or coffee, which they found to be noticeably strong. Most of the passengers were satisfied with the dining. They visited pleasantly together, so the three made do with what they were served. None of them felt the meal was particularly edible.

Taking a moment as they waited for their dishes to be removed, Robert inquired about the other four missing volunteers for the expedition.

"None of them showed. All of us were sent invitations and travel plans, but as long as it took you to arrive, we guessed by that time none of the other invites were going to show," Trish explained.

Another odd notion. Delven had just told him of six members while in Cairo. If he knew only two were going with him, why didn't he tell Robert?

Throughout his dining experience, Robert couldn't help but overhear a gentleman seated behind him. He had been exceedingly loud for much of the evening and prone to lean back far enough as he spoke to bump Robert's chair.

Sitting across from Robert, Trish looked over his shoulder whenever it occurred. He could tell she was as annoyed as he was. After the fifth or sixth bump, Robert turned to tap the man on the shoulder for his attention.

He was immediately answered by a quick swivel of the man on his one-peg stool. For the quality of the train ride, he was lavishly dressed. His charcoal three-piece suit had a paisley cream vest, and several gemstones inset into a gold tie pin. His face was rotund, covered thinly with a waxed-curled mustache and van dyke beard, and he looked to be fifty. He wore no hat to avoid obscuring the centrally parted haircut that ended above both ears in curls.

Ebullient sky blue eyes smiled at Robert as if recognizing a long-lost friend. "Why yes, my charming fellow? What can Renaldo Archibald do for you today? Please try some of this delicious wine I acquired from Bombay last year. It has a delectable aroma of jasmine flowers. It represents spirituality there, you know."

Already a ceramic bottle had appeared from behind the large man, gripped with the passion of a Renaissance painter, and eagerly began to pour into Robert's empty glass before he could react.

In seconds, Robert felt a hand on his shoulder and a full glass of wine in his hand. He barely had time to notice how desperately close Renaldo's chair was to breaking. The flamboyant personality dwarfed Robert's focus for a moment.

There was little chance of avoiding it as the great man laughed loudly and heartily while he began spouting short anecdotes of his past travels.

As each tale unfolded with Renaldo's elegant flair, his body listed and leaned in every direction to drive home his story better. Although no guests were at his table, Robert wondered if it made any difference. Renaldo had the talent to find all things entertaining and had been talking to anyone who would listen.

"... by shooting a tiger," Renaldo continued when Robert returned his attention to him. "The great beast leaped up nearly as high as the elephant I rode upon and tore me from my saddle. Unfortunately for the tiger, I had reached second place several years earlier in the high caliber division of the Gascony-Cecil Grand Marksman Series finals..."

Robert was clamped firmly by Renaldo's meaty hand but turned just enough to see Trish hiding her laughter behind a thin, red napkin. She wasn't going to leave when there was entertainment.

A few times, Robert tried interrupting Renaldo's stories, but his voice was muted by Renaldo's booming voice.

Suddenly, Renaldo took a breath and looked directly into Robert's eyes with an intensity of a hunter staring at his prey.

"I'm hunting something," he began, his breath wafting of brandy and wine. "I caught wind of it while hunting pheasant and boar along the southern edge of the Reinhardswald. Germany," he added when he didn't see the recognition on Robert's face.

"It's taken me years to track it this far. I'm not certain, but I believe it is an entirely new species. Some derivative of a sea octopus of sorts. Bizarre creature."

Like sails losing wind, Renaldo calmed down and settled back on his creaking stool that bowed against his immense weight. The two stared at each other for a moment.

He felt suspicious of Renaldo Archibald. Renaldo had enough money to travel in better accommodations just from the quality of his suit. So far, the quality of the train was comparable to a broken-down donkey. Robert was surprised Delven didn't have a more accommodating travel method. He recalled the caravans at the outskirts of Cairo, comprised of numerous camels, each decorated with fine silks and topped with a large shaded canopy overhead. The cameleers overseeing the passengers had shown great care and interest in their needs.

Car attendants had already passed by their tables to light tiny candles tucked inside frosted glass holders as the sun disappeared behind the dunes. Dessert had not been offered, so Robert lit a cigar Renaldo gave him and sipped the coffee he knew would keep him awake all night.

"... on its trail. I found it easy to follow with something I came across in western Germany some years ago," Renaldo said while flicking the tip of his cigar and sending ash to the wood floor like snowflakes. "It's really an ingenious invention. Works entirely on its own. No need for electricity! I must show you."

From his size, it was difficult to tell if Renaldo had stood up until he gestured toward the back of the train where the sleeper cars were latched. He either was unaware of his surroundings or didn't care that his bulky backside pushed plates and glasses from a couple's table behind him. Their bitter glances went unnoticed by Renaldo. The portly figure squeezed through the exit and into the next car.

"I guess we should follow," Sinclair said as he looked to Trish for approval from his indecisiveness. Trish acted like she was not interested and shrugged her shoulders, looking out the window momentarily before getting up from her stool. The one peg fell like a toppled tree to the floor, the clatter amplified by a brief pause in conversations. She pretended not to notice as she strolled after Sinclair.

Robert followed the two through the series of cabin cars. He thought it hadn't felt like the train was this long as they entered the last one. It turned out that the ninth car was one large cabin.

It was as if the opulence of the luxury train had been gathered and concentrated only in this one car. An upright piano had somehow fit through the narrow doors. It rested against one wall while a small cocktail bar, which put the dining car to shame, completed the furniture set on the opposite side. A chandelier hung from the raised ceiling in the center of the room made of polished gold and Baccarat crystal. A full tiger's fur and head stretched underneath to solidify Renaldo's story.

Various 19th Century antique furniture had been brought in for what appeared to be only decoration and no practical use. Renaldo stood among a few maps on the walls focused on different regions of Africa.

A cherry wood secretary took up the corner beneath the hanging maps, and he slipped the door open to it. Several small niche holes were along the back, each stuffed with quills and tightly rolled parchment, but Renaldo picked up the only thing resting on the desk.

It had the overall appearance of a radio with its outer casing removed. Several copper coils were exposed, tightly wound in cylinder shapes, and a magnet hovered perfectly in its center. The front of the device, where one would expect knobs and frequency range to be found, was a single, large Bakelite dial with two switches on either side. No labels or notations indicated what anything did or what it was for.

"A seismograph!" Renaldo Archibald said proudly with a grand pause. When he received no applause, he continued, "Modified, of course. Heavily so, from the looks of it, and tuned specifically to what I am tracking. However, I am not an expert on new-age electrical trinkets."

Like a pack of excited puppies, his sausage fingers wiggled jubilantly above the device as he looked over the different components. One of the two switches was flipped, and the three guests felt their teeth chatter from a strong, invisible force.

With a quick motion, Renaldo turned the dial counter-clockwise, which caused the intensity to go down against their teeth.

"I am sorry," he said apologetically. "I guess I had it turned up too strongly. Unlikely the proximity is that close. It would be right in this very room otherwise!"

He held his shocked expression while gesturing for his guests to take seats. "Where are my manners? I find I lose awareness when I tinker with this gadget."

Sinclair seemed most eager of the three about the device and tried to get a closer look, but Renaldo waved him away.

"Please sit, please sit. I fear too many up close makes it act peculiar," Renaldo said as Sinclair took a seat on a green velvet-lined mahogany chair. With eagerness, his hands gripped the ends of the armrest carved out into eagle's heads.

Robert took his seat as well, momentarily keeping an eye on Trish, who had disregarded Renaldo's request and was exploring the treasures of the wet bar. Once their eyes briefly made contact, Robert slightly brushed a finger against his nose, and Trish flipped a second empty glass from behind the counter.

Renaldo already had begun rattling off details of how the device operated at an advanced technical level while claiming to be a novice with "electrical trinkets," as he called them.

"... added tuning capacitors back here to improve the reception. It's all quite ingenious. The main coils have a large inductance which is necessary to cause the diode to reciprocate..."

Try as he might, Robert found little he could comprehend during the lecture. With a fine crystal glass filled with a beverage that hinted at maple and hickory smoke, he held up his hand. He stopped his host from continuing, much to Sinclair's disappointment.

"As much as I appreciate your hospitality, Mr. Archibald, along with such a fine demonstration of what is sure to become the preferred investment for dentists everywhere, it has been a long day, and we should be going," Robert said, standing back up and showing no intentions of leaving his drink behind.

The device was immediately shut off, and Renaldo frantically waved his arms. "No, no, you mustn't leave yet!" he exclaimed with a sudden look of desperation. "You don't understand. This has brought me this far in hunting the beast. I'm no expert tracker, but this eliminates the need to be a tracker at all!"

A few steps from the door, Robert nodded. "I don't doubt that it does, Mr. Archibald. It certainly rattled my jaw. But right now, the three of us are exhausted and have to figure a way farther south once this train hits the end of the line."

"Robert?" Trish spoke up for the first time in hours. Her glass was resting on one of the mahogany desks scattered around the room's edge and covered in brown aged papers. She was sifting through a few that had captivated her attention.

By the light of a kerosene lamp, they all gathered around Trish. Each page she shuffled through was covered edge to edge with explicit depictions of an invertebrate specimen with numerous lengthy appendages stretching from a central core body. The offshoots were detailed with small oval-shaped orifices. One illustration included the display of an adult male silhouette beside it for scale. It was a leviathan in size compared to the man.

"I'm no expert in drafting technical illustrations," Renaldo said, tapping a finger on the drawing, "but that's the best I could depict of what I'm hunting.

*

Against the setting sun, the old steam iron horse rattled across an endless line of uneven metal beams. Its noise chugged rhythmically into the night and broke the savanna's silence, drawing the attention of nearby grazing herds. With a start, a dozen zebras bolted with fear off into the fading light, tearing through hidden lions waiting to pounce on them. The sudden change of direction balked the lions until they, too, bolted in fear. A dark octopus-like figure clung to the caboose through the dimming twilight like a waiting spider. The train rolled on, disappearing into the darkness, and the creature began to move.

CHAPTER X

Anglo-Egyptian Sudan, 1926

Like stacked razor blades, the moon's glow was sliced by the window blinds as it entered the room. The rhythm of the train's less-than-smooth ride over old, rusted tracks hadn't lulled Robert to sleep as the night rolled on. Too many occurrences with no clear explanation had slammed into his life quickly, and he was on the hundredth journey down the list of them in his mind.

One thing was sure to Robert: Delven had no interest in the hospital or its staff. He was only using it as a carrot to dangle in front of anyone who would follow it. All he cared about was this strange species that seemed to get around quickly or was multiplying. Either way, it felt ludicrous for a few people not trained to handle this situation to be sent on an observation mission to witness the creature for Delven's records.

Well, almost everyone. The party's eccentric newfound companion, Renaldo Archibald III, seemed well aware of their situation and prepared to face it head-on. Before they had retired to their sleeping cabins, he had shown the three his collection of firearms that would easily take down a whale. He was just one man, yet he carried a dozen rifles and shotguns, each with special ammunition he claimed to have made but "was no expert." None of the guns were considered normal for hunting unless faced with gargantuan monsters.

That left the two others Delven had handpicked to join Robert on his trek into the jungles of Africa. On more than one occasion, the thought had crossed his mind that he was taking too much for granted.

Trish knew Delven extensively, but Robert had learned just how well-known he was among his enemies. Genevieve certainly had enough material on him to nearly convince Robert to kill him. Spies were employed on both sides.

At this point of the trip, however, Delven was essentially out of the picture, so there would be no reason to bring along spies for Genevieve, at least not such blatant ones.

If they were hiding their espionage identities, Sinclair had done the better job of the two. Up to this point, he had been a sponge for Renaldo's worldly expeditions. With each tale told, Sinclair eagerly asked questions, followed by requests for another story immediately after. He wasn't very social to Robert, keeping to himself unless speaking to Trish, which Robert by now was convinced they were telepathic. They hadn't spoken to each other since he had woken, yet he felt they had shared numerous conversations.

Outside his cabin, the moon was full and suspended high above the Savannah plains. By now, they had traveled into Anglo-Egyptian Sudan, which stretched vastly in every direction. Only a tiny train station had been built to mark Egypt's border.

A dozen people boarded their train, which raised the question of where they came from. The only road leading away from the station went on for dozens, if not hundreds of miles, with no signs of civilization. All of them had been barefoot.

Deep shadows covered the plains from Baobab and Acacia trees, giving little to see, but Robert knew nature was wide awake. He knew better. During any other journey less foreboding, he would have enjoyed sitting on the caboose's deck, trying to make out night calls of wild animals.

The words "you are hunted" surfaced in his mind after doing his best to forget about it. The tiny piece of paper someone had placed in his notebook had given him a slight edge in preparing himself for possible attacks. If only he knew what exactly was after him. By now, it felt like everything was. His visions had ceased, but he worried they might return. As the journey became more dangerous, he couldn't afford to let himself lose grip on reality.

And therein lies the last item on his mental list of Things Not Going As Planned. After his experiences with the Dreamlands, he had shifted his attempts at excusing his visions as hallucinations. He started to accept the impossible notion that all of it was real. His last shred of defense against it was "How?" What was causing these events to happen to him without the world knowing? Just how many knew? Trish and Sinclair had witnessed similar, and even Renaldo revealed knowing, too.

Something passed across the moon's reflection, and the room went pitch black momentarily before returning to a dull blue illumination.

Curiously Robert turned onto his side and froze. Something was squatting in the corner opposite of him, no more than 3 feet away.

Above him, with legs draped over the edge, Sinclair quietly slept while Trish was in the neighboring cabin.

He stared at the creature, perhaps two feet at full height, crouched on its legs and looking back at him. Its chin was resting comfortably on its knees. Two small, beady eyes pulsed with soft illumination, piercing the darkest shadows.

His .357 hung in its holster at the bed's headboard near the window. He slowly reached out to withdraw it, but the creature shook its head and held a finger to its lips.

Like a smoker's cough, its raspy whisper could barely be heard. With each sentence, it exhaled all the air from its lungs before continuing.

"You leave a trail any fool could follow," it spoke to Robert with a tiny, tight mouth that barely opened. Each time, Robert could see a row of equally little teeth that caught the faint traces of the moon's beams.

Robert wasn't groggy, having not slept but fatigued from the late night. He knew this was no phantom or trick of the mind. Whatever this was, it was as natural as Sinclair's long leg hanging before him.

"I guess that's why you follow me," Kipner said.

The creature reached forward with its sickeningly thin arms, extending its clawed fingers to several inches long, slowly dragging itself like pulling dead weight across the floor.

Enough was enough, thought Robert as he grabbed for his revolver, but his arms were strangely weighted down, as were his legs. Almost his entire body was paralyzed. Only his head and neck were free.

"Don't take it personally," Robert said as he watched the creature inch its way methodically to him and ascend the bed. The side of his shoulders felt the first touch of the dark blue, almost black creature's fingertips, making Robert's body quiver and ripple with goosebumps. Like needles, its claws, one by one, slowly punctured his flesh and used his body to haul itself up onto Robert.

Pain shot throughout his body, but Robert's voice escaped him. He lay there like rigor mortis, his mouth gaping from the shock. His eyes briefly went to Sinclair's leg dangling lifelessly a few inches away. If only he could wake him.

Less than an inch from Robert's face, sprawled comfortably on top of him, the beady eyes of the beast hypnotically gazed with an eager grin. Its body was frigid cold, like dry ice planted directly onto Robert's exposed skin. Light vapors escaped the cold burn and reeked of ammonia and sulfur that singed his nose hairs.

"Some secrets are forbidden," it whispered in Robert's ear. "You have seen too many.

"Your curiosity has led you to a point you will no longer return. Debts must be paid for what you witnessed."

Robert's frozen lungs prevented him from screaming as the creature lunged one of its hands deep into his chest and wrapped its long fingers around his heart like a clamp. It closed its eyes in deep ecstasy while it squeezed passionately.

Quickly pulling back, its arm tore away, leaving the hand severed and clinched around Robert's heart. His chest wound fused close, but he could still feel the beating of his heart restricted by the hand.

Robert fought to remain conscious, gritting his teeth against the invisible force that pinned him to the bed. A light appeared to Robert's right, but he couldn't turn his head enough to see it. It was followed by a loud bang, and the creature was gone.

"Jesus! Oh God, are you okay?" Trish's voice came from the same direction as the light. The restraints vanished along with the creature, and he gasped for air.

Trish's hard-edge attitude was gone for a moment. She knelt beside his bed and touched his forehead comfortingly.

"What the hell was that thing? I could barely make it out in the dark."

Sinclair had awoken and dropped down to lean over Trish.

Taking a deep breath, Kipner shook his head. "I have no idea. It suddenly appeared in the cabin and came after me. Said something about secrets being forbidden to..."

His heart seized up again with the same tightness as before. The pain was brief, however, quickly fading along with traces of laughter in his head.

Numerous voices shouted about a gunshot from the hallway, and a knock came on their cabin door. Renaldo stood in the way, his girth benefiting by keeping the passengers at bay.

"What the devil happened in here? Everyone alright?" he said as he grunted through the narrow door and closed it to the sound of disappointed people behind him.

"For now," Robert said.

"That's bull," Trish argued and looked back at Renaldo. "Something attacked him."

"Oh dear me. I have acetylsalicylic in my cabin. I shall fetch some right away," Renaldo said triumphantly, pushing his way down the corridor.

*

Out of the corner of his eye, just as he returned to his cabin for aspirin, Renaldo caught the same creature that had attacked Kipner, climbing up to the window with something in its hand. Renaldo's blood ran cold as his doubt and self-loathing from his past surged into focus.

Some demonic figure, no more than a foot or two tall, stood against the open window, poised to escape with one of Renaldo's artifacts. Despite what he saw, he wasn't sure if it was another illusion cast from the greater evil that plagued him. His body faltered, and he stumbled as he reached for his rifle, sending it to the ground. At the same time, the creature leaped out into the African night and disappeared.

Shaking as he knelt on the floor, softly whimpering in the silent room, Renaldo fought to regain control of his mind but couldn't. He was exhausted and frustrated to be manipulated so easily. For so long, he had control of his life and destiny. He had sought grand adventure, beautiful treasure, and perhaps a good hunt like his father experienced, but now he felt caged like a kept man. For so many years, he lived in fear of repeating his sinful actions in Germany, and here his life was in danger, and he had hesitated. He couldn't go on living like this. Sooner or later, he would either murder again or lie dead from wavering. Was he really up to this?

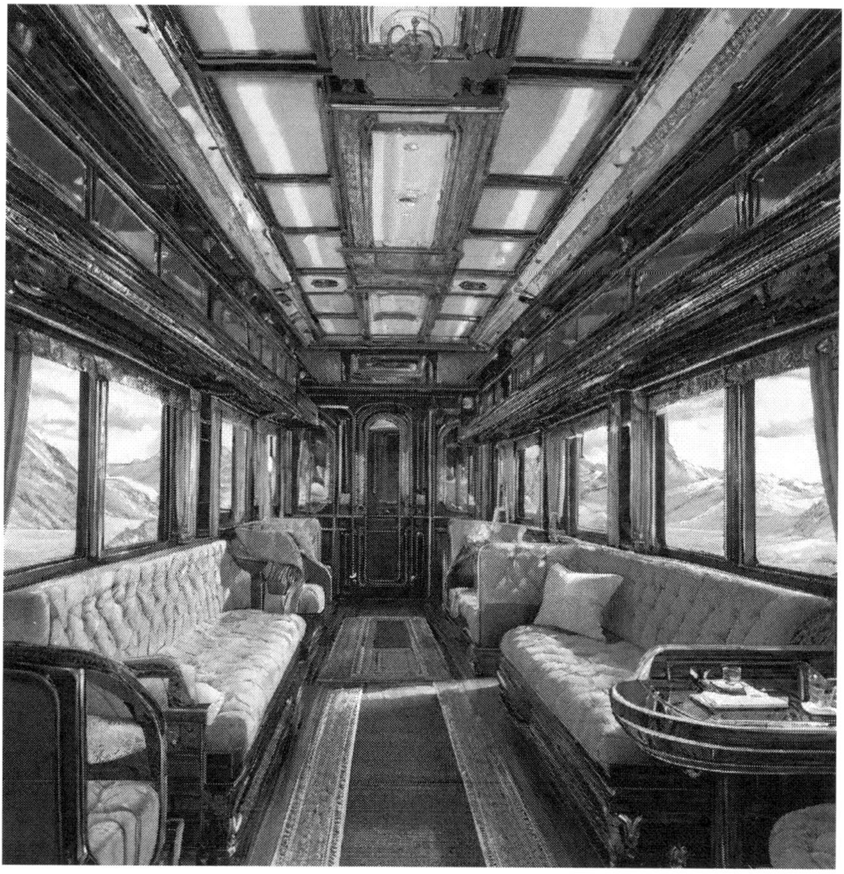

"Yes, yes you are, Renaldo!" he said boldly, groaning as he rose to his feet. "You will not control me. I am my own fate!" Nodding in satisfaction, he repeated the idea several times to convince himself.

He looked out the window to a dark flatland that gave no sign of the creature. It had lifted something from the cabin, but he wasn't sure what. Hopelessly rummaging throughout the room until he passed out from exhaustion, Renaldo could only guess it might have been a cephalopod medallion he had found along the beaches of Calangute in India or a crystal formation of amethyst he brought back from spelunking in the Appalachian Mountains. The room contained so many gatherings he felt would brighten up the place on his trip he barely knew where to begin on investigating.

*

Morning couldn't have come quicker for Robert as the rest of his night was filled with chest pains. Each surge shot throughout, seized his muscles tightly, and stopped his blood flow dead. Trish remained awake to keep an eye on him while Sinclair snoozed.

After a light meal of eggs and toast, the only choice offered for breakfast in the dining car, Robert felt more like himself again - one foot in the grave.

They gathered in Renaldo's quarters after breakfast to discuss further. It had become apparent that their unique events had led all three parties together. Renaldo had acquired the most information, which was minimal.

"Your benefactor left you little to work with, didn't he?" he said after the others had finished explaining their objective. Robert went into more detail about his experiences in London, of how the creature moved without being detected. He noticed everyone shifting uneasily as he described it. Trish rubbed the goosebumps on her forearms. Sinclair stood and paced the room.

Renaldo took notes and nodded emphatically, following up eagerly with questions. His method of note-taking was avant-garde. Hundreds of small pieces of paper, scribbled overwhelmingly with notes, were stashed in every cabin nook. No matter where he stood, he was within arm's reach of sheets of paper to cover sudden cases of euphoria. These were stuffed into numerous pigeonhole cylinders and scattered throughout the cabin. The marvel was how accurate Renaldo's memory was in tracking down the right paper in seconds.

Before he concluded, Robert thought of divulging his visions while traveling on the Orient Express. He was sure by now they were connected to the expedition, particularly the Dreamlands, but until he found that connection, they were nothing more than visions.

"We have an estimation on the direction and how far passed the border the hospital should be found," Sinclair said as he ran his fingers down the map. "If the tracks hold up, we could make it as far south as El Obeid. From there, it's a few hundred kilometers before crossing into the Congo. Should be an amazing sight!"

Sinclair's face had been glued to any window he passed by. There was no mistaking his excitement. Trish had described him as a child visiting the zoo for the first time. Robert learned he carried a Master's degree in zoology from Ghent University and conducted lectures across Europe and parts of Asia.

She had met him during one of his lectures in Florence, Italy, and felt he was too dry and stiff for her liking. Her educational background branched frequently and thinly. While the war had raged in central Europe, she cautiously called Italy home as her eyes kept towards the north. Sinclair had fled to Florence to avoid the dangers in Belgium, masking his travels behind a series of talks at Italian universities.

She would have missed his lecture had it not been for a downpour while sprinting across campus. Dodging into a nearby building, she had interrupted his class after bursting through the doors in the back.

Sinclair had been captivated by her beauty through the drenched and pathetic look and welcomed her to the classroom. Distracted from the lecture, he asked her to dinner before everyone. Trish quickly added to the story that she had no choice but to say yes with all eyes on her.

Once the war had ended, they traveled the continent on college invitations Sinclair continued to receive. Trish had first followed along for the ride, eager to see more than just Italy. Yet, she soon began finding his dry, stiff personality to be sweet and innocent. His passion and knowledge for animals were inspiring, giving her a more focused purpose in life. They had been married for six years.

Sitting in Renaldo's cabin, Robert could see the romantic connection the two showed in subtle ways. Trish had softened up before Robert after his heart attack, as she called it. Throughout the morning, she was always close to Sinclair even though the train cars were small and narrow. Each would glance briefly at the other in a casual, nonchalant way.

Renaldo gave a wink to Robert with a genuine smile and replied to Sinclair, "I'm sure the tracks will be fine, my good fellow. These rails are only a few decades old and become newer the farther south we go.

"In Cairo," Renaldo said as he rested both hands on the top of his cane, "a trader who frequented this region of the Nile gave me the name of a village that trusts Europeans. They don't value any currency, but they are absolutely fascinated by colored gemstones. He said they find them to be fortunes of good luck." He stood up with a groan and moved over to a shelf filled with oddities from his past travels, and withdrew a burlap pouch. Out from it dropped a sapphire, two emeralds, and a topaz onto his hand with a hearty chuckle as if just discovering them.

"Amazing little things, really," he continued after the stunned silence from the crowd. "I am curious to see how the tribe reacts to them. Perhaps they wear them as charms or entirely bizarre means."

Renaldo was a peculiar man. He had been born on October 27th, which he often reminded everyone it coincided with Theodore Roosevelt's birthday, during a torrential storm, which ended with his mother dying from birthing. Grim, as his birthdays reminded him of his loss, upon his 18th, his prominent father was able to gift him a tidy sum to begin his adventurous lifestyle after a successful career in acquiring numerous prosperous mineral mines. As the days passed on their frequently delayed train ride, mainly because of massive herds of wild animals and domestic cattle crossings, Robert learned of Renaldo's wealth through his elaborately fabricated and boisterous tales of grand adventure. Acquiring rare antiquities and relics was at the forefront of each story he spun. A mixture of museums and private collectors shared equal enjoyment to financially carry him through the years. It rang with envy in Robert as he was reminded of what could have been for his career.

He admired and often copied President Roosevelt's hobbies and antics, including big game hunting. The bravado of putting his life on the line against a wild predator thrilled him. On several occasions, as the dreary train continued begrudgingly south along the Nile River, Renaldo would lean off the rear deck of his cabin, holding onto the train with just a rope while aiming a hunting rifle at passing wildlife. He made no effort, however, to gather the dead animals if he was lucky enough to hit anything, stating he was feeding hungry animals.

By the time the whistle blew and the rhythmic chugging of the train's wheels began to slow to a stop in Khartoum, Renaldo had bagged, as he preferred to call it, close to thirty different species. He was greeted with little enthusiasm while they prepared to step off and stretch their legs.

Khartoum was the capital of Anglo-Egyptian Sudan, nestled between the Blue and White Nile rivers which merged to form the longest river in the world. The city's name meant Elephant's Trunk due to the curvature of the Nile where the Blue and White united.

Renaldo led the group off the train with great effort and onto the short boardwalk. Robert watched him take each of the two steps down gingerly and wondered how he expected to keep up with them if they were to navigate on foot.

"My knees sometimes get the best of me," he admitted when asked, "But I suspect our progress will be slowed by the jungle's density more so than my walking pace. We'll be fine, don't you worry, my good man. I've been through plenty of hunting excursions."

Robert didn't doubt his experience. It was how long ago that concerned him. Renaldo's cane allowed for a quicker pace once he reached level ground. There wouldn't be much level ground where they were going.

Their stop in Khartoum was long enough for a quick lunch among the low-profile buildings that dominated the sprawling town. The air was fragrant with apricots and cinnamon.

Much of their lunch conversation was about the upcoming leg of their journey. Renaldo reassured the others of the locals' help as a guide to the border.

"What about a steamer?" Trish had suggested. "I see boats moving up and down the river. We could catch a ride all the way to Victoria. We're past all the cataracts."

The thick porridge of millet and wheat, or Aseeda Dukun to locals, Renaldo had been politely devouring was nearly consumed, and he lowered the spoon into the dish with a satisfying sigh.

"I'm afraid, my dear, that the Sud Swamp makes that option impossible," he said, wiping his mouth with a napkin. "While I know very little of it, I was informed of its terrible danger if navigated. The Romans couldn't even conquer it during their time.

"An influx of aquatic predators and hundreds of miles of maze-like watery passages divided by high tufts of papyrus and hyacinth would make a boat ride daunting."

They exchanged worried glances while Robert leaned back and lit a cigarette he had bought locally. It was harsh, and he stifled a cough before exhaling the smoke.

"Mr. Archibald," he began while taking a slower drag with better control, "I'm marveling at your worldly knowledge." Robert's deadpan expression showed no truth to his words. "Has all this wealth of information come from the single source you obtained in Cairo?"

Their waiter came by to remove the dishes and deliver their check. Renaldo paid without hesitation, then shook his head at Robert.

"Certainly not. I am somewhat obsessed with knowing as much as possible about where I am going. I spent several weeks prior to setting out from Munich studying the geography and cultures of a few countries I suspected I would travel through. Much of my worldly knowledge of this journey, as you so nicely put it, came from a generous and charming gentleman I chanced to meet in Venice.

"He approached me on the docks as I awaited my ship's arrival for Cairo. With him was a satchel that he said belonged to me after introductions. I was startled to realize I had foolishly left it behind at a delightful cafe.

"We both boarded the same vessel, and I quickly learned the gentleman was traveling to Cairo to witness the pyramids in person."

By this part of his story, the four had returned to Renaldo's quarters a few minutes before the train began lurching toward El Obeid. While continuing, he brought out brandy and shared a few drinks.

"To say I am worldly knowledgeable would have been an understatement compared to him. He was simply a genius. I found myself captivated by his grand elegance and sophistication as he delivered answers to my questions time and time again."

Robert smirked at the mention of elegance and sophistication, suspecting the conversation had gone on for hours like two noblemen discussing world events.

"It was such a shame our paths had to branch away, but not until after I departed did I realize how specific he had been in detailing the precise route I was about to take. He knew where I was going before I did. I had only mentioned my ticket to board the train and that my plans beyond had yet to be set. I had subconsciously taken the same course before the realization."

Robert leaned forward in his chair and set the glass down. With earnest eyes, he stared intently at Renaldo, who trailed off in puzzlement. Renaldo's story had made him uneasy as his suspicions grew.

"Did this companion have a name?" Robert asked as he glanced around the room at the others.

"Yes, he had an unusual one," Renaldo replied. "Phineas. It's a Hebrew name, I believe. Why? Do you know him?"

Sinclair said, "You're right. It is Hebrew for the serpent's mouth." The zoologist gave a concerned look as he spouted the encyclopedic information. "Sometimes 'oracle' depending on the interpretation. He was the one who ended the plague that God sent to punish the Israelites for..."

"Okay," Trish interrupted. "It's Hebrew."

"Describe him to me," Robert continued. By now, he was barely sitting in his chair. Perhaps it was paranoia and suspicion of what Delven was capable of. He was beginning to think Renaldo's companion was the same person.

His eagerness made Renaldo nervous. He twiddled his fingertips against each other as his head turned to everyone.

"As I said," he stammered. "He was a sophisticated gentleman. His suit looked brand new, with a red flower against his lapel. He wore a fedora and carried about him a polished mahogany cane. Clean-shaven. Minor scar on the right eyebrow. I believe he was British."

They sat silently for a few minutes, all eyes upon Robert as he was in deep thought. Visions returned to his meeting with Delven back in Cairo. Delven always wore extravagant suits whenever he could, even out in the field. Still, he needed a more astute description besides fancy attire and a scar.

Ever since he left London, one step after another, all things connected with each other, and Delven was the nucleus of it all. Coincidence had fleeted Robert's suspicion. He wondered if he had made the wrong decision not to put a bullet in Delven when he had the chance.

So what was Delven's angle? If he had been in Italy, what was his drive to bring together four strangers into the remote jungle? Robert was all too familiar with his manipulation when dirty.

Snapping out of his thoughts, he glanced up. "There may not be a hospital when we get there."

"Yeah, Robert, it went silent. That's why we're. . . "Trish started to say.

"No, I mean it never existed to begin with," Robert explained to puzzled faces. "Delven wants us to go into the Congo for some other reason. All four of us. He baited me for the ride with the sketch of the same creature I saw back home. He baited you, Renaldo, with his charm. You couldn't resist. And you two?"

The couple briefly looked at each other to decide who would talk, and Trish nodded. "He was arranging for Sinclair's lectures."

"I thought I was more popular among academic circles than I was," Sinclair added. "It turned out it was just the pocketbook of Delven paying the schools to hire me. People showed up, but looking back, I always noticed I would be placed in old, nearly forgotten classrooms as if they were embarrassed. I was too grateful for the jobs to ever question it."

Trish picked up the conversation in perfect rhythm with Sinclair. "Delven attended the last lecture he held. We hadn't heard from universities lately and wondered if something might have happened. He spoke to Sinclair about his future, then proposed this expedition when we had no plans."

Robert got up from his chair and paced over to a window. The train had slowed dramatically across the tracks while a large herd of wildebeests galloped across. Tens of thousands in number pounded the ground thunderously and threw massive dust clouds into the air.

He pivoted to address his companions. "That leaves us in the dark on Delven's motive. We can all agree that, given what we know, the coincidences are peculiar. I've never trusted him in the years I've known him."

"Then why are you following his orders?" Renaldo asked, rolling his fingers across the cap of his cane.

The investigator had asked himself the same question several times along the trip. What was driving him? Was his curiosity so great to discover what this bizarre creature was that he would follow his enemy so blindly?

They sat in silence as the rumblings from the wildebeests slowly faded away into the evening. No one had an answer to Renaldo's question. Something beyond curiosity was pulling them onward, or they were fools with little to live for.

*

The night before they arrived in El-Obeid, Renaldo Archibald III was troubled and had paced the length of the train for hours. Car after car, he wandered in silence, pondering his predicament. He had grown tired of tossing in his bed with the fear of coincidence on his mind, but so far, walking wasn't helping.

Too many coincidental situations befuddled him. In front of his new companions, he had worn his jovial face to hide his concern, but he was growing ever more frightened. Traveling across Europe had been his dream, seeking hidden treasures as his father had when he was a child. Yet fate forced him down a path he felt he had no control over. After what he witnessed in the deepest regions of the Black Forest, he found himself in the company of three people aware of the same thing. Of all the trains, time schedules, and places he could have gone, his life's path fell in line with the courses of strangers that shared his secret.

What they all knew was known by presumably such a small number of people in the world, perhaps only themselves, that the likelihood of them finding one another was virtually nil. Yet here they were.

As he walked, he paused for the fourth time to look behind him in the lonely train car. The hairs on his neck had risen once again, and he felt he was being followed. He had passed no one in over an hour. At this hour, even the staff was quietly gathered somewhere towards the front cars, leaving the train's riders to their slumber.

Something stirred in the dark shadows at the end of the car. There was movement just beyond the last window, where a nook had been built to hold decorations.

Since Europe, Renaldo was confident he was hunting something sinister, something foul. But as the black, ooze-covered spider-like form slid from the darkness into the dull moonlight, he suddenly realized he had been hunted the entire time.

Visions of his hunting rifle formed in his mind as it comfortably rested on an ornately carved wooden plaque back in his car. He trusted no pistol and carried no weapons while he wandered the aisles. Only retreating away from the creature was his form of attack. Daring not to turn his eyes away for fear it would lunge at him, he guided himself with his hands behind his back. He stumbled against a standing ashtray sending its contents across the carpet. There was nothing else for him, so he grabbed and wielded it with two hands tightly, knocking the ashtray itself onto the floor to leave him with the stem.

Plans changed for Renaldo now. The hunter inside him took over, and he began to advance strategically with purpose. He swayed from side to side as he had with some predators to confuse their monocular vision. He doubted this contained eyes at all. The only way to win this fight, he was sure, was to attack first.

It glided with ease down the hall, sending tentacles in quick, straight shots at the surrounding aisle to pull itself closer to him. The motion was methodical and showed no urgency. Renaldo had judged the creature to be more instinctual rather than cunning. The lack of speed made him consider otherwise.

His window of opportunity came suddenly upon him. The length of the ashtray's stand, perhaps three feet, gave him some reach, but the tentacles were much longer. His eyes grew wide, and with a spike in adrenaline, he leaped forward, sending the spear-like weapon deep into the beast's center. The pierce came easy, but he didn't give up and continued to drive the metal further. His subconscious mind observed while no blood exited from the puncture wound, his grip had become wet, but his rage of battle clouded that thought until he calmed down. With gritted teeth, he held the metal stem firmly, bracing himself against the thick carpet beneath him, and watched the life rapidly drain from the creature.

A moment later, the thing lay limp at the end of his makeshift weapon, the tendrils having retracted, leaving nothing more than a black glob of goo. His quick action had prevented being attacked, but part of him felt disheartened by such an easy fight. Had it been defenseless against him, or could it be it was not threatening him to begin with?

He stood there holding the blob dangling lifelessly for several minutes, which bobbed and sloshed like a rocking bowl of liquid gelatin. From his point of view, the shape began to look like a human head and torso. It was curious, but the form bore a resemblance more and more like a human body with every passing second.

And suddenly, it was a human. The person was a male, perhaps in his 40s, wearing the uniform of the train's staff, now soaked with dark red blood from the wound. Beneath the motionless body grew a pool of blood that began flowing into the carpet. The body's weight ripped the stem out of Renaldo's hands, but from the horror he saw, he let go anyway.

"Oh, my God. Not again," Renaldo muttered to himself as he stared at his hands soaked with blood. Had he been attacked by the creature that he tracked? Had his mind deceived him, or had his past returned to haunt him? No, he forced himself the other night to say he was in control of his own fate, not it. Yet he committed murder, again, unbeknownst to him. How could he keep letting this happen?

There was no mistaking the dead staff member bleeding before him. Whatever he saw a moment earlier was never the truth. He had to deal with what was true now.

Struggling between dead weight and Renaldo's obese size, he did his best to deliver it to the end of the car, where he opened the door to the open air in between. It would be consumed by night scavengers and picked clean by dawn. The following day, there would be a search for the missing staff, perhaps an investigation if they were so motivated, but they would find nobody.

Breathing heavily and feeling his age, he wept silently to himself at his horrible act. He was shameful, but he knew no other solution that would not hinder the trip. Where fate was pulling them to could not be diverted or stalled despite his most vigorous efforts. He just hoped God would forgive him when he faced judgment.

Late in the night, the stain was gone; the carpet had been cut away, leaving a peculiar but typical hole. No one noticed it when the sun rose. It was just another characteristic of an old, run-down train.

CHAPTER XI

Renaldo Archibald III, 1876-1926

He guessed adventure and wonder were in his blood. Born to a prosperous entrepreneur who found his wealth in buying deeply remote mineral mines, young Renaldo Archibald III would wait for weeks, sometimes months, for his father to return home from the latest exciting journey he sought in search of his next fortune. Renaldo Archibald, Jr. first struck good luck during America's Civil War after the bad luck of a Southern troop eliminating his troop and driving him into a dense West Virginia forest alone. For days he was hunted through the hills, constantly pursued by the rebels who had killed his war friends.

Stumbling his way over upturned roots and thick patches of soft, black soil, his steps found a covered sinkhole that sent him falling below. The fall sprained his ankle, shooting pain up his leg, and made it difficult to climb back out. His time spent recovering down there was rewarded by the discovery of rich veins of gold exposed to the evening air.

He was bitten by the bug from those riches to many others who had fallen victim. So Renaldo, Jr. sought additional remote locations, driving himself into harsher conditions in hopes of stumbling upon more significant areas. This led the Father of One into dangerous situations, encountering strange and bizarre wonders the world had not witnessed before.

Upon returning home, Renaldo III would anxiously listen to the tales his father would spin for him of his travels from far and wide. Each story woven would be embellished more and more, adding fantastical beasts encountered until his father was fabricating nearly all of his stories. To his son, he had become a legend. As he grew into young adulthood, his future plans always wanted to follow in his father's footsteps. There was a point in his maturity when the truth of the stories' exaggeration came to be known, but by then, the young man didn't care. He would make his travels an adventure.

His father had gained enough wealth by the time Renaldo reached 19, so he didn't need to work for a living. However, his father insisted that he acquire an education before galloping worldwide. He felt exploration and discovery of the world didn't demand a specific focus in college, so he pursued what thrilled and interested him. He sought out philosophy, science, engineering, and history. Although the curriculum didn't favor a recognized, established field of study except for a General Education degree, his father made a discrete donation to assist the administration in creating a "Renaissance" of sorts degree that his son could complete. The expanded range inspired many other students. By the time Renaldo III graduated with his Bachelor's degree, his university had officially offered a Bachelor of Science in Scholarly Studies, as they titled it, due to the increased inquiries of students.

Armed with his newly gained wisdom and a nice stipend from his father to get his feet wet, the young man faced the most challenging decision of his life - where to go first? He had considered accompanying his father for a few adventures, which his sire encouraged. In the end, he wanted to explore alone like his father had.

Most of his life had been tied to America's New England area, and he had already heard about much of the States from his father's tales. New adventures were further away, so he bought a ticket for a steam liner to take him across the Atlantic to traverse Europe with his destination to ultimately be somewhere in Asia. From his studies, he felt the farther east he went, the more exotic discoveries he would find. At least, alien to Renaldo Archibald III.

His love for hunting came later in his life. His father was good with a rifle, having been with the Union Army during the Civil War. The young boy hated the loud explosion the rifle produced, even with cotton heavily stuffed in his ears.

When his maiden European voyage brought him into Germany, he fell in with a gathering of a woodsman who often explored deep into the heart of the Black Forest. During the nights around campfires cooking fresh meat from that day's hunt, the huntsmen spun stories of fairy tales and legends, much like Renaldo's father. He was captivated by each one, filled with danger and mystical enlightenment, claiming the fantastical creatures and hidden, ancient settlements were more profound in the forest.

During those travels, the men of the forest showed him the way of the rifle, giving him new methods and experience that removed the fear of the loud noise it produced. Soon he delivered an outstanding, natural talent of marksmanship and began leading the rest on the hunts as he uncovered an exceptional sense of tracking.

Despite the group moving deeper into the Black Forest, they failed to uncover secrets or hidden treasures. His discoveries only came when he was traveling solo. Perhaps the presence of his woodsmen friends kept the mysticism of the forest at bay. While they assured him that it was inevitable in time, Renaldo kept thinking of his father.

Renaldo was meant to travel alone and eventually bid farewell to his friends to explore more isolated regions of Germany. His prediction proved true only a week after leaving them.

A cold, heavy rain began to fall around him through thickly covered pine trees. The drops hit hard against the needles and dead leaves on the ground, sending rhythmic patterns of nature to his ears.

For several hours, his vision was poor. The extreme rainfall and the close clusters of trees yielded little distance for his sight. Yet through the pine trees, shrouded in thick forest, his travels came across a village.

The buildings were all straightforward, one-room shelters, but each was constructed from natural stone and topped with wood bark coated in heavy moss. From inside, each told a story of the previous inhabitants.

As he explored, he learned they didn't pack up and relocate. However, all across the ground in the wet, dark mud were bare footprints mixed with huge canine paws the size of a bear. Essential tools and instruments were left behind with no one in sight.

Nowhere could he find signs of violence, though. There were no splatters of old blood or damaged clutter, but the town was not well-defended. None of the buildings had doors. Instead, they had draped heavy leather skins across the openings, which would do little to stop predators.

The night was already thick from the dense forest, and Renaldo grew weary of the day's travel. The various shelters would keep the rain off him while he slept, but he feared a return of what made the paw prints. There was covered firewood near several houses that provided dry wood to burn. Soon, he had a moderate fire burning near the entrance of a building he had chosen for the night. He was confident that if the fire could stay lit, predators would keep their distance, and he could leap over easily should he have to evacuate quickly.

But the night made him restless in the forgotten village. Several times he partially awoke drearily to moonlight cascading through the window, but only upon waking a third time did he catch the unwonted phenomenon. There was no clearing above the heavy old pine trees to allow moonlight to come down, and the rain foretold a whole night of overcast weather.

He rose from the hay-filled bed, stretching his arms sleepily, and approached the opening. His fire had fallen to hot coals that gave off a welcome warmth against the chill night air, but his eyes were fixed on the scene that chilled his bones that night.

Shimmering blue visions of figures moved throughout the buildings and went about their business as any day. They were wavering translucent apparitions, their shapes softly swaying in the midnight darkness. Each one dressed in clothes of nature that dated centuries ago. The women were garbed in leaves and fur from shoulder to hip, while the men wore heavy leathers draped over their shoulders. Their effulgent glimmer gave the moonlight glow through the window. Isolated, they barely were detectable in the dark, but he could easily walk around without stumbling into objects in the presence of all of them. It was as if the moon was full and shown brightly down upon them.

All of his attempts at communicating or gaining their attention failed. They didn't communicate among themselves or stop to socialize with one another. They walked in a trance and followed the motions of the day as if memory alone drove them.

Though strange and disturbing as the sight initially had seemed, Renaldo soon found no other ideas to pursue. He hoped to find something he had overlooked the night before when daylight broke. He had encountered an authentic ghost town filled with remnants of the past that vanished with no record. Whatever tragedy befell them was not apparent.

After restocking the fire with larger logs, the rest of the night, he slept on the floor of the house he chose after discovering his bed was now occupied by a sleeping woman that softly glowed in the darkness.

He was nearly killed in the morning by a great beast that loomed over him.

It was enormous in size, towering over him like a horse. It had the likeness of a wolf but with black tentacles erupting down its spine, moving with life and pinning him down. Eyes solid white, they writhed with tiny worms just under the surface like a parasite. In place of teeth, its mouth was filled with thin, small human-like fingers covered in tiny, black hairs and smelled of foul death.

With incredible speed, the creature plunged its alien mouth onto Renaldo's shoulder. No other time had he witnessed more pain than the bite it delivered. It was more intense than buckshot and lingered to the point of shock. The numerous fingers, equipped with needle-like hair follicles, drove themselves deep into his flesh and began to wiggle feverishly.

The fires had died almost entirely again, and if it weren't for Renaldo's quick action, his grave would have been in that simple cottage in Germany. His arm was extended from the position he had slept in near a branch still smoldering. With all his might, he plunged the stick deep into the beast's side, exiting the other side. Blood ruptured from the animal, engulfing the young man to near suffocation. He gagged at the taste, failing to avoid it flowing into his mouth when the beast dropped heavily upon him. The wind was knocked out of his lungs from the weight, and once again, he feared he might have met his doom.

After great effort, however, he twisted the branch enough to wiggle his way out from underneath. He struggled to his feet from the exertion. The door frame supported him while he regained his breath and allowed him to scan the rest of the village for more beasts. To his fear, he was surrounded by patrolling creatures of the same size. They hesitated to advance on him while keeping their eyes glancing in his direction.

Renaldo made no hesitation and reached for his hunting rifle, a Spencer repeating carbine he had purchased from one of the huntsmen. Each aim was brisk and accurate, firing down upon the rest of the beasts and sending each one to the next life. Some attempted to flee, but his rifle bore down on them before they separated themselves too far. Others growled and tried charging at him, but a wide swing from the butt of his long rifle drew them back enough to give Renaldo time to bury a bullet in each.

By now, the bite on his shoulder was screaming at him, but his rage and fear for his life temporarily hid the pain while he finished them all. With his smoking hot gun, he stood above the dead carcasses that spread throughout the town, sending the clash of gunpowder into utter silence.

He tended to his wound for a moment, gently wrapping it with a strip of his shirt and wincing in pain the entire time. The flesh wounds were deep and numerous across his shoulder, forming a series of disturbingly sickening and unnatural holes. He doubted the dressing would hold.

His attention returned to the carnage, and he dropped his rifle. The stick he used to kill the first was now speared completely through the woman who slept in his bed, now fully formed in the flesh. The enormous fur shapes were nothing more than villagers dressed in the same rugged clothing he saw the night before as ghosts.

There were tales of werewolves among the hunters, but he saw no werewolves a moment before. Stories of creatures with no wicked tendrils jutting from their backs or mouths full of skin-crawling fingers. This was a thing of nightmares no mortal could conceive or should ever witness.

For the moment, he convinced himself they were some bestial formation that could make itself appear human, thus relieving his conscience of guilt. He had fought for his life. They were creatures not meant to be seen by mortals, and the idea gave him shivers. They were not simple villagers. But the massacre before him played tricks in his head to make him think otherwise.

Along with the creatures, something else was new to the village. A vardo, a wooden wagon built for living, was parked at the edge without a horse or ox to pull it. Strings of ribbon hung from the roof's eve, and a small metal smokestack rose above. Snaking slowly up from the rim of the metal pipe was thin wisps of smoke.

As he drew near the front door, there was the faint sound of an accordion softly playing from within. With his ear cautiously pressed to the door, he guessed it came from a Victrola.

Tentatively he knocked but received no reply. Once again, he attempted to gain attention with a knock. If anyone was inside, they avoided receiving visitors or were hard of hearing. He glanced around in a moment of hesitation.

The hairs on his neck stood up as he felt watched, but no ghosts or beasts were anywhere.

When he tried, the door was not locked, and he slowly cracked it open, listening for any warning not to continue further. He received no answer and opened it fully.

Bookshelves filled with leather-bound novels lined both walls from front to back, leading to a small bay window at the rear. A wood stove was the centerpiece, currently crackling a small fire from inside and giving a comforting warmth from the cold bite from outside.

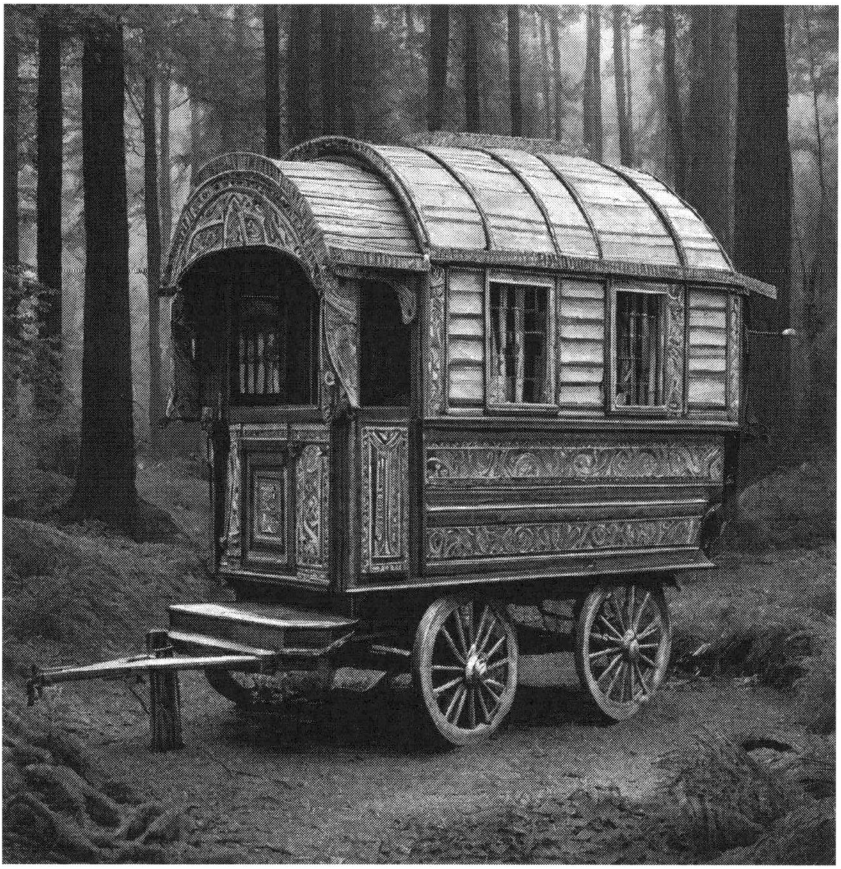

Behind the stove were a round table and a high-back, tuft chair. A skull of some horned animal, along with an extinguished candle, rested on the table, and poised on its short hind legs in the chair was what could only be described as ghoulish.

It was hellish indeed. Crouched in the seat, it stood no more than three feet, but fully erected, Renaldo surmised another two. Like the skull resting before it, its cranium was decorated with horns curved like a ram around long, pointy ears and accompanied by additional straight and ribbed horns over a foot long.

There was exceptional intelligence in the harsh, yellow cat-like eyes as it stared with a sheepish grin. Long, slender fingers bridged themselves as it studied its visitor.

As the day was overcast, the shadows in the vardo were heavy. The creature gestured with a finger to the unlit candle, causing it to erupt into a glorious blaze before settling into typical candlelight. All the time, the beast never took its eyes off Renaldo.

The young man's blood was ice cold at sight, and he was lost for words. The shock of his world had suddenly twisted sharply around, and the realization left him immobilized.

For several minutes, as the candle's flame slowly danced side to side hypnotically, the two stood tensely in silence while the ghoul seemed to scheme.

Renaldo was overwhelmed with the blunt truth of all he had witnessed that day. Seeing the cunning in its eyes, Renaldo guessed it empowered those outside, whatever they were. Regardless of his own wisdom, he felt inferior standing before the ghoul.

After overthinking his situation, Renaldo finally regained control over his legs and stepped into the room. The motion caused the ghoul to flinch, but it remained otherwise. Even so, ever gazing at Renaldo.

The old, dry floorboards ached with each step from the young man as he approached the stove to get a closer look at the creature behind the desk. Its eyes blinked so infrequently it reminded Renaldo of a crocodile, doing so not from necessity but with dramatic effect.

Renaldo paused briefly to look at the titles of books he passed for anything familiar, wondering what a creature of hell could possibly read. Not only were they all unknown to him, but the words printed on the spines were also tough to identify the language. Some were written with frightening cuneal markings and strange forbidden runes that gave even further wonder about the hidden dark mysteries within their pages.

With what seemed like a year to cross the room, Renaldo stood as close as he dared go before the ghoul. Its yellow cat eyes stared at him with a frozen grin, now close enough to see two rows of thin, needle-thick teeth interlocked together. It presented a deck of cards that manifested before his eyes and rested on the table beside the skull. With a slow, smooth swing of its arms, it motioned over the deck as it kept its eyes locked on Renaldo.

He knew what it wanted but wasn't comfortable dealing with the creature. In all his life, he dreamed of mythical creatures and faraway lands spun in glorious tales by his father. He longed for such discoveries, and the stories had warned him of dangers that lurked in the world's most remote locations. Never in his darkest dreams did he ever guess his adventures would contain such foul creatures of evil!

This was never meant to be witnessed by mankind, but his fear had waned dramatically since he had entered the wagon from a lack of aggression from it. More or less, this was what he had been seeking, and he was exhilarated at the experience.

His confidence rose to match the creature, and he reached down to flip the top card over from the deck. Trying to conduct seances on a Saturday night among coeds had been a joy for Renaldo. He had seen friends at the university toy with tarot cards. Yet these cards were from no tarot deck.

The card he had flipped and laid on the table bore his likeness. It was a painting of him as he posed proudly with a hunting dog at his feet and a rifle at his side. The detail was superb, with the difference being the card's version was older, perhaps by fifteen years. The room he posed in was unfamiliar, with a large wooden wall behind, but little else was visible within the view.

With another sweep of the creature's arm across the deck, Renaldo followed the order with another card turned. This time, the painting depicted a vicious, brutal scene of lions feasting upon a dying zebra, its mouth frozen in an endless scream.

It was disturbing to see an uncanny likeness, but he struggled to understand the second one. It was a graphic image of violence, but Renaldo was unsure if he was meant to interpret the cards himself or take them at face value. He was not violent, having never been in a fight. Or perhaps the card meant a destination he would soon reach – Africa? Curiously he went for a third card, but the creature shook its head and lifted half the deck to offer the one somewhere midway down the stack. It was peculiar that the cards were being dealt to him seemingly randomly. Yet, the ghoul was manipulating this particular reveal.

It was unclear what the third card depicted. A blotted ink spill, devoid of shape, covered most of the card.

Tiny dots speckled across the extended appendages of the splotch forced Renaldo to bend closely. Like a squid or octopus, the image was of numerous narrow antennae or limbs coated with small lesions.

Although a simple playing card printed on cardboard, this image shimmered as if it were a moving picture. A pucker motion of lesions opened and closed like a woman's lips after applying lipstick.

Renaldo felt confused between the three cards. They felt less like fortunes from a tarot card and more random and chaotic in order. He was unsure what to make of them and struggled to identify their purpose.

It gazed up into Renaldo's bright blue eyes in anticipation. He had gotten more than he had hoped, setting out for high adventure and discovery. Deep inside, Renaldo questioned if he was made for this. Was anyone made for this? It was difficult for him to fathom logic in his predicament. Had it traveled this far from civilization, or had it initially inhabited the forest only to be invaded by the villagers?

Then there were the cards that tied to him. What was the reasoning behind them? How did it know he would be here? It might have a taste for human flesh yet Renaldo stood before him unhindered.

Never completely taking his eyes off the creature, Renaldo took a second look at the books on the shelves. He hoped a reader would catch his eye and shed more light on the cards. His finger tracked down the shelves slowly, sliding over the ridges of each leather spine, until it stopped on "Gthugthane: Prodigal Knowledge of Forbidden Waste." The odd title would have been overlooked had it not shifted, on its own, when Renaldo touched it.

He recoiled, but when the book didn't move after that, he pulled it off the shelf and opened it.

There was nothing out of the ordinary about the cover. Stretched in black dyed leather, it bore no insignia or markings on the surface other than the title on the spine, which had been stamped in red. The professionalism in its entirety made the contents questionable, however.

Each page had been handwritten or painted in a delicate, tedious derivative of a copperplate manuscript. Ink color varied between black and red, filling pages with chaotic ideas and philosophical concepts that caused Renaldo's brain to immediately ache.

He pressed a hand against his temple, bending over as the pain swelled and throbbed. There hadn't been much time to ascertain details before his head surged. Still, he understood its purpose was revealing secrets, potentially dark historical events, that had gone unknown by mankind for eons. While he could not recall specific content, vivid words such as "stygian," "crepuscular blood demands," and "caliginous wickedness" rang in his mind as he awaited the pain to subside.

The creature crouched and nodded slowly to the young man as he held the book of evil dread. It wanted him to have it. Despite its mouth being widely grinning already, it stretched open further to extend its smile of pleasure, exposing dozens more needle-sharp teeth.

His headache quickly subsided, and Renaldo couldn't help returning to the book and ignoring the potential consequences he had just experienced. However, there was slight discomfort this time, and he could pour through it more thoroughly.

Time passed as he stood there reading through the book, page by page, unable to put it down. The words at first were beyond his vocabulary. In time, his mind consumed them all and followed the disorganized, disorienting text.

He followed the horrific truth that supported what he witnessed that day. The world was shared by others, the book described, that often slept and dwelt in isolation for what humans conceive as thousands if not millions of years but a mere heartbeat in time for them. Upon particular circumstances, mortals and forbidden sights cross paths, often resulting in the mortal's demise.

It was too much for him, but a force compelled him to complete the reading. When he had finished, considerable time had passed. He had neither slept nor eaten but had no desire or need. Several days later, when he emerged from the dark depths of the Black Forest back into civilization, he would learn months had passed.

The ghoul allowed Renado to leave the area unscathed, but not without the book he had read. He doubted he could open it again but couldn't get rid of it. Part of his mind sequestered his experience to a safe amount of his brain where it wouldn't be forgotten yet safely tucked away. It allowed his jovial, boisterous self to nurture and thrive on later journeys.

Some things were not meant to be understood, he thought to himself while wandering the world. The saying gave him peace of mind not to overanalyze things that were impossible to comprehend fully. His world was expanded to include the possibility of other things among him not meant to be witnessed by mortal eyes. Holding that thought close to his heart was vital as his discoveries led to different dark, dangerous experiences.

It wasn't for several years until Renaldo finally connected the ghoul's cards to him. There was little in the case of doubt to their meaning once he found himself stalking the strange, octopean behemoth witnessed on the third card he drew. Finding himself returning near the Reinhardswald in Germany, he had caught loose rumors, perhaps closer to drunken tales, among several villages close to the borders of Denmark. A weaving of stories throughout the area formed together to give him an eerily specific location for its lair.

Until he lay on the soft, moist moss-covered grounds of a shallow hollow staring into a large cavity burrow under a tree stump, Renaldo had not spotted any supernatural entity save the ghoul and wolves. During his travels, he uncovered wondrous sights. He explored breathtaking regions, some accompanied by strangers he befriended and others entirely isolated. Never did he forget the potential of coming across another monstrosity.

On this day, he had pushed himself perhaps too far. His only companion for this expedition had been a pack mule. It had been mortally wounded by a wolf three nights earlier before Renaldo could get a shot off. He was forced to abandon all but the most essential supplies he could carry, and those supplies had already grown thin. He had been confident after studying various charts in this region based on the stories he had been told. He soon realized how easy it was to get lost or how challenging it was to pinpoint an exact spot in a dense forest.

Regardless of his troubles and the rumbling of hunger in his stomach, his hard work had paid off on a heavy mist-filled morning. A drizzle lasted an hour when he woke, and he was worried he would have to delay yet another day for ideal conditions. But he knew it was most likely as good of conditions as he would get.

The first sight of the beast had nearly sent Renaldo to an early grave. It possessed deadly quiet mobility; he had no idea how close it had gotten behind him before it pounced. Like a thick shower of molasses that moved as fast as a bullet, the black ooze lurched down Renaldo's body, engulfing his head firsts and surging quickly to his feet. He was suffocating and immobile for several seconds while the membrane rippled against his flesh. All over his body, he felt the sickly sensation of the lesions attached and sucking against his skin. They pulled violently, drawing out large welts everywhere, and although he felt no cuts, it was as if the creature was draining him like a leech to weaken him.

Fortunately for the brave hunter, Renaldo wasn't entirely pinned, only immobile. He could reach his cigar lighter and flick it to life. The flame was small but sufficient to aggravate the creature, and he was spat out. He quickly rolled on the ground towards the nearly cold campfire and swept a gathering of hot coals with the butt of his rifle onto his attacker. The black mass rose to a total height of over twelve feet, then tumbled over like a wave and shot off, jutting hundreds of tendrils out to anchor onto vegetation and pulling itself through. Renaldo was alone for a few seconds, and the creature was nowhere to be found.

After he packed his things, he set out towards it, aiming to be better prepared for the second round. Stalking it was not easy. He saw its direction when it fled, but beyond that, he had no earthly idea where it went. Intuition led him to the tree in the hollow. As he scouted, a growing foreboding crept over him. At first, he thought he might be hunted by wolves just out of sight. Eventually, he found himself carefully climbing down the steep embankment of a sunken den that bored deep underground. There was no assurance other than his gut feeling that it was hiding down there, but he trusted his senses and waited as long as necessary.

Hours slowly pressed on, giving him little to work with. The mist gathered around thicker as the day rolled on into twilight, sending the hollow into a deep, dark abyss. His eyes were already growing heavy from being forced to hold still and stay poised with his rifle, and he knew he couldn't keep it up much longer.

Frustrated and exhausted, Renaldo devised a plan and started a small fire near the burrow's opening. He hoped it was enough to keep it down there, if it was at all.

Despite his best efforts, it came at night and attacked him through his dreams. Rather than physical assaults, he was assailed. At the same time, he slept, sending terrible sights and evil visions while preventing him from awakening.

He heard a voice, deep and rich, that vibrated his bones as it spoke to him as if some godly power unleashed its wrath. Sending visions of his past, he watched himself attack innocent villagers, gunning them down individually as they ran for their lives, screaming in terror. It spoke of his delusional episode, describing its ghastly work of creating such illusions of monstrous creatures to fool him into murdering them all. Ultimately, it was purely for the chaotic satisfaction of sheer horror the animal thrived upon. It willed itself upon the weak mind of Renaldo, giving him false visions of a threat to hide innocence.

Throughout the night, he was tortured by these nightmares, unable to end them. By morning his mind could not distract from the idea that he murdered innocents in cold blood. He had been manipulated and controlled, but ultimately he pulled the trigger and ended people's lives.

His mind was wrecked, and the experience jarred his confidence. It caused him to question whether his visions of the supernatural were true, which made him scared to death that he would make the wrong decision and either end someone's life or be killed by the real thing. In his days, he had faced angry, dangerous animals, escaped vicious attacking tribes, and avoided certain death among hundreds of traps. That night, he learned the true meaning of hopeless vulnerability.

The grand allure of wild adventures that led to wondrous treasures his father had explored was far from the fate Renaldo had been dealt. Rather than glorious excitement, he had become exposed to such a sinister secret that he wondered if it was even worth continuing. How could anyone go on living in a world where powers beyond your control could trick you into committing deadly sinful deeds unknowingly?

Nothing shook his guilt of murdering that day. It festered in his mind, and he carried doubt with him for years, questioning his judgment with every rifle shot. While the thing was now long gone, the fear nearly drove him mad, and, over the years, his mind slowly protected itself by developing a false, jovial personality that concealed his insecurity. He wondered if he could deduce the next sighting as accurate. He trusted his first action would be the right one.

Recovered from the attack and returned to civilization, he knew he could go in only one direction. As long as the beast lived, he would always be in fear and self-doubt, never to have the confidence he once wore proudly. It was responsible for Renaldo's pain and swore vengeance upon it.

He felt like a fool to follow such a vague signal, but the three cards burned in his mind fiercely and wouldn't let go. He didn't know what he ultimately would find, but Africa was his destination. Although the purity of adventure like his father lived had been tainted, Renaldo was determined not to let his dream die.

Perhaps, he wondered as he made arrangements for a luxurious, yet comfortable train car to await him in Cairo, he needed help killing it. The only question was, could he convince them he hadn't lost his mind.

CHAPTER XII

El-Obeid, 1926

A week passed without another heart attack, and Robert's concern about it reoccurring waned. His sleeping had even improved. There had been no future visions of the Dreamlands. His strange experiences throughout Europe had not followed him into Africa. He wasn't sure if he should be relieved or suspicious.

A harsh brief jolt brought their train to a stop, and the small station was engulfed in a cloud of white vapor from its release. From the few passengers, it would be a lonely return trip to Egypt.

Several dozen passengers had made it to the end of the 4,000-kilometer railway. Robert politely pushed through the small crowd into the station, a single-occupant building with two teller windows facing the train. The red brick walls and wooden ceilings regularly flourished throughout the buildings in town. The Andalusian architecture reflected ancient Islamic culture. It was operated by a single British employee who was busily ruffling through stacks of mail. The building was surrounded by a large wooden platform that stood a foot off the red clay dirt. Half as large as Robert, Cargo crates were neatly stacked near a corral filled with livestock.

As Robert wound through the small crowd, he thought his imagination had gotten the best of him. Taking a second glance behind, the tall, dark figure of Captain Harold Tee of the Jack Whistle had walked past him without any sign of recognition. His uniform gone, he looked as ordinary as the natives of the town, albeit a few inches taller. Accompanying him were two individuals Robert didn't recognize, each holding the handles of a large steamer trunk.

Robert forgot his companions for a moment and drifted after Harold, reaching out to tap him on the shoulder. It caused the man to stop abruptly in his tracks without a hint of being surprised by the sudden touch from behind. He turned to face Robert, and there was a moment of uncertainty from Harold before he recognized him and showed the warm smile from the last they met.

"Mr. Kipner, you are here," Harold said with his smile locked to his face. He extended his hand to Robert with unusually long fingers. Robert gripped the hand and noticed Harold's engulfed his. He didn't recall it being so long before.

"Yes, I am here. I would never have expected to run into you in El-Obeid. What happened to the Jack Whistle?"

The two with Harold had yet to stop or notice Robert's interruption. They were loading the cargo into the back of an unpainted Ford Huckster. The trunk bore no markings on it, but it had multiple locked latches.

"The Jack Whistle is in excellent condition, Mr. Kipner, not to worry. I am just making a delivery that required my personal assistance," the captain answered. His French accent was gone, replaced now with a Russian dialect. "Now, if you will excuse me, Mr. Kipner, I must fulfill my expectations, or I shall be reprimanded."

Harold released the handshake and abruptly turned to enter the truck with the two in the back guarding the trunk.

As if things weren't odd enough, Robert thought as he watched the Huckster shake to life and drive off. Just before the vehicle buckled on, there was a moment Robert swore the trunk bounced on its own. Then the truck disappeared into the streets.

The town of El-Obeid, despite the small train station, was good sized, with several tens of thousands calling it home. It had a sprinkling of Catholicism amid a solid Muslim following. Centered in the heart of the city was Our Lady Queen of Africa Cathedral, initially built piece by piece in Italy and in the direction Renaldo led them. Its front facade, a peppermint stripe pattern of mauve and taupe, gazed upon travelers with its rose window.

Not far from the cathedral was a large stockyard filled with Butana and Kenana. Several dozen were being led into open-faced barns to be milked. One of these barns was Renaldo's destination, and he ducked his head through the low doorway.

The four were disconnected from the culture surrounding them inside. Many farmers stared silently from around or under large cattle at the sound of sloshing milk spraying into wooden buckets.

The heat radiating made the stench unbearable. Robert's shoes sunk a few inches into the mixture of mud and manure as he stumbled to keep up with his guide, who seemed to have no issues traversing through the barn. They passed unpainted, obliquely angled fences and troughs barren of water.

Renaldo reached a set of stairs that led them up to an airy loft filled with hay and countless rats. The vermin showed no fear, often lunging if they got too close.

"You sure act like you've been here before," Trish said as she kicked at an exceptionally aggressive rat. "I thought we were talking to a tribe?"

He continued to the back of the loft without answering. He found a sickeningly skinny old man busily packing hay into a wooden mold. His arms were skeletal, yet he moved with youth and wisdom, wrapping heavy string around the tight rectangular prisms.

Renaldo attempted to greet him twice, first in English, then Arabic, but the old man seemed too preoccupied to notice. Renaldo was finally answered in broken English during his third attempt, "Why do you pester Abu?"

Hay continued to be strung together and stacked as he made no eye contact with them as he spoke. His endless task, as exhausting as it was to watch, never burdened his breathing. With each toss of hay, he remained calm and collected as if it were effortless.

"Good afternoon, my dear fellow. Your brother, Majid, informed me that you would be interested in an additional job as a guide?" Questioning looks spread between the others. How could anyone be so accurate in locating someone in such a remote town without prior experience?

"Majid died five years. You told by the wrong man," Abu said without missing a beat in his craft. Another person, equally thin but not as tall, came up the stairs behind them carrying more straw. He dropped the massive load onto the wooden floor near Abu and left.

"I'm sorry to hear that, but I met someone who claimed to be your brother in Cairo. I didn't catch his name, but he certainly knew you. If he was an imposter, I am not sure he would send me all this way on some red herring. Perhaps you can still help us. We require a guide who can lead us to the Belgium-Congo border. Do you know the way?"

Continuing as if he didn't hear, the laborer said, "No man go that way. The land is dangerous. People get lost. Go other way."

Below the loft, a large herd of cattle was being led into the barn. Robert stepped closer, and the laborer stopped to look at him directly. A broken chorus of moos grew louder, and they barely understood his last few words.

"Ask him about Majid's job when he was alive," came a voice, unlike Abu, from his mouth. Robert could see himself reflected in the eyes that had eclipsed into onyx. His eyes were intense, not the dreary tired expression he had carried before.

None of his companions were reacting to Abu's impulsive behavior. They stood indifferently behind him with their arms at their sides. Their eyes looked past Robert and Abu.

"Ask him about his brother Majid. He lost his brother to an accident," came the voice again from the man. Robert could hear his voice change as if controlled by a ventriloquist.

From a blink, the laborer returned to his work. Robert could hear his companions stirring and shuffling behind him with life again. Their shoes ruffled against the scattered straw, and one cleared his throat.

With a quick glance over his shoulder, Robert wondered if they had witnessed the same thing he had, but they wouldn't look him in the eye. Even Renaldo, who usually had a brilliant smile glowing across his face, looked melancholy.

Turning back to Abu, he caught a brief glance from him. He had taken his eyes off his work for the first time.

Robert took a deep breath and suddenly felt the all-too-familiar pressure in his chest return. It had been a steady, gradual increase of a vice-like squeeze, and each beat struggled harder to pump.

"Majid was in a bad accident," Robert stated matter-of-factly. He didn't give Abu time to argue. "You two were guides together. Took foreigners out in the wilds and showed them the fauna. Then a bad thing happened that cost your brother's life. He was swimming and drowned."

He had spoken without his control. He talked to Abu like a puppet as his heart was tortured by the unseen hand, unable to form his own conscious thoughts into words.

Struggle as he could, something was navigating the conversation in a peculiar direction.

"He swim fine," muttered Abu. His voice growled with frustration. "Animal eat him. Outsider pushed him off boat." By now, he had given up raking hay and looked at Robert.

"Was that it?" Robert asked. "And you couldn't see yourself continuing as a guide without him. So you turn to shoveling hay all day in a dilapidated barn and let your brother's dream fade. I understand. It's what Majid would have wanted you to do for the rest of your life."

The native peered deeply into Robert's eyes, a myriad of wrinkles gathered, showing a harsher life than he deserved. The palms of his hands were worn, and his knuckles reminded Robert of walnuts.

"My brother wants a better life," Abu said. "Not hard work." He sighed in relief as he gazed around the humid, aromatic barn. "I have a boat. Take you to the border. But..."

He trailed off, a flicker of a tragic memory forced into his mind, then shrugged off. "Come dawn, my boat. It tied down at docks. Find me. Bring stones."

Leaving a heap of hay untouched as more was being brought up, Abu headed elsewhere, oddly more nimble than before. There was a slight bounce with each step that grew the farther he walked away. He practically walked on air as he disappeared from sight.

Renaldo's smile returned while he peered down the stairs after Abu.

"Well now," he said, "I didn't mean to offend the poor chap about his brother. I thought my apology was commendable. To simply walk away is highly irregular. I regret we are now at a standstill. Perhaps the city is large enough that we can find another guide."

Trish and Sinclair nodded and gave doubtful sighs while taking the steps down past Robert. Kipner stood there puzzled. They hadn't witnessed any of his conversations.

His clenched heart receded to a comfortable rate. Only a heart attack is what they presumed, as Robert didn't feel the truth would settle well. He had no idea what creature had been in his cabin or how to treat his ailment. They would know less. What difference did it make?

At the bottom of the stairs, Robert's feet stepped through a dark transformation that morphed all that surrounded him. The motion was sickening to watch and played mind tricks on his orientation. The barn was shrouded in a desaturated vision that swirled a cloud-like image across every surface.

He reached out to the fence for support but discovered it lacked substance, sending his hand through it. He stumbled forward and fell on the ground, solid, to his relief.

"You've always lacked willpower, young Kipner." The voice was nearby, but Robert couldn't see anyone.

"Ever since I discovered your unique conductivity, I suspected it would consume you. There was little hope of showing you the methods I have learned in my studies - you were always a step behind. Pity. I would have enjoyed accepting you as my employee for good."

Kipner listened as Delven's voice manifested into the familiar outline he had seen in Cairo. He stood out brightly against the swirling masses, unaffected by its effects. Robert's skin had been touched by the strange moving patterns, giving him a strong desire to scratch his arms.

Getting to his feet, he found his grounding and remained steady. "You always enjoyed talking in riddles like some fairy tale gnome," Robert replied. "It has always been mind games with you. Manipulation mastered. I'm doing this job for myself, not for you anymore."

A snake-like smirk crested Delven's face, and he hung the head of his cane on his forearm. "I know, Mr. Kipner, I know. Your curiosity has always been admirable, and I respect that. It is in our nature. We are driven by the unknown in hopes of discovering.

"We can't help ourselves, especially now with what we know, you and I. We seek out for different reasons but for the same solution," Delven said.

Robert's .38 was in his hand without remembering having drawn it from its holster. He had a bead drawn on Delven's heart with the hammer pulled back. Delven didn't flinch or look worried.

"What is it that's over there?" Robert finally asked. "What keeps following me that plays tricks in my head and speaks for me?"

Delven slowly circled around Robert, seamlessly passing through the barn's fences with a slight shimmer. His hands gestured overly dramatically with each word.

"In an effort to avoid such a cliché response, I shall not use the word 'inevitability.' Instead, consider this. European explorers have come across tribes in Bolivia and Paraguay who have been in total isolation from the world. They are the Ayoreo. Incredibly primitive by our standards of living, but to them, ordinary. How would you imagine their reaction after learning there are dwellers of this world as advanced as our civilizations? Perhaps they would regard us as gods. After all, we possess sciences and technology that are beyond their comprehension. Would it appear magic to them?"

His circular journey around Robert completed, he pivoted abruptly on one foot like a soldier standing at attention and stared intently into Robert's eyes. His eyes were full and bulbous, pitched black and glossy.

"Mankind is a primitive tribe, Mr. Kipner," Delven whispered, leaning in closely. "And you and I have awoken to learn there are dwellers of this world more advanced. Far more than ours. That is what is out there waiting for us to learn their ways and use those powers for our own! We are ambassadors for mankind, my good fellow."

Around them, the swirling was becoming more violent. The surfaces grew darker and blended together, forming an empty void of nothing. He was being pulled towards the focal point of everything merging.

"Ah," Delven said, standing solid against the drawing force. "Our chats are always interrupted too soon. Travel well, Mr. Kipner and I look forward to watching it unfold. Mind the natives."

The world collapsed into a pinpoint of blackness, with Robert following along helplessly. The pressure on his ears spiked momentarily, and he took the final step off the stairs right behind the others. No one seemed to have noticed.

CHAPTER XIII

El-Obeid, 1926

The African blue moon gently caressed the Savannah grasslands and sparked the calls of nocturnal creatures. A soft murmur of casual conversation challenged their distant melodies, complimented by a symphony of silverware throughout the plaza as the dinner hour approached El Obeid.

At least one guest enjoyed the evening meal accompanied by a gathering of street entertainers nearby. Renaldo took in the scenery well, cheering loudly for a trio who played a traditional folk song. For his dinner, under a brightly colored canopy close to the street, he had selected millet porridge with mashed fava beans. He roundly attempted to assure everyone within hearing it was a staple dish in the area.

After seeing the slight mineral color in his glass of water, his three dinner guests had chosen cinnamon tea. Only Renaldo was enjoying the taste of his meal. The fish Robert ordered was more bone than meat, and he couldn't identify what side dish had come with it. He missed the dining experience from the Orient Express as he cast his eyes out along the plaza filled with nightlife activity.

Trish and Sinclair had shared a lamb dish over a bed of rice, but most of it remained on the plate when the waiter removed it from the wicker table. Neither one seemed to mind going hungry as they tried filling up on tea.

The mood had been mellow for the evening save for their jovial traveling companion, who seemed to take in every sight with wonder. Renaldo showed no signs of slowing down either. He had been adamant about leading them on tour along the streets as if he had lived there his whole life. It was surprising to Robert just how much he claimed to know. Every turn since they had met, Renaldo was an expert at generally everything or claimed to be. It worried Robert despite being unable to resist the charming man. For someone who had made an impromptu journey into Africa, Renaldo traveled with experience. His answer was always to be well-traveled.

Trish stood from the table and wandered away into the plaza after the plates were gone and their bill paid. Sinclair had a look of concern on his face but didn't pursue it. From what Robert could tell, neither had said a word the entire dinner.

As Renaldo was impervious to having one less guest at the table, Robert leaned toward Sinclair to ask about Trish.

"She's just frustrated at our pace," Sinclair answered. "Her idea was to fly on some cargo airliner, but Delven's reluctance has made the trip longer than she feels it should have been. I tried reassuring her we weren't in any rush, but I think she suspects treachery."

"By me?" Robert asked with a smirk on his face.

Sinclair shook his head. "No, and not him either," he said, gesturing to Renaldo, who tossed coins into a basket for the performers. "We're at the mercy of Delven for the time being without anywhere else to go. She's getting impatient and frustrated that she can't sniff out when the betrayal might come."

Robert leaned back in his chair and crossed his arms. "She's good at that?" Trish had yet to show many skills, but few opportunities had come up.

"To a fault. She predicted my loss of lecture bookings before it happened. Before it became public, she knew about the strange happenings off the coast with sea merchants. Always bad news, though. It's an odd phenomenon she's had ever since I met her. Whenever she stares off into space as if a thousand miles away, something wrong usually happens."

Somewhere in the plaza, among the sea of people milling about, some camels became restless from a pack of hyenas crying out just outside town. The commotion drew their attention from the conversation.

"Here she comes," Sinclair stated as they spotted her approaching the camels. His face grew dim as he saw her expression.

"Uh oh. I've seen that look plenty of times before. She's made up her mind on something. Good luck changing whatever it is."

She carried a satisfied smirk along with a bold, eager stride. Her chair was pulled out and quickly spun backward as she plopped down on it, legs spread on either side of its wicker backing.

"I have a plane and, more importantly, a pilot who can fly it," she said triumphantly and took a sip of her tea. Her eyes went to all three men, lingering last on Sinclair as if daring him to challenge her.

He did not respond, and Renaldo's delighted eyes showed no intention of arguing, so Robert spoke up.

"We already have a guide. There's no place for a plane to land where we're going anyway."

Without looking at him, keeping her eyes fixed on Sinclair, she said, "There's a landing strip at the hospital used for emergencies. Delven mentioned it before we left. Just a grass field, but long enough for a pilot to put us down safely. He'll be ready in two days. Even with the delay, it'll be quicker than taking the imaginary pleasure trip with Captain Hay Shoveler."

Among the three, Trish believed Robert's story of Abu the least. She neither saw nor heard anything. It was too suspicious and farfetched for her to rely on being accurate. She needed solidarity in her experiences to be able to follow.

Robert thought that she would be a tough nut to crack. He wasn't in favor of flying. Although having never been in an airplane, he had read enough about barnstormers and daredevils to know their lives were limited. While there were rumors one of the barnstormers planned on flying over the Atlantic next year, he was suspicious of the aircraft's integrity. If something happened, it was a long way down.

"And what if Delven lied to you?" Robert said, coming back from his momentary nightmare of plane crashes. "There's nothing but jungle if he's wrong. There might not be enough fuel to come back."

Trish turned her eyes to look at Robert. "I trust Delven as much as you. Probably less. Even if there isn't a place to land, Eddie says he still has enough fuel to return."

The name perked Sinclair's attention. "Eddie?" he repeated to Trish's enthusiastic nod.

"Rickensomething. He said he flew in the War and has been seeing the world ever since with his Jenny. It might be a tight fit, but he said he has a seat strapped to each wing."

The three men exchanged puzzled looks. Sinclair tried to pass the torch back to Robert with a brief eyebrow raise. He knew not to approach the conversation from any direction.

"Trish, I'm not so sure about..."

"Look, we have been on this trail for weeks now, and we're still not even close to the border. I don't know about you, but enough's enough. Let's find out what this is all about and get back to our regular lives. I don't mind traveling, but taking a desert train excursion is not my idea of transportation," Trish interrupted.

"And sitting on the wing of an airplane is?" Robert rebutted. He wondered if she was cut out for this kind of fieldwork. So far, it had been a pleasure cruise compared to Robert's travels. There had been a few archaeological trips in his earlier years where sleeping among wooden crates aboard a leaky ship was the most enjoyable part of the voyage.

Trish rolled her eyes as if riding on wings was an everyday event. "It's no more dangerous than sitting in the cockpit. You'll be strapped in just as securely as Eddie."

"You are already on a first-name basis with this...pilot?" Sinclair asked with a hint of jealousy in his voice.

"Captain, actually," came a voice not far off. The table guests turned abruptly to see a man whose smile rivaled Renaldo's confidence. Just standing there, he gave off an aura of such dominating assertiveness even Robert subconsciously smiled back.

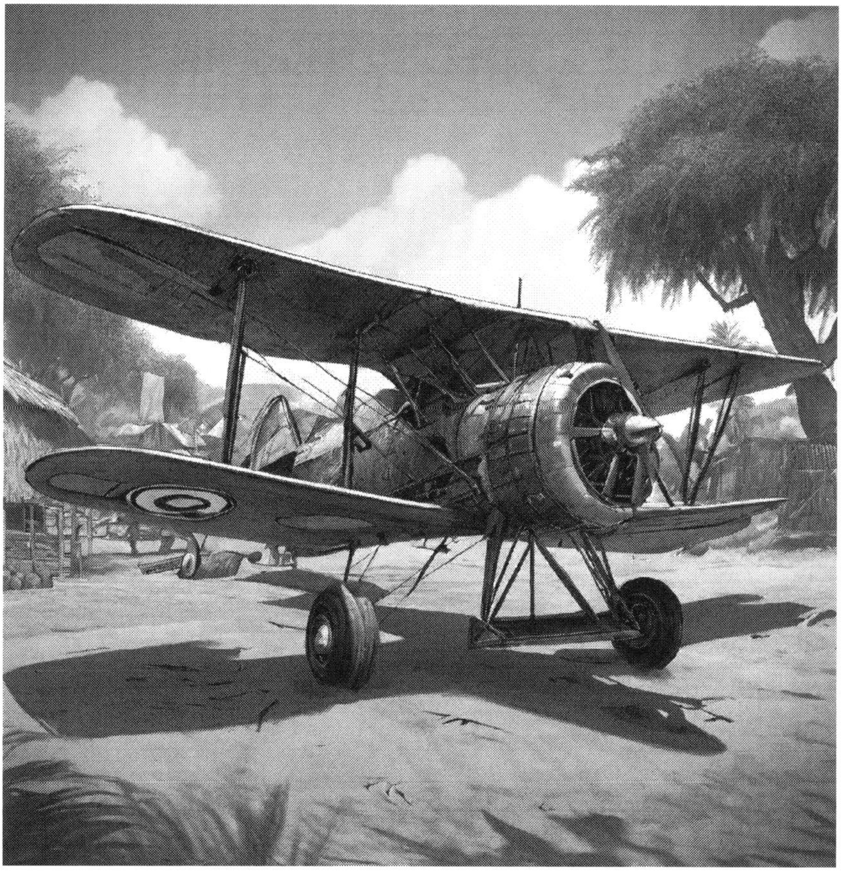

"Captain Eddie Rickenbacker, 94th Aero Squadron, at your service, lady and gentlemen!" He gave a sharp, crisp salute to them. Renaldo's enthusiasm clouded his accuracy as he stumbled to return the greeting with inexperience.

The glow from Eddie reflected onto Trish as she gave no effort to hide her enamored expression. Robert raised an eyebrow at Sinclair but was too busy looking at Trish to notice. Sinclair did not share the same joy she had about "Eddie."

"Captain Rickenbacker," Renaldo said while standing and offering his hand to shake. The captain's smile never wavered, and he gripped the man's hand firmly, shook it twice, and released it with promptness.

"Please, Eddie is fine. We're going to be getting closely acquainted on the journey, so no formalities are necessary. Besides, the last War we'll ever see ended almost a decade ago, along with my ranking. May I join you?" Eddie inquired while drawing a nearby chair and wedging between Robert and Trish.

"Eddie, I'm not sure we all have decided yet on taking you up on your…gracious…offer. We already have a guide waiting for us in the morning." Robert hurriedly shifted over as Eddie showed no concern for close proximity.

"Oh? That is not what I heard from your delightfully fair lady," Eddie said without taking his eyes off Trish. The two were exchanging glances that could not be cut with a knife. Sinclair began to turn red as he tried to form words into sentences, but his jealousy grew harsher.

Robert had had enough of this and placed his hand on Eddie's shoulder to guide his attention away from Trish. To his astonishment, Eddie was much stronger than his stature led on to believe. Despite Robert's efforts, his shoulders were solid muscles, and he did not move an inch. It was as if he tried to move a statue.

"Now, now, Sir," Eddie said, turning slowly towards Robert. "No need to be pushy. I hear you just fine. So you have a guide who'll take you through crocodile-infested waters. Whose brilliant idea was that?"

Ignoring the question, Robert said, "We'll be in a boat the entire time. I feel much safer on the ground than in your death-defying machine."

Eddie scoffed at the description. "It's hardly any deadlier than some rickety wooden boat that could crack at the smallest rock in the river. I've flown countless times and have never had a close call with death. I came closer to the end while driving without 4-wheel brakes than I've ever been flying."

"How much did she promise you?" Sinclair finally spoke up, his voice rusty and jagged.

"She said ol' Kipper here would make me an offer," Eddie said with a returning smile and a harder-than-necessary pat on the back. "What do you think? A reasonable offer will do, nothing too fancy. Why, just earlier this year, that flight company, Delta, took a few fellas from Salt Lake to Los Angeles for 90. How about 50?"

Robert answered with a long, drawn sigh of frustration. The man didn't even know Kipner's name. It had been a long day, and Robert was tired of

Eddie's arrogance - his confident aura had long lost its effect. The travel plans had suited him until Trish had interfered with impatience.

Suddenly something dawned on Kipner as he studied those seated around the table. What had begun with two companions now potentially became four in number. Delven had said there would be six, and Kipner had just realized that six was quickly approaching the further he traveled. If that was the case, perhaps he was meant to go on this ride and come across two more before the journey's end, but he had had enough of fate leading him along on a leash and wanted the control back.

"I'm sure you're a fine pilot, and if Trish wants to take you up on your offer for any amount, she is more than welcome. I'm staying on the ground." Robert rose from the table with Renaldo switching glances to Eddie, then he with indecision. He fumbled with his fingers awkwardly.

Trish nonchalantly called Robert to stop as he walked off, but her attitude shifted to irate as he ignored her. She stood up with authority, shoving the chair back and tipping it over.

"You stop right there, Kipner. Now," her voice was ice cold, filled with a lethal warning not to challenge her.

Robert finally turned around to address her but said nothing, waiting for her to speak. It threw her off enough to soften the edge.

"We need you along," she said, with each word calmer than the last. "You know more about what's going on than I do. This all has gone on long enough, though. I'm too deep to turn back now, but I want this to be over. Please, Kipner."

Her voice had moved dramatically to almost sobbing. Her rage and emotions dwindled her composure, and she was on the verge of crying. There was something about this trip that was getting to Trish, Robert thought, or perhaps she knew more than she led on. The urgency in her voice as she pleaded with him made Robert concerned that there was a time factor he was unaware of.

For several seconds he stood watching her, studying the look on her face. He hadn't learned enough about her, but his long career as an investigator taught him she was sincerely desperate. He was convinced it would be suicidal. It didn't change his distrust of some barn burner sailing a plane built for two over a dense jungle.

He knew he should have compassion for her but remained stone-cold and finally shook his head.

"I hope to see you at the site. Safe travels," were Kipner's final words to them as he drifted off into the city to find a place to sleep for the night. No one behind him called out for him again.

Since he held no loyalty to Montgomery over this so-called expedition, he cared little about keeping with them. It had been just him all his life after leaving home for college. His family was fine, albeit a bit stricter than he cared for. They supported his change in college to become an archaeologist. It had been a matter of desired self-reliance that led him to fend for himself at the earliest point in his life.

Back in his element of working alone, Kipner felt almost relieved and a bit excited. There was pure adventure awaiting him, and it was good to be back in the environment he once loved to be in. If the three found their way to the hospital alone, all the better to greet them there.

With the night sounds shifting back to the crescendo of African wildlife, Kipner found a simple but comfortable place to stay. The fact that the owner had a license to sell araqi legally might have influenced his decision, too.

*

He found Abu waiting for him aboard a boat tied down at the river's dock. The Savannah sun had not begun cresting the horizon, and the air was still crisp. Three rock pigeons cooed together and demonstrated their tightrope abilities near a burned-out street light.

Abu's boat was better than the leaking vessel Kipner had expected. The locals called it a felucca, a fast, lateen-rigged boat used as far north as the Mediterranean Sea. Its hull had row portals and was equipped with oars. Judging from the boat's two travelers, Robert guessed he had a prime seat at one of them. He questioned the boat lacking a motor, but Abu scoffed.

There was a behavior of expectation when Kipner arrived – Abu didn't even look up at him. There was no telling how early he had come, yet Abu showed no sign of fatigue. Pulling ropes, tying them securely, and clearing space of small wooden crates were taken care of without pausing.

"Thanks again for considering taking me along. Looks like the others skipped out for a plane ride," Robert said, navigating through tangled rope and planks. He received acknowledgment once they had traveled upstream for an hour.

During that time, Abu had singlehandedly rowed himself. He had slowed the boat to almost a standstill. When Kipner tried to sit at the rows, he was given a disgruntled sound from Abu. He made no other sound to Robert, in fact, until the river widened significantly near the city of Malakal. Even so, creeping along the point of the White Nile where the current moved lazily.

The sails were lowered, but the ropes were rigged so that Abu could bring them back up quickly. The sound Abu made was a simple command not to speak. Robert was surprised to discover the reason for the silence when he spotted a large, oblong head crest the water's surface a hundred meters away.

The small boat was considered trespassing to the hippos as more heads popped up. Compared to the size of the animals, the vessel looked like a small raft. Kipner took out his binoculars to get a better look at the magnificent beasts and picked up the sight of locals standing along the river's edge. They were all shouting warnings for Abu to come ashore or change their heading. He showed no interest as he slowly continued rowing along the water.

Through the binocular lenses, several hippos were floating ahead of them near their course. Robert's urge to speak up was immense, but he kept his mouth shut and left his fate in the hands of the small, old man.

The mosquitoes were unbearable, biting endlessly against their skin, so Robert took out his repellent and tried his best to coat himself. Abu slapped his hand away when he offered some despite welts along his arm from the bites.

Something rippled the water a few paces off starboard, but Robert couldn't see deep in the reflecting waters. A trail of bubbles rose up from below, which quickly expanded to large mushroom shapes. Whatever was down below was surfacing rapidly.

The sails dropped with expertise, and the winds filled them fully. Abu continued to row but allowed the two sails to accompany them to increase his speed significantly. Robert sat at the bench behind him without asking and took the two vacant oars. Abu showed no sense of urgency in his behavior but moved with such fluid assertiveness. It made Kipner nervous, and he glanced over his shoulder.

A giant hippo was gliding smoothly across the break of the water's surface and gaining on them. Its head was fully exposed a foot above the water, cutting like a wedge.

Neither the sails nor the rowing gave them more distance as the beast lunged to the back of the boat, dropping its chin down on the wood with all of its weight.

The front end shot up into the air. Kipner fell backward toward the water but held the lip of the boat with his fingertips. Abu wasn't quite as lucky and tumbled over his shoulders and into the dark water.

Swinging his arm behind him, Robert reached out desperately to grab his guide, but he submerged before his hand could get a good grip. Abu hadn't surfaced a few seconds later while Robert scrambled back onto the boat. The sails were still up but not controlled, and they quickly took him away from where Abu went overboard.

There had yet to be any lessons on sailing from his guide, and Robert had only observed for a short while. He had no other choice but to try to bring the boat back around closer, so he grabbed the tiller and turned the rudder to one side. The riverboat coasted smoothly to port momentarily and began making a perfect circle. The wind continued favoring the direction they had been heading. The wind and rudder fought each other to a stalemate and drew the boat to an awkward stop where the slow river's current took over.

There was nothing else Robert could do with the boat, which was useless without Abu. He shoved the iron anchor off the side and leaped off the ship's stern towards where Abu was last seen. There was little time to think of what he had just done and the danger he had put himself in.

Below the surface, the water was filthy and murky. Thousands of tiny pieces of grass and muck floating around were disorienting. Each time he surfaced, he tried to recalculate where he thought Abu went under. However, the longer he fought against the soupy water, the more attention he drew from the river's inhabitants.

Something significant dragged against his toes in the darkness below. He tried to ignore his imagination peering through a forest of papyrus and ambatch, and spotted the arm of Abu sinking. Robert surged ahead, kicking hard with his feet above him to dive deeper below. The unconscious body of Abu came into view, and Robert lunged forward to grab his arm.

An enormous object hurled at him out of the corner of his eye with such a blur before he could react. The hippo clamped down around Robert's torso, launching him out of the water.

The jolt was excruciating, but Robert's grip on Abu was vice-like, and the two were launched into the air. The splash surrounded them with bubbles, and Robert couldn't tell where the beast was. He held onto Abu as best as possible, but his mind was geared on instinct as everything moved too quickly to contemplate.

With solid kicks, Robert surfaced again and grabbed a gulp of air but was quickly pulled back down by a large mouth. The first attack of the hippo's tusk had punctured his abdomen, and he could feel the flesh of his calf being torn by the second bite of the hippo while it dragged him deeper.

What little oxygen he had left in his lungs had escaped, and his head quickly throbbed and ached. The glow from the morning sun above dimmed dramatically to darkness, and he felt the grip release his leg. It had been a slow release, its mouth lingering closely to Robert's leg as if daring him to move. Abu brushed against him, but he knew it was pointless to keep holding him.

His eyes adjusted very well to the darkness of the deep Nile River, an impossible task. He began to see large shapes floating lifelessly around him. The hippos' carcasses, riddled with exposed lesions and hollow eye sockets, seemed frozen against the current. Each one was severely rotten and half eaten like an underwater graveyard.

The lack of breathing went unnoticed as his toes dragged against something that moved below him once more. This time, his sight caught a more prominent figure than the dead animals around him. It darted squid-like and swiftly behind several hippo carcasses, reemerging before him like a leviathan to a ship.

All attempts of disbelieving were forgotten by its immense proportion. Robert was a few feet from its eye, larger than he was. It was impossible to fully comprehend the creature's size like an endless black wall stretched in every direction.

He could feel the presence of a voice inside his own head that wasn't his. It spoke to him. He was unfamiliar with the language, and the sound was alien. It spoke with words lacking vowels that appeared in his head like guttural jargon, yet they infused his memory and wouldn't let go.

Whatever he was experiencing felt as natural as his life back home, yet he was not needing to breathe and floated in a substance that felt thick like translucent mercury. It felt smooth to the touch as his arms moved through it.

The message was finished being delivered, and the creature abruptly disappeared even further into the depths below. While Robert knew little of the geography of the Nile, he was sure it was not this deep.

Buoyancy still felt neutral to him, but his body was returning to its normal abilities, like breathing and needing light to see in the dark. Grabbing Abu, he began kicking up past the dead hippos with an unpleasant feeling of each lifeless body bouncing off.

The scorching pain from the puncture wound returned rapidly, and he fought against going into shock.

By now, Abu had been equally lifeless as the hippos below for several minutes. Robert pulled him onto the boat, leaned him forward, and tried to smack the water out of his lungs.

Leaving Abu, he tended to himself. The wound on his stomach was fierce. He ripped Abu's shirt and jammed it firmly against the opening. Thoughts of infection and bleeding out plagued his mind as he quickly thought about how to prevent death. There was not much for first aid, so he used twine from the boat to secure the crude bandage. It wouldn't last long, but for the moment, the bleeding stopped.

Robert couldn't help but wonder if he had made the wrong decision not to travel with the others. Something horrific had convinced him to persuade Abu to go on this journey against his wishes. It had been an exhilarating moment that felt purposeful as if his path was chosen by going in this direction. He hadn't questioned it, but he hadn't felt a desire to. It was as if he couldn't resist the temptation.

After a few minutes of fruitless attempts to bring Abu back, he sat longer, letting the current slowly drift the boat south before slipping the body into the water. An attempt was made to row the boat to the shore, where the natives pointed and mocked, but he found the chore cumbersome and lost the fight against the slow but strong river. The sails picked up and kept him steady, so he had no choice but to let them take hold. He wasn't sure he could launch it successfully were he to beach it, so a water burial was the best he could do for his guide.

"I'm sorry," Robert said somberly out loud and watched Abu disappear back below the surface. "I'm sorry I used your life so carelessly. I hope you find your brother in the next life."

Despite the sensation yesterday, he felt lost and empty. He took advantage of Abu, using sensitive knowledge of his brother, which was shameful, and he thought it. Where had it come from?

The sun rose above him as the felucca slowly moved against the current by rowing. White ripples formed along the river's surface, but no roaring sound of rapids were heard. Abu hadn't told him how the rest of the White Nile was laid out. Perhaps he intended to sail a portion of the length before abandoning the boat and walking the remaining distance. Without a motor, the journey would be a harsh struggle. He was in no condition to row, even if he wasn't injured.

Renaldo had possession of the map, and Robert could only recall fragments. His impulsive behavior last night resulted in the foolish decision to travel without a map. He had relied on Abu to know the way. Judging from the numerous natives who had gathered along the shore and watched him being attacked by hippos, he felt confident that it had been Malakal. That meant Lake No couldn't be much farther. Beyond that, he remembered Renaldo describing a vast swamp named Sudd in Arabic. There had been a significant city marked on the map somewhere far to the south that he placed began with J, to which he would need to disembark if he hadn't already and head due west to the Congo border. He hoped he lasted.

So for the moment, he felt he could breathe a bit, knowing that the river should take him where he wanted to go unless the swamp was hard to navigate.

He chuckled as he reached into a pocket that generally would have a flask of whiskey but came up empty-handed. His arms weren't cut out for extensive rowing, and his stomach screamed in agony. He could not navigate, even if he knew where he was going. Rowing was the only option as the winds shifted in favor of downstream, leading north back to Egypt.

Taking a break after a half hour of rowing, exhausted and sore, he had no choice but to anchor near the shore and search the boat better.

A felucca, in Robert's opinion, was an odd vessel. The bow and stern were arched higher than the center point, with three-foot-tall railings at either end to help support each rower. The oars were attached to tall stems for a standing person.

In the center, the central mast pierced a large box, and Robert discovered dried fruits, meats, and a few small barrels of water. Of course, Abu would have prepared better than he did, Robert thought with a soft smile.

After a light lunch and wrapping his shirt better around his stomach, Robert returned to rowing up the Nile, keeping his ears ready for the sound of rapids or hippos.

*

High overhead, the trailing sun descended in the west, but it radiated just as intensely as in the Sahara. The dry desert heat gave way to thick, heavy moisture that challenged Robert's lungs. Each gulp of air left him gasping as if breathing underwater.

Shade was available just under the sail, and although the clearance was perhaps a foot at most from the deck, the necessity to row upstream forced him to stand aft side. He was not in shape to paddle so much. A life filled with drinking and smoke was not fitting for such a prolonged activity in the sweltering heat.

He took breaks often. As the day dragged on and he felt he was getting close to Lake No, he grew bolder at attempting to go ashore and stretch his legs and back. It had been several hours since he last saw a person, and even the animals were scarce, save for birds and mosquitoes. There were mosquitoes every square foot he traveled, and his can had long since emptied. They focused on his bloodied makeshift bandages, drinking deeply against the soaked cloth. It drew attention to the pain while he tried to ignore it. He knew he was in serious trouble.

Spotting dry land was becoming just as infrequent, too. The swamps he recalled seeing on Renaldo's map had arrived. The massive, umbrella-like acacia trees were replaced by tall grasses of barthii and papyrus and engulfed by endless water in every direction.

As he dodged large grass clusters, his boat wound its way in a sharply curved route. While paddling further into the wetlands, he began spotting small animals. A raft of otters squirmed over each other as they closely watched him politely wave while drifting past. Occasionally he caught sight of a Nile monitor lizard feasting among river lilies.

Beyond the curious critters, his voyage went peacefully for a change. He reflected how two long train rides and one short camel trek through the desert should have provided him with the same peaceful feeling, but every turn had been nearly disastrous.

Deep down, he hated his decision. He wondered about the other companions as the sun began slowly disappearing. There had been suspicion toward all of them, but the journey had shown a better side of them all. Even Renaldo's endless stories of past adventures were missed.

It was unsure how meaningful their relationship was up to that point. It came down to the inability to trust Eddie. Trish had been so strangely love-struck that she could not give any rational thought, and Sinclair was too frustrated to provide any help. Her behavior in front of Sinclair was concerning. It was suspiciously peculiar.

Perhaps they had the right idea, he thought as he looked for a dry place to shore his boat for the night. Nestled within sight of Lake No was a small clearing with tall grass lying flat. It would do nicely for some padding under the hard ground.

There were enough bushes to start a fire but not enough branches to maintain one at any time. With the amount of moisture in the air, he doubted if anything would burn. Even so, he gathered what he could and did his best to burn something with the lens of his binoculars while he still had light. The flames twisted slowly with heavy smoke as the embers ate the twigs and sticks.

Food was left to make a decent meal and wash it down with lukewarm water. It was filling but far from satisfying. He gobbled it down quickly and brought out his notebook to pass the time while there was still some light.

A short section had a few mentions of a pygmy tribe in southern portions of Anglo-Egypt near Uganda. It wasn't much, mainly descriptions of their size range and a few minor lifestyles. Written along the margin was mentioning how the Bambuti tribe frequented the northeast parts of the Congo. During the wet season, which was easy to guess from the endless swamp water, Bambuti returned from being in remote parts of the jungle to trade with villages near the border.

He wished he had bothered to make more notes then, but he wasn't even sure when he made the notes. During his earlier years of college, the subjects were so general that instructors would jump all over the globe during their lectures. He was lucky he even noticed it.

A steady breeze picked up from the west, upsetting the dismal little fire that struggled against it. The pages fluttered like a startled quail. The gust wasn't brief either and sent a steady stream of force against Robert as he worked to remain seated.

It wasn't comfortable against his eyes as he squinted in the swirling mass of grass and wet dirt speckle. All around him, the water's surface pushed tiny ripples over itself as it danced away from the wind. Through narrowed eyelids, Robert could tell the water's edge near his little nesting ground was slowly receding away. It was too quick to be a tidal effect.

A submerged dark-skinned foot became exposed as the water continued to push back. The foot was attached to a leg, which in turn was attached to a body, but the attachment chain ceased there. It was a half-eaten man garbed in a tribal warrior armament. A carapace-like cuirass partially protected his chest, although much smaller in the area covered. Adorned with beads, it had been pierced directly in the heart.

Remnants of a forgotten warrior, Robert thought as he watched through the whirlwind. Fighting to see better, he leaned in closer as his eyes caught a tattoo or marking on his skin below the chest piece.

It was trivial to remove the armor - the ropes holding it around his shoulders were rotten. He slid it off to see a squid or octopus primitively drawn on his body. Branding created it, causing the lines to slightly bump out. It began to bleed from hundreds of tiny pinprick holes that soon coated the strings and then coagulated into a complex, crusty surface.

The wind howled beside him, yet he unconsciously ignored it while his attention was on the peculiar bleeding. After hardening, it separated itself from the man's body with a puckering sound. Now freely lying on the dead man's chest, its solidity looked more man-made, like a charm or pendant.

Perhaps his curiosity led him to pick it up, or it might have been his endeavor to uncover past secrets as a learned archaeologist. Robert held it gingerly in both hands studying the piece closely.

A tiny circle of the material fell away near the top and left a hole where string might be threaded. He reached over and plucked up a long reed and formed a loop.

Suddenly he finally caught himself and stopped. There had been undoubtedly a deep desire mixed with some unknown force compelling him to place it over his head. He wasn't sure what caused him to break the trance, but now he felt more consciously aware.

Robert stepped back to the water's previous edge. The exposed man was returning to his watery grave. The minor wind typhoon had, at some point, reduced itself to a small whimper.

Somehow his infant-sized fire held vigilant, and he squatted back onto the ground, still holding his new find. It didn't feel like it would crumble anytime soon. In fact, it had taken on more of a gemstone like a sapphire or amethyst. Even more peculiar was the tune it made in the softer breeze. Like wind chimes, it trickled chaotically across the scales giving no recognizable melody.

Dangling it in front of him by the grass reed, he listened to the notes carefully and started to feel the tug of desire to wear it again. He was aware of what was happening this time, although he still found resisting challenging.

As the evening sun ultimately settled below the horizon and left him to the chill night, the necklace rested comfortably around his neck. It wasn't clear when it occurred, and he was also unsure when the sun switched places with the moon. He had spent an unknown amount of time kneeling on both legs and looking down at the ground, nothing in particular. Wildlife came and went, passing him widely in fear and uninterested in attacking.

He felt a sense of peace, and the pain from his wounds eased. To his vision, the ground had parted, giving him a clear picture of a stone pyramid-shaped building well hidden by vegetation. It possessed a light hint of jade green along its stone edges and stretched up several dozens of feet. A front entrance typically was wide open and inviting to anyone, but now it was entirely concealed by plants. His hand motioned for them to move, and they obliged. There was no sense of movement from his legs, yet he moved gracefully and effortlessly into the building.

Through a series of connecting tunnels that could not be solved without a guiding map, he ended his vision journey in a sanctuary of sorts. The walls were ordinary and showed no interesting patterns but were close enough to feel cramped. A marble statue of Ganesha, the elephant god of Hinduism, sat in the center of a room decorated with four jade pillars. Inside, his eyes adjusted to total darkness as if wielding a lantern.

Yet it wasn't Ganesha, Robert thought as he looked closer. The elephant had numerous trunks, perhaps a dozen or more, and giant bat wings folded against its back. Its feet and hands were clawed, and its gaze was a solitary eye that stared intently at him.

He wasn't sure where he was or what he was witnessing, but he felt a sudden release of the pull that had been leading him along. Reaching up to the statue, which stood perhaps twenty feet tall, he began climbing. The cyclopean eye contained a red jewel; despite his better judgment, he wanted to see it closer.

The statue provided convenient handholds as he ascended as if it were meant to be climbed. The height of it all didn't faze Robert. His eyes hadn't deceived him. There, perfectly fitted in the eye socket of the statue, was a ruby the size of his palm. His hands held a different trunk that he could now see were tentacles. Fear gripped him as his mind flashed back to the ominous beast that had started this journey from London. He quickly broke out in a cold sweat, and he knew his grip wouldn't last forever, so he acted fast.

Where had the crowbar come from? The pry bar was in his hand without a need to dig for it in his backpack, but he didn't remember bringing one on the trip. The flat end jammed itself between the gem and the statue as he worked its way loose.

Approaching gunfire startled him from below, and he nearly lost his own grip. The bullets ricocheted off the statue, sending a few chips flying. Another shot came much closer.

Readjusting his handle on the statue, Robert shifted his body to look down. From his point of view, he vaguely resembled Ronan. Beside him stood Delven Montgomery. A gunman held a Browning that was pointed in Robert's general vicinity.

The look on Delven's face was that of pleasure and wickedness as he laughed hysterically up at Robert. Occasionally he would point at him with his cane as if guiding the gunman.

Bullets continued to fly as if the shooter was endlessly feeding the pistol, so Robert began wiggling around the statue to the other side. Delven's laughter grew louder over the report of gunfire.

"What are you doing, Delven?" Robert asked rhetorically. "How did you even get here? Let me come down first if you want target practice at the squid elephant."

All at once the gunfire ceased. Robert cautiously peered around from the back of the statue to see he was alone in the room once more. Shimmying to the front, there was no indication of any gunfire. The figure was in the same shape with no chips from bullets.

Nothing made sense to him, but that would sum up his entire journey. His thoughts returned to what Delven had told him about the Dreamlands, and he wondered if he had somehow returned unknowingly. It didn't feel any different, although the entire experience was dreamlike.

If that was the case, he was back at his campfire while his mind was focused here. The thought of a lion killing him while he was vulnerable pushed him back to his original task of jarring the ruby loose.

His pry bar still in hand, he made easy work of it and soon was barely holding the monstrous jewel.

The delicate chimes returned to his ears, but this time a low vibration mixed with it. It melded with the notes and then took a life of its own. Soon he could hear the buzzing of an engine approaching.

A blue-gray sky appeared above him from the morning sun, and his gaze went from the giant ruby still in his hand to a biplane flying overhead heading west. Two seats had been mounted on the lower wings, and it flew low enough to spot the rotund figure of Renaldo strapped onto one of them. Instinctively

Robert waved up at them, but no one aboard bothered to return the wave if they even noticed him. Within seconds the plane disappeared over thick trees, its motor fading to silence.

The plane wasn't supposed to be flight ready for two days. Had he been in his vision for that long? His stomach said yes, and he worked at putting together another bland meal.

He hoped to have a good head start on Trish, but his time-lapse had cost him.

Or had it? Despite all logic, he held the largest ruby perhaps anyone had ever seen in his hand. Why continue on at this point? Its value was probably a considerate amount to a museum where it belonged. He could retire in some warm temperature retreat.

No, he thought. There was more at stake than he knew, and he was hell-bent on finding out what that was. The necklace now took the shape of the odd multi-tentacle elephant he had witnessed in the temple. He wasn't sure if it was guiding him or luring him. Either way, his vision seemed to indicate he was making Delven mad enough to shoot at him, so that was enough motivation for Robert to pursue further.

CHAPTER XIV

Anglo-Egyptian Sudan, 1926

Sleep was unnecessary as the day broke above the motionless swamp. Robert had been rejuvenated from the dream-like state he had experienced. Unlike his energy, his wound remained and had grown dark in color. He had guessed if the plane had remained on schedule, he would have been unconscious for close to 30 hours. Besides a ravenous appetite and thirst, he felt well-rested and could embark immediately after breakfast.

But the feeling was short-lived after rowing a short distance. The sensation of a long night's rest gave way to the reality he'd lost blood, and his strength waned. His mind was sharp, but he fatigued quickly. Given his location, only finding the next village was his best choice. He cursed not being able to stop in Malakal. Rationale thought had left him in all the sudden tragedy and chaos.

The waters of the Sudd continued to surround him well into the day as he found his way to Lake No, a widening of the White Nile. All the time rowing upstream, he had been trying to remember the details of the journey into the Congo from Renaldo's train car. For his life, he could not come up with the town names. He knew the Nile would bend to the west for a few miles before returning for its final stretch to its origin. That would be the closest point to the border he would reach before heading off on foot.

Hippos occasionally crested the waters, spurting out a misty spray before submerging, but he encountered no angry ones. The rowing had become the real trouble. His shoulders were aching more than he cared to feel, and he wasn't sure if his arms could finish the trek. With every stroke of the oars, he felt his stomach wound worsen. A few times, the thought had crossed his mind to come ashore and walk the remaining miles. He told himself it would mean more of a delay as he pushed on.

Everywhere he turned, he would catch the eyes of a crocodile drop suddenly below the surface. On more than one occasion, he had to swat his paddle at a venomous snake trying to enter his boat. And those were just the animals he spotted.

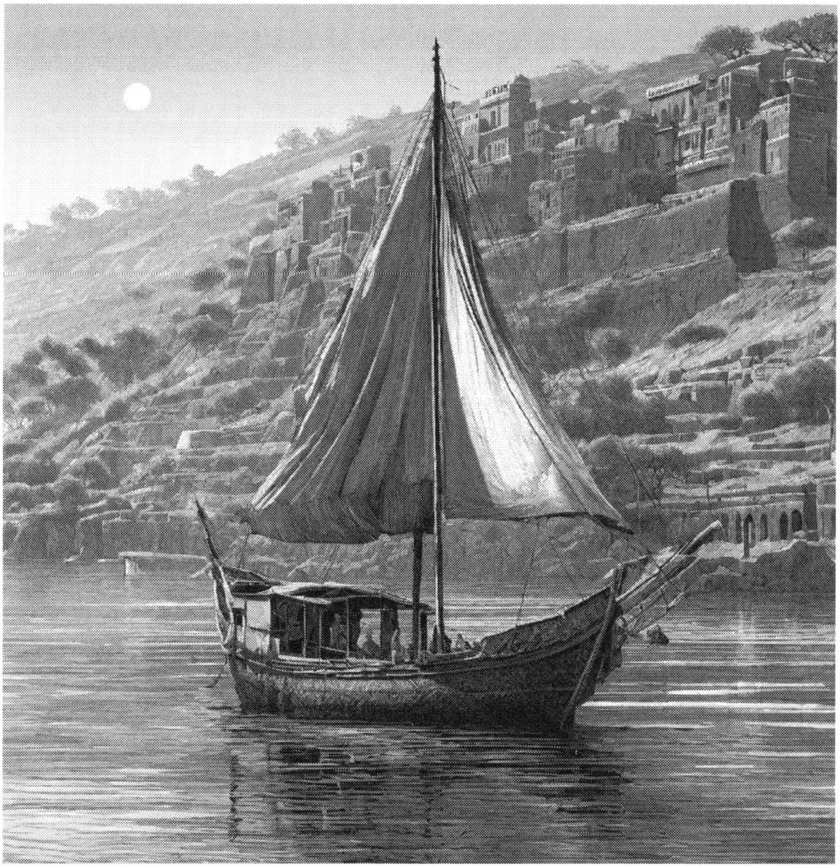

This part of the river was full of people. Even so, without the ability to communicate in their native tongue, none of them wanted to help. Pointing to his wound only made them recoil and abandon him in fear of attracting what he had. The coloration looked infected.

No one appeared to be happy to see Robert. He received long stares from everyone he passed until they were dots.

Whether it was relief or dread, Robert finally reached the bend he needed to get off the river. He had no landmarks to go by, but he could see that the rapids grew too powerful to row ahead. He knew he couldn't continue forever anyway. His body ached too much, and he was severely weakened. His feet sunk fully from the soft, saturated soil when he stood. His legs trembled, and each step was a battle.

He took as much as he could carry what was left of the rations and water. The two oars dangled listlessly in their stirrups for the next person to come along.

Latitude 1.3 Something cut east and west across the middle of Africa, Robert thought. It wasn't clear if he even was headed in the proper direction. He could peek at the sun before heading onto land, but the sunlight was regularly blocked by the mighty Entadrophragma excelsum trees.

"Try saying that just once," he said out loud as he pushed through the dense plants. To the best of his knowledge, he had never heard of the name before - it just came to him. By now, he could take strange occurrences like that. What concerned him anymore was the small inkling there may be something catastrophically wrong with him. Having odd gifts never came free, even the supernatural kind.

Without a compass and a machete, progress was dismal. There were no clearings - only endless plants packed in tightly. Behind the next plant were dozens of others with no place to go. No matter how many stories Renaldo told of the dense jungles of Africa, Robert couldn't fathom the tremendous effort needed to get through them. His vision began to blur as he walked. It wasn't clear to him whether it was the festering wound or the numerous spiked plants and biting insects that wickedly attacked his skin.

There was a chance his path from the river could lead to one of the border towns. So far, that chance had been nil. He wasn't sure if he could travel along the border, so he grew more frustrated at his circumstance and dove into the thickest.

One advantage he found by traveling through the most challenging part was when he needed to lay down to rest. He needed only to lean in any direction, and the dense vegetation would support him upright. Robert was grateful for the fact as his shoes crunched with a meaty sound against the thousands of insects trying to scurry across the ground. He hated the thought of lying entirely flat among them. Even so, they would quickly crawl up his legs, and a fierce battle followed between him and them on whether they could reach more sensitive areas.

Tree after tree, leaf after leaf, Robert aimlessly continued on in a dream-like trance as his mind faded. A break in the trees above occasionally gave him a better guess at the direction. Something inside of him gave him confidence he was headed the right way. It wasn't the strange knowledge or powers he had experienced that he was sure of. The feeling came from his gut of time past being an investigator. Here, in the steaming jungle, constantly bit by flying bugs, the feeling was comforting, not from the joy of avoiding being lost but from a remembrance of normalcy before the adventure began. The days had become lost to Robert, trying to recall how long ago he had left his office and Natasha.

By the fourth hour, with drooping eyes and shambling steps, Robert was pretty confident he was being hunted. There had been occasional twigs breaking with scuffling leaves. He had feared it might be a gorilla since it showed little desire to remain silent. The theory was eventually replaced by the certainty of a person. Pygmies were the right size for the rustling plants, or perhaps he just wanted to think they were following him.

Endlessly he searched on, thankful when he spotted a clearing and could re-calibrate his direction, with little concern for the dangers that were probably in every order. He could remain in denial if he remained oblivious to potential mortal danger. However, it was only a matter of time before he spotted something that would shatter that mental shield.

The solitary rustling sprouted into two separate areas, one on either side and kept to his pace. Frequently Robert would need to stop to get through a particularly dense patch of leaves and vines, or the high humidity forced him to take another swig of his rapidly depleting water. Each pause resulted in his two traveling partners stopping momentarily as well.

He had tried to call out a few times but didn't know common languages in this part of the continent. No response was made towards his greetings, but neither did they veer away. Whatever they were, they kept a safe distance from him even if he walked toward one of them. He wondered how they could see him quickly through the vegetation when his vision was highly impaired.

The ground had sloped upward as he entered some highlands for a while now. It wasn't clear if he was venturing through the foothills of a mountain range, but he felt winded the more he walked deeper in. All the while, the sky gave a consistent stream of rain that soaked his clothes. The wetness was the only comfort as the rain felt hot on his bare skin.

Lunch came at the first clearing he found. He nearly collapsed from exhaustion. He rummaged through the pack in search of whatever he could find. A can of sardines, crackers sealed in wax paper, and dried plantains was left along with a tiny portion of water from a canteen. He tried not to think of what he wished he had, such as a full canteen.

There was no point in cooking his salty fish. He focused more on putting them down quicker than their texture or temperature. The foul smell that filled the air when he cut open the can with the attached key was overwhelming. He quickly gobbled them down. The fish's rich salt, the musky scent were immediate, and he suspected the smell might attract predators.

During that time, his mystery companions, as he grew to refer to him, had gone quiet. With food in him, he felt the drowsiness of fatigue taking over. He had traveled too long for his condition. A lack of a good meal and blood was taking its toll, and he felt it. Lying on the ground, he fought to keep his eyes open a moment longer, hoping to see one of his stalkers. He closed his eyes and drifted to sleep with the empty sardine can still in hand.

It took several minutes before a long skinny stick timidly reached out from the wall of plants, poking the sleeping man. Gripping the shaft was a child-sized arm, dark in complexion, which snatched the tin quickly out of sight. There was the sound of the can being rubbed and then sucking fingers.

To the right of the clearing emerged a child-sized man standing only a few feet tall and entirely naked. He used a similar stick as the other while he waddled and poked Robert, who was too exhausted to awaken.

The scent of sardines was caught by his nose, and he perked up at the cluster of plants that concealed the other. With a growl, he leaped into the plants.

From within the cluster came a scuffle that had no intention of being discreet. High-pitched grunts echoed by shrieks tore through the foliage and burst into the clearing with chaotic ferocity. The swirling ball of Pygmies rolled sporadically across the way like a pinball against bumpers. Robert slept on, deeply slumbering to fatigue, as the two rolled over him numerous times.

There was a struggle between the two for the sardine tin, and neither looked more dominating. Fierce though it was, no severe damage was being done on either side. Blood wasn't shed, and the punches and kicks were in areas easily deflected. Their energy was as high as their tenacity until they finally calmed down. One had pulled the tin out of the other's hands but discarded it after learning it was empty. They briskly chattered to each other, then turned their intense eyes to the sleeping man.

*

When Robert finally opened his eyes sometime later, he stood two small figures, one atop his chest, peering at him and chattering quickly.

During his studies as a young man, he had learned Pygmies have their own language, three in fact. However, none of these three were known to Robert, so he sat there dumbfounded about what to say. While they spoke with incredible speed, their big, dark brown, almost black eyes darted all over like a child barely clinging to attention.

The crude bandages from the shirt had been replaced with large green leaves. They were neatly tied around the waist, and he could feel a soothing dressing reminding him of cream pressed into the gash. Although sore, the sting and biting pain was eased for the first time since being speared by a hippo's tusk.

With a start, they stopped talking. Their little eyes were locked on the necklace Robert wore. As curiously timid as children, they slowly took steps toward Robert, with urges to reach and touch it.

It wasn't sure if they regarded it in fear or awe. Their expressions looked hypnotic, and Robert worried they had fallen into the same vision journey. Both kept exchanging looks and chattering with renewed vigor. Robert held it off his chest and let it swing in the air gently for them to have a better look. They darted back a few steps, then crowded around in closer.

By now, Robert could guess their fascination with the strange symbol like a holy relic. The octopus-like creature looked almost mythical from its numerous tentacles. It could pass as a legendary animal that roamed the jungle nearby. He had never heard of any creature remotely similar. That may be part of its fascination.

Standing up, he tried communicating by pointing to his mouth while it was open. They repeated the motion but kept their eyes glued to the necklace. He pointed to the empty can and then his mouth. All he got was mimicking.

He was getting nowhere with basic hand gestures, so he tried drawing a simple stick figure in the dirt with a fish going into its mouth. He emphasized the drawing with his pantomiming. Nothing seemed to attract their attention.

From above, he could see that both Pygmies had some decoration on their bare backs. He bent around to get a better look; they were identical and familiar. Each had an inverted triangle with three symbols surrounding them. They were the same as Genevieve wore on her robe during his trance-like vision. Whatever the symbol meant, he began to guess the two had a religious connection to the medallion. Some deity was behind it all, and he thought of the colossal entity that towered overhead in the vision. It was undoubtedly god-like in awesomeness.

Finally, he left the clearing with the charm leading the way in his hand. It was a mini parade. Like curious kittens, the two Pygmies stumbled their way after staying as close as they could. For the moment, Robert was more entertained than caring about where he was headed.

Something ahead snapped the Pygmies' attention out of their daze and forced a sudden retreat. If they had been scared of his charm, they were now mortified. Each tripped the other's feet as if trying to deliberately slow the other down to escape.

They had better senses than Robert. He heard nothing. The two little men scrambled into the thick brush to hide. There was silence ahead, and he crept forward slowly to get a better look.

Sparse, open fields laid before him in a significant depression crowned by surrounding mountains. Vegetation had been stripped away to make room for a large metal building. The entire facility was elevated at least ten feet by I-beams sunk firmly into the moist ground. Stairs led up to a bulkhead hatch. Large viewing windows wrapped around the western side of the building with several antennae stretching from the room above. A communication wire joined the tip of the tallest one and disappeared to the east through the dense trees.

A great beast, much larger than a horse, sauntered around the building. It was four-legged and covered in a slick, black membrane that stretched tightly against a well-defined muscle structure. Several thick, flexible extensions jutted from its back near the shoulders and waved like feelers as if searching for something.

The black membrane ended near its face and left an elongated skull exposed. At this distance, Robert could not determine if its eye sockets were empty cavities or heavily shadowed. Its head lowered to the ground and wavered side to side like a bloodhound finding a scent.

Well beyond the building near the other edge of the large clearing was a heavily flattened section of grass that could pass as a landing strip to a small plane. There was no plane anywhere in sight. It allowed no room for error at either end where the jungle took back over.

It was too far to make out any sign of life inside the building, but there were no closer hiding spots. Even moving might inadvertently cause a noise the creature could hear from this distance. He wasn't sure of the animal's intention, whether it would run off at the sight of him or charge, but it was too risky to test it unless forced to.

Squatting behind the last line of bushes before the clearing quickly fatigued Robert's sore knees. It was too uncomfortable to keep his position, but he knew his situation was as sticky as he felt. The hot jungle sun brought a drenched sweat over him in an open area.

Beside him now squatted the two Pygmies, out from their hiding. Their beady eyes peered sharply at the giant beast below. Neither carried weapons and would be defenseless if confronted. It was a wonder why they were still there.

The motion came from the right side of the clearing, that drew everyone's attention. The animal jerked its head up and whipped to attention. Three armed men emerged from the cover of the jungle. Each carried a 30-caliber rifle with a Thompson machine gun strapped to their backs. Their garb was a dark green uniform showing no emblems. One was ahead of the others by a few steps and had grown a heavy black beard.

All three rifles were pointed at the animal before they stepped into the clearing, but the bullets were shot too late. Its movement was supernaturally quick, and leaped most of the distance without a running start. Like a coiled spring, it launched airborne and landed only when it reached the lead gunman. The sheer weight of its body was enough to crush him instantly. As it landed, the waving antennae lashed down on the remaining gunmen, attaching the tips to their faces. Spheroid-shaped bulges formed and traveled up the antennae from the gunmen to the beast. With each new bulging shape, the gunman's heads would lurch forward as if being violently sucked of their insides. They grabbed blindly at the appendages for several seconds before their bodies went limp.

The tiny hands of the Pygmies moved to rest on Robert's legs as they quietly gasped at the sight. Robert could feel the quivering fear in them both. Its movements and sheer immensity shredded any barrier in Robert's mind. His mind tried suppressing the fear he shared with them but failed quickly.

Despite its exceptional speed, Robert noted it took its time when feeding. Rather than devouring the bodies like a crocodile, it took small careful bites and overly chewed the meat before swallowing. It would arch its back as if howling at the moon when it opened its wide mouth, allowing the morsel to be flipped back into its throat.

The procedure looked like the animal would be occupied for a considerable time, which gave Robert a suicidal thought. He guessed he was about 50 yards from the bottom of the stairs. He couldn't imagine the door being locked. It was just a wheel hatch. It might cause him to become trapped with the creature lingering outside, but he was unsure what else he could do.

Delven had asked him to learn what had caused communication to cease at the hospital. Judging from the creature's presence and ferocity he witnessed, it could be the answer Delven was wanting, but it didn't fit the sketch he had received. This had to be the place, assuming no other buildings existed. It looked nothing like a hospital.

A sighting of some supernatural creature is the probable reason for the hospital to no longer communicate - they're all dead from it. It brought up questions if that were the case. Did the faculty lock themselves inside and die from starvation? How did they close the door if the beast killed them? Could this be all he really needed for Delven?

Begrudgingly he knew he needed more information, and it would require him to get inside the building unnoticed. He let out a quiet sigh as the two Pygmies glanced up at him with fear and concern in their eyes.

The beast fed. Its attention seemed to be in pure euphoria as it devoured the men. Even after several minutes of Robert convincing him this was a good idea, it had only managed to consume the top half of the initial gunman. He had plenty of time. He hoped.

Keeping low to the ground, he carefully pushed the leaves away from him as he tried to watch both the animal and his footing for noisy twigs. The bushes were not deep, but the slope leading down into the clearing was alarmingly steep. There weren't any walkways or trails zigzagging down. Vines hugged the ground entirely down, but he knew it would not be easy. He gingerly pulled one as best as he could without making much noise, but it wasn't the same as his entire weight pulling on it.

A step behind was the Pygmies as they cautiously stepped along with him, their necks strained outward and peering at the abomination eating. They leaned down, grabbed a vine without looking, and held them in their hands but remained still.

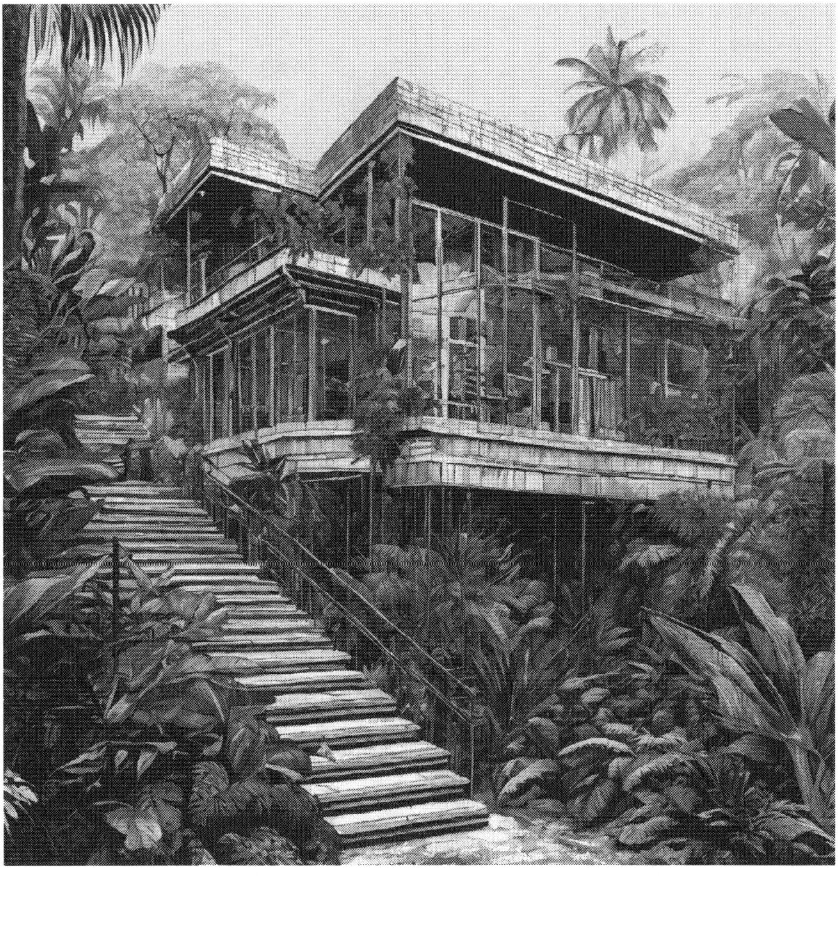

"You don't want to go down there," Robert whispered to them. While their eyes didn't move from the creature, they softly chittered at him in a determined reply. Robert shrugged, figured he had lived a nice life, and began lowering himself down the slope.

The vine stretched initially to his weight but held firm. Another vine was grouped with the first to add support, and his confidence grew with each foot lowered. Every few feet, he paused and looked over his shoulder to ensure the creature was still eating. It didn't matter, he thought as he approached the ground. He would be killed before he could do anything with its leaping ability.

To Robert's surprise, he made it to the ground without making enough noise to give himself away. The Pygmies showed expertise as they rapidly descended utterly noiseless. Often they needed to wait for him.

When Robert turned around, his heart sank as he saw the vast open field before him. The creature was immense! What he had initially thought of as a horse in size was more like a small home. It had finished eating the first victim and had moved on to the second. For whatever reason, it was increasing its speed. Robert needed to make a move quickly.

Still hunched over, he started to the bottom of the stairs, which looked far more than 50 yards away. With each step, his eyes made it look further still. It was agonizingly slow, but he felt he might reach it before dinner.

Just ahead and above him came a gentle but noticeable metal squeak that froze him in his tracks. The wheel on the door was turning. There was a brief moment when all things stopped: Robert looked at the creature, and the beast looked back at Robert.

With his injury from the hippo, he couldn't make the run in a sprint regardless of the new dress. He knew he could not reach the stairs before he was caught. But there was not enough time to gauge and guess.

A stone smacked the beast's skull and ricocheted off the hard surface. It snapped its head towards the direction of the stone's path to lock sight with one of the Pygmies. Both had stones in each hand, launching them relentlessly toward the animal.

Robert took a step towards them, unsure of what to do. Somehow he knew they were buying him time by distracting it, but Robert couldn't let them share the same fate as the gunmen.

His second step was taken, and a rock from the other Pygmy flew directly at him. When he stopped walking, the stones stopped coming at him. Communication had finally been made between Robert and them. Out of the corner of his eye, the beast launched itself up into the air as before, but the two Pygmies anticipated the motion and stepped back into the vines and disappeared inside them.

There were more vines at the base than Robert had noticed before, and the creature landed in front of them, clawing at the vines with numerous appendages. For the moment, the Pygmies looked to be protected by the vegetation. He took no more time and bolted to the stairs.

A shattering scream of frustration boomed around him from the creature behind. Robert's blood ran cold when it was answered by a chorus of similar-sounding cries that echoed in the surrounding mountains. What were these beasts?

As he reached the base of the stairs, he desperately grabbed the rail and swung around 180 degrees to face the steps as a horrendous sharp pain clamped on his hand. The creature had managed to catch up to him so quickly, Robert thought, but he could see the one still by the vines. A second one?

The pain sent him into shock from the fear of the creature beside him. One of the tentacle-like arms flashed down to black out Robert's vision, and he immediately began to suffocate. His air was instantly sucked out of his lungs and tightened to prevent him from drawing anymore. He felt lightheaded and fought weakly against losing consciousness.

Somewhere in his mind came a voice he had often heard before. It spoke to him with a casual confidence that surged through Robert. The words were similar to what he had heard deeply submerged under the waters of the Nile, but this time he understood them. It wasn't a comprehension of communication but a signal to his brain of command.

He recognized the place he had traveled to before - the Dreamlands. Though his vision was dark, he began to see around him in a shrouded mist that gave way to the clearing. High overhead were clouds traveling at incredible speeds with no wind to propel them.

The creature stood before him, with its appendage gripped on Robert's face, but he casually brushed it aside. Something empowered him while here, and he felt invulnerable. He brandished no weapon, but suddenly, he held a sword that was as black as the creature before him. With a quick thrust of his arm, the blade penetrated into the flesh of the dark animal and spilled what made up the beast inside.

Still frustrated at the clearing's edge, the original animal perked up as it watched one of its own be slain so quickly and disappear into the dark jungle in a few mighty bounds.

Robert's heart clenched and seized, and he felt the familiar grip of a hand squeeze against the organ. His vision of the Dreamlands melted to color as his mind returned to his world.

His legs gave out from under him, and he collapsed on the stairs and closed his eyes to wait for the pain to release. Small, delicate hands touched his chest as the Pygmies rushed up to him. Their chattering began as before, in monotone, as if chanting while they made circles around Robert's mysterious necklace.

The emblem began to glow in reaction to the Pygmies' words, and soon his chest relieved him. As the pressure on his heart subsided, so did the glow of the emblem.

Panting for air, Robert leaned back on the stairs while the two Pygmies relentlessly patted his arm in congratulations. The words of Delven returned to him that spoke of his potential and how he essentially was wasting talents that he didn't know he had. As Delven was attuned to the Dreamlands, could he have been referring to it?

Judging by the light reflecting off the tips of the eastern mountains, Robert knew he had little light left of the day, so he hustled up to the door. The hatch was still closed, but its wheel was loose. He still had to muscle through the initial rotation before releasing the seal that the airlock door had created. A rush of stagnant, dry air escaped around the edges when he pulled it open.

He could hear no sound inside as he stepped over the threshold, followed by the two Pygmies. He took his chances against more creatures visiting at night and closed the door behind him.

His small roundish friends cautiously stepped in and peered around in great wonder. Their chattering, though impossible to understand, sounded as spellbound. Squatting down like a catcher to get eye level with them, Robert tried speaking in English about how much safer it was inside than out with the strange beasts roaming.

The room he stood in was for communications. A desk was against the wall to Robert's right and just below a large window overlooking the jungle beyond. Various communication devices were covering most of it, providing the means to send and receive audio messages and telegram notes. Despite the sophistication and available telegram blanks nearby, there were strangely no received messages lying anywhere, including the bin.

Trash had been lazily tossed between the electronic clutter. He spotted a Kits still in its wrapper and peeled it free to pluck it in his mouth.

He could hear the two Pygmies stirring with sudden curiosity at the sound of the candy being unwrapped. The candy was a reasonably new product released only a few years prior. Its yellow texture wafted the light banana scent to Robert's nostrils. He wondered how difficult it was to send luxuries to remote locations. The personnel at Delven's so-called pop-up hospital had good connections.

With the temptation too great, the two Pygmies waddled up to him with outstretched arms, both chattering loudly in a demanding tone. Robert grabbed a second piece after rummaging and split it into two. They chewed happily.

For the first time since El Obeid, he felt out of danger. His brain reminded him of the wounds he had received from the hippos the other day. The makeshift bandages the Pygmies had created were holding well. The stinging was all gone and no longer sensitive to the touch. Hence, he began searching the place for any medical treatment he might recognize.

It was more eerily silent with the door shut. He couldn't even make out ambient noise. The candies were quickly consumed, and his companions returned promptly behind Robert, ever cautiously and without sound.

The comms room had an inner hatchway that swung on heavy hinges like the front. It was open, and he stepped through.

Following the comms was a small first aid station in the adjoining room. The chair for the patient was relatively new and in good shape. Beside it was a physician's tray holding several instruments in an orderly fashion. A row of cabinets patterned with an L shape was around the far corner with overhanging cabinets. To his left was another hatchway door that was closed.

The interior design was unusual for the building's location. It was structured high off the ground to avoid any flash floods, and the local animals wouldn't get through a more traditional door. Unless the natives had artillery or powerful tools, they weren't getting through a simple lock. Robert had only seen bulkhead doors aboard ships. It was unclear why they would be needed here.

Strange, expensive doors weren't the only puzzle he attempted to solve. As he searched the cabinets in the second room, he saw telltale signs of being recently inhabited. There were medical supplies that still had a shelf life. Half-eaten food in the garbage had only minor mold. Whoever occupied the hospital hadn't been gone for long, but they had been long enough. One would expect them back by now.

Even for an untrained physician, Robert found some antiseptic and clean gauze and made himself comfortable on the patient's chair. Where the hippo's tusk had pierced his stomach hadn't been as deep as he feared. After peeling back the leaves, it was clear and healing rapidly. They had applied some mucus-like slime that was drawing out any apparent infection. He was amazed by the rapid improvement and decided to only wrap it with the gauze and leave their work alone.

His leg was cleaned and dressed, and he felt he could put more weight on it. The Pygmies felt more comfortable inside the building and began mimicking Robert's motions by opening the lower cabinets. By the time Robert had finished wrapping his wound, the Pygmies were eagerly making a clutter of things as they tunneled their way inside the cabinets from one end to the other. At one point, he heard one yelp in pain and then tumble through one of the cabinet doors. A scalpel was gripped firmly in one hand and sucked a cut finger with the other.

"Hey, be careful with that. It's dangerous," Robert said. He had grown frustrated from their language barrier in a short time, wishing to ask them questions. While the two little ones didn't appear too concerned, their behaviors were impulsive and inquisitive. Rather than stopping to question, they generally looked to act first and chatter with each other after the experience.

This was true as the other crawled out of the cabinets and hovered over the injured Pygmy. A brief chattering soon led to him scampering back into the previous room and returning with an umbrella left by the door. Instead, they began pulling and tearing at the fabric and wire lining until it snapped entirely off, leaving the metal shaft and handle.

A moment early, it appeared the two were bickering over umbrella ownership. Within a few minutes, the Pygmies had securely wrapped the umbrella wiring tightly around the scalpel to the end of the umbrella rod. Triumphantly they presented their new spear to Robert.

For the moment, Robert smiled at their clever ingenuity. The primitive lifestyle he had witnessed showed significant advancements in critical thinking fueled by a curious imagination. He couldn't help but feel happy they had run into each other. Having them around was welcoming to the lonely journey.

Nodding his approval of their makeshift spear, he continued to explore the remaining facility, which turned out to be larger than he had gauged from outside. The portion resembling a hospital was further back. Patients were led into a corridor joined at one end by the first aid station and passed a series of operating rooms. With each one he passed, Robert let out a whistle in amazement. Delven had not shaved any pennies on the development of the place. Each room was more accommodating than the finest hospital rooms back in London. Adjustable gatch beds lined with rails were accompanied by a water basin, a private curtain, and a small instrument station. Some rooms had windows, but the vegetation was so closely pressed to the glass that it gave little view and little ambient light. But each room was immaculately clean and spotless.

The doors down the corridor continued the same style with water-tight sealable hatches. Although paper envelopes stuck to them to hold medical records, they were all empty. In this part of the facility, he found no signs of life.

Another closed door at the end of the corridor opened into the staff quarters. Its first section was made into a lounge room with divans against a few walls, more cabinets filled with dry goods, and a dartboard hanging above a radio.

The radio was on and receiving a broadcast signal. Until Robert opened the lounge door, he hadn't heard a single sound, and now he clearly was listening to See See Rider crackling out of the speakers with a steady, constant signal.

Like frightened children, the Pygmies stood momentarily behind his legs, then slipped past and approached the radio. They leaned in and peered into the speaker and around to the back of the device chattering all along.

Robert joined them and sat down in front of it, listening to the song with a peculiar look. How in the world was the radio being powered, let alone picking up a radio signal out here?" he thought. He sat fascinated for several minutes, marveling at the first song he had heard in over a month. Next to him, the curious duo poked, prodded, and occasionally chattered directly into the speaker. When the song ended, a man with an American accent announced they were listening to Crazy Blues Hour on WEAF. He introduced the next piece of music, and a gritty rhythmic song echoed in the room.

Robert's confusion continued to build as the unanswered questions kept stacking. An American radio station? How was it even possible to reach this far?

By now, the Pygmies had given up trying to communicate with the radio and climbed on top of it to reach the darts still embedded in the board. Six in all, they pulled each one out. They started experimenting with them, sending them back into the board and the surrounding wall before discovering they could be thrown.

The left door opened to a bunk room with four beds on both sides and footlockers at the ends. Each bed was made with fresh, clean sheets. The room lacked dust anywhere, perhaps due to the sealed hatchway.

Some of the footlockers had locks, but the ones without contained nothing. Returning to the lounge room, he found a fire extinguisher in one of the cabinets and used it to force the locks open. There had been a need for the extinguisher's use as it felt empty.

Three lockers contained a few sets of men's and women's clothing and framed photos of couples and groups of people. One container, in particular, had a person's journal, which he sat on one of the beds and opened.

It began, "Jane Collinsworth, 1925. March 17. I arrived at Marconi Station this morning to serve as chief physician. Mr. Montgomery has so far been beyond generous in my travel accommodations. He insisted on restocking my medical bag with the latest instruments and tools, although I kindly attempted to decline. My wages, perhaps, are the only thing that has surpassed his hospitality. I am still in awe of the amount he offered.

"The station is peculiarly structured above the ground; that is, it rests on vertical beams that keep it over ten feet in the air. I am unsure as to the reason behind this design, but I suspect I will learn from the existing physicians already at the site."

Robert's mind began to sift through the journal casually as Jane's entry notes continued expectantly and ordinarily. She had been hired by Delven in the spring of 1925, and her last entry was three months ago. That made him pause momentarily as he calculated the time elapsed from when Delven caught word the station had lost communication to the present day. There was an entry regarding the communication problem the week prior, so roughly 90 days had passed. To Robert, that felt a bit brief.

Jane explained the telecommunication wire had been paid for and installed through Delven's finances. It provided both an audio broadcast and a telegraph by Morse code. At some point, the connection had died.

Robert began moving backward in the journal. Several notes were written in such haste and disorder he could barely make out the words. They progressively lost form, as if Jane had forgotten how to write. The style mainly was scribbles and odd symbols and shapes by the final entry.

There were numerous mentions of the creatures he saw outside and several other unidentified species with bizarre descriptions. The station had not been penetrated by any of the animals. However, the windows frequently had fish-like flying creatures latched on and using a single long tooth that would scrape in circles across the pane in an attempt to cut through.

The final entry was not conclusive to the journal or her work at the hospital. Although frantically written and barely legible, Janet expressed her fear of remaining there from the increased attacks of the "creatures of nightmares," as she described them. She mentioned they were growing in size with each new assault, but the journal was not closed. It was too abrupt to ignore.

Communications had been cut somehow, but he had been hired to investigate the station. Without bothering to read every entry, Robert could tell that it left clues about what might have happened to the staff. With no sign of blood or a struggle, he couldn't assume they were all killed by the local wildlife or strange beasts. It remained a mystery.

The back of Jane's book had a compartment holding loose sheets of paper or perhaps pressed flowers. He pulled it back and found a hand sketch of a familiar emblem. It was the same inverted triangle with three symbols drawn along each edge he had encountered several times in his journey. Each emblem looked like a rune or glyph, less hieroglyphic and more symbolic. It had been the third time he recalled coming across it. Its significance drew his curiosity to new heights. What did this represent?

In the other room, the sound of the darts thudded nicely against the wall or, more often than not, actually on the dart board. The two had developed some sort of understanding of the game's concept before being instructed on how to play. They were happily chattering at what sounded like cheering from time to time.

Robert turned the sketch over. In Jane's better handwriting, she read, "Native tattoo on her back. Bushongo? Baluba?"

His thoughts returned to the Pygmies' tattoo. He only was familiar with the Bambuti tribe that frequently traded with outsiders of the Congo. He wasn't sure of their tribe, as there were many, but her thoughts might be along the same line.

He had been optimistic Jane's diary would have shed some light on something to cause the entire staff to vanish so abruptly. He tried thumbing through the pages multiple times to see if his eyes caught a word or exciting phrase. No other staff member kept a journal.

The keen investigator's ears suddenly picked up the lack of noise from the other room. The Pygmies seemed to never stop chattering at one another and had gone silent. He made his way to the doorway but was met by the two backing slowly into the room. They stared straight toward the comms room.

A few seconds later, Robert heard it, too. Far down the hallway, through the first aid and into the comms area, Robert could just make out the squeak of the hatch wheel turning to open. Although he could see the first aid chair through the corridor, the wall beyond blocked all view of the main entrance.

The Pygmies had latched onto his pant legs and were quietly but desperately pulling toward the back of the room. Something terrified them, but as skittish as they were, it could be anything, including the staff returning.

Yet he paused before stepping into the corridor, holding the hatchway. Something did feel a bit off, although he wasn't sure what that was. Voices came from the front door as the hatchway swung open. It took a moment to identify they were speaking in Hungarian, but one of them was distinctly familiar - Genevieve. Whatever she said to the other two was unpleasant as she barked viciously at them. Robert felt the wave of ferocity coming from her mouth while footsteps quickly came from down the hall.

It was peculiar how she managed to arrive at the same time he did unless he was being followed. He decided not to have a friendly conversation with her since he had failed to kill Delven. He doubted she knew he was there.

Backing up with the Pygmies, he nearly tripped on the hatchway into the bunk room. He saw a man dressed and armed like the three outside.

Cursing under his breath, Robert was not in a good position. Each door had made too much noise, so he couldn't risk entering the adjacent room from the bunk.

They all had a crossbar that could be lowered to secure the hatch from opening. It would reveal his presence, but the locked door would be impassable from the other side.

Before he followed Plan A, he glanced around the bunk room and saw a return vent near the corner. It wasn't secure, but it fit snugly enough. He hoped it would remain in place. The vent had to lead somewhere and was large enough to crawl through. He took out the multi-tool he had packed back home and quickly worked on the screws to loosen the screen. The Pygmies wasted no time crouching in with Robert after he replaced the screen. He suspected they would discover the loose vent soon and hoped he had found an escape route long before then.

The voices were challenging back and forth with short orders, echoing off the thin walls. Genevieve was lashing out about keeping quiet though her voice rang louder than the rest. It was clear by now they were searching for him. He had no time to calculate how she could have arrived so precisely on time and accurately on location for him.

He had never seen a vent that wasn't directly linked outside until now. Instead, it opened to a secure room without doors. A sizeable metallic box occupied most of the space and was armed with numerous thin metal conduits jutting outward. One led to the lounge where the radio had been plugged in. At least he found where the power was coming from, although he needed to figure out what he was looking at.

Generators had been around for many years, but the size of this one was perplexing. He wasn't sure how it was creating power as quietly as it hummed, but underneath, a wide cylinder led into the ground. It was wide enough for him to fit if he could step inside.

Down the corridor, the gunmen's footsteps approached cautiously. Their Hungarian conversations had gone silent, and their footsteps were barely detectable.

"You are hunted," drummed in his head as he fought to control his breathing. He had felt hunted the entire journey. Now the time had come to escape.

The Pygmies had proven to be experts at stealth. Robert nearly forgot they were there, huddled silently in the dark corner of the hidden room. With their beady eyes, they watched Robert closely with expectation. They were in survival mode in a strange environment but followed his direction.

Thinking of no better option, he turned to the strange generator. It had an access panel that a screwdriver could remove, revealing a narrow cavity lined with more metal pipes. At the back of the nook was a steel disc widely punched in the center to grant passage below, but he could neither fit through the niche nor into the cavity. He wasn't sure what it was designed for. The hole possessed no piping or wires - just an empty spot roughly two feet wide. Somewhere below ground, coming from the pit, his ears picked up humming. Its rhythm made him think mechanically.

A small hand touched his shoulder, and he almost shouted from shock as he turned to see the Pygmies crouched beside him, also peering in the nook. One gently pushed his shoulder in that direction.

Into the darkness, they both went without hesitation from the ease of space. They didn't need to duck their heads as they stepped up to the hole in the floor.

Outside he could just make out shuffling feet. They had made it into the bunk and were making their rounds. Through the vent, he could see the men, clad in dark green uniforms, slowly heading towards the back and inspecting between and under each bed. He knew they would most likely discover the loose vent in seconds when they turned back. He had but a few seconds to act.

The Pygmies had disappeared into the darkness. Robert couldn't hear them land, and he had run out of time, so he laid on his side and, using the nearby wall, pushed hard against it and wedged his body between the pipes. With his torso turned on its side and arms stretched in front, he could get a hand on the lip of the hole. He discovered the steel disc was friction fitted and slipped out in his hands. With it removed, the two-foot gap was considerably wider. He had broad shoulders; he wasn't a twig.

There was no going back at this point. Most of his body was wedged so tightly Robert could not get a full gulp of air from the restriction. His shallow breathing rapidly sent alarms through his body. Somewhere past his feet, he heard the scraping of the vent opening and Hungarian shouting.

His body felt a surge of adrenaline from fear and anxiety, and he pulled himself further down with all his might. Most of his body was in a pitch-black hole.

Scuffling feet scratched along the floor behind him, and his shoes were grabbed. At least two pairs of hands were holding them, and for a moment, he thought the shoes might slip off and let him slide away.

With a jolt, his ankles were pulled violently back. The ripple shook his clothes, and he watched his multi-tool among a few coins slip out of his pockets, disappearing into the darkness below. With each inch, he felt his ribs grind painfully. It had been easier going in than coming out.

He was dragged into the bunkroom. There was no point in resisting - he could feel two people kneeing into his back and one at his throat. The men grunted like they were struggling to restrain him, lifting him off the ground with his hands bound.

Through the lounge and down the corridor, they went to the front room, where he was greeted by Genevieve. None of her goons in the room, two more than the three grabbing him, were familiar to him from their last encounter.

Her expression was filled with disappointment. Sitting on a wheeled chair by the comms desk, legs and arms crossed, she looked up at Robert with narrow eyes.

"What could he possibly have to offer?" she asked, raising her eyebrows. "Your entire adult life has been a joke of an excuse because of him - pitiful and worthless. A secondary career, poverty-level wages, and yet you have made it here. For him. How is he driving you on?"

Robert rolled his head to the side and glanced out the window, almost expecting the same gardener clipping iroko plants. There was a strange fragrance coming from somewhere, though. Its origin couldn't be pinpointed, but it reminded him of Natasha's perfume.

His eyes returned to Genevieve. Her hair was still pulled tightly in a ponytail, and she wore a dark skirt suit that could have been the same one as before. Her high-heeled shoes struck Robert as odd for a jungle excursion.

The entire situation made little sense to him. How did she get here so quickly?

She waited patiently for his answer. He sighed slowly.

"I no longer work for Delven," he said simply. He knew it wouldn't be enough for her, but he didn't feel like spouting more than what was needed.

She scoffed at the answer. "Don't bother being coy with me, Mr. Kipner. You made it this far. I don't know what he has offered you, but whatever it is, you can expect my offer will be more favorable."

"What, you'll offer me fifty thousand this time?" Robert said, and he felt the grip of the men holding him squeeze his biceps harder. He smiled up at them, "Good instinct, boys. I was just about to slip free."

"The chance for financial gain has passed," she said. "It is your life that is at stake now. I'm tired of your sarcasm and casual, careless approach. I will ensure you carry out your task this time."

She glanced at one of the guards, and, with a nod, Robert was dragged outside and down the stairs. For a moment, he hoped one of the strange beasts would return and remove a few of the guards for him, but his luck, what little he had left, was nowhere to help him.

Parked at the foot of the stairs was a peculiar vehicle. It resembled a truck, but its rear wheels had been replaced with a metal segment belt to create a makeshift half-track. Its front wheels were broader and more prominent in diameter than conventional vehicles back home.

Only two of Genevieve's goons climbed in the truck's bed and half dragged Robert in while Genevieve delicately stepped into the cabin with another. The remaining two went back inside the building and closed the door.

The ripple of the motor jarred his teeth as the truck came to life. Over the engine's noise, Robert could barely hear himself think, let alone attempt to ask any questions. He suspected that time had passed for now.

To his surprise, the vehicle moved extremely slowly but diligently out of the clearing and to the north. Front headlights illuminated their way but proved useless as the car pushed through dense foliage. At times it sounded like the engine was overworked and overheating, but it somehow broke through to a dirt road.

Figures, Robert thought to himself as he glanced down the road. He could only make it out a few feet before the darkness clouded his vision beyond. He suspected his walk into the facility would have been a lot smoother had he known of the road.

Whenever he leaned in towards the cabin, he would be encouraged in a less than polite manner by the goons around him to sit upright. Frustrated, he uncomfortably sat still as the truck bounced abruptly over large roots and rocks.

Wherever they were headed took time, although it could be a few yards away at their traveling speed. His mind wandered to Trish, Sinclair, and Renaldo. There had been no sign of their plane landing nearby, so they had either crashed or found another spot to land. After learning of this hidden road, he wondered how much civilization had been constructed this far into the jungle.

Now that he didn't have to think of his survival from hippos, starvation, or giant exotic animals, he realized how exhausted he was. The rhythmic humming of the truck didn't help either. The repetition played havoc on the weight of his eyelids, and he soon drifted to sleep.

CHAPTER XV

Congo, 1926

Matching the sound of his pickax was the wail of a jungle bird seeking a lover. The coarse, wooden handle tore against his raw red skin from overuse. With every forceful pull down of the tool, another small boulder split apart; another chunk of black soil was scraped away.

The work would be laborious even for a seasoned rock splitter, and he had just started. Before him lay a wide slope covered in an ancient avalanche of rocks and overtaken by the jungle overgrowth. Most trees in the area had been knocked over by the landslide and never recovered, giving way to a clearing of hot sunlight that soaked Robert through his clothes in sweat.

Nearby a small troop of men dressed in green uniforms went about with operations. None appeared to be doing any actual work. A series of large-scale tents had been erected, providing a destination for them to walk to. One of the tents contained Genevieve.

A friendly chit-chat wasn't offered to Robert by her when he was brought out of his deep sleep. Instead, he was roughly dragged over the side of the half-track's bed to where he was now and had been for days. Robert thought crudely and horribly uncomfortable from the heavy weight of the iron resting on his shoulders. They assured them he would not escape by locking a metal collar around his neck attached to the only surviving tree in the large clearing.

Being forced to produce hard labor had not occurred to him as punishment for not fulfilling her request. His back screamed at him, along with the generous wear and tear his body had endured ever since he reached Africa. From his heart being squeezed regularly to knife wounds and tusk goring, it was all rapidly taking its toll. The prolonged work in the high humidity was quickly winding him down.

He could only know that his arduous labor had lasted well into the afternoon from the blaze of the sun's position. It was becoming increasingly difficult to stay focused and land his blows squarely.

Only the goons had spoken to him after waking up. "Break and dig," they told him after handing him a pickaxe. He thought of burying the tool deep in the man's cranium, but would only give him brief satisfaction before he was destroyed by the others.

Hours turned into days, but Genevieve remained in her tent while he was awake. Each night when it was too dark to strike a stone, he was shoved into a giant tent filled with more of her goons and grunts.

Robert didn't blame her for remaining under shade. He was becoming delirious from heat stroke. He could see Delven Montgomery, white fedora and mahogany cane in hand, striding out from behind a large boulder with confidence as if he had magically transported from elsewhere. Hallucinations set in once again, but this time he didn't suspect they were as supernatural as the others.

Robert's hallucination approached him with a smile as he gazed down at him. It reached out, and Robert felt the hand of Delven pat his shoulder assuredly.

His vision spoke to him. "Ah, Robert, there you are. And look here, you managed to get back to digging for hidden treasures after all these years!"

Robert stood silent, staring with a desperately dry mouth as the vision, appearing very real, strode past him and entered one of the larger tents. Several goons stopped him with their machine guns lowered. No guards kept an eye on Robert, so he stood there and followed with his eyes, unable to turn around entirely from exhaustion to track the man in white's movement. At least, Robert thought it was from exhaustion. His feet really could not move like they were glued to the dirt.

Genevieve's voice came from within the same tent before emerging. "Delven, you aren't welcome here anymore. That part is over between us. I would advise you to jump back home while you are whole." Her eyes scanned slowly to the side and locked on Robert, who was blistered on his lips and unable to move.

"Get back to digging, Mr. Kipner. You haven't found anything yet." She turned her attention back to Delven.

Delven didn't skip a beat and said, "It looks to me like we continue to share information." He did a grand sweep of his arms to emphasize the dig site. "Or should I believe that you accidentally stumbled upon this location and felt the need to send your elite digging force to work?"

A few chinks at the closest rock were enough to satisfy Genevieve and permit him to listen further. At this point, his impacts on the rock posed no threat to their well-being.

With narrowed eyes, Genevieve said, "I took what was rightfully mine and used it. I saw no reason to share anything more with you, given that you did not intend to divulge the region. We had a deal, and you broke it. From this point on, you are walking on thin ice if you interfere with me."

No amount of threat ever seemed to stagger Delven. Taking her words casually, he found a chair nearby and sat down with the grace of a young gazelle despite wearing a full three-piece suit in the sweltering heat. In each encounter, Robert had seen Delven wearing the same white attire. Except for Cairo, he had only spoken to him while in the Dreamlands. Strange even more so, he wasn't sweating despite the intense oven temperature from the jungle. That started a peculiar thought in Robert's mind as he listened.

"My dear Genevieve," Delven began as he crossed his legs and rested his hands on his cane. "You knew where to look; I held nothing back. See here," Delven turned and pointed his cane at Robert. "You knew where to bring him..."

"No thanks to you," she said. One of the men in green brought over a cup of water and handed it to her, and she took a long, desired drink.

Delven shrugged. "On the contrary, a thank you is in order. I assured you he would pass right under your nose; all you had to do was follow the scent. And you did just that. Here we are. I don't see a need for the animosity."

Reaching into his suit, the guards raised their weapons, but he ignored them. Out from an inner pocket came a circle of stone with thin strips of leather wrapped tightly around to form a pattern like spokes on a wheel.

He raised it up as Genevieve folded her arms, awaiting its explanation. "Now, if I were to do this, however," he said, remaining perfectly still and holding the piece to his eye like a monocle. Robert watched as everyone around Delven jerked to a stop as if held by an impossibly strong force. Their arms and legs were held fast, but their facial expressions remained free.

"Then I could understand some animosity," Delven said with a hearty chuckle. The device showed no special powers or effects while he held it, which was brief before putting it away. Delven tilted his head and smiled charmingly at Genevieve as she struggled against the invisible restraints.

"What have you done, Delven? This goes well beyond even your tricks. Now you're going to bring them into the fight by tampering with their things. Are you prepared for that?" Genevieve asked through gritted teeth. She gave up, knowing fighting was useless, and relaxed against the force.

Getting up from the chair, he approached her uncomfortably close. His warm breath, a putrid whiff, blew across her nostrils, making her nearly retch. The smell was rich with ether and ammonia.

In a hazy state of mind, Robert tried to keep conscious as he listened to the two banter. At some point during the chat, he suddenly realized the iron collar around his neck was no longer locked. It loosely dangled on his shoulders.

For a brief moment, Genevieve's eyes flicked toward him, and he feared she would notice and order a guard to secure it again. This time, she made no indication and just as quickly looked back at Delven. Perhaps it had been her doing to free him, but he was unsure how she could have done so at a distance.

The clues that had ensued since Delven had arrived had culminated into a theory Robert was willing to test. Delven couldn't travel so freely around with little effort in the world. He frequently appeared and vanished within minutes of seeing Robert. That, along with the magic trick of Robert's iron collar, gave him the idea he wasn't necessarily living the moment in the world he knew. It might have sounded strange to Robert a month ago, but now he was sure he was tricked into believing the Dreamlands as reality. There had been so many lifelike moments before that felt so real he couldn't distinguish one way or another. Still, after his travels and experiences, he was sure enough to risk his life on the bet.

He could make a move. Gauging his distance, he knew he could reach Delven in two enormous strides if he bolted. Montgomery had behaved peculiarly in each of his recent encounters. There was a quick, nimble step in his walk. He appeared to be far more agile than he should be at his age.

He thought of himself sneaking up behind Delven and landing a solid blow to the back of his head, but why make his plan so real? Robert found himself a few inches behind Delven. With no movement, he had been transported to the location he had visualized going to. He was in the Dreamlands, after all! His theory had been confirmed, but he wondered for a split second how long he had been here. Were the Pygmies as real as Delven and Genevieve, or were they native to the Dreamlands, only appearing when Robert was connected to it?

Robert raised his hands in a double fist and was suddenly smacked between the legs by Delven's cane. He went down immediately from the excruciating pain, and Delven looked over his shoulder and down at him.

"Tsk, Tsk, Mr. Kipner. I always watch you. Everything you do, I see. It has always been so. You had your chance, but I'm afraid now you will finish what Genevieve felt so clever at doing. Get up," Delven spoke with a commanding voice; his charm vanished.

The words had force behind them that pulsed through Robert's body. It was as if there was a power over him, but he had heard a peculiar musical tune through the voice. The medallion he wore quickly hummed like wind chimes, and the sound of Delven's dominating voice was silenced. Robert was free once again.

Delven's body was abnormally dense, and despite putting all his strength into it, he didn't budge. Robert feinted to rise but charged into Delven's abdomen. His shoulder landed solidly as he lifted up with his legs into Montgomery, noting the sensation was like pushing one of the boulders nearby.

Robert could feel the stone disc Delven used to freeze everyone in his jacket pocket. His hand slipped into the bag in the skirmish, trying to use his body to conceal his theft attempt.

Immediately Delven's grip came down around his wrist, and Robert felt a searing heat on his skin. His flesh began to cook with rising steam. A sharp sizzle hissed like bacon on a hot skillet. There was a great desire to give up, but he heard a voice echo from all around, booming against the mountains of the Congo.

"Wield your power; he is weaker," came the voice, resonating like screams in an empty room. The sound was powerful, and Robert grew bolder and overwhelmed with a need to take Delven's relic.

Pushing through the heat as his wrist liquefied, his fingertips slipped into the inner jacket pocket and barely brushed the stone's surface.

The pain vanished, and he was suddenly back overlooking the clinic. This time, the Pygmies were missing, and his exhaustion from breaking rocks all day and the blisters on his palms were wiped clean as if it had never occurred.

Standing up and taking in his surroundings, he could tell. At the same time, things looked familiar. There were differences this time than before being here. The airstrip lay beyond the clinic, but a biplane was parked quietly at one end this time. He clearly could make out the makeshift seats mounted on the wings. It was Captain Eddie Rickenbacker's plane.

Quickly he rummaged through the leaves and briefly retraced his steps to the campsite where he had met his little friends. Nothing was present to tell they had been there. The empty can of sardines was nowhere to be found. It was as if he had only dreamed them; perhaps they had been entities of the Dreamlands after all. It saddened him to think that possibility as short as their friendship had been. They had risked their lives for him without the ability to even communicate properly. If only he could thank them.

Returning to the clearing, he rushed down the stairs and ascended to the hatch door. The door opened by Trish before he could. He could see her, Sinclair, Renaldo, and Eddie through the windows of the comms room as he made his way up.

"Robert!" she shouted with relief and overjoy. "You made it!"

She leaped out to hug him with surprising affection while he glanced over her shoulder to the others. Renaldo was grinning ear to ear with a look of pride as if his son had returned safely from war. The other two appeared more puzzled.

"You look like hell, Kipner," Sinclair said as he was led inside and to the first aid room. The state of both rooms remained identical to the boxes of KITS candy at the comms desk. They were unopened.

Trish sat him down and looked at his stomach wound from the hippo tusk. No evidence of the Pygmies' medical dressing was present, as if it never occurred. Yet, his wound had healed significantly though not entirely.

"Mercy, did you get stabbed with a sword?" she asked as she rummaged through the cabinets and found the medicine to treat the injury. She gave him a shot at something, and Robert relayed what he had experienced leading up to the Dreamlands segment between Delven and Genevieve. He felt his mouth loosen as he spoke, giving out more detail than usual. Whether it was the serum Trish injected or his secret joy of seeing everyone again, he was unsure but didn't care.

Renaldo entered the room to listen and handed Robert his flask, which was happily and eagerly accepted. "You had the better journey, my boy," he said as

Robert returned the flask. "I didn't think we would find the infernal place before we ran out of fuel."

Eddie was standing in the hatchway leaning against the frame and glanced at Renaldo. His dark expression indicated a history of unpleasantness behind Renaldo's words.

"We got here, didn't we? Just like you paid me to do. Which, by the way, I am still waiting for. I want to leave before sundown," Eddie said, folding his arms.

Trish, finishing up Robert's wounds, replied without looking at him, "I already told you. We need a ride back, then you get paid."

"That's not what you said, Darling, back in town," he grunted, which sparked Sinclair's attention and moved into Eddie's space.

"That's the last time you're going to refer to her as Darling. That is your last warning," Sinclair growled in a low voice.

It startled Robert. What had happened between the four of them in such a short time? It had only been a couple days. Sinclair had been a pacifist the entire trip, with a quiet, subdued tone. He spoke confidently, and Eddie backed down and raised his arms in defense.

"Okay, okay, never again," Eddie said with more sarcasm than probably was necessary. "That still doesn't change the fact there was no mention of a return flight. Besides, I can't take you all back anyway with him in the picture."

With a groggy head mixed with booze and the injection, Robert was not as sharp but didn't seem to care. The pain in his joints and muscles was gone at the moment, and the lightheaded was welcomed from all the turmoil that had bogged his mind lately.

"Who said I was flying back?" Robert slushed out as best as he could form words. He was feeling sleepy.

Behind Trish, he heard several voices talking at once but couldn't make out anything. Trish leaned in and whispered to close his eyes and rest.

*

"That doesn't sound like either are physically here, then," Trish said. Robert had slept for nearly twelve hours and woke early. By the time he had found coffee in the lounge, the others had risen. The place was still stocked with enough dried goods to cook an edible breakfast before they gathered among the couches to discuss a plan.

To the best of his ability, Robert tried explaining what he thought the Dreamlands were and his experiences. Until now, he had kept his theories locked away in fear of being called a fool, but the situation had dramatically shifted. He needed help to move forward.

There was a moment of silence as the group took in his confession before a round of accepting faces looked at him. Of them all, Renaldo was the most cheerful at the idea. Trish and Sinclair showed less than good thoughts, but in the end, it was apparent something sinister was forming, and they wanted to be in the middle.

"While we were awaiting your arrival," Sinclair said, "we unlocked that door and discovered some interesting findings."

It was the door Robert failed to open in time before Genevieve's troop barged in. Behind the closed door was a library with floor-to-ceiling bookshelves surrounding a desk. Books lay everywhere, and the desk was covered in papers. Nothing looked in order, like a mad scientist's scattered brain.

"Whoever was stationed here were hardly medical physicians," he began. "Most of the loose papers are notes written by the so-called staff in an effort to locate a lost building. There are charts of the area, and most of these books are either pertaining to various occult lore or a random historical retelling of African folklore specializing in this part of the continent."

Taking a book off the shelf, he opened it. He showed copied images of humans huddled around a sixteen-sided building. Primitive as it was, the humans were not clearly sapiens. There were strange, grotesque features throughout each that brushed against the tetrapod of the animal kingdom. Their backs, lined with numerous narrow fins, were curved like question marks as they waited for something to happen.

Above the image was a technical drawing with dimensions of the same charm hanging around Robert's neck. He pulled it out from under his shirt for the first time, revealing the oddity to them all.

Renaldo perked up at sight and remarked that it was identical to the one stolen from his train car by the same demonic creature that had attacked Kipner. Whether it was the same or a duplicate was anyone's guess.

After Kipner explained how he had found it and what it had done thus far, no one felt comfortable being near him with it.

"Nyarlathotep," Robert attempted to sound out the word written beside it in the book. "I have no idea how to pronounce that. What language is it?"

"It's not in any language we know," answered Sinclair, again slipping into his matter-of-fact personality. "It could be the name of the strange building. It comes up frequently in their notes and other books. Whatever the place is, it has great importance to them."

"To Delven and Genevieve," Trish followed up. "I bet it's what they hoped you would find in your dream. Have you ever seen anything like it before on your digs?"

It had been years since he had been on any dig site, and none revealed such a peculiar structure. The numerous sides included a multi-faceted roof that possessed no standard angles. All of it was chaotic and made Robert feel uneasy.

Renaldo had refused to step foot in the room and spoke to them from the couch. "You somehow know, or they wouldn't take such an interest in you, my dear fellow. Somewhere up in your extraordinary brain lies something locked away even you aren't aware of.

"Back in Austria, one of my closest and treasured friends often talked at the club about how secret chambers make up part of the mind."

Everyone turned to look through the hatchway with intrigue as Renaldo unfolded another tale. His tone was much more severe than before, and his smile had vanished. He spoke not with a sign of lightheartedness but with foreboding.

"A brilliant man of the mind, he explained these chambers, a term he coined for us to ease our confusion, could become accessible during dream-like states or hypnosis. Among these states, he mentioned sleepwalking or lucid dreaming, where one retains consciousness and is in control of their actions. I would surmise to say your experience in this Dreamland may grant that access."

"Which would explain why Genevieve took me to the dig site while connected to the Dreamlands," Robert said as he patted his shirt for cigarettes, subconsciously having long since run out. Eddie handed him one and lit it with a match. "I was exhausted from the heat, and my mind drifted as I wandered around the site. She hoped I would move to some specific spot tied to this building they were after. But it doesn't explain how I came to possess such a nugget of knowledge."

Renaldo answered with a shrug and said, "Who knows? Perhaps you are the only person on this glorious planet who knows where this place is." But you never revealed it to either since Delven interrupted.

Eddie sat in a chair, kicking his feet up and joining Robert in a smoke. "I saw a road not far from here leading north before we landed. Not many of them are in a jungle."

Of all present, Trish had been mostly quiet. She looked more concerned and hesitant than Renaldo. She bit her lip a few times.

"Something on your mind, Trish?" Robert asked after catching her bite her lip for the fourth time. Her eyes darted away from him and towards the ground.

"I...I just feel we are about to rush into a trap," she finally stammered. She stepped out of the room and went to get a glass of water, but she only held it in her hand.

"I know Sinclair told you about my visions if you want to call them that," she continued. "The closer we have gotten to where you're supposed to be, the weaker my connection has become, and it's frightened me. Whatever is out there is clouding my mind, and I have no idea what we're about to get into."

"That may be so," Robert said, returning to the couch and taking a very long drag to finish the cigarette, "but either way, I can't allow either of them to get any further on whatever they are involved with. At this point, I don't even care what they are after, whether it's the discovery of an ancient building or some old relic lying inside."

"I've been stabbed, shot at, beaten, dragged, and punched because of both of them, and I have had enough. I am going after Delven and will finish what I should have done before."

Renaldo sat up sternly on the couch with a look of disdain. "My dear fellow, perhaps he is a dastardly no-gooder, but that doesn't call for lethal violence!" Renaldo looked hurt from hearing Robert's proclamation. His lifestyle came from social graces, and although he lived for the thrill of the hunt, the laws and structure of the land lay dear to him. He knew the true evils of the world and refused to embrace them.

Dabbing his cigarette butt in an ashtray, Robert shook his head and let the smoke shoot out between his pursed lips. "We aren't talking about a dastardly no-gooder. Delven is a different breed of life that I would call fiendishly evil. He has been hell-bent on ruining my life, forcing me down a predestined path that I followed. I never was a threat to him or a competition in the field. Yet he went out of his way to destroy everything I worked for. I followed a more arduous path I didn't want because of him, and until now, I didn't know why.

"He didn't want me to find this location before he did. It was a remote chance, a needle in the hay, but a chance nevertheless that I could subconsciously stumble across it. He couldn't allow that, so he wrecked my career to buy him time to narrow it down, and now he's pinpointed it down to a small area nearby."

"Now he needs you to show him the rest of the way," Trish said as she drew her knees up on the couch.

Robert nodded. "This isn't some extravagant archaeological discovery. Given my recent enlightenment of existing secret worlds that behave like our dreams, I can only guess this is much more extraordinary."

Looking back to Renaldo, he tried giving a reassuring look. It reminded him of Natasha after he tried apologizing for yelling. This time, however, it worked. "I am not going to kill Delven."

Renaldo let out a sigh and returned his great smile back to his face.

"Not unless he gets in my way."

*

Dusk had arrived just above the trees for a brief time, and Kipner found himself outside the facility before heading to Genevieve's camp for one last smoke to settle his nerves. Beside him sat Renaldo, merrily puffing longingly against a cigar he scrounged up from inside.

The large man drifted the smokey vapors from between his lips and savored the taste, then looked at Kipner, who was staring a thousand miles away.

"You are the man for this, my good friend," he said comfortingly. "Fate brought you here, and it will guide you to where you are destined."

Kipner raised an eyebrow softly and returned the look. "Destined to be buried in the ground?"

"Naturally, for all of us. But I would like to think not tonight." Kipner chuckled briefly and stared back into the dimming jungle. The two sat in silence for several minutes as they continued their smoke.

"My fate has not been good to me," Renaldo said, dropping his positive side and revealing his true, hidden conscience. "I have committed atrocities that follow me like a great weight is dragged behind or draped on my shoulders." He spoke but a whisper.

The cigarette of Kipner brightened from his inhale, but he sat in silence like a priest to a confessor.

"I see things or rather think I see things. Horrible visions that, what I gather, you frequently see as real. My curse is they aren't real, only illusions of the innocent, brought on by that beast I hunt. It has made me murder poor, defenseless people. I cannot shake free from the guilt."

Slowly Kipner nodded, exhaling the long drag and stomping out the butt. "For the longest time, I shared that curse. But in the end, it's all real because I have the scars to prove it. So do you."

Renaldo questioned his statement, wondering how he knew, his hand heavily moving to his shoulder. He felt under the shirt's fabric against the numerous depressions scarred against his skin from the strange wolf attack in Germany. Those marks stayed with him for the rest of his life. The detective was right. He wouldn't have the scars to show if they had been illusions. The voice had been a ruse to further manipulate his mind all these years.

"And Delven's responsible for bringing that thing upon us all for so many years. That's why we went this far," Kipner said, standing up with a grown, patting his friend on the back reassuringly and heading towards the camp. "That's why he needs to die."

CHAPTER XVI

Congo, 1926

The night sky sheltered the Congo jungle like a black satin sheet. Robert sat high on the same hillside he had chopped and hacked away in his dream, easily concealed from the ground thirty feet above Genevieve's camp. Everything looked exactly the same from his Dreamland experience.

The realism of being inside the Dreamlands was baffling. Unless something directly defied a worldly law like physics, it was unnoticeable. He could not distinguish which campsite was authentic and which was the dream. He realized the entire duration had been fake only after returning to the clinic. He had no prior knowledge of how the tents were arranged or looked like. The Dreamlands projected everything identically to the smallest detail.

A few hours had already passed into the night while Robert leaned against a tree along the edge of the landslide. He wanted a warning when their plan had begun. From his vantage point, he could see down the approaching road about a hundred yards.

Eddie had been convinced, by Trish, of course, to remain and help, pinning his service to the Great War as an example of his sacrificial characteristic to aid for the common good. He offered his plane as the second phase of their plan.

It all began with Trish and Sinclair entering the camp to speak to Genevieve in her tent. They would approach from the road and attempt to bluff their way in as new hires for field research at the facility down the road.

Should anyone recognize them, they would surrender themselves and offer information on Delven's next move. They hoped the guards knew of him and how important any news of his plans would be to their employer.

After a quick scouting of the camp, Genevieve and her crew were alone without a sign of him. Regarding Delven's current location, Robert speculated he was near since he could project himself clearly through the Dreamlands.

That theory was loosely based on assumptions, Robert thought, while keeping an eye on the road. He had been in Turkey when Delven had reached out to him from Cairo, some 1,600 miles away. He would be another thousand miles further from Delven than that tonight, but he wasn't sure of the limit of his power. His knowledge of abilities that surpassed mankind's limits was at a master level, and Robert did not want to underestimate him.

Once Genevieve was occupied, the rest of the goons would be removed by a series of dropped sacks from Eddie's plane above. They had discovered chloroform in the first aid station and filled several small pouches. They hoped the impact would send the powder into the air, but it was anyone's guess was whether it was concentrated enough to ease the guards unconscious. Even Renaldo genuinely admitted he was no expert in the matter.

With the distraction in place, Robert would envelop into the Dreamlands and hope his instincts would quickly find the entrance. He was unsure if Genevieve or Delven would spot him after entering like before, so they took no chances. Once he was inside, he had no idea what he would do. The entire plan was poorly thought out at best, but no one was clever at scheming.

Two dark figures walked down the road toward the edge of the camp. Neither traveler had carried a light source to conceal themselves and get as close as possible. Only one man was on watch as most others slept in their tents.

A lantern was lit by a match at the guard post that comprised a single folding chair. The lantern beamed above his head, and he called out to the figures.

One of the travelers waved and spoke something to him as they approached, but Robert's position was too far away to make it out. Their conversation lasted several minutes at quiet levels, so he took that as a sign things were going well.

Silently the guard escorted the two, illuminated now to be Robert's companions, into the large tent.

"Here we go," Robert whispered as he watched them disappear behind the flap. He just hoped Genevieve would give them enough time so he could find whatever he was looking for.

Through the loud chorus of insects and night birds, Robert could just make out the hum of a plane. The trees were too tall to allow any sight as they approached, but the engine's noise was quickly getting near.

Years of combat flying experience as an ace pilot taught Eddie how to minimize the sound, and he dropped each pouch quickly. Like an arrow to its bullseye, the purses landed perfectly along the ground in a row near the tents. Soft puffs of air-popped as each bag burst open, sending the white powder up and all around.

Somewhere on the other side of the landslide hid Renaldo. He was in a position for when things turned sour. Beside him laid enough ammunition to threaten several countries. He wasn't too eager to pull the trigger unless forced to. Hunting ferocious beasts was one thing, but he loathed the thought of killing another person.

Meanwhile, Robert crept down the slope, being as careful as possible to avoid causing another landslide. Each step felt like his footing would slip out from under him. He desperately reached out to grab a nearby tree branch on more than one occasion as he lost his balance. A handful of rocks and pebbles were sent tumbling down below.

Once at the bottom, he began to let his mind wander. He wasn't sure how to trigger the Dreamlands each time or how to touch that remote part of his mind, but he hoped the process was that easy.

He had never been sure how he continuously tapped into the strange place. It had always picked opportune times. He remembered the medallion he wore around his neck and pulled it from his shirt. It began to pulsate in his hand and shimmer into a dull luminescence. Like before, he felt tempted to follow the commanding chime-like sound that beckoned him. It wasn't. The world around him took on a violent front, sending dark clouds swirling rapidly across the sky and whipping him with wind gusts.

After being attacked by Ronan's blades in Cairo, he was a victim of some brutal sacrifice with Genevieve as the master. The entire moment had become a vision and not one of the Dreamlands, but it matched his current.

His eyes turned skyward and, to his horror, spotted the same colossal, world-sized monstrosity towering high overhead. Its strange, whip-like head slowly swung like an inverted pendulum, and he heard a low siren wail that was horribly off-pitch calling from it.

Around him, the harsh winds thrashed about, yet they didn't affect the tents a few dozen yards away. Whatever this was, whether it be the Dreamlands or another realm altogether, he could not say. Regardless, he was no longer entirely in control of his actions.

There was a gradual pull, like an invisible rope had throttled his neck and tugged him to take a step forward. When he did so, the power grew in intensity until he was walking. The force sent him back up the slope, and he began to pick his way among the large boulders and loose gravel.

The sensation was addictive. With each passing minute, releasing the medallion still clutched in his hand felt less desirable, now glowing brightly in the darkness. The illumination never caused his sight to flinch or squint. It was as natural to him as daylight.

Pushing up through the rocky, precarious landscape, he continued finding the right spot with each step that gave him solid footing. The voice kept speaking out in a strange language navigating his movement, which made him look directly at the correct rock to step to.

Scaling the entire landslide passed by him effortlessly. His feet crested the apex and came to a narrow fissure that had formed from the separation. An Olympian could leap across, yet it descended deep into a dark void below. Through the edge's heavy shadow, a series of chiseled stones jutted out of the wall just below the lip, which made a shallow staircase. None of them were supported underneath and only allowed half of Robert's foot to be planted, yet no fear was found within him as he stepped onto the first stone. He took them like one would gracefully descend a grand staircase in a ballroom. His emotions had been locked away, imprisoned to give room for new feelings of overwhelming confidence he had never felt before.

The journey seemed longer going down than it had been climbing up. The fissure didn't narrow towards the bottom like a crack. It was more like a slot canyon, and soon the light from the medallion bounced off a flat, smooth rock floor.

Across the gap, a part of the stone face cliff was a green jade pyramid that he had witnessed in his dream before. Plants hung thickly across its surface, doing well to conceal it from a passing eye. His vision from the swamps of the Nile was proving to be hauntingly correct. Each detail of it precisely matched what he had dreamed. Stairs led up the pyramid into the cliff's face, pausing midway where a bloody altar now rested. Just behind was a dark, silent opening to the building. The altar made his stomach turn over as he thought he could still feel the sensation he had during the hallucination.

High above, against a dark sky, he heard his name calling out to him. The voice was familiar. He had heard it many times before but could not picture who was speaking to him. From a distance, it was unclear who it was, but the person was beginning to follow him down the dangerous stairs. It didn't matter to him because his focus was directed to his current course of action and nothing else. Whatever power came from the medallion felt good, and he obeyed its will.

Before he could continue, though, he knew he wasn't alone at the bottom of the fissure. Something was lurking just out of the light's reach.

"I command you to step forward, Delven," Robert spoke. His voice was not his own, and it startled him. It boldly resonated several octaves deeper and tore out with power behind each word.

From out of the darkness stepped Sinclair and Trish. He wasn't sure whether it was more peculiar how they got down there or how they knew where he was. The veil separating reality from whatever world he was connected to had long since dropped, merging the two. His perception of differentiating the two was impossible. He needed to prepare himself for anything.

The murmur in his head, channeled from the medallion, surged to rekindle the fire that had driven Robert this far. His attention was still attuned to those standing before him in the light.

Both smiled encouragingly. Trish took a step ahead and stood within a foot of Robert.

"Robert, be careful. Delven's in there," she said, glancing in the dark doorway above the pyramid's steps. "He arrived last night and is already preparing something. Genevieve said..."

"Genevieve?" Robert snapped to look at her. The murmur within was now screaming in anger like a child to a neglectful mother. It was demanding Robert's attention, but he controlled himself.

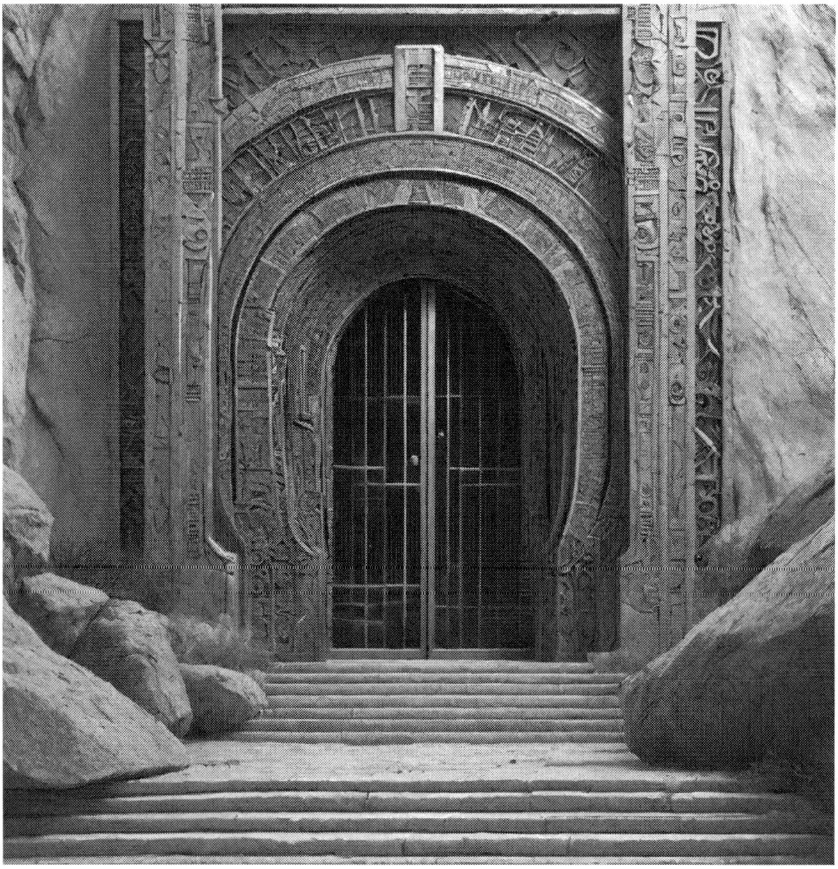

"We spoke to her like just like the plan, and she told us everything. Robert, Delven's betrayed everyone, including her. He's planning to use you with whatever is inside there for his own power," Trish explained.

"And you believe her? She's playing both sides. I wouldn't trust her any farther than I could throw her," Robert spit back. "Remember, she was the one who dragged me into the Dreamlands for her own gain. To find this place. Well, I found it, and I'm putting a stop to this."

Trish's expression abruptly changed unnaturally. She narrowed her eyes, lowered her head, and curled her mouth into a bizarre, twisted smile. "You don't know what's inside. You're in over your head, making moves without caution. If you go in, you aren't coming out; I promise you that."

From her voice, it no longer sounded like the caring Trish that had journeyed with him across the continent. Behind her, Sinclair joined in with a menacing look on his face. His goofy, cartoon ears and nose did nothing to deflect his dark attitude.

"Go on, Robert. You're wasting time out here. We'll follow your lead," Sinclair said over her shoulder. Seeing them both staring with brooding eyes above a sharp ascending smile gave Robert shivers. Their behaviors were like two devils awaiting his signature on contracts. From caution to eagerness, neither showed sincerity towards his safety.

Not far above them, the recognizable voice got closer. They looked up to see Renaldo, rifle in hand, pointing it at Trish.

"That is quite enough, you two," he said after completing the last of the stairs without bothering to watch his step. Renaldo was not joking. There was no mistaking the severe tone of his voice and the stern look on his face.

Curiously Robert looked at the gunman and remembered who he was. The hazy memory of his traveling companion jolted back to the front of his mind like a gust of wind to fog. "What are you doing, Renaldo?" he asked.

"Never you mind, my dear fellow," Renaldo answered, his jovial words conflicting with his voice. "These are not who you think they are."

Before Robert could question him, Sinclair and Trish rushed them both in such perfect timing as if mentally linked. Trish barreled into Robert, sending him on his back. He heard the sound of Renaldo's gunfire but couldn't determine where.

Trish had surprisingly powerful strength. Her legs wrapped around him while she pinned down his wrists. Her movements were inhumanly fast, and Robert was helpless in a fraction of time. She landed brutal head butts against his forehead, opening his head and releasing a steady flow of blood down his face, partially obscuring his vision.

The onslaught continued. Her knees slammed into his thighs in between head butts, and he was losing consciousness rapidly.

The screaming voice from the medallion latched onto his weakened mind once again, taking back control and giving him a burst of strength, unlike anything he had witnessed in his life. His arms quickly sent her somersaulting over his head.

Getting to his feet was easier than expected with the power of whatever guided him. His forearm wiped the blood from his face, but he could feel the stream cascade down his temples.

Behind him were the smooth, click sounds of Renaldo's bolt action rifle finalizing a new bullet in its chamber. He was smiling with the look of a carpenter after the last nail to a house. It was a moment where hesitating would have resulted in certain death, and he had taken action and got lucky.

More importantly, he was sure of himself with the trigger's pull. Somewhere within, a confusing voice faded, and Renaldo Archibald III felt genuinely free of the plague that followed him.

"There is no need for more of this squabbling," he spoke to everyone, his breath heavy between each word. Robert could see the lifeless body of Sinclair draped unnaturally on the stairs, his head pierced cleanly by a gunshot.

Trish made to charge back at Robert, but Renaldo's gun made her rethink her actions. She showed no concern for Sinclair, Robert noticed. Whatever suspicion he had between the two romantically had either been a cover or...

"They're conjurations from Delven," Renaldo said as he confidently strode alongside Robert, his rifle pointing from his hip. "After seeing you gather your medallion and ascend the mountain, I paid attention to Genevieve's tent, which had grown oddly silent. These two emerged, and I saw their bodies and Genevieve's on the ground. They proceeded to murder many of the guards quickly, with some apparatus.

"Despite my certainty, I..." Renaldo said momentarily, hesitating in remembrance of the train staff or the numerous villagers years ago. "I did not want to make another mistake. These visions you see are real to you but often illusions to me. What I witness as monstrous, at times, have been clever illusions over innocent victims created by the very monster you and I chase. When I was convinced these two were not our real companions, they were out of range of my rifle. I don't know where their weapon is now; one of them probably still has it on them."

There was a look of relief on Renaldo's face that felt genuine to Robert. It was as if a heavy burden had been finally lifted from him, but Kipner knew not what.

Trish gritted her teeth in a snarl as Robert approached her and frisked her clothes. In her back pocket was a small hand mirror. He removed it, but before he could look at it closely, the commanding voice in his head spoke to him in clear, specific English.

"Keep your gaze from the mirror!"

His eyes snapped up to meet Trish with disdain.

The mirror was safely wrapped and placed in Robert's pocket while he glared at her. Their demonic expressions and abilities had never been shown until now. He trusted Renaldo perhaps more than Sinclair and Trish though they all had given him several reasons to trust them all.

"What are you and what is this mirror?" he asked.

Trish's grin spread unnaturally wider, reaching her ears. "Incomprehensible to the soft flesh of this world." The mouth gaped open without lips, and her skin stretched tightly across the skull and appeared like a large lesion across the face.

What the creature was, Robert wasn't sure. It glared happily at him like a hungry beast knowing its prey was helpless. This wasn't Trish. Perhaps some phantom-like Renaldo claimed. Indeed, though, it was not part of his imagination. This was real. Somehow.

The odd smile dramatically curved into a V. She resisted answering until a quick rap of Renaldo's gun barrel on her head changed her mind.

"It was a gift," she said through gritted teeth, "from the Forsaken Queen, given to us by the Grand Numen."

There was so much more to learn from the new world he had discovered. The darkness would make him hesitate if not for his uncontrollable curiosity. The names meant nothing to him for now, but he was already anxious to find out who they were.

"You two expected me to believe you aren't Delven's puppets? He has considerable powers, and conjuring you two would probably be effortless to him," Robert questioned.

Trish spat some blood out from Renaldo's blow. Could it really be called Trish? Robert saw nothing to give him the reason. This was nothing more than some doppelganger in the image of Trish. It was not of this world.

"That was Rathkyak's idea," it said momentarily, looking at the body resembling Sinclair. "You carry something valuable to the Grand Numen, and he was convinced he could get it from you. Gain favor for him."

Could this Grand Numen be a title given to Delven in the Dreamlands? There was no telling what he had done there during his travels. Numen was Latin for a god, which would explain any of Delven's extraordinary powers he has while within the realm. These two creatures were without question under Delven's command.

But if so, what did he carry that Delven might want?

Robert raised his eyebrows in disbelief at what he was hearing. "Get it out of me? What exactly did he want, my liver?"

It perked its mouth and shook its head. "It's unnatural. The pain in your chest grows stronger."

Since the odd creature appeared in his cabin on the train and squeezed his heart, constant pressure was applied. The reminder made his heart press briefly. Each beat of his heart was a struggle. He could feel it pound against his chest, but before that frightening night, there had been moments of pain around his heart that he had passed off from an unhealthy lifestyle.

"Did he tell you what it did?" Robert asked. Renaldo whispered of wasting time with it and that he should get going inside, but Robert was too curious to let it pass.

It shook its head no in response and kept its eyes on Renaldo's rifle.

"My dear fellow," Renaldo said, breaking him from his thoughts. "I shall remain here to keep this abomination from causing any further troubles. Go on ahead and do what you must. I will come to your aid if you should call for it. And, Robert, do be very careful. Mr. Montgomery should not be underestimated."

The medallion beckoned him to enter. Given his distrust in Trish, he had undoubtedly listened easily to the voice that lingered in his mind while he wore. It had led him all this way, warned him of the mirror, and, after Renaldo's encouragement to go inside, spoke to him in agreement that he should make haste.

Nodding one last time to Renaldo and staring at the beast for several seconds, Robert walked up the steps and approached the entrance. The door was nothing more than a large slab of stone with the familiar inverted triangle surrounded by three symbols he had seen so many times before. Yet this time, the depiction was incorrect. The triangle was pointing up, and the three symbols were not in the correct orientation.

Around him was deep-shadowed darkness, and he could barely make out the symbols. He tried his lighter a few times, but it had been too long since he had refilled it, giving only sparks as he flicked the wheel. His medallion immediately surged brightly in response to the light that bathed the pyramid's surface. The illumination revealed the triangle was embedded into a stone circle, and a ring surrounded it with the three symbols. He chuckled at the possibility of it being so simple and tried rotating the circle and ring to align correctly. There was a brief struggle to move them both as a stone ground against stone, but the door suddenly dropped into the floor like its supports beneath had pulled away.

"They don't ask how," he said out loud and stepped inside.

It was a tight access tunnel where the top of Robert's head barely cleared, and the walls often brushed against his shoulders. The walls and floor were perfectly smooth, with zero blemishes or seams. It was carved from solid rock. Whoever had done the work was an expert at chiseling stone.

As he walked on, he wondered about the structure's origin. How old could this be? How much did it take to build such a place? Who was it made for?

He struggled to guess how ancient it could be. Chiseling such a large piece of rock would have taken generations to fulfill. Their simple precision turned away the possibility of dating to Mesopotamian. Their ziggurat constructs were stone steps rather than carved from large stones.

The closest structure of this size that came to mind was ad-Deir, an elaborately carved temple in the ancient Jordanian city of Petra, estimated around the first century. However, even at that point in history, there were no advanced civilizations near where the Congo to have the means to build such a structure. The chance for a rock this size to be discovered in this area was essentially nil.

It took some time to cross-traverse the tunnel, just long enough to become aware of the time it had taken. By now, the enclosure was buried so deep underground Robert could conclude with high probability that it was placed down here and not covered by some ancient landslide. Up ahead, the light fell upon an opening that led into a large chamber. Immediately he recognized the place from the dream he had experienced before.

The room was domed with a high ceiling that faded into darkness towards the top. Around the lower half was a series of symbols and markings Robert didn't recognize except one – the same one on his medallion. A tall stone statue carved in a cylindrical column was visually the same cyclopean monstrosity that was in his dream. To a casual glance, it really could be mistaken as Ganesha, but its numerous trunks, tentacle-like each coming to points, showed something alien and not of this world.

As large as it was, the statue was dwarfed by the monstrosity of yet another statue that dominated the center of the room. The detail was so intricately perfect it fooled the eye into believing it was slowly breathing. Taking up most of the floor, it was a crouching, smaller version of the same gigantic entity that took up most of the sky outside. Its hands were perched on its knees as if to stand up with extraordinarily long fingers that reached the ground. Each fingertip was split into several smaller, finger-like appendages. Its chest bore the embedded carving of the same inverted triangle surrounded by the three symbols that had reoccurred repeatedly in his travels. Now he could see what kind of a god would attract so many followers.

His heart began to pound far more than any amount of adrenaline. He could feel the tightness around it, preventing it from pumping freely. He became lightheaded.

In the past vision, he had scaled the strange column statue to acquire a ruby and avoid being shot by Ronan, but little things made him feel something was different this time.

The medallion began to chime with a tinny sound that lured him closer to the enormous crouching statue. No longer speaking to him, the voice sent more emotions and feelings of desire that continued pressuring him forward.

Refusing the temptations was too complicated as he felt weaker from the projections in his mind. They weren't something he could resist but perhaps control. If he only reached out and grabbed it in his mind somehow.

From what once was a lifeless statue emerged into a breathing vessel, its tiny tendrils wiggling at its fingertips. Before him was the origin of the voice, an entity, unlike anything he had ever witnessed. Its grand presence demanded immediate servility, and Robert gave it willingly without any ability to resist. Its existence was overwhelming, sending pounding surges inside his skull that pushed Robert to his knees. If there ever was proof of a god, it stood before him with controlling powers.

A doorway formed between them when Robert reached the being with a semi-circle crest. Through it was an alley that led into a large open city square. On the other side, Robert saw St. Basil's Cathedral. People were strolling across the court in various directions and oblivious to Robert watching them.

"Moscow?" he said out loud in awe at the sight before him. It looked like he could simply walk through and arrive.

"Moscow, London, New Delhi, Venice, New York," came Delven's voice from behind. Robert whirled around to see the white-suited man standing just inside the room from the hall, his patented smile caressing his face.

"Any place and any time you desire. One of many marvels that lay before us," Delven said as he briskly approached him. His cane tapped loudly against the stone floor in rhythm to his black polished shoes. If he displayed a feeling of youth in his step, it was now more than ever.

Robert glanced back at the mystical doorway. People were passing by the alley without a single glance down it. The sounds of birds and distant car horns echoed in the dome room. Whatever caused the sight made it feel genuine, Robert thought.

"It is real, Mr. Kipner," Delven said, arriving beside him and gazing into Moscow. "Merely think of somewhere or some time, and you are off to chase your dreams to your heart's content."

Kipner slowly turned to face Delven as he spoke to him after reading his thoughts. The idea of the creature's theory began to sink in. Something had been placed inside him. Could that be how Delven had kept spying on him all these years? He could read his mind?

Delven shook his head and said, "Not spying, Robert. Observing. Waiting with excited anticipation. You possess a power that few in this world can fathom. I've told you how you have always lacked the confidence to step up and take control of the inner power. To seize it and bend it to your will."

Robert's chest continued to burn inside, and he laid his hand against it in reaction.

"The pain's from a necessary insertion to ensure you were safe until the time was right. Look here."

Reaching out, he placed his hand a few inches from Robert's chest. It took everything in Robert's strength to remain standing as stinging agony shot through his body violently. Delven's hand began closing slowly as if squeezing a lemon. After a few seconds of unfathomable torture, he released his grip, leaving Robert in shock.

"It's a simple agreement I arranged while in Poland some time ago with an odd fellow from who knows where - possibly Saturn or Hell itself, for all I know. Come to think of it," Delven said, grinning with astonishment. "You were there, or should I say, eventually there. It was always a late arrival for you, even in class. Somehow you were one step behind me. I wonder why, indeed?"

Delven winked boastfully at the remark, turning his attention back to the statue.

"A lot can happen if you sleep deep enough, Mr. Kipner, but the method is indifferent to what is before us," Montgomery said without hesitation.

"What is this power I have then? It's not slipping in and out of the Dreamlands - you handle that well enough on your own. Why did you need me here?"

Outside the room and down the long corridor, numerous feet were tapping against the smooth floor. It had no resemblance to any human.

Wiggling a finger, Delven scolded in a patronizing way. "Asking too many questions at once like a confused child. Was it ever a wonder how the strange and unusual always followed you? Give it some thought for a moment; we have a few more seconds."

He had never questioned the oddities like the broken clock in his office stuck at 11:17 or the laundromat matchbook he had found in his suit. Taking it in as a whole, it might be disturbing to the casual person, but to Robert, it had been a fact of his life. It didn't explain the why, though. Perhaps the occurrences had been so frequent in his life that they had felt ordinary.

Tapping noises down the tunnel continued to approach. Robert turned with Delven to see the grotesque monstrosity that had started it all for Robert back home. Dozens of tentacles, each puckering deeply, edged the creature ever closer. Its haunting gaunt, hypnotically locked Robert's attention. Had it followed him all this way? Meanwhile, the voice in his head returned with encouragement to control the beast and bend it to his desire.

At the room's entrance, it stopped and lowered itself as if to pounce but held its motion still in waiting. It began to hum a low, steady, vibrating screech like a swarm of insects.

"Ah," Delven said as if the sight was expected, "it would appear the time has already arrived. Your question will need to be answered with a demonstration."

Leaving Robert to stand there, Delven walked over to the vulture statue and began slowly circling it, casting his eyes up and down in search of something. He stopped momentarily and reached up to a carved symbol at eye level. He pressed his hand into the stone as if liquefied, retracting a circular metallic bracelet from within. It contained a rhombus-shaped cavity a bit over an inch long. He slipped the bracelet on his wrist and returned to Robert.

"Mr. Kipner, it has indeed been a long journey. This expedition and our lengthy relationship date back to your early years in college and I, a simple professor. I can understand a certain amount of resentment towards me; perhaps a tiny portion holds merit. However, in the larger picture, all my decisions and actions were necessary to arrive at this location within our lifetimes."

Delven approached the portal gateway, still portraying Russia. He gestured with his arms widely in grandeur at it.

"Just look at it, Robert. Go ahead; think of a place you would love to be right now."

Robert stared darkly at Delven, then turned his eyes to the portal. Instantly the sight of Russia was replaced by his office back in London. Natasha was sitting at his desk reading a book with a glass of his Scotch within arm's reach. She never looked in their direction.

Smiling, Delven nodded with satisfaction. "Well done, Robert. Well done! I am sure you are anxious to return to her. She fancies you beyond her tasks as your secretary."

"So that's it then? This was what you manipulated me for? A one-way teleportation doorway in the deep parts of the jungle. It's a nice trick, Monty, but it's severely limited, and I bet only I can turn the dial," Robert said. He let his mind wander, flashing different places that came to mind, spinning through them more rapidly with each location. Finally, he brought it to where they were, giving a mirror reflection back to them.

A flicker of anger at the sound of the nickname temporarily broke Delven's character, but he recovered quickly. "Always a sharp young man, Mr. Kipner. I arranged for you to reach this chamber with me. Something inside you controls the portal. You can turn the dial, as you so put it. Why though? Heaven knows. You have been able to control strange phenomena for presumably all your life. I witnessed it repeatedly while you were a young college man, but I was unsure how far it reached.

"After years and years of traveling across the globe in search of enlightenment to your bizarre ability, I discovered, at last, it was a grand gift, bequeathed to you by a living god. It was around this time of discovery that I also received a gift from another god. My God. With it, I learned of these wonderful chambers hidden across the world - nay, across space and time!

"But you were the missing element! You were to show me the precise location of the first portal. I would take it from there, of course."

Working to keep his breathing hyperventilating, Robert groaned between gritted teeth, "Why send me on such a risky trip? I was almost killed dozens of times. Then your little plan would have failed."

Delven shook his head. "No, I was quite confident of your survival. I spoke to those Beyond, far wiser than any human or all humans combined. Their intelligence is unfathomable to our simple minds. They foretold of your success employing six companions aiding your journey."

Robert furrowed his forehead. "Yeah, about that number. There were only two when I got on the train. What happened to the others?"

"They were all with you, Mr. Kipner. Perhaps not at the same time, but you were with any number of the six at nearly all times if you think about it."

There had been Trish and Sinclair, then Renaldo joined his crew. Eddie had been hired to help them reach the clinic despite Kipner declining, but they should still be counted. Then he came across the two Pygmies that saved his life. In all, six had, in one way or another, affected his journey to bring him here.

"As to why you were chosen to receive such a boon," Delven picked back up where he had left off, "is beyond mortals to ever comprehend, but a boon, some physical piece, has been placed within you, specifically your heart. I wasn't quite sure until I arranged for a midnight visit to see for itself. It confirmed my suspicion when it felt something nestled inside your beating muscle as it gripped it tightly on your train voyage.

"And this," Delven gestured to the portal, "is not as limited as you think. There are others like it. Many others! Not just in space but in time! The knowledge of their locations shall soon be known to me. Even better, I believe anyone in possession of what you hide inside can wield their power."

With a quick motion, the palm of Delven's hand swept onto Robert's chest. The connection immediately fused, preventing Robert from escaping. The pain returned a hundredfold, but the link was outstanding, holding him dangling while his knees gave out. Kipner could not just grit his teeth and suffer through it this time. His leg strength failed him, but Delven's remarkable strength held him standing; his legs hung like a puppet.

"Don't worry, Mr. Kipner, you will be dead soon," he said as his eyes intensely bulged out from his face with a sharp focus. His gaze was intense and determined with immense concentration.

Robert was helpless, loosely draped in midair. Desperately he begged to be killed and end his suffering. Yet, Delven continued his ritual, adding odd consonant-heavy words to empower him. Robert felt his heart slowly pull from his body, and he stared in shock. He wanted to kill Delven more than ever, but he couldn't find himself to get free from Delven's grip.

With great effort, a simple rhombus-shaped gemstone, shimmering in color not a part of the world's spectrum, split a hole out of Robert's chest and floated into the bracelet's empty setting, fitting nicely. The open wound shed no blood.

Delven regarded the bracelet lovingly. "Think of this as a means of turning the dial without needing you anymore."

With what little energy Robert had, through the pain, he gritted his teeth in anger and lurched at Delven. Robert was immediately sent to the ground with a casual flick of Delven's wrist. Kipner felt straps tied around his wrist and ankles.

"Now, now, Mr. Kipner. We must relax for this next demonstration. Be at ease."

Turning his back on him, Delven raised his bracelet in a commanding gesture and watched in splendor as the doorway's vision changed from location to location by his will. His hearty laughter echoed loudly off the walls of the domed room.

The massive statue-like creature in the center of the room continued to stir slowly as if awakening from a deep slumber. Delven had shown little surprise or notice of its movement the entire time.

Exhausted, Robert lay watching Delven. He felt nearly dead and could barely move. From behind him, Robert felt something extract an item from his backpack. Curiously he rolled to see a pair of beady black eyes above dark, stock legs and holding the hand mirror Trish's doppelganger had.

The two Pygmies, unusually silent, crouched beside him. One held a stubby finger to his lips and held the mirror out for Robert to take. The other was fiddling with Robert's lost multi-tool that had dropped out of his pocket while being hung by his bootstraps. With the tool, the little guy could hardly contain his joy as he extended the tiny saw from the multi-tool and freed Kipner from the straps that bound him.

Knowing not to look at the mirror was the only thing Robert knew about; he thought of forcing someone else to gaze at it. He tested his idea by flickering it toward the tentacle creature still held back by some invisible force. It was rapidly sucked into the mirror, shrinking to slip inside the reflective surface smoothly.

The humming from the awaiting beasts began to take on form and substance. Robert could hear their aggression and anger from being held back by whatever force kept them at bay. Yet through his medallion, he understood where the true power came from, and a plan formed in his mind.

Delven turned at the commotion, eyes widening at the sight of the mirror.

"No! How did you...stop, you fool...you have no idea of its power...Nooooooo!" The look of surprise and horror was the last memory Robert had of Montgomery as he, too, was drawn into the mirror. Trapped inside, his body was torn apart by the nightmarish beast, which silenced his screams. The sickeningly familiar pucker sound intensified as it feasted on his body.

Little was left of Delven Theodore Montgomery III when the feasting had completed, except for the bracelet that did not pass into the mirror. Montgomery was right - Kipner did have the power. The limits were beyond his comprehension. The source of it all, he now knew, was the origin of the voice speaking to him even now while he stared defiantly at the colossal statue.

Somewhere at some time, a boon had been given to him. By what, he could only guess, was the very thing that was trying to awaken before him. There was a deliberate and powerful connection between them. He was initially tempted to gain the upper hand before it seized him instead.

He understood the nightmares were phantoms, dangerous to only those who gave into their reality. The strange gemstone had only given him the protection needed to arrive safely there.

The portal closed because he commanded it. He realized Delven had learned of this secret years ago but could never overcome his fears to control what Robert could so easily. His time was always limited before his fears overcame him, so Montgomery would have lost the battle against the terrors of the Dreamlands. It was why he had departed so abruptly on the train.

Unless he possessed the gemstone Kipner had carried within his heart, cleverly placed there by the creature who had struck a deal with Delven. He knew Kipner was protected by gods until he discovered the hidden temple, but Robert never needed it.

He removed the gem from the bracelet, which shimmered into a red ruby. The bracelet returned to the liquefied panel Delven had withdrawn it from earlier. Robert followed his past vision to replace the gem in its rightful place. These were relics not meant for mortals and belonged hidden deep inside this temple of a god.

Something rumbled, and the god-like being returned to its previous position and solidified to stone.

He sighed deeply and turned to an empty chamber. To his profound sadness, his little friends were gone. Only an open tin of sardines lay at his feet. Part of the Dreamlands, he thought. He hoped one day, he might get the chance to thank them. Smiling to himself, he headed outside, recalling his multi-tool was still missing, too.

*

The morning was already aging close to the afternoon when Robert woke. It had been a calm, relaxing sleep that he hadn't experienced in several months. There was dizziness behind his eyes and an ache in his chest, but otherwise, he felt alive.

Renaldo and Eddie, what was left of the expedition, were gathered around him.

A few exciting trinkets and relics were found back at Genevieve's camp in a chest. None of them demonstrated the strange behaviors Robert had witnessed.

After a large meal, the three gathered around the hospital's lounge to discuss Robert's experience and the thought of returning to civilization.

"I was delighted to find you in as good health as you are, my dear fellow," Renaldo said as they each lit cigars found among Genevieve's men. "When I heard that dreadful creature traipsing down the corridor and Delven's voice, I feared the worst."

The creature of Trish's form, gagged and bound, sat nearby with its eyes like daggers stabbing at them. It had been seething mad when it came to, after another firmer rasp on the head by Renaldo's rifle. Its mood swings had been violent, and they feared it was no longer under the control of Delven's relics or bargains, perhaps making it even more dangerous. Captain Rickenbacker agreed to take it to the nearest British detention center in Khartoum, where it would be shipped off to anyone's guess.

When they had wrapped up and the plane was packed with Eddie, Renaldo, and the beast, Robert was offered to expedite his travels back home. He politely declined, a little too hastily.

He shook their hands and thanked them for their help, lingering with Renaldo the longest.

"The hunt is not over, my dear friend," Renaldo said as the propeller began spinning. "Our devilish creature, ghastly tentacles and all, continues to roam in our dreams and nightmares. You may have banished it, but I fear it will find its way back. I aim to finally make my mark." Renaldo gave a genuinely large smile and hugged his friend one last time.

Nodding with a smile, Robert handed him the carefully wrapped mirror. The hunter took it gingerly in both hands, his mind full of thoughts and questions. He now knew what it could do and agreed to investigate it further with a few close colleagues.

"I'm no expert in magical relics," Renaldo proclaimed, "but I believe we will solve its mystery and put an end to the nightmare once and for all."

The roar of the plane rolled out of earshot and disappeared over the tree line leaving Robert to the sounds of the jungle.

He made his way back to the pyramid cut deep in the fissure. Any place, any time, Kipner thought as he stood before the door. From the anguish he had suffered for years, witnessing things he was not meant to see, between the heavy booze and sleepless nights, he wondered if it was preventable. Who knew how long this extra-reality had existed?

At his thought, the door whirled into motion and came still showing a red-painted desert filled with plateaus. In the distance, slowly rolling along a well-made trail, was a long line of wagons led by Native Americans heading what looked to be westward. It gave no indication of exactly where or when.

He remained momentarily staring through the door, wondering whether he was up to the challenge. He knew the consequences of stepping through; there would be little chance he would find his way back home without finding another similar door or returning to this one in Africa. If he could, however, find a means to remove this lingering plague, perhaps it would be worth his sacrifice.

Breaching the portal, Robert Kipner was erased from existence from his birth in 1884 to 1926.

Somewhere in the dark of the temple came the voice of ultimate existence.

"Consequences? You know not of consequences or sacrifice. The price has now been paid."

Book Two

CHAPTER I

Maryland, 1830 & Virginia, 1861

Nervous footsteps made an abrupt turn at the end of a small corridor and once again passed by the open bedroom of a concerned midwife sitting beside a dying woman.

Polite conversation among weary guests was kept subdued in the front room, but their words rang through the soon-to-be father's ears. Words like "doubt," "troubled," and "pity" rose above the others for the poor man who had struggled with maintaining optimism for the last several hours.

There had been little to worry about when he woke that morning, expecting nothing more than time spent down the street at Thurmont's dilapidated church. Several newcomers had moved into town, and he was eager to meet and encourage them to attend his sermon. Lately, he had witnessed a decrease in attendance when a rather zealous mountebank deceived a few dozen folks into venturing into the wild for a new life of religion.

His wife, however, had other plans for him that day as their child chose to emerge into the world unannounced. The midwife had warned that the child might be born that week and to be prepared at any moment for the worst. When the contractions began, it was clear early on it would be a challenge.

News spread quickly through town, and several church friends paid them a visit.

So far, there were only cries and whimpers of pain from the bedroom upon the hundredth pass of the man's pacing.

Outside, the beautiful day in May had begun expectantly. Matthew Riley herded three cows down the road toward William Hardy's butcher shop. Mrs. Gwen Lane, the town cobbler's new, much younger wife, tended to her flowers outside their home. However, their eyes darted apprehensively towards the Kipner's residence, then politely diverted away. Something amiss was brewing inside.

Mary Ann had a typical pregnancy. She was expected any day by her midwife and the town physician. So far, all indications were predicting a healthy birth. Throughout the months, she had felt terrific, even energetic, with little fatigue and soreness. Everything, according to her, was fine.

The folks of Thurmont disagreed. They heard James Kipner's church had caught fire the night of their conception. Then during the pregnancy, strange woodland animals would circle their house at night and sniff at their bedroom window. Mary Ann couldn't have milk brought inside because each bottle would spoil when it crossed the threshold. These oddities added to questions of dark magic originating from the Kipner family, which had indeed been the reason James' congregation had dwindled over the past few months.

Only one midwife was willing to help, Mary Ann's mother, Heather. Even she was concerned for the safety of her daughter and the future grandchild.

Herbal remedies and natural methods were frequently found throughout the bedroom surrounding the expectant mother. There had been enough times mentioning curses and hexed luck in conversation that James forbade speaking of it in their home. Her warnings had an impact. Even so, and she continued bringing roots, fungus, and mixed concoctions she swore would resist any dark elements in the area. She rubbed luck charms, repeated prayers, and made strange hand gestures.

Heedless of her efforts, the rebirth of Robert Kipner on the 28th of May, 1830, was violent, and Mary Ann nearly lost her life that day, delivering her new baby to the world.

Bizarre formations swelled overhead of the Kipner's home as the delivery began. What would be an otherwise perfect spring day rapidly transitioned to heavy overcast in a matter of an hour. Winds from the North, an unusual direction for the area, swirled down the town's streets and danced around their home. Most people who had no critical business to attend to retreated to their homes and secured their doors.

James dashed into the bedroom at the first sound of a baby's cry to see his wife cradling their new baby boy with Heather smiling beside him. His mother-in-law showed severe signs of exhaustion and breathed heavily while sitting in a rocking chair. To James, she had aged twenty years just that day. Furthermore, Heather died of natural causes and maintained the same old appearance later that week.

Something clung to the side of the house outside like a fungus, dangling down from the eave and peering with eager fascination through the window. It watched with small, black beady eyes at the baby and smiled wickedly. The streets were empty to have witnessed its presence, but no mortal would have seen it anyway.

Young Robert lay peacefully within the comfort of soft blankets in a deep sleep. He was surrounded by genuine love, yet his loved ones were in the dark of the twisted truth regarding their lives. They were unaware of the price their newborn had paid for his decision to be there.

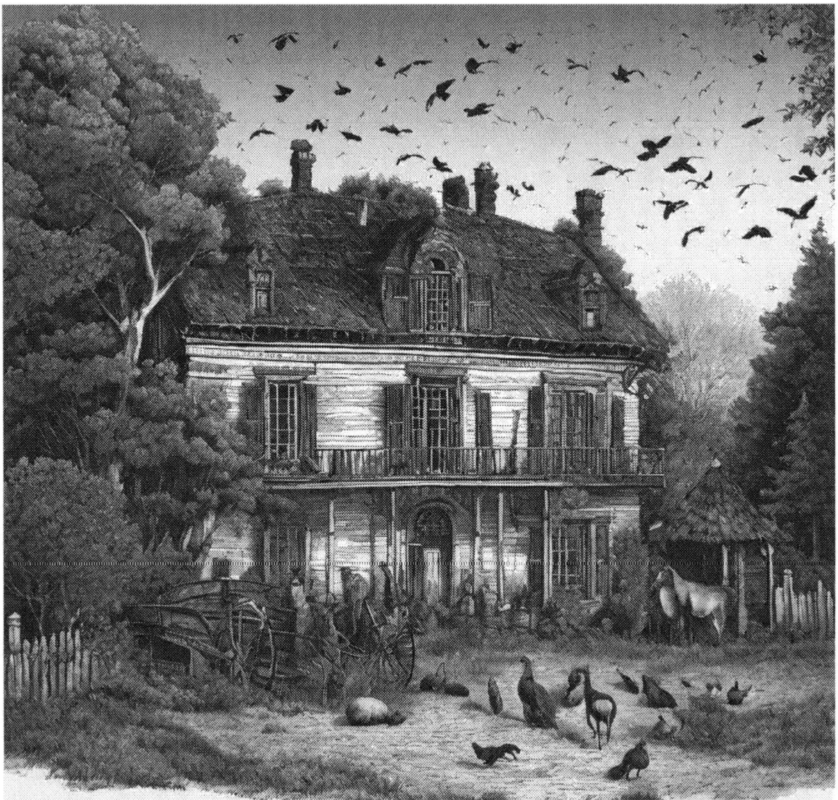

"Sleep easy, my little one," said the creature from outside, gazing down upon him. "Your turmoil will soon come. Bold of you to assume no price would be demanded, but, oh, the consequence you paid for today."

*

What remained of the 2nd Battalion, 2nd Infantry Regiment, arrived from up north near Manassas, Virginia, towards dusk in July of 1861. They had come from Barnaby Hollow, a stretch of low-bottom dry bed that once gave way to Tippen's Creek.

Just that morning, young men, primarily boys, watched body parts rip and shred off friends and brethren as they tried to hold back Lee's Army of Northern Virginia in vain. Only a few managed to retreat and escape with their lives. Despite their protests, their officer, a major general named Pope, gave orders to march south and join up to aid what was left of the 13th Infantry that was failing to keep Vicksburg.

Fatigued and battered, they talked darkly with sick humor as they denied what they had witnessed. In contrast, others sat and stared in silence into the flames.

Wind tumbled through the black silhouette of the leaves against the evening sky, sending the crisp temperature plummeting into a chilly night. The soldiers wrapped themselves tighter with thin coats, leaning in as close as they could tolerate the snapping heat of the campfires.

Dark, blunt jokes about amputees soon transitioned to the wishful thinking of homes and mothers. Nothing felt comforting or soothing to the minds of the battle-torn soldiers as they listened to the approaching storm. Beyond the campfires, more agile men scrambled to reinforce some of the army-issued tents in light of the impending weather.

Those closest to the ridge of trees that hugged the northern side of the army's campsite heard it first. It ripped through the trunks and crackled in the indistinguishable darkness. Everyone perked up at the crackle, rattling pattern of multiple black powder rifles. So what was being fired upon? It wasn't far off, but it was far enough the soldiers needn't dive for cover. To their knowledge, this was their only regiment in the area.

Commanding officers rounded a few night owls already listed for patrol and sent them into the woods to investigate. The group was a close bunch of friends all out of Ellicott City up in Maryland, self-dubbing themselves Huckleberry Hucksters or just Hucks. At first, having them all assigned to the same Infantry, let alone a Battalion, had been a challenge. Even so, through a few favors their fathers' connections granted, the Hucks had been firing rifles shoulder to shoulder with each other.

There had never been a true leader among them. No one bossed anyone around. Five of them, treated as equals all around and proven to be fearful as long as they were in numbers, were closer than most brothers. More misfits than soldiers, their preference among the troops and officers came from their witty, sometimes raunchy, humor and quirky, yet accurate, method when firing a rifle at exceedingly long range.

Numerous reprimands targeted at them had been lost in paperwork due to officers not wishing to lose such brilliance on their line.

From a young age, they mysteriously developed the strange ability to see in the dark better than most. They often could work as a pack without light or lantern.

So that night, they roamed through the tall pines of Virginia, rain pouring down between flashes of lightning, to a small farmstead assaulted by a small troop of soldiers from the army of the Other Side. Bursts of powder ignited among the rifles as they engaged in battle with the house residents.

Tucked away behind the protection of the trees, the Hucks watched the handful of men reload and fire against the wooden walls of the old farmhouse and shatter the glass windows. Throughout the building, darkness reigned and silence dwelt, but outside, the rifles repeated once more at an otherwise empty home.

Among the boys of the Huckleberry Hucksters rose a broad-chested, solid-chinned man with sharp blue eyes. To his compatriots, he was nicknamed Wraith, but to his mother, he was Robert Kipner.

Before another range of bullets could be sent into the riddled home, Kipner nodded to his brethren, raised his Sharps rifle to his shoulder, and aimed at one of the soldiers in the clearing. The rest joined him in precision firing. The Hucks were outnumbered by three, but they knew to be quick on approach to finish the rest with their pistols.

Under the freezing downpour as the wind buffeted their soaked bodies, the Hucks turned five figures cold. Each dropped nearly in unison with a soft thud against the soaked, soft soil.

None of the three remaining alive bothered to turn toward their attackers.

They didn't even react to their numbers dropping by more than half. Instead, they moved more desperately to reload their rifles, keeping their attention on the farmhouse and sent another round of bullets.

Curiously the Hucks approached the last of the soldiers with pistols drawn. Each one had drawn a bead, but they could reach them and push the barrel tips against the enemies' necks.

Yet the three moved even faster to reload their rifles with attention focused entirely on the house. Each was breathing heavily, nearly hyperventilating. They struggled to send as many rounds of ammunition as possible like their life depended on it.

Their eyes were wide and wild with utter fear.

Instead of killing them outright, the Hucks tried removing the weapons from them, which was a difficult struggle. None showed violence toward the Hucks, but their grips were deathlike.

Subduing was their only option, hoping one would explain their actions to an officer. Among the three, one rambled in Spanish, clearly stuttering with such rapidity that, had the Hucks understood the language, none would comprehend what was being said. It took some force, but they could be bound to return them to base camp.

The Hucks couldn't make heads or tails of what had caused the soldiers such a fright. The five stood silently for a moment to listen for anything coming from inside the farmhouse. Even so, the harsh storm buffeted against them and shrouded any noise that might be heard. Wraith tried shouting against the storm, his strong lungs able to power a commanding voice when necessary. Even so, no one from inside returned his call. It was a deserted homestead.

Another Huckleberry Huckster, known among the boys as Ghost, said he would search the house while they took the prisoners back. A few disagreed until Revenant joined him on the search.

Wraith nodded and sent the prisoners back to camp when one dropped down through the wet ground.

He disappeared with such speed, Kipner knew he didn't fall into a sinkhole.

He turned behind to witness the ground bulge from the prisoner's body just below the surface and dragged violently towards the house. Once at the front porch step, the prisoner erupted from the ground and vanished into the darkness.

Despite being bound at the legs, the two remaining prisoners jolted towards the forest edge away from the house, whining and whimpering with fear. Their legs entangled and both fell into growing pools of rainwater, sending them into a crawling frenzy.

The Hucks cautiously paused to question each other. In the shadows of the house, they all swore something was wrapped around the ankle of the dragged prisoner like a whip. It had happened so fast they were still determining what they saw.

With pistols still drawn, the five left the two soldiers to their fate and approached the house. Even in numbers, the sight had rattled them to grow fear inside them. Kipner, above all, was the most fearful though he wouldn't admit it. He didn't see a whip. It was more like a thick, fleshy appendage like an animal's tail.

Revenant and Ghost first stepped onto the front porch and peered into the house.

The front door was gaping open with countless bullet holes. Beyond the threshold was utter darkness; even the Hucks couldn't penetrate. None of them were used to bringing lanterns, so they ventured in blinded hoping to spot a light source inside to illuminate.

Bringing up the rear was Wraith. Kipner had talked himself out of admitting fear and seeking more soldiers to help investigate. He knew the others were just as scared, and although they had no true leader, his wise mind and large structure had often given guidance or assurance to the rest of the crew. This time he didn't want them to lose what little confidence they had left by his confession.

He never forgave himself for that fatal mistake that night.

When he reached the porch, two of his best friends were out of sight in the house. His other two companions, Shade and Specter, 19 years old twins, were steps behind them and dissolved into the darkness.

At the door, Kipner reached for his pocket to find a match he often used to light a cigar with, but the rain had soaked them useless. Before stepping inside, he paused to notice he heard no sounds from the room where his friends were. He called out for them, but he received no reply.

That made him cock his pistol and slowly step through the door, but that was as far as he could manage his feet to move him. He stood in total darkness. To his left along the wall was a four-pane window through which he could see some illumination, but its ambient light went no further than the glass. The sight was peculiar to him.

Behind him was a wide open door, yet no light poured in. An invisible curtain hung over both openings to block out the night.

A flash of lightning tore through the sky above the house, briefly sending the forest into a flickering moment of broad daylight, but his room remained pitch black.

Even so, nothing stirred inside to give any noise. With one hand reaching out, Kipner fumbled slowly across the room, searching for a table that might hold a lantern.

To his deep relief, his hand nearly knocked over a kerosene lamp that was missing its glass globe. He felt a box of long-stem matches nearby and quickly ignited it.

Immediately he wished to extinguish the flame. He turned to inspect the room, which was Victorian in decoration. Taking up half the space, originating in the corner, was a monstrous form comparable to a tree with pulsating flesh for bark. Its cylindrical body rose from the floor to the ceiling. It branched out in numerous appendages that hugged the top of the room. Root-like legs slithered across the floor in all directions, several of which had wrapped around his four companions. Each was restrained and slowly drawn to the trunk-like body where numerous large maws eagerly awaited.

Kipner froze. His mind could not comprehend the sight, trying desperately to give logical reasoning behind its existence. Instead, his mind collapsed on itself, refraining from running in fear.

Revenant and Ghost were already partially consumed by the creature, their upper torsos enveloped within the hungry mouths, soaking the area with pools of their blood. The twins were near the same fate. They had been lifted into the air to mouths higher up the trunk. These had projected several long whip-like tongues now wrapped tightly around the throats of Specter and Shade.

His gun was out and cocked, but it took all of Kipner's mental strength to pull the trigger. His fear had convinced him it would prove useless against it, and his anxiety was right.

The first bullet ricocheted off one of the snake-like branches. Kipner quickly unloaded his sidearm on the monster with a brief fanning and stood in horror as they did nothing.

Ghost and Revenant were swallowed entirely, and those tendrils that were occupied with them were now free to pursue Kipner. His feet were still locked to the floor as his hands shook with tremors. By now, he knew there was no hope for his companions. The tongues securing the twins had easily separated their heads from their bodies; there was no doubt to Kipner how immensely powerful this apparition was.

His fate would have been sealed with the other Hucks had it not been for his mind snapping out of it when the tendrils reached him. He was only a half-step inside the door frame and quickly darted back outside.

However, that wasn't enough to get him out of danger, and the whip-like appendages surged quickly at him.

Kipner took a mighty leap off the porch and dashed out into the storm, splattering through deep puddles of water and heading toward the forest's edge. He wasn't foolish enough to look behind, but he heard the screams of the two prisoners still crawling towards the clearing's edge as something grabbed them.

By the time Wraith reached the trees, their screams were silenced.

It was against his orders, but he refused to report to his officer when he returned to the base camp. Instead, through deep hysteria, he grabbed his belongings and attempted desertion.

Those few awake at that hour intervened, restraining him to the point of sedation until he calmed down. His report to them eventually reached the division's commanding officer, who disregarded him as shell shock and ordered him constrained until further observation. In the meantime, he sent more troops to investigate Kipner's story.

By the time they became overdue, Kipner had leveled his head and was more coherent. It began to cause unease among the remaining soldiers as their numbers had dwindled first from battle and now from claims of a monster. His immediate officer decided to investigate himself, taking with him a large troop and forcing Kipner to join them.

The massacre sent the Wraith bolting into the trees and abandoning his duties as an American soldier. When they had reached the farmhouse and entered the clearing, thin protruding wisps of flesh erupted out of the old house in every direction, securing everyone and dragging them inside. Kipner never forgot the screams of terror coming from them. His only means of survival was hesitating momentarily and not entering the clearing like the rest.

There was no way of knowing how many men were killed that day by whatever was in the building. Even so, Kipner only thought of his dearest friends and the horrific sight of them being consumed. The vision could never be washed away from his mind. Eventually, it toughened him through the years, but he came to understand horrors abound seemingly where ever he went.

CHAPTER II

Texas, 1875

With Hell's fiery, the rattle of his spurs drew closer. The air was thick all around him, shrouding the figure like a phantom harbinger seeking to harvest souls. He carried two polished silver pistols nestled firmly within rawhide wraps. His steps were a heavy shuffle, dragging each heel of his boot across the dry, dusty earth below.

A thick fog had settled late in the evening - unusual for this part of the country. It drifted across the ground like a guard wandering a prison with eyes watching in all directions.

Beneath the moonless sky of Texas slept the silenced boondocks of Hobgoblin Creek with a crescent ridge of rocky hills to the north. In its hay day, Hobgoblin Creek had risen to brief glory at the discovery of silver. Like the boom towns out west, its riches fueled the imagination of poor, dead-end miners hoping to climb out of the hole their lives comprised of.

With those hopes came greedy people seeking to swindle each dime from those lucky in the hills. The town of Hobgoblin Creek thrived brightly in a relatively lawless society.

Yet the broad-shoulder figure standing in the cool night mist stared across the field to a barren community, forever silenced by an unknown reason. Little news had spread for such a growing town, sending word only to Houston by happenstance. A bounty hunter out of Coffeyville, Kansas, had passed through Hobgoblin to discover everyone gone. Claims came that his visit had been brief due to an unsettling feeling of the town's presence.

Had the town been settled closer to anything other than nowhere, there might have been more interest in the matter. It only caught the curiosity of the lone figure because unsettling feelings tended to have a sinister origin, which was his sole interest.

Perhaps a bit morbid, its cemetery greeted each arriving newcomer first. The figure drew a cigar from his shirt pocket while standing at its iron gate, which rose above his tall frame. The small light bursting from his match after striking against the iron illuminated his rugged face.

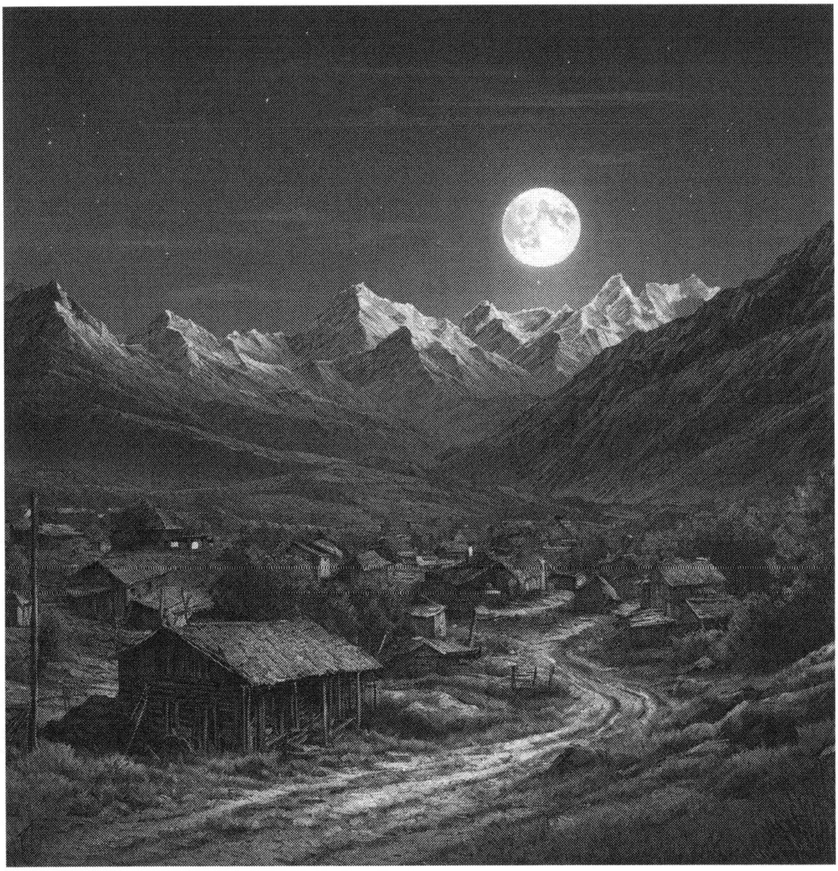

It had seen many years, but the lines across his skin fooled folks to add a dozen more than 45. The thick, overgrown mustache showed little gray and hung low nearly to his chin. When he spoke, which in his solitary occupation was seldom, little movement of his mouth was visible beneath the bushy monstrosity.

Across his brow sat a black Stetson that he was as fond of as the next cowboy to his hat. It stretched broadly to either side and shrouded his face in a dark shadow that made him unrecognizable at a glance.

Even from this distance, the acrid, rotting smell of the fog reached Kipner's nostrils and forced a light cough. To try and limit his exposure, he tied a dark blue bandanna around his mouth and tucked the dangling end into his shirt.

Its use would be more mental assurance than practical use: the fog was deadly over time.

Roy snorted at the scent of death and nervously scraped the ground with his hoof. He knew danger was close, but he wouldn't need to be convinced to get any closer.

There was a better chance of the Missouri Fox Trotter surviving by being left not tethered near the town's welcome sign than leading him into town. The horse had faced numerous beasts that were not meant for this world and fought like a fiery demon each time. Even so, Kipner affectionately patted his old friend on the neck and stared him in the eye in an unspoken loving goodbye. Roy would find his way home if it was more than a few days before anyone returned for him.

The gates to Hobgoblin Creek's cemetery resisted until he gave a forceful shoulder against the bars, and its foot dragged heavily through the hard pan dirt. Throughout the gated area stood white granite tombstones that gave off a soft glow when Kipner approached each one. He recognized the stone as Devil's Rock, more commonly found since the Harrow.

The words chiseled on them were a scattering of departed dates, but they all fell within the same year.

One in particular reads of Gordy "George" Harding, who died at 32. "O Lordy, Gordy, two sips too much tonight."

Each of the graves had been disturbed. Thirty in all, the holes dug had an empty, opened coffin lying at the bottom. A single shovel lay resting against a dead tree caked in dirt.

While Kipner silently wandered the scene examining the open coffins, he heard a soft wail that gradually rose from within one of the tombstones like a solo chorister. He took a few steps away as the single note amplified in the silent desert air, joining monotone notes of different pitches. However, the more distance he placed between the tombstones, the quieter it got until it was silent again.

The U. S. Marshal grunted as he peered at the other tombstones surrounding him. Each one seemed now to lean in his direction, but he shrugged the eerie scene. The moan was a warning, though, to be mindful. Hobgoblin Creek was, indeed, unsettling.

*

It began sporadically, mixing with superstition and American folklore, causing small patches of fear throughout the country. A Spotting or Sighting, as some were starting to call them, were unnatural freaks of nature, mysterious occurrences bordering beyond the realm of tall tales and entering mankind's world. These Spottings could be anything from dark, hairless figures hunched over half-eaten cattle or shifting mounds of partially recognizable townsfolk that would do their best to bite their neighbor. Some blanketed the realm of understanding. A farmer up in South Dakota spoke of watching his son, eleven years old, become engulfed in a pitch-black cloud that floated along the ground in the breeze. His scream was abruptly silenced, then he was gone.

For most of the country, superstition still thrived, but those who followed it were mindful of avoiding falling to bad luck. The majority of the country hadn't witnessed the things few others had. So they carried a lack of understanding behind the truth slowly spreading across America.

But for those who witnessed any kind of Sighting, those who knew the danger that was slowly awakening kept their doors locked at night, salt across their threshold, sharp poles in their chimney, and barbed wire across their shutters. The Harrow had come.

*

Putting the cemetery behind him, the Wraith drifted into the quiet town led by the light from his cigar. His spurs rang loosely with each step as he gauged the village. It had grown to fit the valley it was in, wrapped in comforting arms from the Quitman Mountains that overlooked the wooden buildings. The main looping road pierced through the structures and was the only surviving avenue for the town.

Small junctures, now washed out from flash floods, once extended toward the hills beyond.

He glided down the center of the road, casting a cautious eye to either side as if expecting to be greeted by the town. He passed expected businesses: a blacksmith, a cobbler, a general store, and too many saloons. Each building stood eerily silent in the dead of night, their insides filled with voids of nothingness.

The sudden absence of people had drawn him to visit the town. He ducked his head in a few buildings whose doors were still open, some swinging gently in the night breeze, and while he found no bodies lying, he saw plenty of signs of inhabitants.

Cash registers were filled with money, mail was ready to be sent, and food, now rotten, was prepared in dutch ovens. He found guns on the ground throughout the town as if people suddenly dropped them. Brooms lay abandoned on porches. Everyone appeared to drop what they were doing and leave. Yet there were no footprints that gave that indication. The ground was dry and cracking from a drought, but repeated traffic would still exist somewhere.

Deep inside one saloon was a glowing ember on a table which caught Kipner's eye as he dropped his cigar stub to the ground and stomped it out. The batwing doors slightly shifted as he stepped onto the porch, and he eased them both open slowly, studying the room closely.

The owner had been a proficient hunter in a younger life. Heads of wild game frequently hung around the large area. Wooden booths lined the inner walls while round tables cluttered closely together towards the entrance. The bar was unusually long and curved, with an impressive display of pigeonhole shelves for spirit bottles. A series of brass beer taps, positioned along the longest counter stretch, pointed skyward to an open loft above.

The ember floated and bobbed in a small area above one of the wooden chairs that matched the green felt card table in front of it. The glow was faint yet familiar to the tip of a cigar. It moved with rhythm, darting in closer over the table and then back above the seat as if driven by the invisible strings of a puppeteer from above.

Keeping a watchful eye, Kipner strode over to the bar and, seeing no one there to stop him, helped himself to a mug of beer, sliding a flat stick across the rim to slosh off the foam. He wasn't surprised the beer tap still worked. The story behind the town's mystery began forming in Kipner's mind.

There were several chairs at the card table, and he drew one for himself and gently laid the mug on a nearby chair to avoid the felt.

The glow from the ember gently brightened from time to time, and each moment the light faintly illuminated the translucent outline of a face. Across the table, he heard the scuffling of wooden chairs moving on their own to position themselves beside him. Cards slowly appeared on the table and were shuffled and then cut.

Kipneer had grown up in a unique part of Maryland, an early focal point for supernatural activity. From there, his life had traveled vastly, each as highly concentrated as the last. To his knowledge, no other wearing a badge had experienced the Harrow or believed it had begun.

By the time young Kipner was a teenager, Spottings had already been reported in the area. Significantly fewer believed the origin was something yet to be discovered. Many had blamed Native Americans, thinking they cursed and plagued the land when relocated. Some felt it was a sign for more missionaries to head out west and spread the word of God.

Kipner had initially thrived on the experience, eagerly seeking out mysterious stories the folks around his small Maryland hometown of Ellicott City had spun. He had seen more than his share of bizarre sights before he enlisted during the Civil War. Even so, his memory of watching his closest friends brutally dismembered during the War broke him, which drove his mind to a darker place, one of hatred towards the unknown that plagued America.

Those in power had been skeptical before the War. Even so, enough of Congress' families had witnessed some Sightings by the time the South surrendered that a deliberate but subtle effort was formed to understand the phenomenon's origin. Kipner was the perfect candidate. His heroic bravery was well recognized and rewarded after the Civil War despite abandoning the army, which presented him with a position as a federal marshal with the unique duty of investigating the quietly growing threat of the Harrow.

By the time he had reached Hobgoblin Creek and sat before a table of ghostly spirits, he had become well-seasoned with the supernatural. In fact, several connecting occurrences had been repeated to give Kipner a means to document and offer solutions to more common elements. This document was quietly distributed to those entrusted by the government and soon became known as the Harrow Doctrine. On page thirty-two, he listed expected behaviors for unsettled spirits. The best way to deal with them is to treat them as living. Sometimes, the suggestion actually worked.

Before him, the spirits formed into loosely translucent soft, glowing white figures as they held their cards and sipped invisible shots of whiskey.

"Your bid," came a whisper behind Kipner's ear, softly brushing against his skin and sending goosebumps down his neck. The dealer stared with hollow black holes directly at him expectantly. Kipner could feel the same empty voids from his competitors to his side, equally awaiting his next move.

He hadn't expected to gamble, but he had thought wisely to bring a few coins and hoped it was enough for a hand or two. Knowing they spoke, he only wanted to make the hands last long enough to understand the town's fate.

The bet was small but suitable for the table, and a series of coins appeared and bounced with a satisfying sound against the felt.

He suspected bluffing would be unnecessary against the apparitions. Even so, he naturally held a poker face when dealing with a Spotting. Fear, he had come to believe, was nourishing to anything unnatural.

The cards were shown to all, and Kipner immediately became suspicious of his circumstance. Any of their hands would have won, but his was worthless.

Another hand was dealt, this time by the spiritual gentleman seated beside him, which resulted in a similar collection of cards as before. With the series of betting, Kipner was finding his wallet growing light quickly.

"I think a round is called for, boys," Kipner offered and waved to the lifeless bar to signal for more whiskey. The movement around the table hesitated momentarily, and Kipner took his opportunity while shot glasses materialized before him. Inside, a light green liquid slowly shifted from side to side.

"Seems to be troubled times in town," he began as he held the glass in his hand to cheer the others. They stared intensely at him in anticipation. None of them made a motion to their drinks. It made him uneasy at the thought of downing whatever was in his hand. He hadn't expected it to get this far and was making it up as he went.

A putrid, reeking aroma wafted from the rim of the glass to his nostrils that burned the hairs in his nose. The spirits waited and watched him.

Testing his options, he slowly laid the glass back on the table and gestured to rise but froze immediately when a series of pistols suddenly appeared, hovering midair, and pointed at him.

"Your deal," the whisper returned behind him, breaking his nerve momentarily. He wiped the sweat off his brow, returned his Stetson to his head, and then took his seat.

"Fine, to the other side, I'll see ya," Kipner said with a sigh and dropped the strange liquid into his throat, trying to swallow as quickly as possible.

The remaining drinks were downed in unison, and the deck of cards slid in front of him.

The sensation of the drink was more than he was anticipating. It felt as if a small hand was slowly pulling itself down his esophagus, inch by inch. It bulged grandly, expanding his neck until it disappeared into his chest. Even in his stomach, he could feel the presence of motion swirling with life.

You fool, he thought to himself. He let himself get caught in the moment and trapped in a situation where they had the upper hand.

All of this is for a few questions he probably still needed to be answered.

"Boys," he tried again, "I'm just passing through. Maybe I can help, maybe I can't. But while I'm here, you might as well ..."

"Your... deal," came the voice again, this time more forceful than a whisper. Kipner could feel the voice's teeth lightly scrape across his ear as it spoke.

Looking at each one at the table, Kipner sighed and took the cards to shuffle. With several flicks of his wrists, the cards were dealt, and another round of bets was made.

Another series of cards, nearly unbeatable, came out to which Kipner lost a third hand.

Was this a trick?

He was nearly out of the money he brought, and they seemed to show no signs of letting him walk away even broke.

It was clear to him they were cheating each hand, materializing whatever cards they needed.

Then a thought occurred to him, and he decided to put it to the test. When the deck returned to him, as the last of his money was on the table, his thoughts went to the cards. They were not real, so what was driving them? Could he manipulate them?

He dealt the cards, making slight flickering motions with his wrist as if drawing from the bottom of the deck while being discrete. Each card he visualized in his mind, including his, then bet heavily with all his remaining money. His bet was matched and then increased by each spirit, forcing him into the situation he had feared when he sat down.

Among his possessions, Ulysses Grant had honored him with an engraved pocket watch after the Civil War commemorating his wondrous deeds. Its case was sterling silver and read "Wraith" inside, a name he had carried throughout the War.

Gingerly Kipner placed it at the top of the giant pile of coins and bills.

"Call," he challenged to the table with the thought of the cards still focused in his mind.

One by one, the phantoms laid their cards down, each identical to the last. Despite a traditional deck, they each had three aces and four eights, far exceeding the number of each suit.

Kipner had a royal flush, a numerical series of cards of the same suit, and the highest-ranking hand of poker.

Manipulation had triumphed, to Kipner's surprise, and he grinned while drawing the pile toward him.

He had heard the legend of a gunfighter murdered during a poker game. His hand became known as Dead Man's Hand, filled with aces and eights. Kipner thought it was fitting.

His company at the table vanished immediately, leaving him to recall the odd sensation in his stomach that grew too uncomfortably. It spread through his body, filling his blood vessels with the strange, eldritch power. He wanted to retch and bend over, hoping it would exude from his body. Instead, it reached the boundaries of his body, and he felt his brain seize. He fell to his knees and rolled onto his back, gripping his head in pain.

All around him, swirling manifestations emerged with vigor. As his torture grew, so did the energy behind the visions, coming better into focus with each agonizing second.

Finally, the pain relieved him, and he lay panting on the saloon's wooden floor. Several figures were huddled over him, peering down with the same ghastly hollow eyes as his poker friends.

He was able to sit up slowly and gazed around the room. It was illuminated with the same dull green his drink possessed, and patrons were all watching Kipner intently throughout the saloon.

Getting up was difficult, but he got back on his feet. None of the translucent figures moved or spoke. They only stared directly at him.

"I'm not here to cause any trouble, folks," Kipner addressed the crowd. "U.S. Marshal Robert Kipner. I came to investigate what happened to Hobgoblin Creek. I'm looking for any clues you can provide."

Suddenly their drinks were placed on the tables, and they all stepped toward him. Those closest reached out to put their hands on him, and his body temperature dramatically dropped. His skin where they touched turned light blue as a soft frost formed and burned.

Kipner jerked his arms back and stepped toward the front doors, and the entire room slowly began to follow him out into the street.

Outside was a large gathering of similar entities that approached him. They were all to the south towards the edge of town, so he quickly went farther in.

None of them were quick. Kipner didn't need to run or panic; he wasted no time moving. Exactly where he was running was another question.

Some appeared ahead of him, and others blocked his forward movement. His options were growing thin quickly.

The only place he could go was a town bank whose doors were ajar when he inspected them. He paused and looked back at the growing crowd.

They all surrounded the building, preventing him from leaving but gave no threat as long as he entered the bank.

They had led him there. He suspected the clue he was after was here.

As he thought of lighting some lanterns, wondering if the kerosene was still viable in any of them, the same green glow erupted throughout the room in the lanterns, casting a bright but heavily shadowed light throughout.

For such a small town, their bank was lavish. It was entirely stone rather than wood like every other building, and there were seating areas in front with weight scales on nearby tables. Towards the back were barred teller windows, a sight he would never see except in much larger cities.

He helped himself past a door that took him behind the windows and inspected a back office, presumably for the bank's owner. As if the person simply got up during work hours and left, the room was in a state of operation. Papers were signed in a stack for sales, ledgers were resting open on a desk, and a six-foot diameter vault was embedded in the back wall.

"A vault? Here?" Kipner asked out loud.

Nothing added up correctly for such a rural, isolated town. It was clear every ounce of silver came here and never left.

He paged through some of the ledgers, sifting through the signed papers, and began to piece together the oddity that made up Hobgoblin Creek.

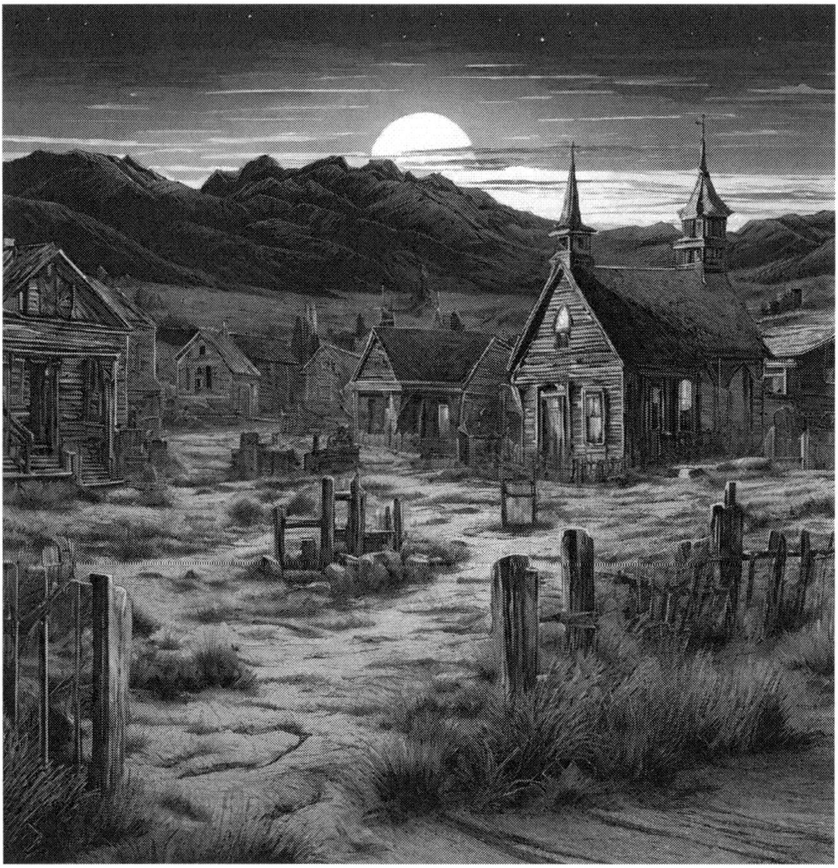

Every document he could find showed an abrupt ending in 1875. The entire town's operation had only lasted, what appeared by the records, two years. He traced the papers back to the city's birth to find an Austrian immigrant family, the von Lists, who originally owned the entire area. Over the following years, portions of that claim were sold to various townspeople to the point that the family owned only a ten-foot cube of land. What puzzled Kipner further was that the von List's signatures for each portion matched the receiver's signature as if the same person who gave the land received the land. That struck Kipner as suspicious, mainly if the mines were still producing silver.

Kipner took another glance around the room. He was curious about what was behind the vault but needed help inspecting inside. Suddenly, the vault door made a thud sound at his thought and slowly became ajar. He approached and heaved the door open with both hands, grunting at the sheer weight to reveal nothing inside. It was void of any currency or anything else for that matter. The vault lacked shelves or storage bins and was just one empty room.

That didn't add up to Kipner, mainly when the remainder of the town contained virtually every possession the townsfolk owned.

When he returned outside, the throng of ghosts appeared specifically to encourage him to continue on a direct path once again.

"You could just tell me," Kipner said as he stepped off the boardwalk and onto the street. "Or I guess you just talk over poker."

The night grew late, and Kipner was operating only on adrenaline. He hoped where ever they were taking him was a nice comfortable bed so he could address this all in the morning under the blessed sun.

The wind picked and breezed down the road toward him, carrying a whirling newspaper that danced in circles until it landed on his boots. Once it rested at his feet, the wind ceased.

"Subtle," Kipner said as he grunted to reach down and pick up the newspaper. Its pages had been separated, only the front and back cover pages, but he soon understood why.

The main story read of a growing disappointment with the von List family, who wished to maintain ownership of the List Mines despite a generous offering from the entire townsfolk to purchase it. The article mentioned the son, Guido, inheriting the claim and offering to allow others to operate the mine. However, 90% of the findings remained in the von List family.

Towards the end of the road, approaching the edge of town, there was a once immaculate home that now laid dormant and dilapidated. It was larger than most buildings in town, with several stories of dark wood. Old brick outlines told the story of an elaborate garden that used to decorate the front lawn. Now broken shutters lay across the ground, paint cracked and peeling.

After stepping onto the makeshift porch, the few boards buckled and groaned under Kipner's calf-length wellington boots. He could already smell death that lay behind the door long before he turned the knob and pushed it forward.

The main foyer was reasonably well-kept. A fireplace, too small for the room's size, had a few logs in the nearby basket but was otherwise cold. Two tall cabinets adorned the back wall beside a closed door, with two more doors heading to Kipner's right and left. Someone had sunk a water pump near the cabinets into the ground and placed a wash bin under the spigot.

His boots scuffled across the dust-heavy floor, leaving behind two long continuous lines and kicking a small cloud in the air. Both cabinets were locked when he tried opening them, but he carried a few iron lock picks with him for just occasions. They had been made for novice locksmiths, and occasionally Kipner got lucky enough with them.

Beyond the cans of sardines and a box of baking soda, strange to be locked securely, was a series of pigeon holes, many containing rolled sheets. Through the various papers, Kipner learned of the house's inhabitants.

Something had been stirred with agitation, and it awoke. One was a distress letter written by Guido von List to his uncle McMannon in Kansas. The date on the paper was from a few years prior. He was scared of heading into the hills, but he stressed it was not from the bandits. He begged his uncle to wire enough money for him to buy a train ticket away.

Most of the papers that followed were of a different tone. They were more commanding, with a powerful voice that no longer feared death. He went on to speak of a great power he had found within and intended to draw from it to change the minds of the townsfolk. Instead, he boldly proclaimed the town was foolish to reject his offering, though he didn't mention what type.

Something made a sound from behind one of the doors to his right that stole his attention from the letters. With confidence, he strode over and listened quietly against the wood. The bed springs of an old mattress creaked slowly in protest, then went silent. Footsteps dragged across the ground toward him from the other side, and Kipner drew back away from the door.

Less than a half mile away, a storm had quietly built itself up, and lightning struck the ground with unnatural force, sending rippling thunder waves across the desert to the rickety house. The walls shook, but Kipner kept his attention on the door.

From the crack beneath, soft tendrils of smoke trickled into the main room, slithering with a snake-like motion toward him. They moved with purpose but no urgency, each splitting into additional appendages and becoming more finger-like. They weaved through themselves, joining then parting away, always heading in one direction.

Kipner gave it as wide of birth as the room allowed, but the smoke shifted to match his path.

Outside, the rain began to fall, rattling against the dry wood roof and slipping over the edge. Cracks across the dirt road began filling with water with nowhere to go.

The marshal needed to find out about the phenomenon - it had not been something he had seen before. It was unnatural, with shifts of gray from light to dark, and each time it tumbled like a wave over itself, the colors swirled and flowed.

Behind him, he felt the solid metal pipe of the pump, and he shifted to one side. The smoke wisps gathered together as it moved to the mouth of the pump, smoothly flowing inside. Kipner watched in puzzlement as the rest of the smoke completed its course and disappeared into the pump and down below. Hesitantly he tried the pump, but only dirty, brown water emerged.

Kipner was curious to know if the slithering wisps were a part of some supernatural power or were a supernatural entity itself. He guessed it could have been both. The sound of footsteps in the bedroom brewed the notion it was the son in the letters.

While he had experienced varying degrees of unusual mysteries since being a marshal, each day presented new challenges of forces beyond his imagination. He had no idea what this particular creature was.

The water pump returned his attention as a thick, black molasses-like liquid oozed slowly. It was like overcooked coffee, rich and bold, that saturated the ground and spread like roots just under the ground's surface.

Outside, the thunderstorm arrived and rolled slowly across the town, sending down sheets of sharp raindrops and flashes of light that flickered in the dark night. The poor old house was riddled with holes, and Kipner was soon soaked to the bone.

The rain was frigid through the cold, chilled night and shivered his body.

Spreading across the floor to outside, the darkening threatened the town in a short amount of time. Mole-like tunnels emerged and pushed ridges in every direction, tightly weaving a branch-like pattern. Only the ghosts were affected. Whenever any extension became close to the wandering apparition, they would be violently pulled into the mound of dirt, followed by the eruption of a decaying, blood-caked hand through the ground. One by one, the ghosts vanished instantly, drawn down to whatever created the ground disturbance, and emerged as shambling, shuffling creatures of the dead.

Making out any details in the town's street could only be granted during the flashes of lightning. His vision was hampered entirely by the sheets of angrily pounding rain and thick, turbulent clouds above. Yet in the darkness, Kipner could sense movement reaching up from the road.

Long, towering, misshapen figures rose above his height across town. No longer could he see any ghosts softly illuminating. The growing plague just below the surface continued claiming them one by one, replacing each with a physical form that loosely shifted their way in Kipner's direction.

He immediately felt that helpful intentions were long gone and should not remain standing in the doorway. Staying indoors would only seal his doom, giving him no way of escaping, so he dived into the torrential storm, throwing his shoulders up in defiance.

The number of shambling forces was staggering in a short period. Through sloppy mud, Kipner stumbled while avoiding figures that would rise suddenly before him. Dodging one way or another gave him little choice. He was at the mercy of the town's curse. Victims of the black ooze came from every direction. He could see more emerging from the buildings he ran past in the bright lightning strikes.

There was no gentle guidance such as the ghosts offered. Whenever Kipner dodged too slowly, arms extended from the mounds with sickeningly long fingers that swiped and grasped at his clothes. Much of his shirt was already torn from the sharpness of their fingers, and he felt a few deep scratches across his shoulder. He needed to escape the town, but they came from every direction.

He went to the town center, where the bending road peaked in its arch.

He could sense he was surrounded in the dark with his back against the cold, wet stone of the town's well. It was here that dodging was no longer an option. With uncanny speed, Kipner drew his Colt pistols in desperation and began unloading heavy lead at the impending creatures knowing his bullets were vastly outnumbered.

With superior accuracy shooting from the hip, he kept death at bay briefly. The motionless bodies began forming a makeshift bulwark before him that slowed the lively creatures beyond. He fed his hungry guns in preparation for another round of assault. The strange sensation in his gut suddenly returned. It was more intense than before, sending him to his knees with gasping pain. After an eternity, the pain became tolerable, but the effect remained. It spread similarly to the first time throughout his body. This time he clearly saw his blood vessels glow beneath his skin, a pale green that reminded him of the apparitions. Soon his entire body was covered with hundreds of tiny appendages of his circulatory system giving soft light against the dark night.

The two pistols still in his grip were encased in the illumination as if they were an extension of his body.

However, it had given the figures time to breach the barrier of bodies, and through instinct, Kipner began firing back.

Each bullet exploded with a fiery green light, leaving long trails that slowly dampened and faded out of sight. The impacts were violent and compelling, sending each approaching creature into small piles of ether.

The battle raged for several minutes as Kipner continued trying to unload his weapons and push back the force. Despite the sheer number of these shuffling, lifeless mounds of flesh, it was clear to him that, somehow, he was driving them back. After each kill, the remaining creatures drew slower and slower until, finally, they stood still.

He rested his blazing green guns, realizing he had not reloaded them for quite some time. Flipping the cylinders out of their chambers, they were both empty and cool to the touch as if they had never been fired.

The underground plague was retreating, pulling itself back as it had come towards the small shack. Each creature caught near the retraction was vaporized, leaving nothing more than a tiny ether pool.

What was once shrouding his skin along with his pistols now darkened and was gone. He wasn't sure at the moment what was in that drink the ghosts had given him, but for the moment, he had to credit his life to them.

While the rain came down, the frequency of lightning and billowing winds lessened to a more tolerable shower. He was able to gather himself off the muddy ground and watch the last of the sprouting ridges disappear into the building.

Inspecting the inside once again, he found no signs of the ooze. The water pump was dry to the touch. Stepping into the bedroom where it had originated, only a broken mattress was found. There were no footprints on the dusty old floorboards.

Whatever he was dealing with, it showed considerable power. Transformations, controlling corporeal forms, and presumably possessing enough power to murder an entire town was perhaps only the surface of what he was facing. Until now, he knew von List had a vendetta against the city and an acting pursuit to control all of the silver in the area. He could understand why von List would monopolize Hobgoblin Creek's principal, and probably only, source of income as an act of vengeance. Even so, he was unsure why he had gone so far beyond as to murder everyone if he did.

Kipner hadn't ruled out an outside source as the reasoning behind the town's fall. It was riddled with powerful dark forces that seemed to funnel into the water pump in von List's home.

From a heavy shower to a light sprinkling, the storm finally blew itself out and relieved the town until another day. It had done a number on some of the homes, sending shingles onto the muddy street and branches through a few windows. Kipner zig-zagged his way to the place of his Last Stand, where his pistols took their own life.

The town's well was nothing unusual except for the peculiar wooden ladder that leaned against the inside leading into the depths below. Usually, one was constructed for anyone who unfortunately fell into the water, but it typically wasn't left there. It was too deep to see the water's surface below, and out of curiosity, Kipner dropped a lit match.

The curiosity from the water pump was drawing him to the ladder, wondering if there was something other than water down below. He looked up momentarily to the surrounding hills hidden in the night's darkness. Somewhere up there, he guessed, was a long mine shaft that tied up with the town's underground water. However deep it was, it went beyond the visibility of its fall. Only von List had access to what the ledger had read, so whatever he had done to the town might be down the well.

He stepped into a general store to retrieve a lantern and strapped it to his belt. It took the struck match and gave a soft orange glow that pushed back the night. Satisfied with the light it shed, he swung his legs over the well's rim and descended the ladder.

Each step was slow. He was ginger with the rungs as he trusted none of them. The whole ladder could collapse on him from his weight. His old boots scraped against the rickety footholds that echoed off the stones.

If water was at the bottom of the well, it was considerably further than one town should hope. Granted, the area was notoriously dry year-round. Even so, rainwater often would quickly seep through the cracks and form an extensive water table somewhere below - just not this far down.

His lantern light bathed the stones in a gentle amber glow. By now, he was at least fifty feet below ground. The ladder's integrity at this length for such a simple town was impressive. They apparently had a solid carpenter at one time.

The echoing sound of his descent softened, and he glanced down to the bottom of the well's wall. The hole continued into darkness along with the ladder.

Dipping below the last layer of stones, Kipner tightened his grip on the rungs. His lantern's light terminated into a seemingly endless void from a vast cavern. His little ladder was all his solidity from feeling the enveloping nothingness. What was this madness? None of this was naturally built by the townsfolk. Drawing water would have taken hours and been enduring with each bucket.

With flapping wings, something buzzed him from the darkness behind his head. It was no small nocturnal critter. If it had been a bat, it ate well from the size of the sensation.

Holding on with all his strength, he whipped his head from side to side, trying vainly to see any other diving attacks. The silence throughout the cavern rang in his ears, and he continued his climb down.

His situation was grim. After leaving the well's support, the impossibly long ladder bowed greatly against his weight. Trying to ease his way slower made no difference.

There needed to be more confidence in Kipner's actions.

As the wood creaked, he took another look down and found relief from the far boundaries of the lantern's glow. He had seen the water table thirty feet below the well's rim. The ladder disappeared into the murky underground lake.

Cresting from the water near one side was a small island with bones and human skulls. A cairn of stacked stones that tapered to a point formed the island's centerpiece.

Crunch after sickening crunch, Kipner tiptoed cautiously across the island to get a closer look at the pile of stones.

It wasn't built for an adult of average height. The stones reached his belt, so he guessed between three and four feet, and it stretched close to the same length. Most of the stones were river rocks, smooth to the touch and flat, allowing several hundred to be used.

Kipner kept his distance and circled slowly. Leaning against one side was a crudely constructed symbol or perhaps a periapt made from more bone and unknown material. Its size would comfortably fit into a person's hand.

While he stood there contemplating the strange oddity, a chorus of men's voices began singing a harmonious single note, deep and ominous. It rose in volume the longer Kipner watched the object, tempted to remain fixated. He tried backing away, thinking back to the gravestone outside town, but the noise did not lessen this time.

Something rose from the cairn to match the rising chant. It was a shadow in form, slightly translucent and vaguely humanoid in shape. It seeped into his mind and locked his motion still. Paralyzed not with fear but from the power of the creature's restraint, it reached out. It caressed Kipner's cheek tenderly, drawing him in closer. It melted the chanting into a whisper that was both soothing and alluring.

"How I have waited for a second vessel," it spoke. "Your flesh has strength...your blood, quenching. Sleep."

A trance befell Kipner with such force his eyes closed before he could consciously fight it. Exhaustion overcame him as if he had walked all day in the sun. Somewhere inside, cold fingers dragged him down and wrapped around his organs.

They squeezed. Rapidly increasing with strength, the invisible talons compressed against his vitals, buckling his knees and sending him to the bone-covered ground.

His body tightened, and his mouth gaped open. There was no freedom to scream from the pain - he suffered silently. Across his body, his skin burst into lesions from unseen blades and exposed tissue below.

"Mmmmm," the creature moaned with pleasure as it closed in. "You teem with life. I shall covet your flesh and use your shell for my desires."

Kipner contorted into an unnatural pose, cracking his joints and stretching his muscles beyond their limits. He attempted feebly to counter the creature's unfathomable power, but his mind was too tired to fight back. With quick whipping motions, his body went into convulsions, smashing the nearby cairn with powerful kicks of his legs and exposing the crumpled mess of a corpse hidden inside.

A sudden light momentarily drew the apparition away as Kipner's side arms came to life. The glow from the lantern dwindled as it slipped from his hand and rolled out. The oil from its base poured out, spreading a small trailing fire that briefly roared up.

They flew into the air with purpose, rising without a hand to guide them, and hovered with their barrels aimed at the dark menace. Kipner hadn't reloaded them but shrouded in the green light, their hammers cocked back and repeatedly fired at the real Wraith. Exploding phantoms, purple wads of luminous ether shot out of the guns. They penetrated it, splitting the creature into smaller shreds of shadow.

Throughout the cavern came a shriek that would ring in Kipner's ears hours later. It tried retreating to the cairn, its outstretched arms withdrawing from Kipner's body and releasing his paralysis. Even so, the cairn was too damaged to offer protection. It turned, exposed, toward its adversary with malice and fear.

When he had been promoted and sworn in as a U. S. Marshal, he had been issued dual Colt Single Action Army pistols. They had been a nice improvement from the single Remington he had bought on his own dime, which was all he could afford from the poultry wages from the War.

Their quality was significant in design. Their side plates were silver inlaid with a gold scorpion just past the cylinder, and the barrels had three wide inlays of gold near the end. There was a comfortable grip to each made out of dark mahogany that was soft in hand. They balanced well and felt light when held.

Until that night, they had never performed in that way.

Soft drips of moisture fell and rippled the underground lake calmly while Kipner recovered from the attack. Facing an eidolon wasn't something he had hoped to find down there, and it had caught him off guard. The cairn was a common anchor point for them to spawn from, tied forever to a restless soul beneath the rocks.

The pistols hovered in the air, fixed barrels to the specter as if waiting for Kipner to regain control. He got up and eased his hands around the mahogany grips and wasted no time to finish the unholy creature, unsure of how he was capable of destroying such a thing. He was beginning to wonder if a greater power or force was in more control of his situation than he was.

Easing the pistols back into their holsters, he surveyed the area. Any sign of the threat was gone; only the dehydrated corpse remained among the broken cairn stones. Kipner could only assume it was Guido von List.

The rocks covering the body shifted and rolled over one another as the body began to emerge from within, rising in a hunched form barely recognizable as human. From Kipner's light, the face was deeply pocked and disturbed with crevices across its skin and two hollow sockets where eyes once rested. The hands were curled and twisted with severe arthritis that left oversize knobby knuckles.

Its voice was not more significant than a raspy wheeze like someone out of breath still trying to speak. It was cold and rigid like old, rusted iron.

"It is moot. Your venture here is too late. I have gotten what I wanted. There is nothing more." It labored horrendously with each word, pausing in between before continuing. Its withered body appeared to slowly shrink in size as it stood before Kipner, decreasing in mass by the second.

"I know how they wronged you and your family, Guido," the marshal began. "I know they took what was yours for themselves. You shouldn't have gone to the lengths you did to murder them all."

The corpse twitched at Kipner's voice as if it pained it to hear him. "They deserved worse than death, and I gave that to them!" it winced at its explosiveness as it tried to express its raw hatred. "We gave that to them. It was awake when we arrived. It just needed convincing."

Drawing the attention of an eidolon was as dangerous as working in conjunction with one. Kipner had written in the Harrow Doctrine how to attract an eidolon from where ever they came, which required committing a sinister act. The purpose of his book was not to encourage horrible deeds but to recognize and identify those who committed them and put them behind bars.

Collecting all written papers regarding the Harrow, no one truly knew what these entities were or where they came from. Kipner had suggested they had always been here, staying in hibernation, hidden and out of sight, until something caused them to awaken. Only from his personal experiences did he even know what an eidolon appeared to be, but he had witnessed many times before people striking bargains with them to gain powers humans were not meant to possess.

From the notes he left behind, von List's hatred of those in town led him to sacrifice himself as an offering to the creature in exchange for it to lay waste upon the citizens of Hobgoblin Creek. Judging from the sheer number of bones that made the crude island, it had done unspeakable horrors to all of them.

As the corpse of Guido von List shrunk to nothingness, Kipner tried to gain more information about these creatures.

"Did it tell you where it came from? Why it awakened?"

In its last breath, through a series of heart-wrenching coughs that could be taken as attempts of laughter, it spoke. "It was always here. We woke them. My...uncle...told...me."

There was little left of the mummified figure stretched over brittle bone save glistening white teeth and a peculiar leather thong tied around the neck. A tiny, stale body in the fetal position no larger than a mole hung from the string.

As Kipner peered closer, the tiny ornament began shaking with life, vibrating like a maraca. The paper-thin skin could not withstand the aggravation and split open, revealing a smooth stone from within. The dried flesh peeled back, and the stone popped out with force. Against the soft light of his lantern, it was covered with several scratches too deep to be trivial. The markings were laid with purpose but gave no obvious pattern to Kipner. He had little knowledge of ancient or primitive markings and knew nothing of whether it was a language or something else. It could be nothing more than false relics of a diabolic occult. Until he could find an answer, it was coming with him. Something sinister was tied with it all; he meant to get to the bottom of it.

Kipner returned to an empty town. The presence of supernatural visions, ghosts, and ghouls alike, was nowhere to be found.

The toxic fog that had caused his coughing to draw blood to his lips had also dissipated. From house to house, each was filled with a cold avoidance that left little doubt he wandered an authentic ghost town. No sludge escaped from the water pumps. There were no decks of cards that dealt themselves. From below, bizarre and ghastly eldritch powers no longer distressed the cursed town of Hobgoblin Creek.

He crested an overlook of the town a mile outside with Roy, who was happily feeding on some oats Kipner toted along on his saddle. A simple stew of salted pork and dried vegetables soaked in a bubbling pot.

Above, the rising wisps of steam mixed with the thick cloud from his cigar. It helped little against the aches of his aging body after a day of terrors.

Although he had been through countless forms of unspeakable sights, finding a means to escape each one by his whits and pure luck, he could never completely calm his nerve. However, it kept his edge tight, which he accounted for his fortune.

At the end of the day, when he found himself still breathing after another miraculous attainment, he wondered how many more he could find himself on the living end. He wasn't getting any younger. He had just turned forty-five, and his joints reminded him each day he got closer to death.

Roy finished his evening meal and nudged Kipner with its nose, softly blowing a tired sigh when his friend scratched his muzzle. When Roy came into his life as a rejected colt, he showed no signs of being worthwhile on a ranch. Kipner had traded for him after helping Dillon Jackson eradicate what was thought to be a wolf plaguing his farm. The most challenging task Kipner had faced was finding a dead wolf to show him instead of the multi-tentacled feline that was feasting on his cattle. There were still parts of the country unwilling to believe in such monstrosities.

Taking his daydreaming eyes away from the campfire, he took out the cloth-wrapped stone etched with scratches and pondered its origin. Beside it in his hand were two others like it, their markings just as foreign to him. Each one had come from different parts of the country and was hiding near the source of the area's most potent horrors. There was no telling just what they meant. They bared no resemblance to native markings. Kipner had inquired about them at a few colleges but was answered with vague theories and guesses to whom all wanted to keep for studying. He knew they would disappear to some forgotten museum if he listened.

*

The small campfire burned brightly in the eyes of the figure watching the Wraith. Some two miles away, the figure sitting beside the fire was impossible to see from this distance. Yet, the watcher's eyes were so exceptional he could easily see the three marked stones in Kipner's hands.

He stared in deep thought. Another figure, this one ancient, approached from an ever-growing track nearby.

"Pursue?" the figure inquired the watcher, gazing out into the darkness. It leaned slightly and favored the right leg heavily.

The tall watcher was adorned in a suit in the style of New Orleans. He made a murmur while thinking about the question and shook his head.

"He won't know we are here. Even so, send one out, one-quarter mile. Report if he heads in our direction."

It nodded in understanding and hobbled into the darkness towards the sounds of hammer on iron.

CHAPTER III

Kansas, 1875

Coffeyville was a relatively new town of less than a decade of age. A few years ago, it was nothing more than a trading post for Native Americans in the area or pioneers passing west. The Leavenworth, Lawrence & Galveston Railroad coming through town in '71 signaled its actual growth into a city. However, it had not been incorporated until a couple years ago.

Roy sneezed and shook his head as he slowly walked his master past the city limits of the Kansas town.

He was a Fox Trotter, born in southern Missouri, and loved the open country. His legs were strong, and he carried weight over longer distances than Kipner's past horses. There was a character behind his eyes, and Kipner had caught Roy laughing at the right opportunity on more than one occasion.

The Wraith leaned against the bar of the first saloon he came to and selected a cigar from the display case, tossing a coin onto the counter. In kind, the man behind the bar struck a match and offered to light it, which Kipner obliged with a nod of thanks.

If Hobgoblin Creek was a dead town, Coffeyville was a funeral for it. He had only been in town half an hour but already could tell the law laid a heavy hand on the poor townsfolk. Friendly nods, cheerful smiles, and warm greetings were missing. Folks kept their heads low and hustled to where ever they might be going, which was the shortest distance between the two points.

No one casually strolled down the street or rocked in their chairs outside general stores. Kipner called towns like this "scolded."

Kipner never wore his U.S. Marshal's badge out in the open. He didn't like the attention, which typically resulted in petty requests or young brats wanting to prove his worth at the draw. Occasionally he had to reveal it just under his vest, but usually, he found no one questioned his word. In towns like this, he made especially careful not to show his badge if he could avoid it. Folks might have little tolerance for seeing a U. S. Marshal's badge.

It frequently happened, even before the Harrow. Given the right size and location, sometimes a town was run by corruption and tyranny. It might be a crooked sheriff or some hell-bent judge who was two sermons away from condemning them all to Hell. Whatever the case, it usually ended badly.

"Closing time at the top of the hour, Sir," the bartender said as he poured Kipner a shot of whiskey. He left the bottle, relocated the rest under the counter, and locked it.

The sun had not set yet across the flat Kansas plains. Birds were merrily chirping in a tree outside and showed no signs of the day ending soon.

"Seems pretty early to close up shop. Why the early call?" Kipner asked.

The bartender continued loading bottles into another cabinet and locked the cigar case. He just shook his head and didn't look at Kipner.

He had only been in a few towns with curfews, but never this early. Usually, they were for the safety of the people in case a dangerous outlaw had escaped and threatened to return to town.

None of the patrons in the saloon remained. Kipner strolled to the batwing door and gazed down the street into the heart of the town. Folks were few in sight, and those still out were making their way to their respective homes.

Even the saloon's swinging doors had an additional exterior door that sealed up the place tightly at night.

"Do you have rooms upstairs or just for visiting ladies?" Kipner asked as he returned to the counter and poured another drink. He respected the local laws of every town he visited, but this law felt excessive.

The man shook his head and finished his work. He looked uncertain as his eyes darted to a door beside the bar. There was a sense of urgency as he edged himself closer to it.

"Look, I'm just a visitor. I'm not here to cause any trouble. I just need a place to stay. Does this town have a hotel?" Kipner asked. He knew he could find out himself just by looking outside, but he was befuddled at the loss of words from the bartender. They had a fear of speaking too?

By now, the bartender had slid his way back to the wall and arrived at the closed door. He opened it from behind, and as he darted inside, he said simply, "Yes, farther down," and closed the door. Kipner heard the lock mechanism latch a second later.

He didn't lock his saloon up, Kipner thought as he shuffled outside and closed the door for him. No one was in sight. He was by himself on the boardwalk and felt like it had also become a ghost town.

Not far down the street was the town's only hotel, a single-story building that looked to have minimal rooms for the size of the city. It was decorated with hanging advertisements across its front awning of features it showcased. They all had red paint slathered across them to obscure what part they read. Hot baths, clean towels, and breakfast were no longer offered there.

As he made his way across the street, he caught a few faces staring at him from behind the safety of their window shutters. They quickly hid behind if he would glance in their direction but peeked out after he looked away.

The front door to the hotel was closed and locked. Kipner checked his pocket watch to read it was a little past six. With so many he knew watching, he didn't want to pick the lock unless he had to.

"Well, it would seem we have a newcomer to our little town," came a voice behind him. "It's a special occasion when we have a visitor."

A moment before, Kipner was alone in the streets of Coffeyville, and now a lean, young man stood alarmingly close behind. From where he appeared was anyone's guess. Kipner looked around and could not spot any suitable location he might have emerged from.

Not a speck of dirt or dust on him, the young man wore a pinstriped three-piece suit with a derby in his hand as a polite gesture. In his other hand grasped a silver ball-tipped baton to which he made a sharp, whipping motion that sent the wand into a telescopic movement, extending to the ground.

"No need for any special ceremonies," Kipner quickly interjected and offered his hand. "I'm just here for a few days, then I'll be on my way, Sheriff." He gestured with a nod to the man's badge prominently displayed on his vest in high polish.

"An astute observation, Mr...?" the young man asked.

"Kipner. Robert Kipner."

"Mr. Kipner, good. But despite my status as sheriff, I am only acting in Sheriff Polane's stead until he returns," the man said, revealing a deputy badge tucked in his vest pocket.

"Deputy Rawthorne, though most folks call me worse, I'm sure, just not in front of me."

The marshal grunted in understanding without wanting to give his status away. Most deputies he had met were pleasant to be around and often acted like the peacemaker between the citizens and a particularly hard-nosed sheriff. At the end of the day, however, the deputy still was the dog of the sheriff's orders, and the people knew better.

The two walked a short way up the road until they reached a tiny jailhouse and stepped inside. The young man offered coffee to the marshal, who accepted graciously and gingerly held the hot cup while making himself comfortable on a wood chair.

"I'm afraid the hotel closes rather early around here. I'll make sure you have a place for the night. Can't have you staying outside as our guest. Sheriff Polane would not be pleased," Rawthorne said. Both times he pronounced his boss' name, he dragged the word out into two long syllables of "poh" and "lane," it was already getting on Kipner's nerves.

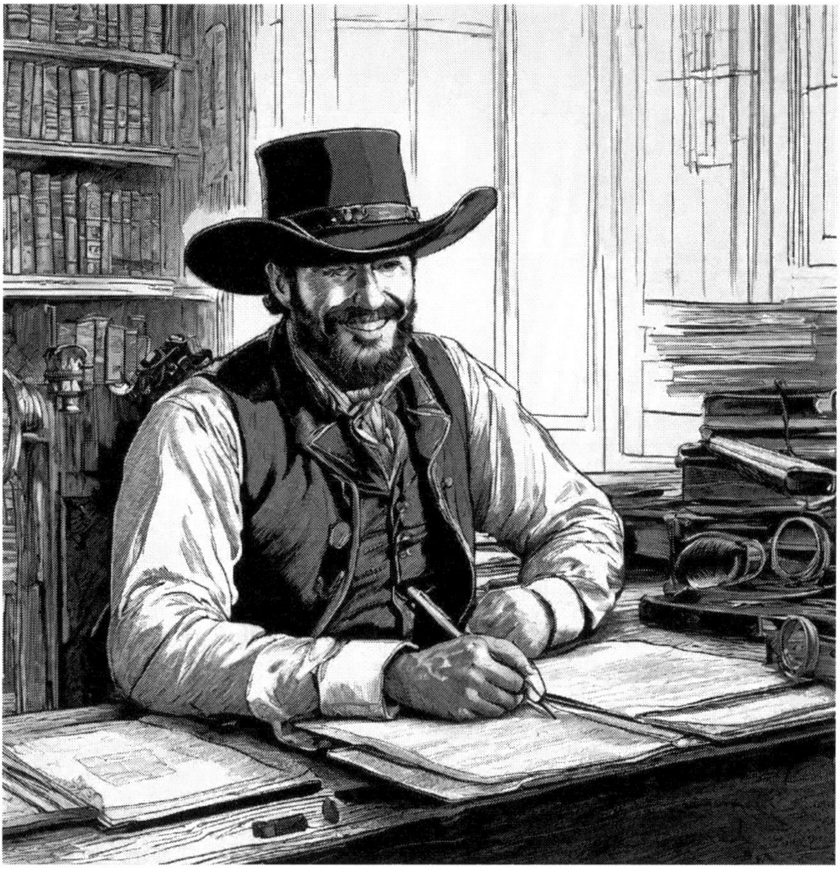

"I noticed everything closes early around here, deputy. Does the sheriff keep a tight shift around here?" Kipner said while he looked around. It was too simple, with one cell and a desk beside a rifle rack. In the corner was a square trapdoor that drew his attention.

"Absolutely. Before Sheriff Polane was appointed justice of the peace around here, it was just one deadly fight after another. He had to pull the rope tight on the folks until they settled down. Behaved like civilized individuals," Rawthorne replied. He had a bad habit of exaggerating words by emphasizing syllables, not just in the sheriff's name. Now it really annoyed Kipner.

The Wraith scratched his chin to delay saying anything, guessing his newly found youngin enjoyed talking more than he.

"Yes, sir," the deputy went right on, pulling a few sheets of paper from his desk and handing it to Kipner. "Those rules are undoubtedly the true blessings for an orderly environment."

That surprised Kipner as he began scanning the papers. He didn't expect a welcoming letter listing the do's and don't's of the town's local laws.

After reading the first law, Kipner knew how dangerous this town was. It read, "Empowerment of new laws is granted to Sheriff Polane in case of emergency. Emergency determined by the empowered authority."

Kipner let out a low whistle as he continued down the page. They were far worse than the ridiculous laws he had seen. It was illegal, punishable by twenty days in jail, not carrying about your business outside. The vagueness was harsh and clearly intentional to give the sheriff a more subjective judgment.

"All citizens cannot own property of any kind," Kipner decided to read aloud. He looked up from the paper at the deputy in expectation to comment.

"Correct, Mr. Kipner. Sheriff Polane found ownership was a common cause for criminal activities. Removing that feature eliminated the need for theft. It was one of the signature laws he put into effect."

"So, how do they acquire anything?" Kipner asked, his eyes still occasionally glancing at the odd trapdoor. He didn't see many jails with basements. Prisons were meant to temporarily hold prisoners rather than to store cargo. From Polane's list of unlawful rules, Kipner was quickly concerned about what was below the floorboards.

"Folks just have to ask. It's as simple as that. Just like assuring you have a place to sleep tonight. Sheriff Polane would not allow anyone to sleep outside," Rawthorne got up and stretched. The front window was open, most likely the only one in town, and the young man leaned with a satisfied sigh against the sill.

"Yes, Sir, Mr. Kipner. This is sure a dandy of a town for anyone staying or passing through."

The overly joyful tone of the deputy was alarming Kipner. He needed to learn more about Guido's uncle, McMannon, but he doubted little could be known if everyone was under a whip.

Before he could ask anything else, a rhythmic clanking of chains could be made out down the road. Kipner couldn't imagine anything could perk Rawthorne up more than he already was. Even so, he became downright jubilant at the sound.

The young man glanced back and gestured to join him at the window. "Here comes the boss!"

Kipner approached the front door and stepped out onto the wooden porch.

Around the area, folks bolted to whatever door they could get to first. A line of people chained together at the ankles down the street shuffled toward him. They were led by an overweight man on horseback, heavily protected from the glaring sun employing a vast brim hat.

Like Rawthorne, the rider wore a button-down long-sleeve shirt despite the unimaginable heat, but this shirt was on the verge of surrendering to his barrel chest and gut.

He might have worn it when he was fifty pounds lighter. Most of his face was hidden by the shadow of his mud-brown colored hat, and the remainder was covered by a heavily grown beard. It was unkempt and uneven, as if he had no intention of making it appear reasonable.

Where most would hang a good pistol, the stranger preferred a sawed-off shotgun on both sides of his hip. The holster's belt looked custom in design and thicker to accommodate heavy slugs, which it was adorned with. While he may not take anyone down from a distance, he cared little for wounding.

He brought the line of chained people down the road to stop in front of the jail. Each prisoner looked on the brink of dying, denied of water in the hot afternoon sun, while they shuffled their feet through the dry, dusty ground like dead men walking.

All the while shouting harsh commands at them, the rider had picked up the sight of Kipner early and hadn't taken his eyes off as he approached the marshal.

"Looks like we have a special guest in our humble little town," he said while grunting to get off his horse. Kipner could swear the horse sighed with relief.

The stranger put his hands on his hips, making it obvious they were near the pistol grips of his shotguns. He smiled handsomely though most of his face was hidden under the fur rug covering his face.

"We sure appreciate anyone honoring us with a quick visit. You'll find we keep a nice, sharp, well-disciplined community filled with delightfully caring folks." Kipner remembered the deputy had a similar opening line earlier. It was as if Rawthorne mimicked his sheriff in envy and admiration.

Behind him, the chain gang was listing side to side like masts of a ship on rough waters. Many of their mouths were gaping open, and eyes nearly rolled back in their heads. A few had fresh gashes and lesions covering their bodies with pale darkish liquid slowly oozing out.

The rotund man ignored their whimpers of mercy and gave Kipner a dramatic confused look.

"Now, perhaps you can shed some light on the conundrum I happen to possess at the moment," he said with his thumbs brushing the curve of his shotguns. "What might you be doing in my humble community?"

Kipner's hands were hanging at his sides. Despite their shortened barrels, he was confident his pistols could be pulled out of their holsters quicker than the sheriff's hog legs. He was hoping it wouldn't come to that. Although he carried a federal badge, the man before him had jurisdiction in town.

A brightly polished sheriff's badge was hanging dominantly in his shirt pocket. That gave him all the control he needed for the town. Unless threatened with violence, Kipner couldn't do much against him.

"Sheriff Polane," Kipner began nonchalantly with a smile, making sure to be deliberate in mocking the deputy who stood behind him, peering over Kipner's shoulder. The mentioning of his name raised the man's eyebrows in response.

"Your fine town happened to be on my route up to Kansas City," he lied to the sheriff. He wanted to keep the element of mystery as long as he could. He suspected he was in the presence of a renegade sheriff who wore his badge too brightly.

"Uh huh," Sheriff Polane replied, staring intensely at his interlocutor. "Mighty convenient of us to have our town on your route. Heading on to Kansas City, huh? Nice place. Have a grandma up there. Resting her soul in Elmwood."

The two looked at each other in a silent battle to judge the other or gain some insight for an advantage. Both held firm poker faces.

By now, the streets were vacant save for the two officers and the line of prisoners. No one wanted to be near the sheriff. Everyone else had retreated into any building they could reach quicker. Even so, Kipner could tell out of the corner of his eyes that most were staring out windows and between closed shutters.

One of the prisoners collapsed in the heat, knocking over another before him. The clattering of chains pulled Polane's stare from Kipner to address the fallen men. He answered by kicking them both with full force, bringing out the crackling sound of broken ribs against his foot.

He grabbed them both by the collars of their ratty clothes and hoisted them up like bags of potatoes.

Both got a face full of spittle as Polane screamed threats at them. Regardless of the intensity of his voice, none of the prisoners showed emotion or pain.

It was as if they were walking dead.

"Looks like you have plenty of work ahead with such heinous criminals," Kipner said to bring his attention back to him. "I wouldn't want to take up any more of your valuable time as I am suddenly reminded how thirsty I am."

Kipner stepped off the porch and headed past Polane toward the nearest saloon, but the sheriff stepped in his path and gently placed a hand on Kipner's shoulder. The gentle touch gradually grew to a firm lock.

In soft words, Polane said, "Sundown, you best be out of my town."

It took more than words to shake Kipner. He had witnessed horrors that had made the average man fall into convulsions from fear.

Polane might hold the town in fear with an iron fist, but unless he had more than a juvenile deputy to help, Kipner was okay with handling the sheriff if push came to shove.

Equally gentle, the Wraith replied, "With such hospitality, I might move on in. I hear the courthouse is vacant." He pulled the other cigar from his shirt pocket and forced the grip to ease with a meaningful step away, lighting it and blowing smoke into the air. His walk took him into the saloon without looking back, but he could feel the glare of daggers from Polane.

"Better watch yourself then. Closely," the sheriff muttered loud enough to be heard, then forcefully encouraged the front man on the chains to walk into the jail.

*

It had been the first night in weeks Kipner was fortunate enough to lay on a bed rather than a blanket against hard soil. He was looking forward to a pleasant night. He hoped the unusually tight law Polane administered in town would give a quiet evening. Typically he could sleep through the usual ruckus in a western city. Even so, Polane ensured that everyone was well aware if he flashed his badge at any night.

The night was somewhat young, approaching midnight when a small family of three broke down in their wagon just at the edge of town. Hailing from the southern Oklahoma town of Durant, the simple couple and seven-year-old son hoped to find better farmland in Nebraska. Their wagon had barely made it this far before two wheels broke over a large rut Kipner had noticed when he arrived the day before. Stranded in the middle of the night, they had chosen to settle in their wagon and deal with it come sunrise.

Unfortunately, their plan did not match Sheriff Polane's plan. Kipner arose drearily to the sound of shouting coming from down the street. He stepped out onto his hotel balcony dressed in his union suit for a better look. Not far away was Polane, holding one of his sawed-off shotguns dangerously close to the father's proximity and questioning him at the top of his voice.

Clearly, the family was rattled with fear from the aggression, and the father stuttered fiercely while his son and wife cried.

Kipner watched as the family was forced off their wagon onto the ground, falling painfully to the hardpan. Manacles were slapped on the father and dragged towards the courthouse while his wife and son tread in the heels of the sheriff. It was a wonder how violently short-tempered Polane was, switching so quickly from his casually cantankerous attitude to an all-out belligerent behavior.

But what reasoning behind the sheriff's distrust for outsiders, even casual travelers, was unknown to the marshal. It may be some xenophobia, but it was more to hide something from the outside world. More was going on in the massive jailhouse he dragged the father into than just a lot of holding cells.

It pained Kipner not to interfere, but he knew he had to carefully gauge his next move in town.

So far, he had kept his distance to avoid confrontations that might lead to his incarceration. Even so, he knew he would have to investigate what happened behind the courthouse. He doubted there was another entrance other than the front, so chances are he would have to get in there the hard way.

The cries of the wife and son echoed on the streets for several minutes after the courthouse door slammed closed in their faces, the father having disappeared inside with the sheriff. From one window, the deputy peered out at them, a look of concern on his face. The sheriff returned to the front office, and Rawthorne quickly changed his expression to that of sinister, staring eagerly at the sobbing people. The front door swung back open, and Polane reached for both of them, only snagging the woman before the young son scampered out of his grasp and dashed off.

The sight following sent Kipner downstairs with two leaping strides. Without hesitation, Polane pulled out his sawed-off shotgun and down the boy as he ran away. His motion was swift and savage, with no expression of regret. He commanded Rawthorne to retrieve the body over the woman's screams of agony at losing her boy.

A moment later, before Rawthorne could react, Kipner was out on the street with both guns and locked on the sheriff. He had hoped to discover more of the secret to this town over time, but the sight of murdering an innocent child put the marshal into a temperament that gave him his dark nickname. He looked like a tiger about to pounce with a cold, solid stare.

Polane stopped pulling the woman indoors. The sight of the pistols pointed at him even momentarily stopped the woman from screaming.

His emergence from the hotel was so swift everyone was caught off guard.

There was no mocking smile from the sheriff this time. But his voice was steady and sure of himself. He spoke as a matter of fact rather than boastfully.

"You best return to your room, Kipner," he began. "I will deal with you later."

The pistols remained pointed true at him.

Kipner said nothing in response and let his guns do the talking. He was in no mood to have an idle chit-chat. He doubted there would be an arrest tonight, guessing from Sheriff Polane's attitude. He would not go down quietly from whatever he was up to in the jail.

The grip on the woman was loosened, and she slumped to the ground, sobbing quietly as she watched.

From the window stood Rawthorne, unsure of what to do next. His eyes were wide and went back and forth between the two gunmen.

At last, Polane stood upright and straightened his clothes, returning to his modest behavior and controlling his temper. His blood pressure still boiled beneath his skin, but he kept it hidden.

"Very well, Mr. Kipner. I will deal with you now," he said as he stood in the doorway. Kipner made sure when he bolted out of the hotel's front door that he was distanced from the two hog legs. The bead he had on him wouldn't have mattered either way.

"Just as I suspect there is more to you than a man passing through to Kansas City," Polane continued, "I'm sure you have your suspicions of me. You may believe my laws here are too harsh for your taste, but I don't care. They're my laws, and I hold anyone to them."

He gestured to the body lying a dozen feet from him. "Folks break the law. Punishment can be severe. While this family broke the law, they were going to jail for only a few days. But he didn't accept that and decided to run. That law is broken. We don't tolerate it around here."

"What law did they break to get the treatment you gave them?" Kipner said in a low growl through gritted teeth.

The sheriff momentarily looked down the street at the broken wagon and said, "Sleeping on public property. I don't want to find folks sleeping outdoors in my town. Dangerous at night with predators, sometimes it gets frigid cold, and I won't allow my village to have bums on the streets. The law's for their protection. Besides, the wagon blocked most of the road where morning traffic through. I don't want to have my thoroughfare congested with some broken-down wagon. Obstruction of traffic.

By now, Kipner's temper of vengeance had somewhat subdued though his pistols were still pointed. Kipner hadn't been fired upon. The sheriff should be shackled and punished for what he did to the innocent boy. However, shooting him now would be an act of revenge, and he would not be protected by the federal government.

Polane knew where he stood, reigned supreme, and took advantage of every situation. He knew if he addressed himself as a U. S. marshal, the sheriff would come down hard on him. His badge was affixed to his shirt upstairs while he stood in only his underwear.

"Now, are you done wasting my time here?" Polane asked. "If you want to commit murder, you go right ahead. Two witnesses must testify at the next court hearing, which would not bode well against your testimony."

There was a note in his voice mentioning the court hearing that reminded him of Judge McMannon and why he had come to Coffeyville. There would be no fair trial if he oversaw the judiciary.

Frustratingly, Kipner holstered his pistols and watched as the look of victory flashed across Polane's face. He grabbed the woman by the hair as he nodded with a smile to Kipner and pulled her in. Rawthorne went outside and wrapped the poor boy in a blanket, and carried him down to the undertaker. All he could do was look at Kipner and shrug.

*

Morning came too early for the marshal, and he felt like he had a night of drinking. His head rattled as he rose from the bed and washed his face. The strange experience with the traveling family last night was only one of the numerous disturbances Sheriff Polane solved with arrests. He deduced the safest place in town was either in a cemetery grave or elsewhere.

By his count, Kipner had fourteen people in jail from arrests during one night alone. There was no room to imprison that many people. It solidified his fear of where the trapdoor led.

He tucked his U. S. Marshal badge into his traveling bag. He locked it in the hotel room Rawthorne had graciously arranged to open. He would be suspended if he lost it, but he needed bait to test his theory. He didn't get a chance to ask Rawthorne what citizens had to do in return for asking for anything. He guessed it was some form of payment though not necessarily in cash.

It was apparent the townsfolk were petrified of being around him. Whenever he left the office every morning, people nearly bolted into whatever building they were near and closed the shutters. He would make his rounds early in the day, casually harassing his townsfolk by pressuring them into a harsh condition or simply arresting them for clearly fictitious laws.

On one occasion, he completely seized control of a business because some drunk had broken their window the night before. While the shop owner begged and pleaded, the sheriff warned him not to cause a scene in public, yet another crime. He reasoned that the owner could not administer proper security to prevent such a thing. The matter was settled in the end, with the owner being led into the jailhouse and the shop locked up. Hours later, a different man exited the jailhouse and entered the shop with a key.

When Kipner went to investigate, he was quickly interrupted by Polane and Rawthorne to kindly mind his own business.

Another peculiar moment happened after wandering out of sight nonchalantly for an hour or two.

Sheriff Polane would return with a line of people chained at the ankle and escort them into the jail.

This would happen at regular intervals far too close together to still have such a thriving community.

Sheriff Polane had left for the day after inquiring about Rawthorne. His destination and reasoning were not available to give him.

"Sheriff Polane assists other nearby towns and cities as needed," Rawthorne explained. "His duties range too greatly to detail."

His hotel stay was free when he asked how much he owed. The deputy reiterated the law of no ownership, which included temporary hospitality.

To test this, Kipner returned to the saloon from the day before to find the coin for the cigar still resting on the counter. The bartender paid zero attention even when Kipner tried handing it to him.

Strangely, it was an effective means of operation. Still, Kipner knew the town needed to be more capable of providing all necessities and would require importing and trading goods.

"Sheriff Polane provides all forms of need for the town, Mr. Kipner," Deputy Rawthorne explained. "There is no need to be concerned. It may be unusual for outsiders to adapt to our lifestyle. Still, you can see we have great order and safe conditions simply by walking down the street."

Kipner continued trying to be convincing, but getting anything but a well-rehearsed reply took a lot of work. Because of the strict law, he could only monitor the jail once Rawthorne left so he could inspect the trapdoor, but the deputy seldom was far from it.

Giving up on the jail for the moment, Kipner turned his attention to his true purpose visiting to find McMannon. He wanted to avoid asking Rawthorne so he could keep his reasoning for being there a secret. Still, after several hours of attempting to get any word out of the townsfolk, he gave up and asked him.

"His Gracious Honor McMannon, you mean," Rawthorne began, and Kipner immediately regretted asking. His pronunciation took half a day to get through the title with his exaggerated speech. "Why he is our illustrious judge who presides over the entire southeast portion of Kansas. His district is considered on a technicality that resulted in his reaching almost Kansas City in the jurisdiction.

"Because of this grand range," he continued when asked where McMannon currently was, "he is hearing in Wichita this week. Are you in need of His Gracious, Honorable services?"

A little too hastily, Kipner shook his head. "Not at the moment. I had only heard of him while in Texas. Some bounty hunter spoke high praise, and I wanted to meet him in case I ever needed his help."

Rawthorne stared a few seconds at Kipner, taking in what he had said. Finally, he said, "Uh huh," but did not comment further.

While Kipner wasn't in a hurry, he didn't like waiting. Each day was strangely routine in Coffeyville. People kept to themselves, the sheriff disappeared daily, and Rawthorne guarded an empty jail. No matter how many people were arrested, they were all ushered in, but from Kipner's observation, were never released.

The townsfolk behaved strangely, but even stranger was their typical daily life. There were only so many businesses in Coffeyville, and the rest were residential in some form. Most of the people were simply going from one house to another. Only some actually worked. On several occasions, Kipner followed a few who exited from one building, quickly darted to the next, disappeared behind the door, and locked it. Try as he might, he could only gain entry into the houses with citizens' help. Even more peculiar, his lock picks would not work on the doors after he discovered they all could be barred from the inside.

With each secret learned, he became more frustrated with the oddity of the town. His instinct told him something sinister was amiss. The sheriff had done an outstanding job hiding whatever was happening behind closed doors.

Kipner gave plenty of a head start before following Polane, skirting behind building after building.

The sheriff went through the small town, soon reaching the northern edge where a railroad crossed east to west. There had been no whistle of its approach that surely would have been noticed anywhere from such a small community.

From what Kipner could tell from his distance, no traveling passengers were on board. Little was offered in terms of hiding close to the train.

The station had no building and was comprised solely of a large, flat platform littered with sacks and crates.

The line of prisoners Polane continued feeding into his jail came from the train, and another train would arrive every few hours. He would never engage in the conductor, nor was the conductor ever in sight. It was as if the train was running on its own.

Polane would slide open the large cargo train door and violently pull the first chained people out.

This would go on several times a day.

The railroad traveled much through Kansas and snaked its way through Missouri. However, each train that arrived lacked any identification and could have been the same engine for all Kipner could make of things.

While he witnessed the most likely illegal activity, he thought back to the von List in Hobgoblin Creek and his connection to Judge McMannon here in town. There had been no sign of the "glorious honorable whatever" judge. Still, he had kept on his toes, expecting him to be just as sinister as Polane. It was always dangerous when a sheriff and a local judge were crooked. There was little people could do. Council voting by the town's folks could rule them out, but then it would take the efforts of sending a message to the governor requesting a replacement.

During that time, which could be weeks if not months (or he might ignore the letter altogether), the sheriff and judge would likely make their lives miserable. Most would never dare do such a thing for fear of what retribution might befall them.

"Oh, they're not from around here," Rawthorne answered after Kipner inquired about the prisoners. "Sheriff Potane finds folk elsewhere and brings them in here. I've never been with him at any of his Gatherings, as he calls them. Only his uncle, his Glorious Honor Judge McMannon, will sometimes ride along, but I'm not sure why. His Glorious Honor Judge McMannon is at an age even getting on a horse is a chore."

There had only been a little riding from the sheriff except to meander to the railroad tracks to pick up a shipment of more people.

"Looked to me like he orders from a Montgomery Wards catalog and picks them up at the train station," Kipner said as he helped himself to a fresh coffee Rawthorne had finished brewing.

"In a way, I guess he does," the young man said with a dawning expression. "Where ever he goes, it's where criminals are plentiful. At least, that is what he tells me. Then he arranges for them all to be transported here. Makes it more accessible than hauling them by wagon and risking a prison escape."

Before the fourth night, Kipner was convinced nothing would change. He was beginning to doubt he would get anywhere when he was awoken at night to the usual commotion outside. He was already awake from sleeping poorly all week, so he gathered himself and stepped out onto the balcony of his room. Instead of seeing Sheriff Polane making a scene, Rawthorne exited the jail and disappeared into the darkness down the road.

The sheriff was nowhere to be seen, and the marshal's sharp eyes noticed the deputy failed to lock the door when he left. The lamps had been blown out in the jail, leaving it dark inside and perfect for Kipner to make a move.

He wasn't sure how long he had, so he hurriedly threw his clothes on in the dark and down to the street. Before he crossed the road, he paused quietly to make out any sounds that might come from the direction of the deputy. He heard nothing. It was like a vacuum of silence that echoed in his ears, but that was typical for his nightly experiences here.

There was no cover while he crossed the road, but at this hour, everyone was asleep. All the same, he subconsciously looked around for any signs of motion and then moved to the front door.

He recalled a bar for the jail like the rest of the town, but no one was there to lower it unless someone was just sitting in the dark. As he predicted, the door opened, and he deftly slipped inside.

Since childhood, he always seemed to see better than others in the dark. His eyes adapted quicker, and he could make out more detail than any typical person. His talent moved to third best with his brethren in the Huckleberry Hucksters. Shade and Specter, Kipner swore, could read a book in pitch black. Pulling scare pranks growing up was too easy for them as they could hide in shadows and leap out.

Kipner was blind in the jail. His confidence in his talent drained immediately, and he panicked. There was no explanation; he should be able to see anything. It wasn't that dark inside, but he could not even make out his hand.

Behind him, the door slowly closed shut, and he became disoriented. For the moment, he crouched down and stood perfectly still listening to his environment. There had been a window in the front near the door, but that, too, was shut closed.

His memory was sharp, however, and he let himself breathe and recall the room's layout. The desk wouldn't be far from where he stood, but when he reached out, to his utmost horror, he felt a raw dirt wall that flaked in clumps to his touch. Four walls of dirt were in every direction. This hole was deep. Very deep. How did he even get here?

It reminded him of his parent's root cellar when he was a child, where he would imagine exploring vast underground caves filled with hidden treasures. The memory gave him no solace in his situation, though. The surrounding air was stagnant and stale, with a hint of mildew.

Whoever created the hole had thought of various methods of escaping. Kipner tried leaning his shoulders into one wall and pressing his feet into the opposite to walk up the wall, but the soft mud fell in large chunks. The diameter was just beyond arm's length to brace himself while climbing upward.

His first fear was the walls collapsing and suffocating him under pounds and pounds of soil. He avoided digging his way out for now and hoped his abductor would reveal himself soon.

Sitting on the soft soil was comfortable, and the hole size allowed him to stretch his legs while supporting his back against a wall. He sat for many hours in the dark, feeling his thoughts and memories surge in his mind. At some point in the night, he drifted off to sleep.

*

When he awoke, food had been placed beside him. He had been served cold beans, half a slice of bread, and a shot glass of water. He wasn't the hungriest but ate the meal in case he needed the energy later. The lack of water worried him. He knew the risks of breaking into the jail, but he didn't expect this sinister punishment.

The sheriff showed considerable prejudice against him being in town without knowing who Kipner was. Perhaps, he did know him after all. Rawthorne made it clear Polane knew he was an authoritative figure of some kind, just not what title.

By now, Kipner could guess confidently they had searched his bedroom at the hotel and found his badge. He was sure it would spook Polane to believe he was there for other reasons, all related to the sheriff's operation. There would be little concern from Polane if Kipner died down there. Polane would know a U. S. Marshal doesn't regularly report on their whereabouts.

Time took a lot of work to gauge. He could only hear his pocket watch ticking, and he wasn't at the point of madness yet to sit and count the ticks heard.

More food never came, and he was already thirsty again. His legs ached, so he tried standing up for a bit to stretch. Methods of escaping came back to his mind, and he wondered if making footholds in the soil would hold his weight if made deep enough. Disregarding the cave-in risk, Kipner tried scraping chunks of mud and dirt about four to six inches away.

His fingers grabbed a metal bar. He paused as his hand felt a thin horizontal bar that led to a junction with a vertical bar. He felt no more earth past the bars, just open air. With more fervor, he tore through the chunky dirt, pulling large pieces away to expose more metal bars joined in a grid.

It wasn't long before he discovered his hole was a cage in disguise. He couldn't make out the reasoning for such a ploy. Perhaps it was some psychological effort to cause fear of being buried alive and persuade him to try to escape.

Once he cleared off most of the cage, he stood several feet above the bottom with the amount of dirt he had pulled down. He climbed several feet further to learn the cell had a locked trapdoor at the top.

Several minutes passed, and he realized his unique ability to see well in the dark returned now that the dirt had been pulled away. He was still in a dark room.

He could make out more cages like his evenly spaced in all four directions. The cells were welded at the top to cross beams, suspended in the air. He proved that by shoveling more dirt through the cage bars, sending chunks below. The clumps splattered on the floor a few dozen feet down.

Although not perfectly clear in the darkness, Kipner could make out people in the nearby cages. They all sat motionless. None of them moved, even when he called out for them.

Now that he better understood his surroundings, he began working on a plan to escape. He climbed the side of the cage to the roof and observed the lock was nothing more than a padlock he had picked countless times before. It was awkward holding himself up with just his feet to free both hands to work, but it soon gave way to his skills.

The trapdoor to the cage was rusty but opened with little resistance, and he hoisted himself up to the welded I-beam above. About a foot above the I-beam was the ceiling made of steel plates. Yet another trapdoor was fixed directly above his cage but barricaded from the other side. The beam was his only avenue, so he went to one of the nearby cages.

They seemed to go in every direction as far as his eyes could see. He counted several dozen, which could be doubled or tripled depending on how far out they went.

Unlocking the next cage from above was much easier, and he slipped down to get a better look at the prisoner. He found it peculiar it lacked any dirt, but perhaps the person had already discovered what he just had and cleared it all out.

The inhabitant of this cage was a woman. She had no clothes on and was unconscious but alive. From a quick glance, Kipner could tell she was severely malnourished and deathly pale. There was no color in her lips. There was no sign of ever being given a meal.

He knelt down and tried to gently wake her without startling her. When that didn't work, he lightly patted her cheek and called out. Nothing worked. She was in a deep sleep, or drugged state; very little would wake her.

The inspection was interrupted by their cage jolting in one direction and beginning to move. Ear-piercing metal screeching on metal came from all around as cages slid slowly against the metal beams above. The sound was intense and painful as they slid slowly across the room and through holes in the wall.

More light came from the other side of these walls, and Kipner climbed out of the cage and across the beam to get a better look. The pens moved dreadfully slowly, and he could reach the hole long before his cell reached it.

Before him, down below, was a room of assorted medical apparatus and chemical experiments scattered across several tables that surrounded a large furnace. Next to the burning stove was a mining car filled with Devil Stone, softly glowing against the amber light.

Several naked people, each nearing death, shoveled the glowing stones onto a smooth slab of rock, then crushed to fine ash by a rolling stone. The process looked backbreaking, and they barely appeared strong enough to operate it.

Another man, too old to tell, was going over a letter and mumbling to himself. It was impossible to hear him above the shrieking metal passing Kipner.

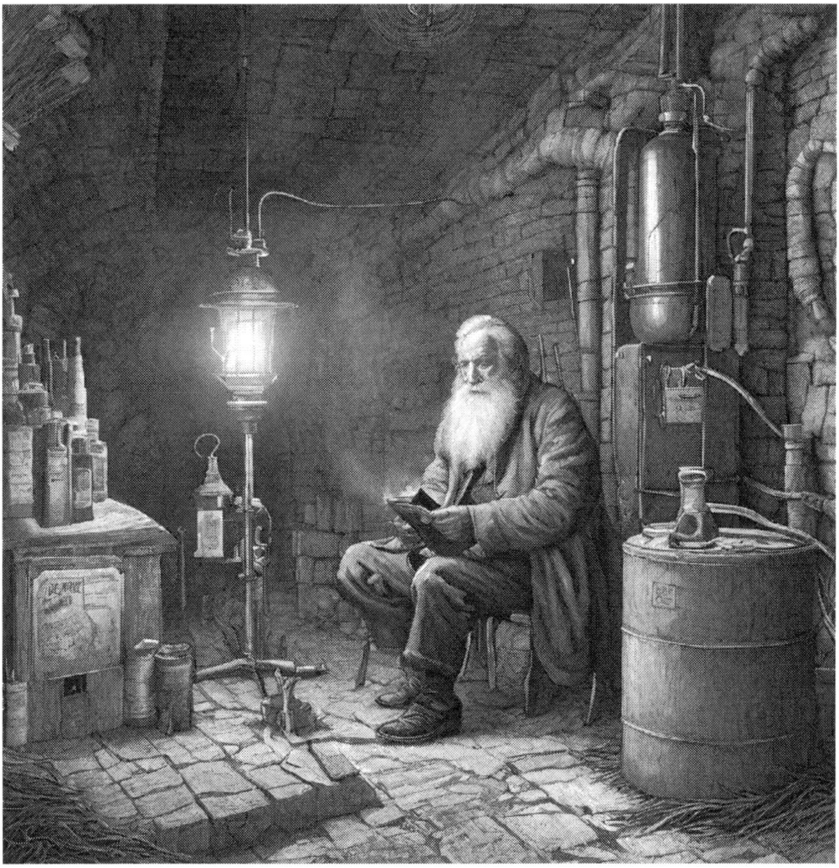

The cages came into the room one by one. They were lowered to where one of the naked people could insert a needle into the arms of the unconscious prisoners that drew blood out through tubes into nearby jars.

When a jar was full, another naked person would gather handfuls of crushed Devil Stone, pour them into the pots of blood, and then place them beside the man reading.

The man blindly reached for a stirring rod without taking his eyes off the letter. He casually spun it within the concoction, bringing the jar to his lips, and drank slowly. He sipped like it was a cup of coffee. The rest of the pots had the same ash deposited in them and placed in an ice box.

Only one victim was needed for this procedure as the screeching metal finally stopped. The two naked people exited the room through a concealed door and left the man alone.

It was all signs of some kind of madman as he peered over the letter. He stood about thirty feet below Kipner. His federal jurisdiction might be different had his pistols been at his side that moment. Carefully poised on the beam, Kipner listened carefully to pick up what the man was saying out loud.

He was muttering to himself as he read aloud the letter, his voice raising with excitement as he continued.

"'...has been with great success!' Excellent news! I knew it! I knew it. 'Continue efforts at fourfold in a fortnight.' Fourfold? That's preposterous! I lack the resources!"

He went from triumphantly happy to raging mad within seconds, crumbling the paper in his gnarled, bony fingers and shaking violently as he sat in a chair. His breathing was heavy, and his muttering continued as he mumbled ideas about gaining more materials. As if he was dictating to someone, he made comments and jabs while reading out loud.

"Suppose Harold owes me a favor. Maybe the post in Arcadia. Ship from Louis and have the boy get it," the ancient man spoke as Kipner dared to get closer to hear. He was slightly fatigued from the imprisonment and lack of exercise, but his legs held up for the moment.

The marshal knew he had to subdue the man quickly but carefully, or he might call upon Rawthorne or even the sheriff if he was still in town. Hitting him over the head too heavily, the man might not wake up again.

To say he was frail would be generous.

Kipner's only way down was through the lowered cage, and he took more time to reduce noise as much as possible. With every inch he made, he dreaded the thought the old man would turn around and see him.

Carefully he stepped onto the floor and positioned himself just behind the old man. His motion slowed to almost a standstill as he came down with the back of his hand to the old man's neck. His arms felt like lead pushing through sand.

"You would be doing me a great favor," said the old man without turning to face Kipner.

"I have been waiting for the reward I deserve after death for a long time. So far, it would seem my ticker is quite strong. I might outlive the boy." He smiled a toothless grin at Kipner as he slowly turned around to face the marshal. The holes where teeth once joined at the gums had grown over, leaving a smooth, wet line of soft tissue speckled with black spots.

Despite the restraint in his arms, Kipner could not resist his mouth and could speak.

"I have no intention of killing you," answered the marshal. "I just want information. I want answers."

The old man struggled to turn his chair around to face Kipner. His eyes were half open, and he swayed slightly as his piercing blue eyes looked up. He looked older than before and incredibly tired.

"I am sure you do, marshal. Polane found your badge in your room. You were right to keep us in the dark as long as you did. I hear the boy would have shot you dead the moment he saw you if he had known. No, for the moment, let's stop being foolish with the karate chop, eh?" the judge commented, and Kipner's arms went to his sides against his wishes. Some mythical abilities had him wholly helpless and ultimately controlling the man.

"You came to our humble little town to find answers about me, Mr. Kipner, and I am considering fulfilling that request. But first, let me tell you a bedtime story," he began.

While Kipner wasn't sure what to expect upon meeting Judge McMannon, he had not prepared himself to see such an ancient, shriveled old man. He was well beyond years of suitably overseeing court hearings and should have retired long ago. But there was considerable vigor stirring in him. In just a few moments of Kipner watching him, McMannon's skin tightened.

The wrinkles around his eyes lessened. Numerous age marks faded away on his skin. In a slow time-lapse, the old man was reversing his age.

He took another sip of his bloody tonic, finishing it with a satisfied sigh. "It tastes as bad as you think but keeps me alive for another year. I still have things to finish before I move on.

"A bedtime story," McMannon said, returning to his original subject. "Not terribly long ago, this fine country was at peace. Explorers came here with high hopes and rich dreams of prosperity. They shared their wisdom with those they encountered, which gave their lives wellness.

"Yet all that time, little did they know a great secret was held from the newcomers. A secret that would jeopardize their lives in years to come."

"All the while, certain native folks of this country carried strange beliefs and rituals the newcomers didn't understand. Their faith believed they kept back evil spirits. Still, Christian beliefs had been too ingrained in the newcomers to have open minds and unravel the secret before it was too late. I don't even think the natives knew their beliefs were true," McMannon continued.

"Then one day, those rotten, backstabbing, backward people unleashed their secret of control over a powerful force to which mankind was not meant to witness. They intentionally withdrew their control over the nightmarish evil they once nurtured and manifested through their dances, chanting, and trances. The country was soon overrun with terrors.

You call it the Harrow. I call it an opportunity of fortune."

Kipner remained frozen in place, but he wasn't fatigued from standing. It felt like someone was bracing him and relieving all the tension.

McMannon continued, "While the country might be going to Hell, plenty of these little beauties have surfaced everywhere."

The cart of Devil Stones sat nearby, and he hobbled over to take one out. "I haven't scratched the surface of its potential, but I came up with a few beneficial uses. Every few hours, my drink gives me vitality that keeps my heart alive."

He gestured nonchalantly toward where the rest of the cages still hung. "As you saw, I have more than enough specimens to keep it pumping for years."

"Enough bedtime stories," Kipner interjected. Being restrained after his brief imprisonment was losing his temper. "Your nephew, Guido, told me you knew where these creatures originated. How they awakened. You're telling me it was all brought on by natives throwing curses on the ground? What makes you think that?"

Over near McMannon's desk was a shelf of a few books to which he withdrew one. It had a blue cloth cover with pressed silver lettering on the spine that was fading. The pages were yellowed but not brittle while McMannon flipped through them.

"I've been fascinated by our primitive neighbors ever since I was a boy," he said, slowly thumbing page to page. "They spend countless hours hooping, hollering, and dancing about campfires, chanting rhythmically. All that effort and wasted energy in hopes that their pretend myths and made-up legends are true. Ah, here,"

McMannon turned the book around, having found a part he wished to share with Kipner. It was an illustration of natives performing a Sun Dance. A gathering of people was circling a fire while others prayed for healing. Some were giving blood sacrifices to the fire on behalf of the community.

Opposite the illustration was a page of native writings too foreign for Kipner to translate.

Satisfied with his presentation, McMannon returned the book to the shelf.

"They've known about the Harrow long before we arrived, Mr. Kipner. They have had the power to keep them at bay, but now they seek to obliterate us newcomers by unleashing that evil upon us all."

The theory was not new. Many people blamed the natives for calling forth all demonic formations that wreak havoc on innocents.

Kipner's father had been a missionary when he was a child. Originally from New York, James had traveled as far as the Mississippi River to spread the gospel of God to natives. In his teachings, his father would show concern towards those he preached to and tried to persuade them to refrain from performing such rituals that might endanger the lives of others. From Robert's recollections from his father's stories, the natives struggled to understand his message. He was among the first to believe the country's downfall would lie on the natives' shoulders.

Kipner had no theories of his own. He was expected to discover the truth behind the Harrow's origin based on facts, not superstitious guesses.

"Another wonderful discovery I have found with this Devil Stone, as everyone calls it," McMannon said as he fondled the glowing stone between his knobby fingers, "is its instability. Highly volatile in small concentrations."

To demonstrate, he gently ground the stone against the edge of the desk, sending bits of sparks to the ground, where they each gave a thunderous pop.

"Not much is needed to set it off," McMannon said with a smile.

Kipner needed to get somewhere with the judge. It was like McMannon became a school teacher and was eager to instruct him on his vast knowledge. For now, Kipner wanted to delay whatever the judge had in store for him.

"Rawthorne said you were in Wichita until the end of the week," he reflected.

The judge nodded in agreement. "He believes so, yes. I can't be in two places simultaneously, but I can't avoid the demand for my services."

He picked up and put down the letter he had been reading when Kipner entered the room from above. "I'm too old to travel anymore, but I still need to keep my agreements secured with others. So I made a deal to be in two places at once."

The ground rumbled gently as if a machine murmured to life far below and then halted. McMannon leaned back in his chair and closed his eyes with a smile, breathing slowly.

"Yes," he said, drawing the word out as if soothed by something. "I hear you. I always will listen to you."

Awkwardly Kipner remained frozen beside McMannon as the judge sat in silence and slowly moved his head from side to side. There was a soundless melody playing that seemed to be for only him to hear.

"I shall," McMannon finally said after several seconds of pausing. "I am yours to command."

Opening his eyes, the judge acted like he saw Kipner for the first time and smiled warmly. The effects of the tonic he had drank before had reached their peak and gave him a youthful yet frail appearance.

"Far, far, far below us, further than anyone on Earth can travel, sleeps Oryx."

Another pause was briefer when Kipner showed no recognition or excitement. McMannon was losing his confidence in his presence the more Kipner was not impressed with his reveal. The proud smile slowly faded but continued regardless.

"Its great powers are past our comprehension, but it has been generous to me. A part of me now carries out my daily duties elsewhere, allowing me to remain here to focus on what I prefer to be doing.

"There are those in this world who seek domination, and I can provide such a path for them by aiding them in copious amounts of Devil's Stone. They're more than welcome to do it. I need but a fraction of what I possess to survive.

"And in return, my boy fetches me the worthless bodies delivered on time." He raised his empty glass jar of human blood in a toast to emphasize his deal. "Petty criminals, citizens who refuse to be law-abiding, and the ilk all come to me now."

In exchange for Devil's Stone to military vigilantes, they would send him the prisoners and kidnapped victims. He would just need an ample supply of stone.

"Hobgoblin Creek wasn't a silver mine, was it?" Kipner asked, drawing himself back to why he was there.

"It was initially when we bought the stake," McMannon replied. "My brother, Guido's father, was the true miner. I was the brain between the two and recognized the Devil's Stone when he came up with a bushel. I knew we had something valuable given to the right people until those inbred townsfolks stole our property right out from under our noses!"

The memory made the judge shake with anger. He began coughing violently for a long time, finally dabbing his mouth with a kerchief. Kipner saw blood spattering against the white cotton when he laid it on the desk.

The glance didn't go unnoticed by the judge. He muttered after he caught his breath, "Consequences of immortality. It's not my blood anyway."

Kipner had had enough of being restrained. He tried to resist without straining to test if whatever power McMannon had on him was still in effect after his coughing fit. He swore it was loosening, but it might be his imagination.

McMannon clapped his hands once together and perked up, looking at Kipner better. "Now, what to do with you? You're the most vigorous specimen I've seen in years, so your blood should be rich in iron and mix well with the rock.

"But we need to do a better job of keeping you where you belong. Now where do you hide that lock pick of yours?" the judge asked rhetorically while beginning his search on Kipner. He quickly found and removed it from Kipner's pocket, leaving it on his desk.

He paused a moment with a thought and slowly turned back to look at the Wraith. His eye had a bright glimmer as if he marveled at the notion it was his idea.

"Unless...you would be willing to open your mind...to other possibilities?"

From below his feet, Kipner could hear the rumble return momentarily. This time, McMannon didn't relish in the pleasure of the moment. Instead, it was Kipner who listened to the call.

It began like a soft whisper or cool breeze against the ear, then blossomed into a voice or a strong thought planted in his mind. He didn't hear a voice like someone speaking to him directly but more like a memory of someone's presence and the various quotes they were known to have said.

The sensation was not unpleasant, and he closed his eyes to focus on it more closely.

There was an idea, Kipner thought, of escaping his situation, but the method was against his code of law. McMannon, despite his brittle age, needed to answer for the crimes he had committed along with his son, Polane. Even Rawthorne had been an accomplice and should be tried as well.

He could be freed from McMannon's bonds, but only if he made a deal with the source that planted the idea in his head. Whatever it was, far below him in some dark, forgotten cavity that could reach the surface with just its mental capability, it presented its offer and awaited the Wraith's answer.

In a flash of thoughts, Kipner envisioned the countless people that had been wrongfully imprisoned down below here in cages, barely fed, and bled to death slowly for the benefit of an evil, shriveled old man who clung to life. He had been tried; there would be no doubt he would hang for his deeds.

At this point, the marshal knew he wasn't getting out of the situation without help, and his life was now in jeopardy. His frustration built up while constricted by the old man's forces was too much to bare.

McMannon's face was shocked as Kipner lunged at the man's throat, squeezing it with both hands and sending the judge's face into deep shades of reds and blues. It was quick and easy, however, because the old man put up no resistance and embraced his death. The last of his life slipped out of his eyes, and he drew his last breath. He smiled at Kipner. It was not of peace or of being at ease but rather malice.

Leaving the body where it fell, he returned his lock pick to his pocket and quickly examined the rest of the books. He selected the one McMannon had shown, the only one of interest or potential value to him, leaving the rest of chemical and medical interest.

Without McMannon, the prisoners would likely starve to death. Kipner felt around for the cleverly concealed door used earlier and stepped into a stairwell above the cage chamber. There were dozens, if not hundreds, of metal trapdoors, all bolted closed. Throughout the large room were naked prisoners, much like he saw before opening each door one by one and lowering a plate of beans and a shot of water to the cages below.

The sheer scale of operation McMannon had to run to create this situation was hard for Kipner to fathom. It was nearly self-operating as he used the same people who were trapped.

Kipner was a federal investigator, but ultimately, he was just as much a protector of innocents as any other badge. None of the feeding prisoners interfered while he went about unlocking trapdoors. However, after opening several, he realized freeing everyone would be herculean.

Despite his best efforts, none of the caged prisoners moved to flee. He had no idea if they were alive or dead.

He was becoming desperate. He wanted to escape Coffeyville, Kansas, as quickly as possible. Deep down, he knew he couldn't rescue them; worse, Kipner knew they would not survive if he sent word for help.

He was in over his head, making decisions that went against every code of honor he held true to his job. Whatever deal he made with What Lies Beneath still rang in his mind. After hearing a strange voice in his head, he just killed an unarmed man.

All around him were naked men and women barely stumbling consciously from cage to cage, dumping beans and water on the prisoners below until it was their time to return to their cell and others take their place. Kipner watched the mindless people, stripped of their lives and dignity, hopelessly move about him.

Overwhelmed with regret and sorrow, Kipner fell to his knees and sobbed quietly in the dark. He felt as hopeless as those around him and knew he had to leave them to their ill fate. It tore him apart, knowing he abandoned innocents.

*

"I know you're in here, you worthless child! So help me. I am going to make you regret running!"

The cold, dark spot a young boy had chosen to hide was cramped even for his small size, but he knew it was difficult for her to reach when he was spotted, which he knew was coming soon. Try as he might, no place in the house could keep him from being found by his mother. It was horrifying.

Throughout the house, the woman with crazed eyes, glassy and engorged, searched for the minor child with a lantern in her hand and a leather whip in the other. The flickering flame danced from the lantern and swept across the floor and cabinet. The creeks of doors opening and closing resonated in his ears and made his skin crawl. He was frozen inside.

"I am going to make you hurt. You know it pains me, but you won't listen, will you? Will you?! Ungrateful, worthless little burden!" the screeching voice boomed too closely for the child to feel safe. The cabinet doors flung open, and a gnarled, bony arm tipped with knobby-clawed fingers surged towards him.

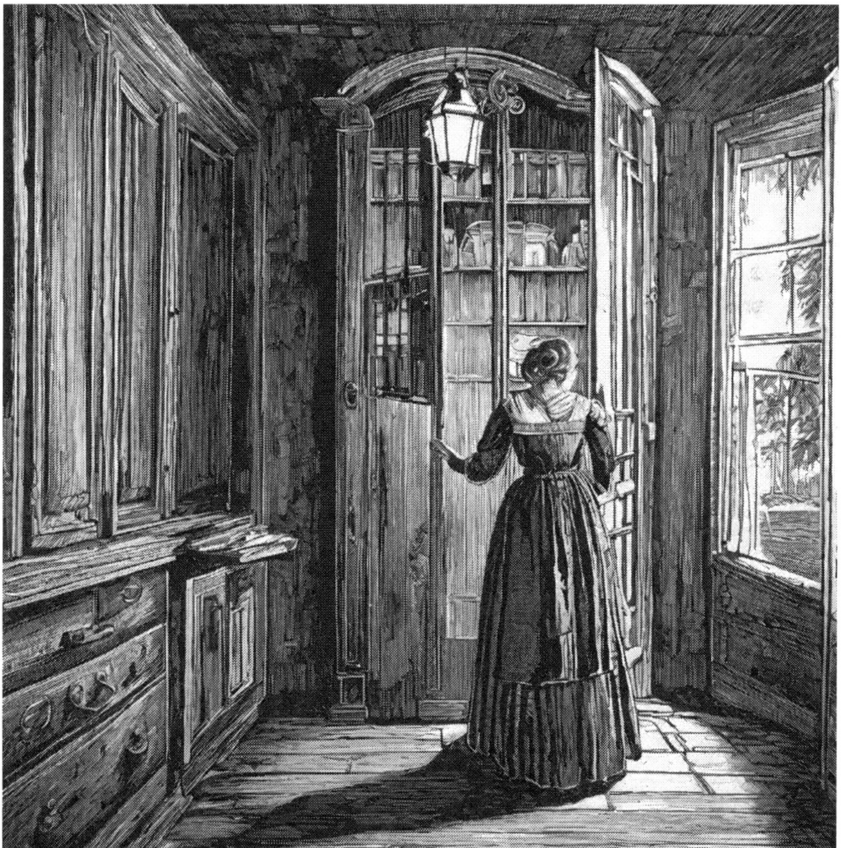

Whimpers and screams came from the boy as he desperately tried to back up more profoundly into the nook he had chosen for his hiding spot. It was almost deep enough. Almost.

He was dragged by the ankle out of the cabinet, banging his head against the cabinet's walls and floor along the way. He feared how bad it would be this time.

She had not always been the source of his nightmares. It felt so long ago, though, like a distant memory that kept fading with each day. His childhood had been restarted, and the previous life he barely clung to was disappearing from him. The vivid childhood he knew now was not the same. It had taken him years to realize what he had done, but the anguish of his consequences led him down a dark path.

His mother was as loving as any child could hope. His father was a preacher, and when he went on missionary trips, she played with him much of the day and provided delicious meals. But his father, James, had not always been a missionary - at least not in this life for Robert. That lingering memory of What Once Was, now fuzzy and unfocused, remembered his father as a businessman specializing in bookkeeping. He had owned one of Ford's first cars though they wouldn't exist for another twenty-five years.

Robert had stepped through a doorway in hopes of seeing how the Dreamlands and monstrosities originated, hoping to find a means to prevent them from occurring. He had been foolish and overzealous to use such a powerful contraption without understanding if it came at a cost. But that no longer mattered.

These days he carried the burden of knowing how dramatically he changed existence with his rebirth, sending his mother into a spiraling drug addict that resulted in an early grave. An entire Kipner family generation of grandparents was wiped from the face of the earth to provide room for James and Mary Ann Kipner to fill the role.

The downfall of Robert's decision to step through the door began when Marcus Whitman, out of New York, met his father in 1842. Whitman was a prominent preacher in the New England area who was known for his successful missionaries. They were well organized and usually large, but they were often far from home.

Robert was approaching the age of twelve when his father said goodbye to him for the last time. Whitman had recruited James to assist him on an extraordinary Presbyterian mission destined for the Oregon Territory after the church James preached at had failed. Robert's father hoped that the missionary would rejuvenate his faith and return with strengthened motivation to restart the church.

They made their way into the Walla Walla Valley, the location of a winter village for the Cayuse Indians, leaving Robert and his mother behind back home outside of Baltimore.

Letters were written, but sending them from one side of the country to another through unsettled land took a long time. Sometimes those letters were lost when the carrier was attacked by wild animals or protective natives.

But the final letter Robert and his mother received from James foretold what would become known as the Whitman Massacre of 1847.

According to James' letter that year, measles had been worse than expected in the northwest. A massive number of Cayuse died, many of which were in Whitman's direct medical care as a trained physician. However, tensions rose among the natives when few white settlers in the mission were affected.

The Cayuse became distrustful and accused Whitman of poisoning the 200 Cayuse in his care. Despite his best efforts, the spread of measles was too great for him to control, especially so far from modern hospitals.

News finally reached the East Coast of the deaths of Marcus Whitman and his wife, Narcissa, along with ten others, including Robert's father. They had been murdered by the Cayuse in the act of tribal law for providing what they called terrible medicine.

Years of separation from her husband, Mary Ann fell into a series of illnesses that made her bedridden for several months. During that time, for her cough and headaches, the doctor administered Laudanum, on which she became reliant.

Violence was all the young man knew from daily beatings from his mother's whip. Years of abuse broke him into a different person. Had it not been for the death of his mother in the winter of 1852, he might not have survived. She transformed into a monster toward young Robert during these moments under the influence.

Instead of adopting the rage his mother unleashed on him, after moving at the age of twenty-two to Ellicott City, he became toughened and resilient. He used his now broad shoulders and muscular arms to help others who couldn't defend themselves. He stood up against tyrannical, sometimes barbarous, people every day. It is how he met and became friends with those within the Huckleberry Hucksters.

He joined the Army in 1853 when he turned twenty-three. He hoped to be stationed at Fort Vancouver to retrace where his father went on his missionary. Insted, he was given less than exciting duties in St. Louis. He watched the Mississippi River slowly roll south daily.

Only when the Civil War broke out in April of 1861 did he get another chance to protect innocents from a strong hand that swept up from the south. Yet he learned quickly it wasn't those firing at him that was the firm hand but the men decorated in medals, safely hidden well behind the firing lines.

CHAPTER IV

Kansas, 1875

There was little sign of life in the marshal. Saddled horses and wagons pulled by bridled animals missed trampling him by inches. Mud and animal dung caked across his clothes and matted into his hair and beard while he lay partially in the road like a drowning man. Both hands clung tightly to an empty bottle of whiskey.

Two hollow, glazed eyes stared into a bright blue sky that stretched over the small settlement of Stonewall in the Black Hills of South Dakota. Gold prospectors spent their days hidden among the peaks and valleys and their nights slumbering among the simple wooden structures that would later become known as the town of Custer.

The Wraith waited to die as he lay in the muck, oblivious to the scorns and blasphemies spat down at him as people walked by. He was numb from the troughs of booze he had consumed after barely escaping Coffeyville with his life.

As he lay like a corpse in the fading sun, his cursed mind replayed the last scenes of his getaway, dodging bullets from an angry mob and one sharp-shooting sheriff.

There had only been one exit Kipner could find in the underground laboratory McMannon had constructed. As he feared, it was the same trapdoor in the jail he had spotted earlier. It had a bolt on the underside, which had been latched firmly when he got to it leading to believe Rawthorne might not know what was going on down there. The judge never mentioned the deputy, so Kipner could only assume McMannon considered him a minor necessity and probably expendable.

Kipner winced at the amount the trapdoor made when lifted only an inch, hoping to avoid a confrontation with the deputy. It didn't matter, though, as Rawthorne had his feet on the desk and stared directly at the trapdoor as if expecting him.

"Well, if it isn't Coffeyville's very own U.S. Marshal," Rawthorne said, exaggerating the U in the U.S. If Kipner wasn't in the wrong spot, he would have rolled his eyes at the comment.

"Do come on out of there, Mr. Kipner, Sir. And please, do it mighty slowly with your hands up."

Wooden stairs took Kipner up and out of the trapdoor with his hands composed above his head. He left the door swung open and resting on the floor.

One shiny new pistol was cocked in the deputy's hand and pointed at Kipner's heart. While holding the gun, his pose was so loose and relaxed that Kipner wondered if he could still get a bead on him.

"I just had a nice chat with the judge," Kipner said. "Seems everything is fine on his end. Not sure what kind of beef you have with me. I thought we got along just fine."

A broad smile as genuine as fool's gold crossed the deputy's face. He smiled and said, "Oh sure, we are just two candy canes.

Kipner caught Rawthorne's eyes darting quickly to the open trapdoor a few times. His curiosity was killing him.

He flicked the guns toward the jail cell and instructed Kipner to enter. The gate closed behind, and Rawthorne's eyes locked straight to the trapdoor. He holstered his weapons and peered down the stairs. One quick look at Kipner, and he descended and was gone.

The temptation was too much for the young man, thought Kipner as he quickly flicked the locked gate open and headed for the front door.

He stepped out onto the boardwalk. Outside, the sun was bright and hazy from the sweltering heat. A handful of folks did their business, but he heard no chain gang approaching.

Right then, he had a choice to make. The easiest solution to his current problem is climbing onto Roy and galloping out of there in a cloud of dust. But something McMannon spoke of nagged the back of his mind. If the whole country's problem originated with the natives, he needed more proof. At the moment, he had a book that was likely a history lesson that would shed little light on the matter.

McMannon's house, he had learned while nosing around town earlier, was the large house at the north end of town. To his knowledge, no one lived with him, and he had no servants. That last fact surprised Kipner expecting the use of the nearly dead prisoners as butlers and maids.

Before deciding, he returned to the jail, closed the trapdoor, and slid Rawthorne's desk over it. "Let the twerp find his way out," he thought as he headed down to McMannon's estate, making a quick detour to pick up his pistols and badge in the hotel room.

Only Rawthorne should have known what Kipner was up to. The townsfolk should have gone about their business having already seen Kipner the past few days, and Polane was presumably gathering another batch of prisoners from the train.

Instead, he watched as the sun sank rapidly below the horizon unnaturally. Within seconds the town had been shrouded in nightfall. His eyes picked up his surroundings nicely, but he quickly wished he were blind. Throughout the homes and buildings up and down the street, he caught pairs of red eyes peering out between shutters, cracked open doors, and around corners. Each pair of eyes was part of some ungodly humanoid.

They scampered out with excessive speed, crawling over any surface like feet across the floor, down the street, and stopped. Their bodies were elongated, emphasized at their necks and arms that stretched several feet. Reminiscent of a pendulum, these rubber-like necks swung to and fro as they gauged and studied the Wraith. The citizens of Coffeyville revealed their true nature.

Each one was lined at the side of the road. As Kipner stepped off the porch, they slowly began approaching him. Methodically in motion, they moved with a smooth determination. Each step was like a leopard slowly stalking its prey.

Kipner was in serious trouble. He had no experience with this type of creature. There was no documentation explaining how to handle them, and now he faced an entire town. Each of his steps drew them in closer no matter what direction he wished to go.

One of the closest ones tilted its head back abnormally far, allowing its jaw to unhinge like a snake. The giant, gaping maw lashed out a whip-like tongue that shot at Kipner's head. Seeing the tongue's shape gave him sudden frightening flashbacks of his youth. He hesitated too long, allowing the tongue to snap around his head and hold him fast.

The strength of one of these creatures was immense, slowly drawing Kipner in to feast on his cranium. Its wide and menacing maw extruded needle teeth outward from its lips several inches long.

Kipner reached for the post supporting the building's awning, giving himself a tight grip. The pull from the tongue was greater, drawing great pain to his neck and fingers. He couldn't hold it for long and let go. With the tongue wrapped around his head like cloth bandages, it was difficult to see, but he could just make out a little between the gaps.

Being punctured by dozens of four-inch needles into the skull was an odd sensation to Kipner. The initial pain was nonexistent. Some towns with Chinese immigrants had brought the practice of acupuncture with them, which he had tried before. The sensation was similar, but only the first fraction of an inch.

The creature's tongue adjusted its grip to allow the needles to press into Kipner's cranium, jolting his entire body into severe pain. He screamed out with full lungs as he desperately tried to focus on saving himself.

At either side were his pistols, to which he grabbed them both and sent their barrels straight up to his attacker's chin and pulled both triggers.

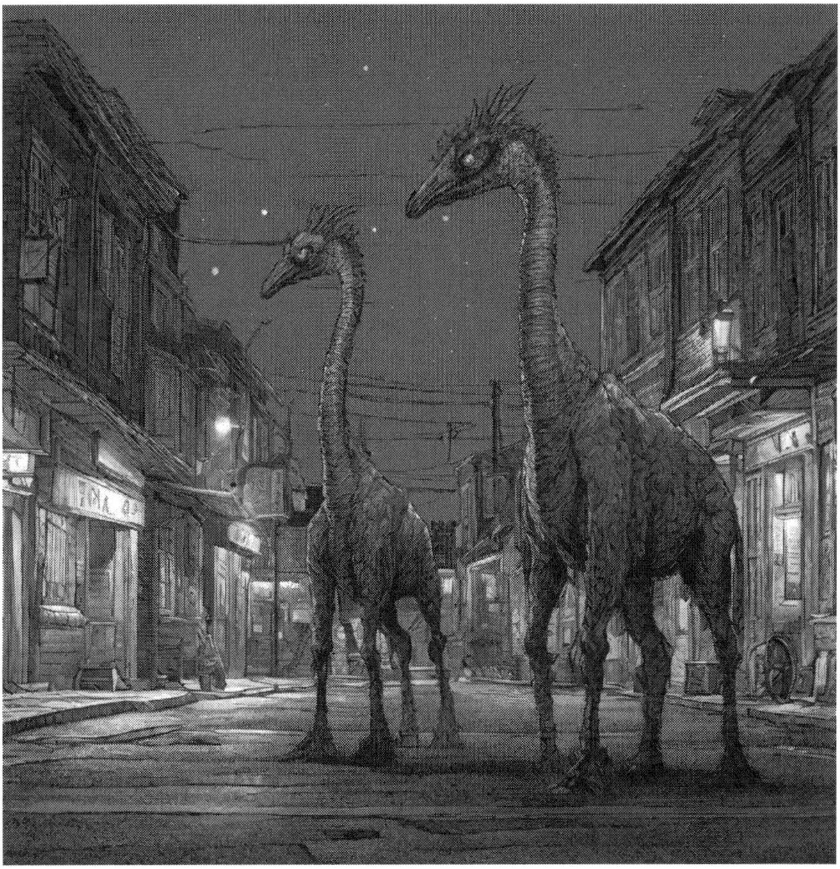

Suddenly the front half of the creature's face was a void as the pieces burst in every direction, releasing Kipner from the death grip and freeing him for a moment.

The rest of the creatures lurched at once, sending their tongues in his direction, grabbing him where ever they could attach. Some tongues expanded at the tip, extending several barbs outward to secure better in the flesh.

Tongues were attached to his shoulders, waist, neck, and leg. Each tried dragging him towards a different creature, stretching his body like a torture rack. His pistols answered each direction, burying a bullet deep in each beast.

When he killed two or three that would release him, two more reached him, biting down fiercely into the flesh of his shoulder, sinking the four-inch long needles dangerously close to his heart.

His knees buckled from the weight of the creatures leaping onto him and the unimaginable pain coursing through his body. He bent over quickly, launching the two on him over his shoulders and onto the ground. In the same motion, he rolled beneath several trying to grab him, slipping past their feet.

The piercing wound on his shoulder felt much worse, and the pain caught up to his mind as he realized the creature ripped a large chunk of his shoulder as it was flung while still attached. He couldn't move his left arm much and holstered his pistol, giving him just a couple more shots with his good arm before he had to reload. It would be impossible for him to perform the maneuver with just one hand.

His roll managed to get him closer to the boardwalk that lined down the front facade of each building, and he scampered onto it and got back to his feet. At least here, he was partially protected from his left while they congregated in the street.

The pain was beyond his mental strength to block it out, and his legs started stumbling. But he got to McMannon's house. Two creatures stood before the door, and he sent one to the ground with a bullet. His gun clicked empty against the second one.

It was too fast for Kipner to draw his other pistol with his good hand, and it was on him again. This one was wiser, and its tongue wrapped around his lousy arm and pulled. Kipner gasped and lost the air from his lungs at the torment, crumbling to his knees.

His injured arm lifted him off the ground, now barely attached to his body. Kipner's vision was slowly dark, and his mind convinced him to give up. He began listening to it, but the voice, he realized with a start, was the same from far underground. It called out to him, providing another offer.

Did he really want to live bad enough to agree to the terms? There was far more danger in accepting its request than the initial one. Meanwhile, in the fraction of a second the dialogue took place, Kipner was hoisted up like a puppet, dangling before the creature with needles pressed against his face.

Suddenly his other pistol came alive and ejected itself out of the holster. As if some invisible force had wielded it, the gun flew smoothly under the chin of the creature. It removed half its head, giving Kipner freedom yet again.

Things moved in such a blur he couldn't recall if he agreed to the Thing Below, but he threw himself at the door and slammed it shut behind him once inside. Like all other doors in town, this one had a place to bar the door from the inside. None of the beasts from outside tried to break it down, nor did they attempt to enter through the windows. They remained hovered outside, however, waiting for him to leave.

For the moment, it seemed Kipner had time to recover. His shoulder was in horrible condition. He likely needed his arm removed, but he had neither the means nor the skill to do so and could only overly bandage the wound and stop the bleeding.

That had been the second time that the pistols had saved his life by operating independently. He couldn't help but fear he had somehow subconsciously agreed with the Thing Down Below. Still, the phenomenon had occurred long before he knew it in Hobgoblin Creek. Whatever caused it must have come before. But what exactly empowered them? They were ordinary pistols from the President.

"We give them life," came a dark, groused voice from every direction. The feeling wasn't like before. There was no voice from within his mind. It was as if he was surrounded by a single entity that enveloped him with sound.

"Who are we?" Kipner asked out loud.

"We are of this world. We are evil. We are good. We are everything."

Never in his experiences as a U.S. Marshal had he been allowed to communicate with these strange, horrific creatures that plagued the country.

"What made you begin to attack America?" Kipner asked, cutting straight to the point.

"You seek the truth of things unrelated to us. We have always been here. They have not."

"It doesn't seem like they've been around too long, then. They don't seem to be too friendly. Causing chaos all over. Outside this building especially. So why did you help me?"

Silence filled the room, and the voice was no more. Whatever the entity was, it was gone. While he had vaguely felt a presence nearby, he felt nothing but the cold darkness that wrapped around him now.

Kipner took a seat to gather his thoughts. Suddenly he discovered the world is inhabited by more than he initially thought.

It was beginning to become exhausting to keep track of it all. None of this, Kipner suspected, was meant for mankind to ever know about. Something had disrupted that pattern, which caused the secret to being revealed to mortals.

His body was weakened by now to the point he could barely walk. He took his chances the house was secure and collapsed on a sofa in the living room and soon passed out.

Hours later, his body woke him from a terrible nightmare of being chased by dozens of creatures outside. It was still dark out, and the building was still surrounded.

Still worn out, he was able to get back on his feet a bit and wander the house. The notion of searching the home as a waste of time occurred to him as he began rummaging around desks and cabinets, finding little.

It was hoped that McMannon had some information or piece of helpful clues that could gain further knowledge of what was going on. He had blamed the natives for cursing the lands before being relocated, but so far, there was no proof in that statement. Even most of the natives who were questioned stated their practices never favored curses or hexes. That kind of religion was more related to Voodoo. Still, the region of influence was primarily concentrated in the deep southern parts of America. The Harrow was witnessed virtually everywhere.

On the ground floor, Kipner's sharp eyes picked up light scratches from a secretary in the corner. The pattern on the wood floor was a perfect curve indicating it was rotated occasionally.

The desk would not move in any other direction and caused a small door to open in a wall when rotated correctly. Kipner found this odd when McMannon was clearly the town's power. Why would he need to hide anything, especially in his house?

Kipner struck a match to light a lantern and took a step onto a stone staircase that spiraled tightly downward fifteen feet to a basement.

A scholar in history would cherish such a sight that Kipner saw. In a large open room were desks, shelves, and cabinets overflowing with notes, letters, books, journals, and maps relating to McMannon's theory of native curses. Kipner could spend months here and only get through some things. Everything needed to be in order, with many papers scattered across the floor haphazardly.

Maps were more accessible for Kipner to analyze quickly, and he came across one of interest. It was hand drawn from most of the United States, with dots scattered in several locations. Each bead was circled, which had an additional wider circle around it. Seven dots spread throughout, but the widest circles overlapped other wider circles. Taking those into consideration, the entire country was inside them.

In small letters, the dots and circles had dates written against them. The dates went as far back as 1830 and progressively increased as they went westward. The first circles around the dots had dates roughly twenty years later, with several being scratched out and changed. The most expansive rings were around fifty years later.

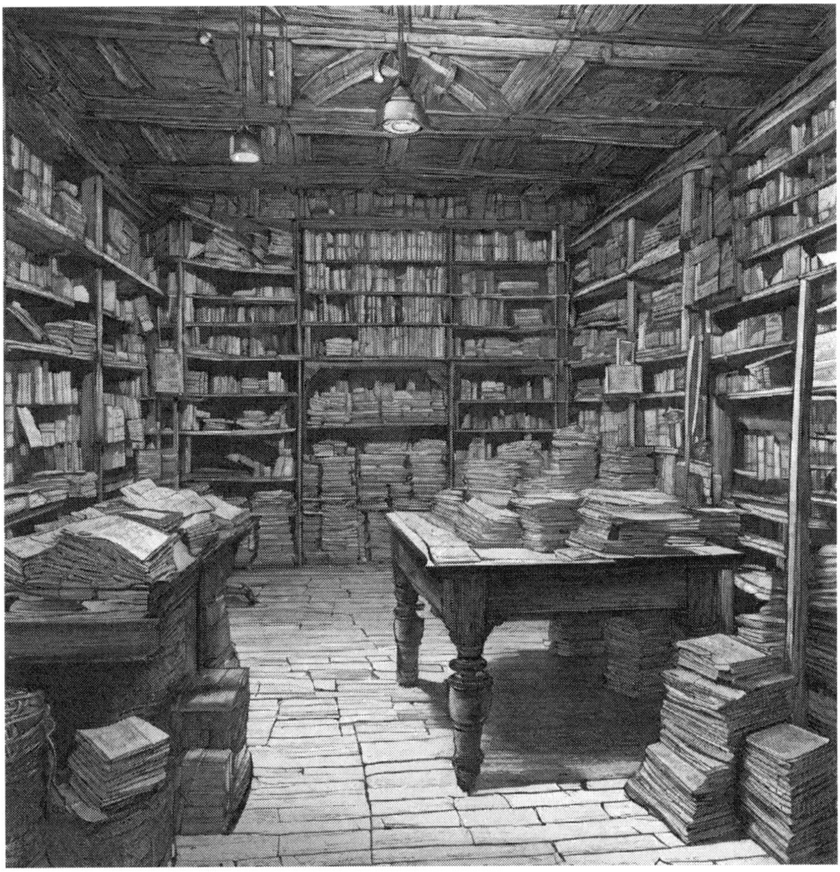

Thinking back to his teen years, Kipner remembered seeing spooky things at night for the first time, but as for his childhood, he couldn't recall any incidents. That didn't mean there weren't any critters roaming the hills just out of sight.

The first circle just barely touched Baltimore. Given his memory, the date was pretty close. Interestingly, there was a dot precisely on Coffeyville and one not too far from where Hobgoblin Creek resided.

There wasn't enough time to sort through all the papers, books, and journals, so he scanned the room for anything that might stick out. One was a small pocketbook of McMannon's listing what he believed to be instructions for rituals and occult incantations. The actual descriptions and words were in a native tongue Kipner wasn't familiar with, but he knew of a few tribes that might. He was curious if they really were curses or something McMannon misunderstood.

Spiritualism was profoundly the theme in his research. Even Kipner had heard of the popular book from the late 1840s from his mother, who dabbled in practicing the movement. The Principles of Nature by Andrew Jackson Davis was among them, combining mystical philosophy and healing practices.

Above, the creatures of Coffeyville paced across the boardwalk of McMannon's house to remind Kipner of his entrapment. Thoughts of his horse came to mind. He had led him back to where a stable for long-term residents at the hotel could safely store their rides. He wasn't saddled or bridled and had never ridden Roy naturally. He wondered if the beast would allow him, but if he knew the situation he was about to put himself back into, Roy would have no problems bolting as quickly out of here. Kipner could just hold on.

Leaving everything but the map and pocketbook behind, he explored the rest of the house. He found a suitable satchel for his newfound treasure. He really didn't need it; both folded and fit within his pockets easily. He was procrastinating the inevitability.

Outside, the creatures clawed and scraped their way from one side of the house to the other. However, they were mainly concentrated at the front of the house. Oddly enough, McMannon never had a backdoor made. Only the front door formed an exit.

There was a second story, and Kipner studied one of the windows at the back. It was a good drop to the ground with hard-packed dirt as his cushion. One sprained ankle, and he was a dead man. He was probably already a dead man, he thought.

All the while he was in McMannon's house, he felt the Thing Below trying to reach out to remind him of the offer. The idea repeated like an annoying song that couldn't be shaken free.

It wanted him to expand its area of influence further. By using him as a beacon or relay point, whatever lay far, far down below, could reach further beyond its range and continue its work of manipulation.

Kipner would be free to leave town safely if he agreed. Otherwise, lingering death echoed over and over in his mind. He could only imagine the consequences of being some focal point of a creature not of this world.

He had already lost much of the integrity he carried behind the symbol of his marshal's badge from the death of McMannon. The decision to die with dignity drove him to the maddening thought of leaping from a second-story window.

Daylight was not in sight, giving a heavy shadow behind the buildings. He could only guess they could see better if he had good vision in the dark. How far this hostile atmosphere stretched from town?

Occasionally, a single beast wandered to the back, slithering its long neck from one side to the other, then gracefully returning to the front. They came back there sporadically. There wouldn't be a timetable of how long he had back there before another showed up.

One thing that was plentiful in the bedroom he was in were bed sheets. He had only heard of making crude ropes out of bed sheets through comedic stories, but his only other option was leaping. He got to work.

He would be completely vulnerable climbing the rope, so the descent would have to be rapid. His useless arm wouldn't be able to fire his pistol while his good arm held on.

McMannon's master bed lacked posts at the corners, to Kipner's disappointment, but he could anchor it to the frame. He tested the rope with a few tugs, but the bed moved reasonably well across the wood floor. To save it from moving, he shoved it against the window. He had plenty of lengths to reach the ground now.

Poised just inside the window sill, Kipner waited for the next random creature to pass through before he would drop down. But the beast never came. Several times he had his mind almost convinced to just go, but he had visions of one of them turning the corner of the house the second he began lowering down.

Minutes passed by, and the back courtyard remained vacant. The nerves in Kipner's body were already thin from his fight and the pain he had forced out of his mind, but his anxiety was through the roof. He began to shake from tensing his body in anticipation.

A slight creak came from the stairs that froze Kipner cold. It was brief, followed by total silence, but the Wraith had his pistol drawn and pointed at the bedroom door. The shakes he had turned to steel for the moment as he gripped the gun. It had always given him a moment of confidence that he could trust. Any bad situation he was in could often be resolved with what he held firmly.

Nothing appeared at the door, and he wondered if it had just been the house settling. Something in his gut told him otherwise, and he slowly approached the door.

Poised to leap through the doorway, something beat him to the jump and wrapped around his head completely, sending him into total darkness.

Uncertainty and confusion made him forget to resist, and he was roughly pulled into the hallway, banging against the doorway. It was horrific how so much of what he was experiencing in this small, random town matched so closely to his childhood fears.

The tongue of one of the creatures lifted him off the ground and let him hang a moment in the air. Kipner could hear sound from below indicating the front door had opened somehow, and more were coming quickly.

With the gun already drawn and pointed, the first two shots were blind and missed the target, but his third was proper, and it dropped.

His Sharp rifle was locked away in the stable next to Roy. There was doubt he would get to it before they got to him, but he dashed into the bedroom anyway and slipped down the makeshift rope. He was grateful to have taken the time to reload his pistols when he was safe in the house, but he was already down to two bullets.

The focus from the front door had drawn their attention for the moment. Kipner tore through the dry dirt towards the stable. Behind him, he heard the creatures pouring out of the same window in pursuit. He wasn't going to have much time.

Roy was already petrified and had destroyed the gate keeping him in the stall. His hooves tore through much of the surrounding wood, and he had snapped the rope tethering him in. It was surprising to Kipner he hadn't burst through the stable door and bolted off.

Kipner lowered his shoulder into the door and exploded inside, further scaring the horse. Quickly securing the door, he took the precious time snatching his rifle from the shelf and leaped onto his faithful friend by the horse's mane.

Immediately Roy resisted the sudden pull from his hair, rearing back and discharging Kipner onto the ground. The marshal winced at the pain from his shoulder but quickly got back up, trying desperately to calm the animal.

Roy stared into Kipner's eyes but stood still. Kipner got back on, and the two charged out of the barn like demons out of Hell, trampling several creatures. They clawed and shot out their tongues, but Roy was at a point of panic, thundering his hooves against the ground and bursting into the clearing.

It took everything for Kipner to hold on to Roy's mane with just one hand while squeezing a rifle under the elbow. He was just as hysterical as his horse, glancing behind to see the pursuing beasts keeping up with Roy.

Kipner knew he would fall off if he turned to fire upon them. Lacking stirrups gave him a disadvantage in holding on, and the rhythmic bouncing of the horse shook him fiercely. He only hoped Roy's endurance would outlast them.

They rode on, seemingly for miles in no particular direction, galloping at full stride across the Kansas prairies until finally, Roy began to slow down. Kipner glanced behind him to see their pursuers had long given up and were nowhere in sight.

With a sigh of relief, he slowed Roy to a walk to let him catch his breath, then halted him for a rest. The horse was shaking with fear as he, too, turned to look behind. The two stood in silence, breathing heavily as they tried to calm down and ease their mind that they were finally safe.

As if by a sign of assurance, the first rays of the morning sun appeared in the east.

*

The nightmare finally ended in his drunken mind as Kipner lay in the muck of Stonewall. He tried another sip from his whiskey bottle, but only the taste of dirt and grime around the bottle's lip was found. He wondered where Roy was. He didn't care, he guessed, at this point. He had put the poor animal through enough pain and suffering. Where ever the old boy was now was probably safer.

The glaring sun bored down on him like a metal rod lunged at his forehead, and he closed his eyes. He hated what he did to himself after each Sighting of the Harrow. They used to be so adventurous when he was but a young man! Nowadays, he wondered if this Sighting would be his last. The only drive he had anymore was knowing not many marshals, or any other badge-carrying servant of the law for that matter, cared enough to find a means to an end with the plague that rung the country like some demonic bell.

His head rang like a metaphorical reference, and he made no indication to ever move again. His booze had already given what Kipner wanted, but now it was taking the cost out of his body.

As long as no one bothered him, he could just sleep here, half in the street and half on the boardwalk, until he felt himself again. He didn't care, though, if it took all month either.

"Bobby? My boy, what have you done with yourself? Again with the drinking. That will kill you quicker than spooks and specters."

The voice was angelic - soft, warm, and caring. It came from above Kipner and reminded him fondly of his father's voice. There was assurance behind it that everything would be alright in time.

The marshal decided to try opening his eyes and, to his amazement, succeeded. There was the silhouette of a man hovering above him with sun rays expanding around his head behind. Perhaps he had died. It was as if an angel indeed came to visit.

"Come on, Bobby," the voice said with a grunt as Kipner was slowly lifted off the ground. "You've almost become the horse crap you are lying in."

Once back on his feet, Kipner readjusted his vision to his savior. He was a portly man in his seventies with a full head of gray hair, clean-shaven, and a genuinely beautiful smile that forced Kipner to smile in reaction.

His grip was firm, and he could easily hold Kipner up. Only two people in the world brought a smile to the Wraith. One was his former girlfriend. This man wasn't as pretty as her.

"Amos!" Kipner said and tried to hug the man but was gently denied.

"It's good to see you, old friend, but before hugs are given, you must be doused and dunked in enough water to fill a lake. Come on, the boys have built a pond not far. Soup might be in your future, too.

CHAPTER V

Dakota Territory, 1875

"Geez, Bobby. I didn't know you sympathized with these monsters. What did ya do, offer them a little nibble on your shoulder for dinner?"

By now, the pain due to the loss of much of Kipner's shoulder had gone numb from dead nerves, but what little pain remained was covered by the small dosage of morphine his friend administered.

That friend was Doctor Amos Sales, a Greek immigrant Kipner had met during the Civil War. Sales found himself mixed up in the War as a field medic, long after his prime, advising young men who had no idea what they got themselves into. Now at seventy years old, Sales had seen his fair share of battles. He was unusually calm and collected, sewing wounds while bullets flew overhead.

In Kipner's line of work since the War, Dr. Sales expected and received numerous visits from the marshal in hopes of yet another miracle being performed. Up to this point in Kipner's career, he had nearly lost a leg, four fingers, an ear, and half his shoulder, all while in the line of duty. So far, he still had everything except the shoulder.

There was a mystery behind Dr. Sales' magical medical skills that Kipner never learned. He had a theory but didn't want to know that it was true. After his mental encounter with the Thing Far, Far Below, he would instead remain ignorant and benefit from Sales' work than be plagued by knowing what he sacrificed to be able to do what he does. Kipner understood sacrifice well.

The doctor gently probed the bandage he dressed on Kipner's shoulder with a satisfied look. It was one of the worst he had seen from the marshal.

"How does that feel?" he asked Kipner gently.

The painkiller hadn't faded yet, so it felt as numb as when lying in the street, but he nodded to make the old man happy.

"Like a night with Lucy. Thanks."

Chuckling while helping Kipner to a more comfortable chair, Sales said, "Lying little brat. Give it an hour, and you'll be clung to the ceiling. How is she anyway? Seen her lately?"

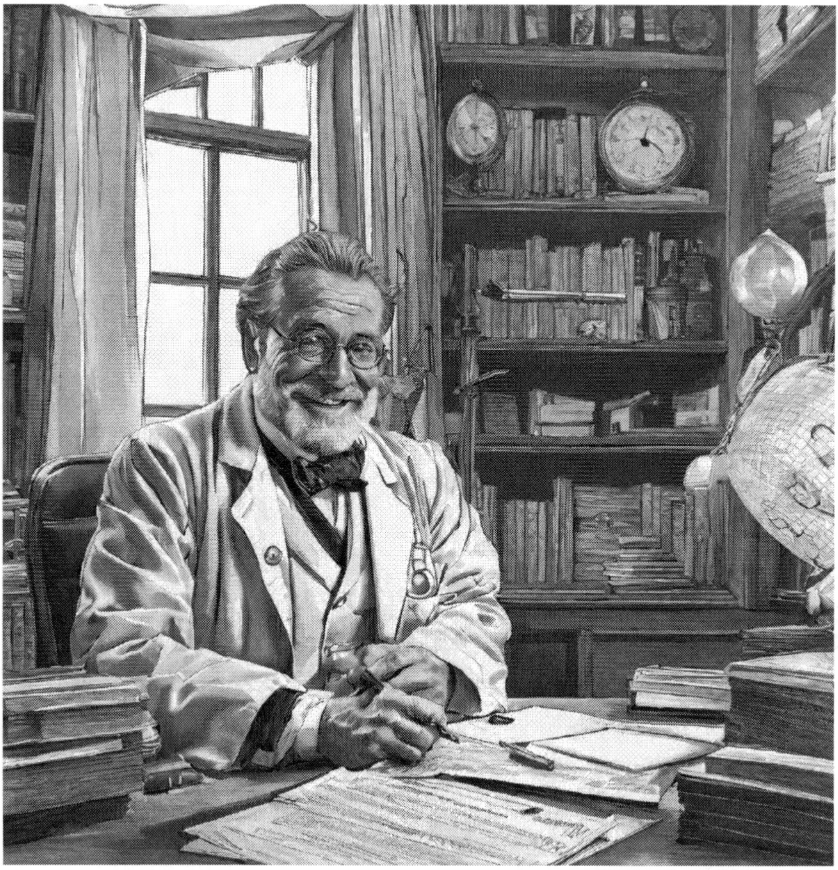

Sales had brought an elaborately designed lounge chair for post operations. It was made from hand-carved walnut, fastened with rich green velvet, and deeply padded with cotton. To Kipner, it was his favorite place to be in the world. It was bliss to his butt.

The marshal's mind eased at the comfort, and he thought of the sensitive question Amos nonchalantly asked. Lucy had been his love lost just after the War during a better time of his life.

The two had meant to be together, but Kipner's sacrifice that changed his parents' life drove him away to keep focused on his job. She went elsewhere and pursued an archaeological career, to Kipner's amusement.

"Haven't heard from her in years," he mumbled drearily.

"You know, Bobby," Amos moved on, letting his inquiry die while performing a general massage over the muscles that especially ached. "One of these days, I'm not going to be around here. I can't keep patching you up. Maybe when that happens, you might consider reducing the intensity of your duties to typical humans."

Sighing more from the relief of his muscles than the repetitive suggestion he had heard dozens of times before, he rolled his neck and immediately winced at the pain. Amos was the father figure he didn't have for most of his life. It was always comforting paying Amos a visit. Still, it was always due to some horrendous injury and not for a casual hello.

"You know I can't give up yet. Not after what I've paid. What I know. They gave me the job because I was the right fit. The only fit. But sure, some days I wish I had taken an easier career. Like miracle worker," Kipner smiled and winked at Amos.

The old doctor had never stopped smiling since he saw Kipner. He had never had a son; marriage hadn't been in the cards either. Kipner was a stubborn man with great humor when he wasn't too beat up. Amos couldn't help but give him fatherly advice whenever he could. He had a lifetime of untapped wisdom just waiting to be given out.

"You wrote the book on it. You could make someone else read it, for Christ's sake."

"Oh, come on, Amos," Kipner said as he buttoned his shirt and gently lifted his vest over his wounded shoulder. "You know, no one ever read my book. It needs more illustrations. Besides, you can't expect to survive from knowledge in a book. It's learned out there in the wild.

"Now, what on earth are you doing way up here in no man's land?" Kipner asked as he lit a cigar, which was promptly jerked out of his mouth and cast into the trash bin by Sales. He tried burning a second in protest, but it, too, was snatched and discarded.

"I thought I would ask you the same," Sales replied. "I go where the work needs me. There's plenty of fighting and squabbling between everyone up here. I'll only stay during the summer months and then travel back to Tennessee. I expect plenty of unnecessary limbs to be removed over the coming weeks. The Black Hills have been owned by anyone but the newcomers for centuries. Shiny yellow stones keep bringing the folks from the east every day. I can't believe you are interested in gold, so what could bring you up here?"

News from Amos was bitter to hear. The more Kipner learned, the more troublesome he felt. Storms brewed across the country as new folks wished to live where old folks had always dwelt. Compromises were unheard of, and if any truce was made, those with power soon abolished it in the way of expansion and a state of mind that went against the natives.

Kipner handed McMannon's pocketbook over to the doctor. "I was hoping this was written in Lakhotiyapi. Thought maybe Flying Hawk could shed some light on my conundrum. Unless another secret power you possessed was tribal linguistics." Kipner nudged Amos with his elbow and smiled jokingly.

"Wa slolyA ota taku," the doctor said with a wink. "But not what you need, young man. This...this list of black tricks and forbidden words, I can't..." He trailed off and handed the pocketbook back with shaking hands.

"I could never forego your duties, Bobby. You're made into a puppet to do the work of political cowards."

Amos rested his hand on Kipner's good shoulder with a fatherly smile of assurance. He was intensely proud of him, and he knew Kipner had grown through a hard life to be a strong man. Through utter terror, repeatedly, Kipner faced them with hopes of one day returning peace to the country. Yet they both knew eliminating one evil would only lead to already existing evils before the Harrow.

Nodding and patting Amos' hand in agreement, Kipner said, "I know. I've been one most of my life. It's the fate that's drawn for us. But for me, it's all I know."

Kipner rose reluctantly from his comfortable chair, embracing the doctor with his good arm. Amos held the hug longer than usual with his mind deep in thought. Finally, he said, "I don't want to think of your fate, old friend. Instead, I'll just think of you playing your old harmonica around the campfire late at night. You still play that old thing?"

There was a brief hesitation before the marshal drew a thin metal-plated harmonica from his vest pocket. Across the shiny plate read "HOHNER" in all capital letters, a gift his father had given him shortly before he left for the Oregon Territory. There was a time he would bring it out at any opportunity for those who would listen. But in recent years, he found less enthusiasm to play it though he always kept it close to his heart.

This time it found his lips, and he played the first song that came to his mind, one he knew would make Amos smile. Beautiful Dreamer. He once played it for his troop during the War to ease their mind before sleep. It did the trick for his old friend, too.

*

On the eighth day exploring the highlands of the Black Hills, Kipner had tracked a large bull elk down into a ravine fueled by a small, winding spring-fed creek. The elk had been unusually clever, behaving far beyond any herd animal Kipner had tracked before. On multiple occasions, the marshal found looping tracks from the beast, extended paths directly down the stream, and zig-zag patterns crossing the water several times. Behaviors would be expected among mankind but not an animal.

He rested his Sharps rifle on a rock as he leaned back and looked down into the small valley below where the elk grazed. This strange world had quickly changed, which sprung a thought while he tracked the beast. It gave him pause to reflect on the experience.

Whatever these sinister, awakened species' intentions, perhaps their purposes went beyond the human race. Kipner had killed numerous beasts that were dramatic mutations from common species, which he only assumed were more of these strange unknown creatures. What if they were manipulating innocent wildlife to further whatever amusement they desired instead?

Far below, still within the exceptional range of Kipner's Sharps, the bull elk slowly made its way along the creek's bank, scouting for rich clumps of fireweed and occasionally poppies. As it ventured further downstream, it slowly grazed in a large, clear circle before moving on, often around several trees or bushes. It nonchalantly would cross the creek from time to time. Casual observers would just see it seeking additional morsels elsewhere. Still, Kipner had studied its movements carefully enough to see differently.

While the elk didn't appear to be deliberately maneuvering strategically, it was as if its subconscious mind was guiding it. Perhaps something else entirely.

He still wasn't sure what the intentions of these astral creatures were, especially towards innocent wildlife in isolated regions of the world. He was the only person in the area...

The realization struck him like a thunderbolt, and he suddenly became paranoid about his surroundings. Could one of the entities be within range to detect his presence and mock him by enlightening the intelligence of his target?

To support his theory, he withdrew McMannon's map and traced his finger to where he was. He was well within the inner circle that immediately surrounded a dot to the south of his location. Somewhere in that spot resided something with powers of manipulation among many other talents. So far, he guessed that each dot represented the potential location of one of these awakened entities of the Harrow, a Sighting.

Inside Harrow's Doctrine, chapter two listed the known abilities these creatures had been witnessed to possess. The list was exhausting to go through entirely, from physical mutations to spontaneous combustion to rapidly shriveling crops to manufacturing painful rainstorms of dangerous chemicals. One of the more horrifying sightings was the conjuration of abominations not of this world appearing in vulnerable communities and massacring every living body.

With every day he spent without a solution to the country's terror, he felt he had wasted everyone's time. Innocents had been frightened and slaughtered by these creatures for decades now, and there was no sign of controlling or neutralizing the threat. Part of that reason was that no one knew where they actually were present. Some believed they were below ground, some right in front of everyone but invisible, and a few thought they weren't even on Earth and contacting other planets like Saturn.

During this time of year, Chief Flying Hawk's Lakota tribe was deep in the Black Hills, far from civilization. It was always a grueling task to find his tribe, as they were highly skilled in avoiding leaving a trail. He needed a lot of answers, and Flying Hawk may have at least one if Kipner could track him down.

At the moment, however, it was ironic to Kipner that he had stopped to contemplate herd animals he was stalking and failed to hear the predator that had stalked him from the tree above.

Directly above him, perched on a branch, poised the most prominent mountain lion Kipner had ever seen. It was abnormally bigger than a typical cat from this part of the country. Its girth matched closer to a tiger than an American cougar. The paws it possessed were massive, with all claws extended.

There had been no warning. Later Kipner would guess his bad luck brought him to the stalking animal already in the tree without noticing.

When it dropped onto Kipner, it felt like a tree had fallen upon him. The beast's sheer size pummeled him to the ground, knocking his rifle from his hands and the wind from his lungs. It screeched piercingly down at Kipner, inches from his face, filling his nostrils with the foul stench of decayed meat from its last meal.

The Wraith wiggled his arms free enough to shield his face from an incoming bite, sending the teeth deep into his forearm instead. Kipner screamed in pain and suddenly yelled with hatred at the creature, trying desperately to use his adrenaline to block the pain. It had no effects on the animal.

From below the waist, the lion raked against his thighs, shredding the leather of his pants away like cotton and lining his legs with wide marks of blood.

With his life on the line, Kipner reacted irrationally at the situation and threw his head up into the cat's jaw, knocking him firmly with a head butt. The aggressive move was enough for Kipner to roll out from under the animal onto his rifle. The Sharps was a lever action loader, and Kipner was so accustomed to the unique weapon he had it cocked as he rolled away and sent a bullet into the beast's gullet.

It did not stop it. It screamed a deep, gurgling cry that mimicked a tiger. Curved claws launched at Kipner, swiping a mighty paw across his face and sending the marshal back several feet. There was no hesitation upon the lion. With his back to the animal, he didn't see it until it snapped onto his throat, clamping quickly down around his windpipe and crushing it.

Flail as he might, Kipner began suffocating as the giant beast, heavily breathing from the brawl, poised over him with its muscular jaws tightly pinched, awaiting his prey to die.

"Xyt Ultiz Er y ghilestriun," came a voice of unknown nearby. It was garbled words, like a madman unable to pronounce correctly. "Llo Trzed mmwyted."

It wasn't a foreign language but an entirely different form of speaking.

As Kipner struggled to hold his breath longer to remain conscious, he funneled his attention to the words spoken to him for a moment.

"Bargain," it finally spoke in a comprehensive language for Kipner.

The struggling man didn't respond, but anything at this point was suitable for him to survive his doom. The increasing pressure of the animal's jaw ceased, but it held his throat as firmly as before. Kipner could barely breathe in short gasps.

"Stop searching," it said. "Return. Home. Now."

The man's mind was racing from the ferocious beast tightly holding his throat, and he struggled to comprehend at first what the voice meant. He wasn't in a position to think profoundly or rationally. Yet it was enough to understand what it wanted and answer a question he had carried with him since Hobgoblin Creek.

He was on the right track! That meant it was critical he found Flying Hawk at all costs.

In response to his thoughts, as if no protection could shield his mind from it, the mountain lion pressed harder and resumed suffocating him again.

"One choice or die," it said with its strange way of giving an ultimatum. Its primitive vocabulary would have been amusing to Kipner had he not needed that part of his brain to devise a plan to free him from the trap.

During that time, one of Kipner's hands had pulled out his Bowie knife at his hip belt and, with all the force left in his body, jammed the thick blade up into the rib cage of the great beast just behind its front leg.

His throat became free, and he rolled back away, recovering to his feet.

The tight grip of his rifle cradled between his two hands eased the muscle memory of pulling the lever down, loading another round stored along the hilt of the gun, and cocking the lever all within a second.

There would be no time to load another or aim the rifle from his shoulder. He let the gun go off from his hip, aiming tightly at the beast's face wanting no more mistakes.

Kipner's specially modified Sharps was built for extra-long distance. Those with exceptional eyesight could mark a shot up to 1,200 yards, but Kipner's vision was eagle sharp. The furthest range he ever hit was over 1,500 yards the year prior, and that was at a moving target. Those witnessing the event had never seen anything like it, believing him to have made a deal with the devil until he showed his U. S. Marshal's badge. Somehow that made more sense to the common man.

Little was left of the giant mountain lion that lay motionless fifteen feet away from the sheer power of the gun. Kipner still needed to get a clear look at the beast. Now that he stood over the carcass, he could confidently guess his theory of the Harrow affecting wildlife was true. No feline of this caliber lived in either North or South America. It would have rivaled the lions of Africa.

Kipner presumed that his action was sufficient of an answer as there was no further speech from it. It rejuvenated him, knowing he was on the right track. A simple sign; he had been asking for one for weeks after what he thought was aimless roaming across the country in search of clues.

After the pleasantness of running into his old friend, Amos, his spirits had further been lifted by finding another good friend. His horse, Roy, had wandered off through town while Kipner binged his demons away, lingering around the gambler's hall and itching to place more bets before Kipner could intervene. There were forty dollars in the saddlebag that Kipner didn't recall having before.

Both Amos and Roy were what he needed to continue pressing on in his investigation. This acknowledgment from the Harrow creature was the cherry on top.

Climbing back onto Roy, who had conveniently removed himself from the mountain lion fight, Kipner clicked his teeth to get the horse trotting north along the valley ridge line. Flying Hawk was around there somewhere.

*

Defiant against a raging storm, hundreds of miles away from the Wraith, the hammers continued to come down upon spikes, driving them deep into the ground and securing yet another beam of iron rail. Around the tireless workers struck bolts of lightning, sending the area into a waterfall of sparks with each tree hit. None of it mattered to them. Their hammers continued to fall endlessly, day and night, without rest. Those who witnessed only wondered how it was done. Those who knew were a part of it, connecting the dots across the map. The rails would amplify the calling. The tall watcher monitored in silence and then vanished.

CHAPTER VI

Washington, D.C, 1866

"Come in, Mr. Kipner."

Two tall wooden doors painted white with gold accents opened in unison, pouring a brilliant candlelight illumination across the blue-carpeted hallway. That is not to say the hallway was also lit with numerous candles along end tables and candelabras, but the elliptical room that had been accessed cascaded in an opulence of light.

Aside from a sofa and a dozen chairs, very little comprised the decor within the Cabinet Room. What was abundant in light lacked in furniture, however. Dominating for attention was a long table, suitable for eight guests, equipped with eight locking drawers for all cabinet members.

Each Cabinet member of the United States was present along with President Ulysses S. Grant, who sat at one end of the long table. Members of the local police force were stationed outside the room to refrain anyone not invited from entering. At the same time, the District of Columbia's U. S. Marshal, Ward Hodgins, stood like stone just inside near the door. All eyes pointed to Kipner as he strode in and sat at a nearby chair.

"Mr. President. Members of the Cabinet. Ward," he acknowledged with the least enthusiasm to the marshal, who did not return the nod Kipner had given.

As I expected, Kipner thought as he stared at Ward. While the two saw eye to eye on protecting innocent civilians, they differed dramatically on who constituted a civilian. Ward had paid his services to the country during the Mexican-American War in 1847 while defending the Mexican army. Until the Civil War broke out, Ward spent most of his time leading volunteers through untamed lands seeking tribes he claimed had hostile intent toward the safety of the United States. In his mind, natives were primitive, savage warriors who wanted to eradicate the white man.

Ulysses Grant puffed on a cigar a few times while studying Kipner's expression towards Ward but let it go.

"Mr. Kipner," he said, "Thank you for coming all this way."

"I was happy to oblige, Mr. President," Kipner replied and accepted Grant's cigar. He struck a match and enjoyed finer tobacco than he was used to.

The president glanced for a moment through a series of papers in front of him, though the gesture was more for dramatic effect. Grant had read Kipner's reports from the Civil War to the point of memorization. He knew Kipner's unique experience of the Harrow and meant to capitalize on it.

"It would appear you have had quite a tale in your young life already. Your entire troop was sadly taken down by what you reported as "odd appendages, not unlike that of an octopus that extended more than thirty feet in length."

Several of the cabinet members turned to whisper and softly grumble to each other. Most of their expressions were either annoyed or disbelieving of what they heard. Few had experienced the Harrow, especially those of the rich who had been mostly isolated in recent years. Whether that was in part of fear the Harrow might be true or their typical aristocratic lifestyle was anyone's guess.

"Yes, Mr. President. My group, known as the Hucks, comprising of long-time friends, all perished. That is correct," Kipner said, trying to lean on the potency of the tobacco for support against his nerves weakening. He had risen to First Lieutenant before the War ended, partly due to his experience that night. Despite his bravery, being in the presence of so many high-ranking politicians at once was unnerving.

"Mhm," Grant said as he pretended to read his reports. Finally, he looked up at the young man, resting his cigar stub into a nearby ashtray. "Any idea of what might have caused such an experience?"

Kipner paused momentarily, occasionally looking at the president but keeping his nervous eyes studying the wood grains on the table. "I've only heard rumors, Mr. President. I don't have any evidence of what brought about the Harrow."

The mentioning of the word brought another round of grumblings between the cabinet members. Their frowns could not droop further as they glanced at Kipner, many shaking their heads.

Now that the Civil War had ended the year before in '65, attention began to turn from it to yet another adversary. Washington D. C. had already received numerous requests for help in various parts of the country where Sightings had been spotted. These often were vague or so far-fetched in the description of what was witnessed that Congress had all but discarded the letters into a bin.

Kipner knew, however, this wasn't going away anytime soon. He had seen signs of it before the War, and the experiences were only getting more dangerous.

President Grant bridged his fingers and leaned forward in his chair. That day he wore a dark charcoal three-piece suit with gold cuff links. His well-kept beard hid yet another frowning mouth, perhaps out of frustration with the country's predicament rather than doubting validity.

"Mr. Kipner, I am facing a national problem most would believe to be a fabrication of tall tales among the common folk," Grant's words were supported by a gathering of nods and additional soft grunts from the gallery. "Despite the naysayers, I would like to have more than rumors, as you call them, about the growing situation of fear among America.

"At some time during this past century, we began to witness a rise in fearful citizens seeking our aid for various incredulous accounts.

"Therefore, as a precaution, I have recommended our Attorney General, Mr. Pierrepont, appoint you federal marshal that will answer directly to Washington for a special assignment."

Among the cabinet members sat a dark-haired man with a thin mouth and sharp, heavy shielded eyes. Edward Pierrepont wore a beard on his face long enough to hide a bow tie accompanying his suit. He had been a Lincoln supporter despite his Democratic background. His reputation as a solid reformer was supported by his views that an African American freedman's right should be protected.

Grant nodded to Pierrepont, who sat upright to address the room and Kipner. "I evaluated an impressively long list of names who satisfy our criteria to be suitable for the position. I mainly analyzed those who had both combat experience and positive reports of Harrow encounters. You were selected.

"As to the accuracy of this selection to properly fit the role that Mr. President has challenged me to fulfill, however, I cannot say with utmost confidence..."

"Your selection, I'm sure, will be admirable for the task, Ed," Grant assured.

"You're name is on Mr. Pierrepont's list, Mr. Kipner, based on your knowledge and experience so far.

"If willing, you'll be given unique authority above a typical U.S. Marshal.

"For starters, you won't be assigned to an existing district. Instead, the country will be your boundary to which you will seek out information regarding this phenomenon, including any indication of how it might be neutralized or, at the very least, reduced to a more controllable state," Grant said and turned to the other marshal in the room.

"Mr. Hodgins will also work on the same assignment with equal freedom and responsibilities. We hope between the two of you, working separately, of course, the truth will be learned." The marshal glared darkly at Kipner with narrowed eyes but said nothing.

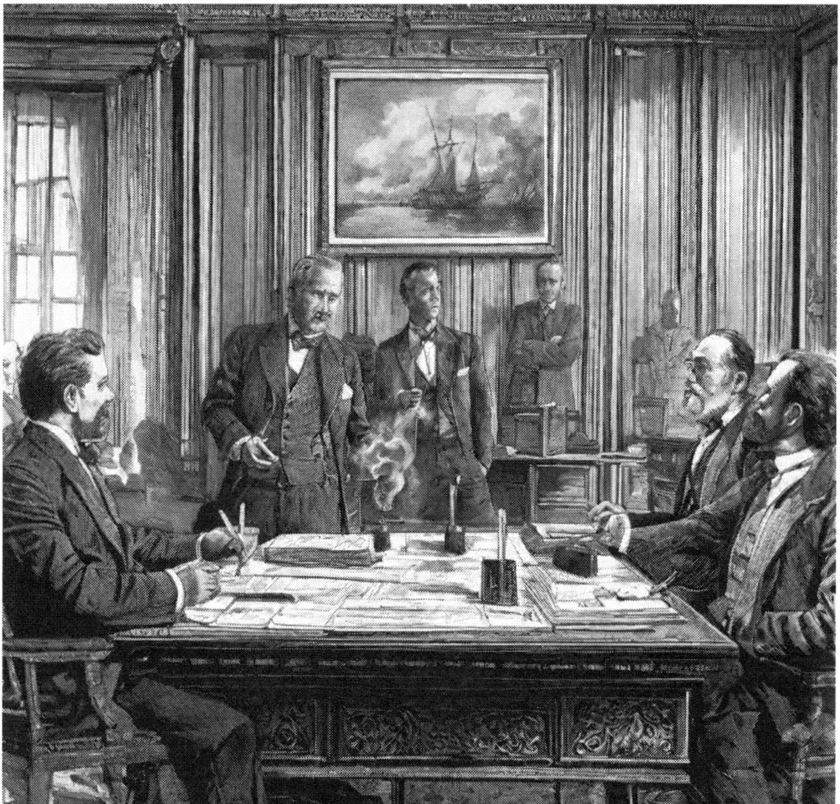

The cigar finished, Kipner extinguished it and gazed around the room momentarily in reflection. When he had been notified to appear before the president and his Cabinet, he believed it to be a mistake or a forgery. Someone had played a stunt that he didn't find all too funny. When the second letter came, this time delivered in person by a carrier of the White House, he became suspicious of their need for him. He had not had much luck during the War and had shown little moments that would result in recognition.

The level of vagueness offered by the men he sat before perplexed Kipner. None of them knew the actual situation, and many didn't even believe there was one, to begin with. The country's best representatives, whose minds were expected to be highly educated, thoroughly trained, and well-developed for large-scale issues America faced, needed to figure out what to do.

Their only idea was to send two men out into the country in hopes of discovering a solution seemingly at random. They would give the marshals a small window of time, expecting they would fail almost assuredly, then proclaim to the country there is no cause for concern as the Harrow was nothing more than campfire stories. It was a fool's errand that the politicians could use as an expendable scapegoat to wash their hands in the matter and move on.

Being in that room disgusted Kipner; he would have left if he could. Judging from the looks of those in the room, especially Ward, who had not taken his eyes off him, Kipner was now an involuntary obligated servant of the law.

"Since this new line of work involves a unique set of duties and expectations, would those present be in favor of an increase in wages for a typical federal marshal?" Kipner said, tossing his hat into the ring. He knew what was at stake; the danger didn't add up to $200 a year.

Grant smiled at the young man, knowing he had talked him into accepting the job. "Of course, Mr. Kipner. We have set aside a budget to satisfy your request.

"Now, we wish to have regular reports sent via carrier or otherwise. Anytime you can do so, please provide anything you might find."

When Kipner finally was free to leave the meeting, the murmurs among the cabinet members were loud enough to quickly pick up pessimistic views of never hearing from him again. Grant only sat there watching the young soldier leave the room just behind Ward, slipping through the door.

The president's dark gray eyes shifted to his appointed cabinet members when Kipner was gone.

Grant's only daughter, Nellie, had been a victim of the so-called Harrow when she was brutally attacked by a dark apparition that crept into her room one night and left her with only a few bones remaining. Grant knew the entire Cabinet didn't believe his claim, having never experienced a Sighting. Most of Congress didn't either. He just hoped it wouldn't be too late by then if they came around.

*

Kipner was escorted out promptly by Ward, who said nothing until they were outside.

The federal marshal was stocky for his height, standing at 6'2", but his girth gave people hesitancy in confronting him. He enjoyed wearing mutton chops that nearly joined at the chin and a derby hat that covered a receding hairline.

"I'm not entirely sure why Ed selected you, Robert," the marshal said as he stepped before Kipner to stop him. "Your record isn't impressive. Your parents are dead. No one could pull strings. So how did you wind up making a list?"

"I send them all Christmas cards every year," Kipner replied and tried to sidestep around the marshal but was blocked. "That makes me reliable."

Ward puffed his chest out and sneered up at Kipner. He lowered his voice and spoke softly. "You know we only awaken once. Your mind won't handle it when you come to realize that."

Before he could reply, Ward stiffly brushed past him and back inside, sending his shoulder into Kipner's side forcefully. It would be several years later before the young soldier fully understood what he had meant.

The day he was sworn into office as a United States marshal was depressingly wet. A storm had passed through the city earlier that day, and lingering showers had kept the temperatures low and chilly. Because of the unusually few members, the preceding occurred indoors regardless of the weather. The ceremony was unceremoniously private, with only those members sworn in, Attorney General Pierrepont and a few minor White House personnel. Kipner noticed none of the Cabinet was present nor Grant.

With badges passed out and papers signed, Kipner was eventually free to leave again. This time, he received a carriage that took him a few minutes east to a small cafe he had enjoyed his last visit. Fate would have it, choosing to go there at that moment, he met Lucy.

She was cute but not beautiful, with golden blonde hair that was always messy. Her skin was fair except for her hands, which were calloused from years of working on her father's farm or digging in the dirt for lost artifacts. Her bright blue eyes demanded full attention from anyone they fell upon.

Archaeology was not a common practice for women in 1866, but she delved into it with such a headstrong mind that few stood in her way. Among her findings, she frequently found herself further and further from civilization, often leading her into native territories. Her line of work was hazardous because of it. With the new developments of the Harrow, her career had amplified in difficulty. Much of her dealings with the natives had been sensational, however. In fact, among many native tongues, she was known as White Dove for the peace she would bring with her.

When Kipner first met her in the cafe that rainy day, she was not looking her best or in the best mood. She had come to Washington as an activist to promote protection for natives across the country. When she was laughed off Capitol Hill, she returned with fire and brimstone to join the growing movements for women's rights.

The rain had driven away customers, and much of the cafe was empty when the young soldier stepped in with a newspaper over his head for shelter. She had been sitting by herself near the window at a table, staring listlessly out with her hands cradling a white cup of coffee.

His clumsy efforts to keep his wet clothes from shedding water everywhere resulted in lightly sprinkling her, which sent her over the edge.

Up to that point in his life, he had faced high-marksman soldiers, strange and powerful entities, and dangerous predators. Lucy, however, gave him the most fright in his life at that moment.

Her fists lashed out, pummeling his chest with such beatings he knew not what to do. Behind him was a downpour outside, and he thought it was best to be soaked than face her another minute.

When the tantrum had subsided, Lucy had returned to her chair, and the sheepish face of Kipner apologetically offered her a meal. Her sharp blue eyes shot at him defiantly, but something about the young man subdued her anger when she finally looked at him. He had a calculated look as if he knew how to handle any situation.

Soon the two were deep in conversation over their current predicaments while enjoying dinner.

The days flew by, and the two rapidly fell for one another. Their chemistry was evident to those few who were in the cafe that day, and they spent the next few weeks together supporting Lucy's cause. Kipner helped Lucy control her fiery temper and remain level-headed. At the same time, she inspired him to rise above and help those without a voice.

Weeks soon turned into months, and Kipner still remained in Washington. He was reporting weekly about exploring the city for clues. Still, he knew he could only stay there by drawing attention to his lack of effort.

"They're using you, Bobby," she said behind teary eyes after he confessed the need for him to set out West. "All they want is a reason to sweep the dust under the rug and forget everything until it is too late."

She gently caressed his face, which always softened him to clay. By now, it was clear to him that was precisely what they had in mind. They would send him out into the wild, force him to face countless evils and expect him to die early. From that, Washington could deny any claim and gently change the focus to more exciting topics.

"I'm not doing this for them," Kipner said, gently holding her hand to his cheek. "Answers need to be found. I've seen what happens when things go unchecked out there, hon. You do, too."

"So you will just go out there and expect to find your answers? It's not that easy, Bobby," Lucy said, brushing back her tears. "I need you. You can do so much more staying here with me."

Long nights had been spent with Lucy, knowing deep down that he was a split man. His love for her had become strong, but the desire to learn why so many lived in fear each day was just as powerful. He could remain happy with her, but it would be short-lived. Sooner or later, the safe world would shrink until the only proper safe place might be the afterlife.

To say she was bitter at him the day he left was an understatement. Deep down, she knew some presence threatened various parts of the country, but she couldn't accept that it would ever become more severe. Throughout history, there were always dangers in the world that posed as a threat. This was just one of the many which would pass like the rest with time.

Her efforts in Washington without Kipner were in vain. She had lost the male voice that was louder in politics. Each year, more women would unite to shout out for their rights. Still, her original passion for native protection faded into a dream.

Nearly ten years had passed since their romantic blossom had been felt. From time to time, Kipner tried to reach out to her, learning she had given up her political goals to focus on her archaeological interests and was working for the Chicago Academy of Sciences.

But his letters were never returned.

*

"With all due respect, Mr. President, this is suicide. It's untamed wilderness throughout most of the country. Add to that the chance the Harrow is real. It's asking too much," one of the gentlemen, hovering around the president, said as Grant gazed out the large front window overlooking the lawn.

The Unconditional Surrender puffed away on a new cigar and savored the smoke in his mouth before he released it into the air.

He grunted at the notion then said, "I'm aware of that, Mr. Chandler, but we need better transportation from California. Crops are thriving out West, and abundant minerals are discovered every week. Resources this part of the country needs."

"Yes, but if we delayed it another year and give the marshals some time to ease the turmoil lands first, it would be safer to build. In the meantime, we can establish more trade wagons."

The room erupted once again with a sea of arguments. Grant lowered his head like a heavy weight as he heard the other Cabinet members disagreeing with the Secretary of Interior for the hundredth time. He enjoyed the challenges of being a president, but some decisions were beyond his tolerance. He faced rapid growth on the East Coast as more people arrived from Europe each day and, through that, increased demand for food. Out West, there were constant assaults between forts and native tribes, battling each other for land in a nearly lawless region. Top priorities went to areas Grant had control over.

"First, we have delayed this for fifteen years from fear of the Harrow's authenticity," Grant said, glaring at his Cabinet members into silence. "I think the delay is strong evidence the Harrow is real. We now have four private enterprises, two of which were originally chartered, eager and willing to take the risk at no cost, might I remind you, well aware of the dangers of the job. In the end, we will have four equally distanced tracks running coast to coast that will forge the United States into an industrial era," the president said.

His speech didn't give him solace, however. He had made the controversial decision to include two companies, both of which had gained an unnaturally large distance ahead of the others. Both companies had a history, but they were so willing Grant decided if they failed, the country would still have whatever rails had been laid.

So far, no one had solved the riddle of how they achieved their high performance, but Grant often would lay awake at night, fearing he had made a devastating mistake in his choice.

CHAPTER VII

Dakota Territory, 1875

Smoke rose above the spruce and red cedar trees in a thick plume. From dozens of miles away, the sight of fire had drawn attention to the marshal. Still, he had hoped to see tipis scattered across an open Dakota prairie. Instead, he saw several wooden houses surrounded by a palisade, licked in flames. From his vantage point overlooking Fort Randall, he could make out soldiers scampering hastily to dowse the flames with buckets of water. It was clear most of the fort was doomed.

Roy was sent into a full gallop. Kipner was within the compounds within a few minutes, leaping off before Roy stopped and aided against the fire. Nearby was the Missouri River, but a lack of buckets to carry the river water resulted in the battle lost. While the fort was not destroyed, it was now vulnerable to further attacks. It would be weeks before the damaged walls, let alone the buildings, were rebuilt.

Everyone was exhausted and collapsed onto chairs and the ground as they watched the last fire burn itself out. Cups of water were passed around to soothe burned skin and dry throats. Somber moods among the men were apparent while their civilian wives cried worriedly.

Kipner had found the fort's commanding officer, Colonel Lugenbeel, who had just been given the duty the year before. He learned from him the attack on the fort had been by an unusual native tribe.

"The Lakota have been peaceful with us for years," the colonel said while sipping water out of a ladle. "I recognized some of them as they tore through the fort earlier this morning. Their behavior was entirely unnatural."

There was a tremor in his hand as he held the ladle, cradling it with both hands to steady it enough to drink without spilling it. His eyes glazed over momentarily as he stared off into the distance. He had clearly witnessed traumatic sights that even damaged a seasoned soldier like the colonel.

"They came for meat. They tore through the place, house to house, dragging people out into the night. Some victims disappeared into the trees screaming, then suddenly silenced. Others weren't so lucky and were slaughtered before the sights of everyone else."

Lugenbeel pointed a shaky finger to a few bloody patches of grass where the fire hadn't charred. Pieces of raw flesh scattered around each pool.

"They craved the taste of us," the colonel continued, his voice barely strong enough to speak. "I have never seen a more diabolic, grotesque sight. They feasted before my eyes on my troop. On my friends!"

Kipner wondered if he would ever be capable of commanding again. Nothing more could be acquired from him. Beyond his testimony, he did nothing more than mumble while looking at the ground with hollow eyes.

A few soldiers were desensitized far enough to communicate more reasonably. These men had gone through some of the bloodiest battles in the Civil War, yet they were not fully healed from the sights that morning.

One particular young man, only nineteen, had wandered to the fort six months before after escaping a brutally abusive family somewhere in Minnesota. His strong will saved his life, fending off the cannibalistic warriors and preventing the fire from worsening.

"A few had passed through a few weeks before," the young man began. "Brought in some furs to trade for oats and wheat. Nothing strange.

"Today was out of the Bible. Like the Devil came after us. They all started taking bites out of us. Ripped them right off the bone they did. Dragged the rest off that way."

He pointed towards the northwest from the fort, and when Kipner showed him the map McMannon had, the young man identified the dot on the map as the spot.

Remaining to help was heavy on Kipner's mind as he sat and watched the people of Fort Randall mill about, scavenging what little remained of the burned buildings. He wished to help them return to a more protective state if he didn't have more pressing tasks.

His thoughts moved to Flying Hawk and the deep concern his life might be in jeopardy. It sounded like his tribe was now a victim of another Harrow entity, and Kipner couldn't stand the thought of his old friend being tortured.

The Wraith had first learned about Flying Hawk shortly before what became known as Red Cloud's War in 1866. It was soon after Kipner became a U.S. Marshal. Leaving Washington D.C., he had found his first travels heading to Wyoming, where he picked up onto the Bozeman Trail. He knew the trail benefited travelers wishing to cross the Rockies. Still, it severely cut through several native tribes, including the Cheyenne and Lakota.

When Kipner made his way through, the two tribes had banded together with the Arapaho to form an impressive force to counter the United States army. Several forts had been constructed in the Crow native territory in response to attacks on civilians, and the natives were sending raid parties against them.

It was a horrible time in the country already. America had been divided for years, constantly fighting between armies and the natives. Now, the addition of the Harrow spelled doom for America. There were so many sides to decide which to stand upon it quickly became confusing.

Kipner knew that the move of European immigrants westward would continue. More people meant more areas they took up that were originally tribal territories. It was an epidemic that was allowed to run uncontrolled. The natives had no voice in the matter.

However, beginning his career as a federal marshal by firing upon the U. S. army was an easy decision. Through his eyes, he saw the power of the government unleash its wrath upon a people severely handicapped by comparison. They were the innocents against a tyrannical, often sinister organization, much like how his mother often overpowered him as a child when she was blinded by opium.

The first encounter with Flying Hawk had been dicey. His small scouting party had ambushed the marshal while camping along the trail and almost killed him. What saved him was, by sheer luck, a patrol party traveling down the path from one of the army's forts. It allowed Kipner to show his skills with his Sharps long-range rifle, sending half the patrol to their graves before they reached them, to which Flying Hawk's party quickly dispatched the remaining few.

From there, Kipner had created a formidable disguise, although he had little doubt to ever be recognized this far west. Even so, he was cautious while he aided the raiding parties, staying considerably distanced from the forts and firing his rifle upon the lookouts while the natives charged in from the distraction. He quickly became a trusted ally among the three tribes, most notably with Flying Hawk.

The young warrior was destined to be chief of his Lakota tribe, and he possessed vast knowledge of his ancestry and history while wishing to constantly learn the ways of the white men that Kipner could feed him. The Wraith learned to use the bow and Flying Hawk the rifle at their respective quality of skill.

After Red Cloud's War, the two had briefly traveled together to strengthen Kipner's chance of success. During this short period, Kipner began to believe the natives weren't to blame for the Harrow but were somehow connected. He was taught various means of protection that were useful during Sighting encounters.

These thoughts replayed in his mind as he guided Roy northwest, which soon led down into a narrow valley. A large flood had once transformed the valley floor into a dense swamp. It deepened alarmingly fast, and Kipner was forced to guide Roy through the duckweed and water lilies while dodging a few aggressively curious snakes. On more than one occasion, Roy saved Kipner from a particular bite by the horse pummeling the snake with its hoof.

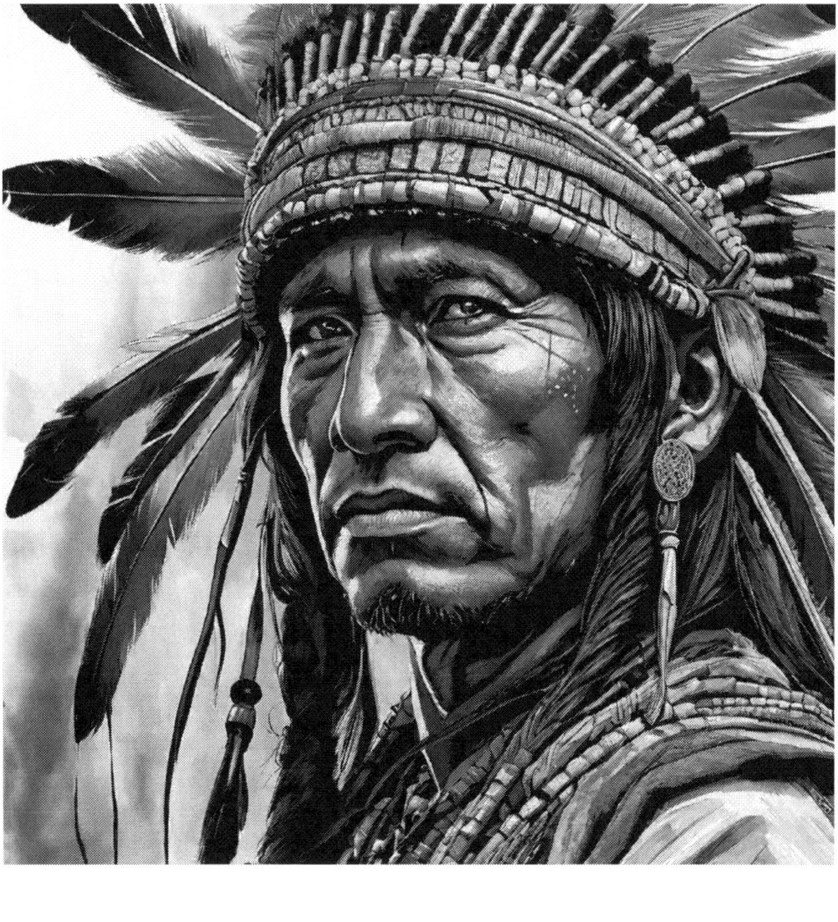

Progress had been less than ideal for the marshal, and his eyes kept turning to the west, knowing the sun was settling soon. He had traveled most of the day searching for signs of the Oglala Lakota people, confident he would come across them now that he had a good idea of direction.

While he couldn't find current signs of the tribe, he came across old remnants of a past group that survived among the highland swamps. Several old huts had been built just above the water level and were connected by primitive rope bridges. Each house was cylindrical in shape with a peaked conical roof made out of old dead leaves that wouldn't resist a light sprinkle.

None of the buildings were significant, but one was enough to allow Roy to get out of the water for the night and onto dry land. Nearby was another hut suitable for Kipner to stretch out on its floor with just his feet exposed outside.

Through the darkness, Kipner's eyes came alive, and he gazed around the hut he was in. The dark wood was rotted with deeply recessed grains worn away with time. Someone had carved deeply against the boards in one area to form a series of markings that would have been unfamiliar to Kipner had he not acquired three stones with the same strange markings already.

They had been found in seemingly random places in the country, always nearby some powerful entity he would encounter or see signs of its presence. Each one had been buried into a small fetish or tiny-sized person used as a charm in a necklace.

There was no way of telling how old the stones or the hut he was in. Perhaps if Lucy was around, she would immediately be able to identify the tribe and date with high accuracy.

Beams of moonlight pierced the light clouds overhead. They gently covered the surface water, creating heavy shadows under the gathering trees. Water ripples formed beside lilies accompanied by tiny bubbles which great larger. The disturbance caused Roy to awaken from his snooze with a start and dance fearfully against the old wooden floor.

For the moment, Kipner leaned outside for the floorboards that wrapped the circumference of the hut were only a few inches deep. Something outside in the water was slowly surfacing. Only turtles would cause any kind of ebullition this far north, and the immense size of the area exceeded anything he had ever seen. The diameter was more significant than all the huts combined.

It froze him in terror, and he instinctively grabbed the door frame of the hut for stability though his house stayed firm. The weakness in his legs fooled him into thinking he was sinking into the muck.

Before him, cresting the surface, emerged a single eye, large enough to stand upon and walk about. Its pupil, a black slit comparable to a goat or frog's eye, looked about the area as if to take in the valley for the first time. Finally, it rested on Kipner.

The night air became cold and crisp as the Wraith was studied in silence by the monstrosity. Nearby, Roy battered his hooves to protest the sight but dared not enter the water. The pupil locked firmly on the marshal.

Buzzing night insects swarmed around him, ruthlessly biting against his skin that quickly formed into welts. They throbbed and grew red with sharp needle-like pain at each spot.

A small idea slowly grew into thought and desire somewhere in his mind. His desire escalated to hunger, but he knew his rations would not satisfy his craving.

The bugs backed off together, and the eye started submerging into the abyss again. It left Kipner with a different look in his eye, one that of flesh-eating. He knew he needed to feed soon, and sleep was no longer a burden. Roy emerged from his entrapment from fear and tore through the fragile old hut, surging into the water in search of dry land.

The Wraith had no hunger for the horse but followed the animal anyway into the night. They pushed through the water for different desperate reasons. All the while, Roy neighing, frightened at what was trailing behind.

As they fought, the ground shuddered, sending the entire swamp into violent ripples while the trees shook vigorously. The valley was too wide to see both sides along the floor. Yet, Kipner witnessed them tower above the trees, higher and higher, and begin to curve overhead and fuse in the middle. The light from the moon was blocked by the curvature, which sealed the two inside and formed a cavern.

His incredible eyes gave him just enough sight in the pitch-black to avoid running into trees. "Devil's Eyes," his mother called them when she was hellbent on abusing him as a young teen. He would hide in the darkest corners of the house at night where little to no light was shown in hopes she wouldn't see.

He never knew how he came to possess such a gift, but he had carried the talent all his life. When he was an adult, he wondered if something had given him the ability. There had been enough people he crossed paths with to know they had made deals with Things they would later regret. So the idea he was granted anything without his consent bothered him from time to time that whatever gave it to him would one day come for the payment.

At last, they found the swamp's edge and stepped onto a narrow ledge that hugged the cavern walls. Now that Roy was out of the water and hadn't been eaten by his companion, the horse settled down to allow Kipner to get closer.

Behind in the water were hundreds of enormous eyes, some larger than a house, all staring at him. Together they displaced the water. Each moved independently, slightly shifting as they watched the man look back.

"What are you?" Kipner shouted out. "What have you done to me?" The hunger bored a hole into his skull, and he could barely keep it from controlling him. Each eye tried trickling into his mind like a thousand voices whispering to let them in.

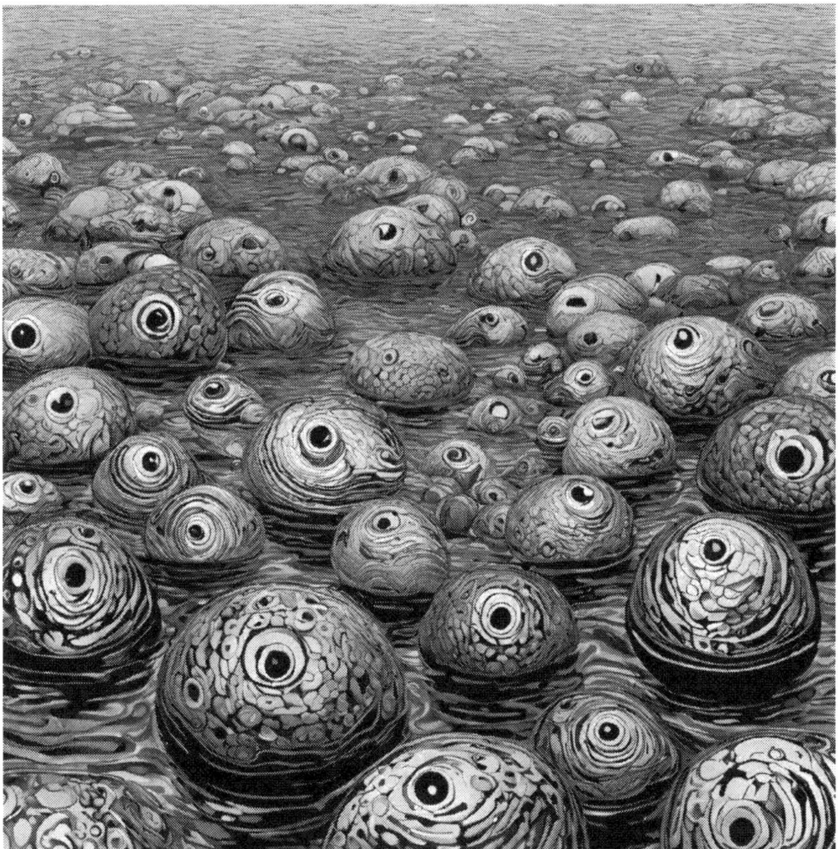

There wasn't much to work with along the rim of the swamp, and Kipner paid careful attention to each step across loose stones and soft soil that wanted to send him into the pond made of eyes.

Green grass had covered both sides of the valley before terminating into the water, but now the blades of grass gave way to solid, rough rock. Its irregular, rough surface would be ideal for climbing had it not curved outward over the swamp.

While his hunger drove him through the night, his eyes picked up a fissure in the wall that continued up and out of sight in one straight line. Its position was in approximation to where the two slopes merged.

Unfortunately, he had no pick axe or shovel to chip away or venture deeper into the crack. He carried no tool that would aid him in excavating; he believed the fissure was a possibility of getting out somehow.

The other end of the crack was found on the other side when Kipner finished his travel around the water's edge. With each step, he was accompanied by his faithful companion and an endless collection of slit pupil eyes. The entire journey took a few hours.

Where the crack ended, it was slightly different. A small cave at the base reached a ways back into the wall the man could push through. However, it needed to be more significant for Roy. He wasn't about to leave the poor animal alone without suitable food. Still, it was the only exit he could find, and he decided to make his way through to see if it brought him out.

Fresh air greeted him long before he finally saw the night sky again. He pulled himself out of a vertical hole covered mainly by large stones. After being in the stale swamp air for so long, the new scent of outside brought him peace for a moment. The valley never existed. Above him was a typical, peaked mountain with no sign of a ravine. Snow-capped above the tree line edge, the mountain sloped dangerously down to the ground below.

His given point was not ideal for any movement other than falling to his death, so he returned to the underground swamp to rejoin Roy. The animal had found its way over to a gathering of lilies and was savoring a sample.

"The Wraith cometh," Kipner warned the entity surrounding him. What he thought was nothing more than a swamp had trapped him within like a great fish swallowing him whole. If all he could see comprised the beast, he was in a religious formation comparable to a mountain. From the outside, it was nothing more than a mountain. The scale was difficult to comprehend, chilling him to his bones. Could this be common - the true power behind the country's disaster hidden right under their noses but of immense size?

His wandering thoughts brought him around the vast cavern again, searching for other means of escape. The longer he crept through the darkness, the more he felt himself slip into a state of mind that demanded human flesh. Each step drew him closer to losing himself entirely. The voices that hounded him coming certainly from the thousand eyes that never turned their view from him, became more familiar than his own. It wasn't long before he forgot himself and gave in to them.

The last thought the mind owned by Kipner remembered was of the great mouth opening above him and being cast out into the world to hunt.

*

Snow had piled heavily over the cold, still, body, leaving nothing more than a lump in the perfect, untouched white. Beside the frozen, partially eaten body knelt the Wraith, who slowly emerged from his trance. Caked blood crusted across his lips, and a gnawed foot was in his hand.

With a start, the mind of Kipner snapped back into focus and control, and he flung the foot away and wiped his face in horror. He had no memory of how he got there. The pure snow silenced the hillside he rested on, amplifying his heavy breathing.

He was close to a small wooden shack hastily put together and wide open to a glowing stove.

Furs covered the floor, and bones hung along the walls and ceilings. At one point, there had been crudely built furniture violently destroyed beyond repair.

No longer did he crave human flesh. His stomach was full. It was too much to take in, and he became ill in the snow. The hot bile melted the frozen white away and gave off a pungent odor so alien to him it nearly made him heave again.

Once he got control of his stomach, his thoughts went to the curse given to him. Now he carried a foreboding dread of losing track of his actions. It was clear from the body he had murdered and desecrated an innocent man. His life could not be the same again.

The cold wasn't bothering him, so he attempted to regain his bearings.

Enough snow had fallen since he lost control of himself. He could not retrace his steps back to the mountain, but he could scale the hillside he was on to get a good view of the surrounding land.

The sun reflected against the snow into Kipner's eyes, blinding him until they adjusted to the winter view. Below, a wide field spread across his view, softly rolling like sand dunes before rising again into the west. There against solid white sprinkled a few dozen tipis like pine trees.

Descending the other side of the hill was more accessible with a gentle slope. There had been no signs of Roy when he came to, but he didn't blame his friend. The animal had learned to trust him only to be frightened by his threatening menace when Roy needed him most. For all Kipner knew, he was already headed back to his former owner.

Like a grain of pepper in a bottle of salt, the lone figure traipsed across the snow toward the tribe.

The warnings from Ford Randall rang through his head as he drew closer, keeping an ever-watchful eye on the tipis ahead of the movement.

His greatest threat came not from ahead but from the corner of his eyes along a tree line. A pack of wolves burst out from hiding and sprinted towards Kipner, who spun around and raised his rifle. He drew a bead and let the bullet fly, sending one of the many sliding along the snow to a halt. There were too many, though, to reload in time.

The pistols at his side came out with both hands after his rifle swung back around his neck. Before he could pull the trigger, the sight of the wolves came closer into view. Running on all fours, they were naked humans decorated in tattoos from head to toe.

Their speed was animal-like, and they galloped with dexterity as if born to run with the aid of their arms.

It sent the Wraith running for his life, but he knew there was nowhere to run. For no other reason than pure instinct, he made a break for the tipis with the savages on his heels. Behind, they howled and hissed in unnatural sounds.

As he grew closer, he spotted a lone figure in the middle of the tipis. It was an elder woman kneeling in contemplation. She was calm and content, with no apparent awareness of incoming danger. Although Kipner yelled in warning to her, she remained still with her eyes closed.

Something shimmered around her like a dome that was tough to pick up unless viewed from a specific angle.

There was no time for the marshal as he skidded to a halt before the meditating woman. As soon as he passed through the shimmering dome, however, he felt his flesh begin to singe. The heat was painful, like a sunburn that was rapidly getting worse.

"You reek of destitute," the woman quietly spoke. "You will not survive within my sanctuary for long."

The pack of savages had reached him, but they had veered off and circled the shimmering globe. None of them challenged the barrier. He stared intently at the threat, watching them snarl like the wolves he mistook them for. Fresh blood smeared across their faces like they had recently made a kill.

He could only guess what they might have eaten.

Every inch of his skin burned intensely with pain, and he knew he couldn't stay within the confines of the woman's safety bubble. His skin showed a dark crack pattern as his flesh began to split open. From underneath, his blood began to ooze out in a thick soup.

"I'm looking for Flying Hawk. He's chief of the Oglala Lakota," he hastily said.

"His mind is not of the Lakota but of the awakened bloom that grows and spreads. They trap who he was in a cocoon of vision and torment his people," she replied soothingly.

It was a challenge to speak in complete sentences. Kipner dropped to his knees in agony and gritted through for a moment more. His body was riddled like plate tectonics shifting across a red sea.

"I'll...help...need...them," was all he could muster out as he pointed to the swarming cannibals.

In response, the woman removed a necklace she wore of a stone that he quickly adorned and rushed out of the protection of the dome. At that point, even fighting to the death felt better than a second longer in burning misery.

To his dismay, the cannibals snarled at him but shied away in repulse. They dashed back into the forest when they realized their dinner treat was off the menu. The elderly woman never flinched or made a movement the entire time.

The painful destruction of his skin fused back together once he was safe from the sanctuary. He possessed no scars or any sign of it happening.

Even the bloody ooze that excreted out between the cracks vanished.

His friend fell victim to the same catastrophe he had had. No telling how deeply he was under the control of whatever nasty Thing trapped him.

Cannibalism was a common element in the region. Kipner had befallen the curse along with the Lakotas. It was as if that was the only goal the titan monstrosity he came across earlier knew.

Inquiring further information from the woman was fruitless, and Kipner refused to re-enter the dome.

He had to find Flying Hawk on his own.

The trouble was, where?

Curiously he inspected the stone around his neck. It bore the same strange markings as the other three. If this one was the same as the others, why hadn't they saved him from the cannibals?

He had dove through the dome before they had reached him. Timing had prevented him from putting them to the test. It needed to be clarified if they would have worked or not.

Now that he had four, he couldn't help but contemplate what might be the result. He needed to locate Flying Hawk immediately.

His stomach rumbled.

He was astonished to feel the pain of hunger so soon after his last meal. As was the last time, the need for human flesh was the only appetizing thought.

He knew he would have to satisfy it soon.

With his growing hunger came a scent off in the distance that wasn't there before. It wafted in the air and danced across his nostrils in an alluring fragrance he found himself following. It was harmonious to any meal he enjoyed, bearing no resemblance to a specific food. Whatever it was, it was irresistible.

The smell took him past the edge of the rolling plains and into a low hollow cradled by two groves of trees. In the center was a tree stump from a fully grown elm. It had been cut by a blade or saw, gnarled and twisted in its life. Between two large roots, each at least six inches in thickness, was a crevice that some burrowing animal carved into and down. It would be a tight fit for Kipner, but he would prefer to find another means of satisfying his hunger.

Like a compass to the north, his attention pulled him to a hole in the stump. Flesh, human flesh, lingered below, and he needed a bite.

He was here to eat whatever was down in the hole. Although his craving was intense, he remained in control of his actions. It was peculiar, but he needed to be able to analyze the reasoning.

Peering closely, the scent became overpowered, and he began digging and crawling down below. The soil was soft, and he quickly kicked it out from behind him the more he dug. The hole was already suitable for a coyote or a giant raccoon, but those scents were absent.

Flying Hawk was just ahead in the hole staring back at his old friend. He was barely recognizable to Kipner. Nearly covered in fur, he had looked to be transferred almost into an animal, with only his facial features remaining, albeit covered equally.

"Flying Hawk, it's Wraith. I know what it did to you. It did it to..." Kipner tried saying, but Flying Hawk lashed out at him with a hand that had morphed into a clawed paw. The marshal needed to prepare or be better positioned to compose himself. The claw marks sliced three significant scratches against his face.

Backing up was awkward in the tight tunnel, and Flying Hawk gave Kipner another swipe to the face in the opposite direction with his left paw before Kipner could escape.

Outside once again, he dabbed his face with a handkerchief to spot a crisscross of blood. It stung all over, and blood quickly dripped down his face and over one eye.

His sleeve stroked much of the blood away from his eyes in time to see it slither from its hiding spot.

His friend was unrecognizable. Mostly covered in matted fur, Flying Hawk had no practice for shaving and looked like a dog with mange. His eyes reminded him of the thousand eyes he saw in the valley with horizontal slits for pupils. At least Kipner knew who was manipulating him now.

A quick shot of his pistol would end the fight quickly, but he wasn't about to shoot his dear friend no matter what he did. The older woman said his mind was trapped, not necessarily gone, so perhaps he could be saved.

Instead, Flying Hawk lunged at Kipner with uncanny speed before the marshal could dodge. The two went to the ground, and the native chief tried lashing out with both claws against Kipner's rawhide jacket. He shielded the blows with both arms, then seized his friend around the throat and tossed him off. Though nimble with speed, Kipner was far brawnier than the chief.

Immediately landing on his feet, Flying Hawk leaped back towards Kipner, but he was ready for him this time and slipped to one side, letting the native glide by. With a flash of his Bowie knife, the Wraith held it against the native's side, sending a long gash down his skin.

This time Flying Hawk toppled end over end and slid against the wet snow. Rich, bright red blood poured from his side as he lay there catching his breath.

It was a safe bet Flying Hawk's mind would not comprehend danger from a modern weapon. Still, Kipner drew his pistols and pointed them at the recovering native anyway.

Beneath his feet, Kipner's boots crunched the snow with a satisfying sound, and he walked up alongside his friend.

"Easy, my old friend," Kipner said with hushed tones. "The old lady back with your tribe said you're still with us. Just roll on your stomach, and let me take you to her. I have a feeling she can help, but you have to let me bind your wild claws."

Flying Hawk rolled quickly, sprang to its feet, and leaped again onto Kipner. The entire motion was smooth, and Kipner was desperately dodging for his life again. The native had picked up Kipner's tactic, however, and extended his paws out, striking viciously with his claws that tore across his exposed hand. The curve of the nail sunk in, and the native's momentum shredded a large section of the back of Kipner's hand off, leaving a sizeable bloody cavity with bones.

Both pistols fell to the ground, and Kipner bent over in mortifying pain, clutching his injured hand.

Flying Hawk had managed to wing his right hand, which was his dominant. Although he could shoot with his left, without the balanced weight, the feeling severely hindered his accuracy.

His hand bled profusely.

Flying Hawk came at him again, each more vicious than the last. Kipner felt the weakness start overtaking him as the white snow around stained crimson.

Once again, he was knocked over by the bolting native, and he felt his back roll over his rifle.

Flying Hawk leaped into the air in an impressive high arc, both claws extended to give Kipner a death blow to his face. The Wraith swirled behind and whipped the butt of his rifle in a violent swing in front of him.

It made contact across the side of Flying Hawk's face, sending him straight down and motionless.

His weight jolted the wind out of Kipner, and he lay there with his friend for a moment before rolling him off.

He feared he struck him too hard against the head and killed him, but the young chief still breathed, albeit in raspy, short breaths.

Kipner bandaged his wounded hand as best as he could, which was nothing more than wrapping torn cloth from his shirt. Even as thick as he wrapped it, it stained red immediately as the blood-soaked the fabric.

At a time like this, Kipner missed Roy. The native was not as burly as the marshal but was still a grown man. With one good arm, he hoisted his friend over his shoulder and trudged back through the several inches of snow, leaving a trail of blood behind. To his surprise and relief, Roy was grazing back at the camp. Kipner never learned how he found the place.

*

Flying Hawk lay still beside the elderly woman. Kipner watched as he and his companion lost their flesh painfully, each section flaking off like dried ash from burned wood. He was in misery, gritting his teeth and trying to block out the pain like before, but he was losing the battle.

When he had arrived with Flying Hawk, she had ordered him to enter her sanctuary and place him before her.

When he attempted to leave the searing pain, he was instructed to stay, too.

"Both of you are trapped within the cocoon of the blossom," she had said before beginning a series of chants.

As Kipner lay down in pain, unable to stand anymore, he felt his flesh continue to burn off in chunks, but just like Flying Hawk, fresh skin lay under the surface. They, indeed, were in some kind of cocoon membrane the old woman was casting off.

Finally, the pain overtook the marshal, and he eventually lost consciousness. His next memory was waking to a familiar face leaning over him. The joy on the native's face was radiant with a golden smile as he hugged the lying marshal.

Kipner had been placed on a cot in one of the tipis, and a fire had been made in its center. Beside the fire sat the old woman, still kneeling with her eyes closed, but there was a pleasant aura about her that was missing before.

"Welcome back, old friend," Flying Hawk said. "Looks like we live for another adventure."

After a few minutes of being conscious, Kipner sat up on his own and drank water from a cup.

The taste was ice cold and soothing to his dry throat, and he suddenly realized he had been without a stiff drink or smoke in weeks. It was not an entirely unpleasant feeling.

"I have no idea what brought you all the way up north this time of year, but I'm relieved to see you, Wraith," the chief said. "Our Elder Mother spoke of months of me entangled with that thing that dwells in the mountains to the south. To me, it was like a day had passed."

Quietly speaking to herself in silent prayer, the Elder Woman continued her practice ignoring the two men.

"Well, to be perfectly honest, I came up seeking you," Kipner said. "I'm still looking for a solution to the Harrow and thought you might shed some light on a bit I found."

Flying Hawk shook his head and smiled sympathetically. "Kip, it has been ten Winter Counts since we started your wild adventure, and you're still hunting for a solution. Has it ever occurred to you that it might not exist?"

His body still ached from the wound on his hand, and for that matter, his whole body still ached from the fight. The cocoon might be gone, but his muscles remained. The Elder Mother had relieved the pain with what Flying Hawk called ksuyeya tincture. The two men had to gather bark from a willow and a mullein root to which she mixed a clear liquid from a plant and water. When applied, the stinging pain subsided shortly after that.

With a sigh, Kipner nodded.

"Some days that crosses my mind. But then, something like this out of nowhere keeps me going."

Leaning with a grown over to his satchel, he withdrew McMannon's book and the three other stones matching his necklace and presented them to Flying Hawk.

"Not sure what to make out of them. You were with me when we found one of these stones, and the markings match what's in this book a crazy old man blaming an ancient tribe for the Harrow had. I've seen these markings in other places too. Up around where I ran into that thing in the mountain," Kipner said. He caught movement out of the corner of his eyes from the Elder Mother but otherwise remained still.

The native inspected each of the stones and then turned to the book. He was well-educated and could read a few languages. Still, after opening the book, he flung it across the tipi in fear.

"That book is dangerous. Lethal. Do not read what is inscribed inside."

The marshal glanced over to the haphazard book and raised an eyebrow. "I respect your beliefs. You know I do, but I have trouble believing reading something will cause anything bad to happen."

"That is the very reason the world is in its state," Flying Hawk answered.

"People are so closed-minded that they refuse to believe things if it contradicts their so-called rational thinking.

"Look around you, Wraith. How can you doubt a book is lethal when you were swallowed by a mountain full of eyes?"

He had a point. He once denied the Sightings as accurate before finally succumbing to the truth. Why would he now doubt his friend's claim? Who knows what the reality that went beyond his comprehension was?

The voice of the Elder Mother crackled like the fire beside her with a gargle in the back of her throat. She spoke with a fierceness that snapped the attention of both men.

Flying Hawk translated for his friend. "The book is from the awakened blossom."

"You said that name before. What is the awakened blossom?" Kipner asked.

"The Elder Mother spoke to you before?" Flying Hawk asked. Kipner nodded, which perplexed his companion.

"When I first met her, I was being chased by your tribal members. She said the awakened or the awakening blossom had trapped your mind."

"Those behind the Harrow? They are the awakening blossom?" Kipner asked her.

After she didn't reply, Kipner inquired about the other tribe members roaming like wild animals seeking human flesh.

According to Flying Hawk, he learned the Elder Mother only spoke Lakota. Despite Kipner's insistence on talking to her earlier, she had yet to learn English.

Instead, the chief translated for him, and she explained the remainder of the tribe lacked the strong will Flying Hawk possessed to be saved. Their cocoon was fused to their spirits, and they would die within her sanctuary.

She said no more that night to them. Until she turned in for sleep, she continued muttering the chant.

They spent the evening talking about Kipner's travels since they had last seen one another a few years ago. Towards the end, as their eyes grew heavy, Kipner brought up the book again. It was late into the night before either friend wanted to sleep.

"I recognized the writing," Flying Hawk said. "It was chaotic in just what little I saw. There were pieces of Algonquin...I'm not sure what the English word would be...symbols, but there was another I did not recognize."

The book was safely tucked back into Kipner's satchel unopened. He recalled what he had seen when he thumbed through it.

"Latin was in there," he said, reflecting on the thought. "I just recognized the words, but I have no idea their meaning. But I know someone who does."

His friend shook his head.

"You still are driven to open that book again. It is going to kill someone. There is a power within those pages just waiting to be unleashed."

With a tired yawn, Flying Hawk rose from his seat and exited the tipi. At the opening, he turned back to Kipner.

"She's not the person you had in mind, right?"

After all these years, Flying Hawk remembered that short period in his life. He had talked about her in their travels after the War, and Flying Hawk had, on numerous occasions, encouraged him to seek her out and perhaps give up the badge.

When Kipner only looked at him, the native knew. A look of sorrow filled his face. "In that case, I had better come along. She will need protection, and the Elder Mother can't travel. I doubt it will be enough."

CHAPTER VIII

Missouri, 1875

In the winter of 1875, Wraith and Flying Hawk slowly worked east toward Chicago. Much of their travels took them out of the method further south to avoid dangerously cold weather. At one point, they had made it as far south as Missouri, which spawned reflections of Kipner's initial station in St. Louis.

He had been assigned to Jefferson Barracks, a prominent military base along the Mississippi River on the city's south side. His expectations for lack of military excitement held true as most of his duties comprised marching and watching ships pass by. Most of his nights had been spent writing in a journal that he found enlightening and confusing.

From time to time, as he put ink to paper, he would realize soon after he had written an event in his life that felt strangely out of place. Names of people he was not familiar with ever having met, like Renaldo Archibald III and Natasha, would form onto his pages subconsciously. He would sometimes jot down memories of traveling to foreign countries on vast steam vessels. What was most peculiar was when he began making rough sketches of images that initially had no meaning. There was a memory of his father standing beside a black machine resembling a wagon without horses. The memory was so vividly painted in his mind that he could loosely replicate it onto paper. Of course, he never shared such sketches with anyone for fear of being committed.

When the two travelers came into the outskirts of St. Louis, Kipner suggested visiting his old barracks and see if anyone he had stationed with remained.

The sun had set long ago when they made it to the gates, and lanterns had been lit on either side with two guards at attention. They were much younger than the forty-five-year-old marshal, so he decided to ease any tension and offered his badge when they inquired about his business.

"The barracks is off limits to civilians. Seek elsewhere for your business," one of the soldiers said, ignoring the badge and avoiding eye contact. Kipner could see both men had carefully re-positioned their hands on their sidearm.

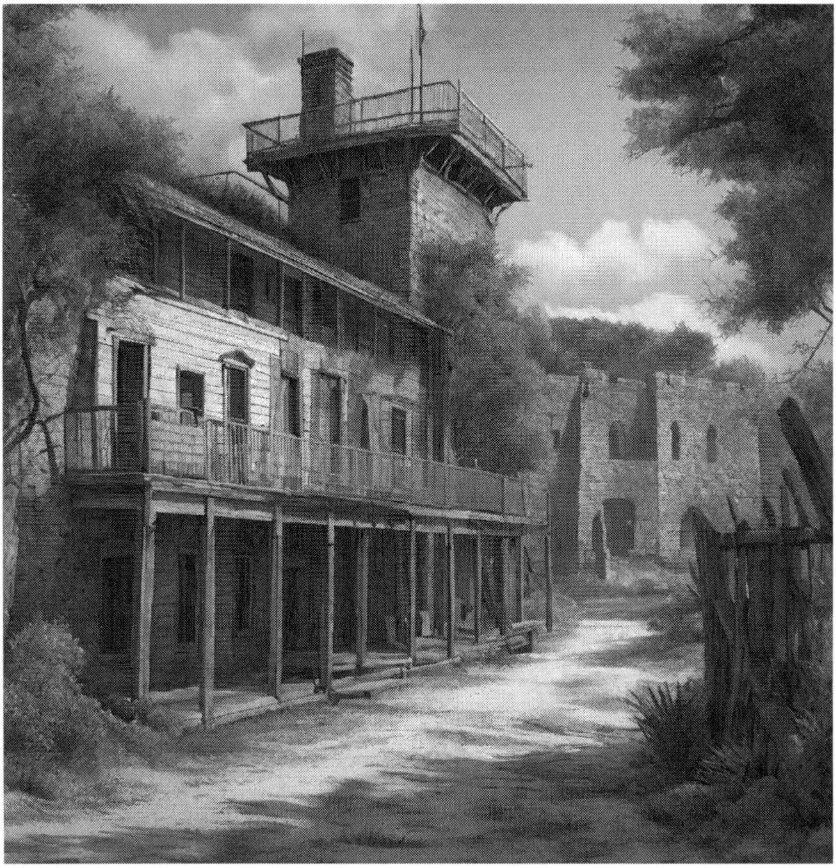

Kipner eased his hand off his duster's lapel that carried the polished badge. After the Civil War, when he was assigned to be there, the need for the place was nil, and he was among just a few who lived there. He remembered hearing the news in 1867 the army's Engineering Department had taken over the facility and was presumed to still operate it. Today it was thought to be a recruitment center for the cavalry. Clearly, something had altered those plans. What good would a recruitment facility be if they turned away possible recruits?

"The name's Kipner, U. S. Marshal," he said to emphasize the sight of his badge. "Used to be a part of Company C of the 13th Regiment, U. S. Infantry, here in '61. Captain Greer commanded the barracks then, though I hear it's governed by the Engineering Department."

Neither soldier even flickered at his words and remained at sharp attention. Their hands remained gently resting on their sidearm. Beside the marshal, Flying Hawk had taken several steps away and looked poised to flee at any minute. He dared not speak and let his friend handle the situation.

"Is there a provost marshal on duty? An assistant?" Kipner asked but was ignored. "Military police of any kind?"

Continued silence was all the soldiers were willing to give to him, and their grips were becoming tighter. He wondered if they would shoot a U. S. Marshal on the grounds of asking questions on free soil.

"Ah, I guess you all are having a private birthday party for one of the men," Kipner said with a smirk. "I wouldn't want to miss out on cake, but I understand if there isn't enough. You boys, have a good evening."

Quietly into the night, the Wraith retreated with Flying Hawk at his side, occasionally looking back at the two guards. The native nervously kept pace with the long-striding Kipner, who walked purposefully.

"Did you really think they would let you in after all these years?" the young native asked as they returned to St. Louis in search of a hotel.

The burly mustache crowning Kipner's upper lip and covering most of his mouth concealed much of his frown.

"If it's just a place for recruiting, yes. The whole area should comprise engineers and not mind civilians coming and going. Those two looked like they were poised for war."

They had separated themselves from the barracks by a few miles. However, Flying Hawk was still nervously looking back to ensure they weren't being followed. The lantern light wasn't even in view.

"You were a few seconds away from being torn to shred by those bullets. I've never seen such aggression over something so petty."

The moment briefly came back to Kipner's mind. He had wondered if they would come to life and aid him in a hard battle if he were attacked or restricted. He felt his guns lightly vibrate in their holsters each inch the soldiers had moved for their weapons.

Both were tired, and the night was late when they found a hotel with available rooms. Something had brought in a lot of visitors, and all but a few rooms were full. The two were forced to share one, and Flying Hawk drew the short end for the wooden floor.

By early morning the reason was apparent why so many guests were staying in town. At the sight of the marshal, people staying in the hotel tried to cling onto the lapel of his coat and beg for his help. They had escaped from the other side of the river in Cahokia near the burial mounds.

"We were overrun!"

"They feasted on all of us!"

"So many didn't make it. So many."

The voices sobbed and cried out for Kipner, who gently regained control of the room. Their clothes were soiled and carried the aroma of filth. Their fingers were black and stained from soil or similar.

"Alright, alright, everyone. Let's calm down and have a seat, and I'll hear all of your stories." Kipner said, pulling himself into a chair. Hawk peeked at the bartender of the hotel's saloon, but he only shook his head sadly.

"Now, what drove you out of town? Too many of what exactly?" Kipner asked, lighting a cigar for the first time in a few months. The thick taste of smoke was harsh this early in the day, or perhaps it had been too long since he last enjoyed one.

He held a hand up at them all as they began blurting out once again their individual problems until a little old lady was pointed out to speak for everyone.

Only a little was worn by the woman. Her dress was made from burlap and a strap of hemp for a crude belt. However, her eyes were brilliant green and hard to gaze upon. They were contrasted dramatically by the harsh creases on her face that told the story of her struggles. She had been through a lot; it was obvious from a single glance.

When she spoke, Kipner and the rest of the company in the room leaned forward to hear her soft whisper voice. It was gentle and timid, like a nurturing mother telling a bedtime story to a sick child.

"Mr. Sheriff," she mistakenly called Kipner by the presence of his badge. "We are being hunted."

Something deep in Kipner's mind snapped at the line, and for a moment, the world stopped for him. The sentence she spoke triggered some odd memory that had significance to him. Something about the phrase frightened him. Along with the fear, he heard a voice say "unawindwa" that, too, felt familiar though he didn't understand.

The old woman continued, "Those of our past have come to kill us all. We have not been honorable to our ancestors, and now we pay the price."

The room erupted with contradictions to her specific statement but sided with her implication. Taking bits and pieces of many of the patrons at the hotel, Kipner heard the ancient burial mounds in Cahokia, just across the river, had recently become disturbed. Holes large enough for someone to burrow through had formed overnight and left empty graves within. Many of the people felt they would be attacked by the awakened dead. In contrast, others believed in less drastic theories of grave robbery.

As harsh as robbing a grave was in the eyes of the law, he wished it was that in truth. He knew all too well the people were facing a more sinister threat. But walking corpses were the least of his efforts at the present time. His duties were far broader than settling the unrest deceased.

"This matter is suited for the city marshal or your sheriff. I'm afraid my duties take me elsewhere. I only stayed here for the evening for rest before moving on."

Cries lashed out at the marshal. He picked up words like "no sheriff," "they're dead," and "missing." Each one surrounding him was filled with sorrow and desperation.

It took Kipner a moment to make a decision despite his better judgment. His task, laid out by the president himself, was to identify and potentially discover a means to eradicate the growing threat to the nation. Every incident may not lead to a solution, but they could shed light on the immediate danger in that area. The map from McMannon strongly hinted there were concentrated pockets spread across the land, which affected the area's folks.

"Alright, alright," Kipner said again with his hands up to calm the mob. "I'll inspect the mounds and see what I can do."

A resounding cheer came from the crowd, and they seemed satisfied enough with his answer to simmer and return to their seats. A few volunteered their rifles as pseudo deputies to Kipner after they realized he was a U. S. Marshal. Still, he made them all promise to remain in the hotel's safety. If anything came for them, they could protect themselves inside or dash south to Jefferson Barracks as refugees. They wouldn't deny a large group that was attacked.

"It is important to find a way to return the bodies to their graves," Flying Hawk said as they crossed the recently completed Eads Bridge, the first of its kind across the Mississippi River for St. Louis. Taking seven years to build, it crossed the more comprehensive portion south of the Missouri River.

"I doubt they will want to go back inside," Kipner said, glancing over the rushing water below. "I've seen plenty of awakened corpses before. They typically aren't much of a danger unless in large numbers. But I've come to find that they don't spring up without some power source. Someone usually tampering with an ancient artifact they found along a creek or cave. The difficult part is finding that individual."

Once across the river, they turned north and followed the riverbank, then veered east toward the location of the burial mounds. They rose above the trees impressively to nearly a hundred feet in the air and could be seen from a few miles away. Neither Kipner nor Flying Hawk knew just how many there were.

"Seventy of them?" the native asked rhetorically as they studied the numerous dirt mounds covering the terraced structures. "There could be hundreds in the area."

The young man knelt down and studied the ground around him, feeling the cold winter air breeze pass over his shoulders. Even from this distance, there had been unorthodox tracks of footprints that seemed to wander aimlessly in the area. None of them had a purpose or direction like a drunk.

Roy broke their moment of concentration as he snorted and stomped his hooves toward their right. Kipner slid his Sharps from the saddle holster, cautiously loaded a round, and cocked the gun.

Three stumbling figures emerged slowly from the tree line to the east about fifty yards away. They began making their way in a loose pattern toward them. Neither of them moved with urgency.

Even during the morning hours of sun, their disorderly manners were uncomfortable to most citizens encountering them.

The two watching the shambling figures slowly approach agreed they could avoid the confrontation and loud gun noises if they hustled further north. Flying Hawk had brought his favorite horse, Cloudy Day, a gray and white Appaloosa with a Grulla blanket pattern across her hip which, up to that point, had tolerated Roy at best. Given the situation, however, she preferred riding abreast of her counterpart more than dealing with the bodies that gave off a terrible odor.

They galloped further north, drawing closer to the mounds to get a better look. Kipner had no idea how to locate any source of what had disturbed the bodies, but he hoped there was something to find closer to danger.

The area around the mounds had been cleared off and laid relatively flat and hard-packed from the cold winter weather. Remnants of decent snow stilled gathered in large patches. As they came up close to where they could make out numerous holes scattered across the surface of each mound, the ground shifted to a cracked sediment that continued to further compartmentalize as they grew closer. These cracks, some three feet in width, wedged several feet downward. Soon they came to a wide fissure; the horses were at risk of failing the leap.

"I've never seen cracks like these before, Wraith," Flying Hawk said, glancing around at the imposing force. Like fingers gathering around the throat, they were choking them slowly.

"You and me both. I need help to spot a good safe path. There are no means of reaching them from this side. Let's try going around along the east edge."

With considerable difficulty, they tread cautiously along the narrow cracks in a wide arc, watching nearby tree clusters or the mounds themselves for any movement. The noonday sun removed any heavy shadows except directly under trees, which gave them plenty of visibility.

Cloudy Day had a knack for finding obscure paths. She had come from out west in Arizona. She was traded to Flying Hawk after several years of guiding riders into the canyons of the desert. With little effort, Flying Hawk loosened his grip on the reigns and let her find the right path.

Suddenly she balked going further, but they saw nothing ahead that might be a danger. More cracks laid in their path, but even Kipner saw a few areas they could safely take.

Then Roy picked up on the scent as well and began whining. Something made numerous clicking noises from within one of the cracks ahead. Those were accompanied by the cracks all around them.

Drifting up from the depths within came swarms of bird-like insects with oversized proportions. With wings spread wide, comparable to a hawk, two sets sputtered wildly to hold up a tagmata body. The oversize head was amplified with a foot-long proboscis that pulsated slowly. Its skin was pinkish in hue with a sickly green fading in around the edges. The swarm, numbering a few dozen, gazed at the two riders with sixteen multifaceted eyes that blinked rapidly.

Each chittered at one other with two small limbs emerging on either side of their mouths, which took the shape of an upside-down V. These tiny extensions tapped each other like a drummer with sticks so rapidly the sound was humming-like. There was intelligence in their behaviors, making clear signals to each other and acknowledging the requests and orders.

Flying Hawk and Wraith faced an unbeatable foe. The Wraith's pistols were already held firmly in his hands. The twelve before him would become thirty, and he would need to reload. He knew this species came in immense clusters, sometimes numbering in the thousands.

Within the pages of the Hallow Doctrine, the strange bugs were called Upolios. Against many scientists' wishes, Kipner gave names to the unknown discovered species. He welcomed others to publish any information before him.

The purpose of an Upolio, as far as Kipner could deduce, was to absorb various neurological signals from a human. These messages the bug would intercept could be interpreted somehow into thoughts they could comprehend. When a swarm invaded a town, they were observed afterward to display behaviors similar to the victims. Once consumed, Upolios leave a long trail of dead bodies in their wake. The obvious sign of an Upolio attack is a gaping hole in the body's forehead.

Flying Hawk held his Tomahawk high above his head, poised to split a few, but Kipner warned him.

"We're outnumbered. Start backing up. We need to find shelter, or we're dead."

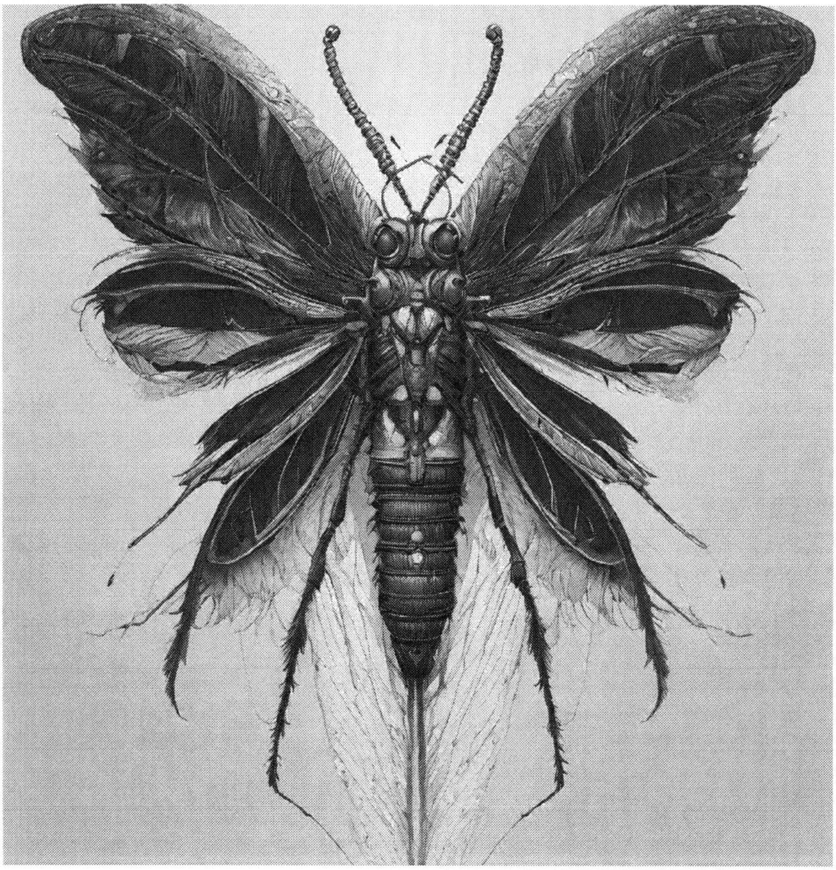

Huge expanding cracks brought the familiar humming from more bugs heading to the surface. With the burial mounds, nothing showed promise of protection. They would have to infiltrate one of the sealed entrances.

Kipner led the way over to the nearest. Passing by, they looked unnatural in predominantly flat terrain, and any opening access took significant investigation. This particular mound had been partially excavated from traveling anthropologists, and now a wood door was mounted with a padlock. When it had been constructed, any access was blocked off by dirt.

"I need some time," the marshal said as he extracted a few metal pins and set to work on the lock. His native friend swirled around to face the oncoming group. Beyond them rose another series of bugs.

Among his tribe, Flying Hawk had risen to chieftain through his prowess and wisdom of the citizens of America. He knew English well enough to prevent traders from swindling them. Numerous towns still refused him to enter their limits, but he was able to work with larger cities. Their tribe became profitable and benefited from modern wares all because of him.

What really showed for the young native, however, was his blurring skills with the Tomahawk. Even as a small child, he could move quicker than seasoned warriors. With each swing, his blades whirled with a unique sound that put fear in his enemies. One factor was weight. Flying Hawk's arms were sizably noticeable. He benefited from wielding a dense weapon weighted perfectly for his mobility. Few could even lift it, let alone swing it with control.

The air around him picked up as his blades spun in his hands, and they whistled in low tones like the grunts of an angry grizzly bear. Like a martial artist, Flying Hawk set his Tomahawks into motion and began slicing through one Upolio after the next.

No matter his best efforts, he was attacked from all sides. Upolios showed clear intelligence in tactics and constantly communicated with each other. They shifted and readjusted their attack to counter the native's moves each time. He could tear through them quickly enough, but each swing resulted in additional bugs filling the void.

Insects chittered loudly against Flying Hawk's blades. His heavy weapons created satisfyingly wet sounds as another Upolio dropped in halves.

One of them had weaseled passed his chop and latched onto the center of his shoulder, an impossible spot for him to reach even fully extended. The creature's mouth was vertically split open and shot out a transparent barbed quill that punctured the young man's flesh. It had a life of its own, biologically sentient, and forced its way passed his backbone cover to the spinal cord. The sharp tip had three splinters that trailed behind and prevented being pulled out without significant damage.

The initial prick was so minute he could have mistaken it for a mosquito bite. When the barb was deeply embedded, it acted like an anesthetic and removed all sensations. If it had attached itself while he was asleep, he would never awake again.

The blades of Flying Hawk swung on. His energy was still sharp. The absorption from the Upolio would soon kill him, but for the time being, he suffered no adverse effects. It was unsure how long he had, but Kipner had popped the lock.

A second bug found its way onto Flying Hawk's chest, and its barb plunged quickly inside, dangerously close to his heart. When pushed into an artery, the tip was so sharp that it sealed the wound to avoid internal blood loss. Like a mosquito full of blood, the body's hue darkened to red.

Too many were attacking him immediately, and his body was soon crippled against the weakening suction. His vision was obstructed by dozens of swirling masses that flung themselves in cyclonic rotation. As the numbers of Upolios increased the decibel level of their constant chattering, mixed with the dizzying motion, he soon became disoriented and aimlessly sought to find his companion. The roar of the buzz flooded out any shouting that might have come from Kipner.

His thigh was latched by another Upolio, then another. Much of his body was snared by now, sending him to his knees from the relentless sapping of his body. He lashed out a few more times in vain. By now, his swings were slow, and the bugs easily predicted and countered.

He dropped face down near one of the huge cracks and slid over the edge from the weight of a motionless body. Head first, he fell, drawing himself into the dark abyss below, but one of his ankles was suddenly gripped by a hand. It was accompanied and reinforced by a second hand. The unconscious native hung like a trophy fish on display above death.

The hero slowly tugged against the dead weight to inch him back up to the lip of the drop-off. With both hands tightly gripping the ankle, he had no means of protecting himself from the onslaught of the Upolios. One after another, he could feel the initial pinprick of their barb into his flesh and begin feasting on him.

His vision was growing dark, and his eyelids became heavy. He tried taking a few deep breaths to control his weakness, but it was too much. It was too much to endure, and his grip began to loosen.

Just above him came a series of pistol shots, and he felt the sudden decrease in weight at his holsters. It was difficult to see what was happening as everything was directly above him, but gunfire was clearly apparent.

With the sudden resurgence of strength, he pulled his companion out from the dark depths and back onto the surface. Although most of his body was numb from the numerous incisions, he could feel the weight of the bugs draped across his body. A few shots of pistols and the weight slid off and didn't return.

Two pistols returned to the Wraith's holster with full cylinders as if they had never been fired. The heat of the barrel was cool to the touch. Yet in every direction, he saw splattered, exploded bodies. There wasn't much left of each carcass either.

Flying Hawk remained unconscious after the bugs were removed, each body loosening its grip on the embedded barbs and leaving him like a porcupine. Kipner, too, had several independent barbs remaining across his body.

Their attachments acted like hypodermic needles and pumped the blood like a fountain. One was anchored to an artery in Flying Hawk, and his blood squirted fiercely into the air.

The Wraith didn't know what to do. He tried pulling his own quills out, but the barbs tugged at his inner parts and tried to take a piece of flesh with it. The pain was excruciating and nearly sent him into shock. He gasped for breath at the sharp intensity that exploded throughout his body.

Little more could be done with them, so he tried clotting the wound and dragged his friend over to the mound entrance he got open. The Upolios had given up the onslaught for the moment despite their numbers. He had no time to dwell on what had just happened trying to prop Flying Hawk against the mound.

Kipner lowered his shoulder into the swollen door, forcing it to swing inward to a dark tunnel ahead. He got a good hold of the scruff of Flying Hawk's shirt and grunted to bring him inside and close the door behind him. If any Upolios returned, he wanted to ensure they had difficulty reaching them.

Inside the mound was a turnbuckle that helped it swing open. It hissed and whined as the door flung closed and bathed the two in total darkness. Kipner struck a match for one of his bullseye lanterns and let it burn until the very end of the stick, then ignited the soaked wick. The flame flared momentarily, then soothed itself into a trance-induced dance.

For the moment, they both were safe. The quill-piercing Flying Hawk's artery was under control. The remaining quills were only fixed in position but not imposing any threat without the bugs attached. Still, they would be very painful and challenging to remove.

The Wraith thought back to his experiences in the past. He had come across Upolios, but they only sought gains by death to the humans they attached. They weakened him, but he wasn't convinced his life was endangered had he remained a victim. His expertise today felt the same as before, but they seemed to need to take more to benefit.

Flying Hawk hadn't moved since he dropped into the ravine. Against the dim lantern light his body was riddled with bone-white spines. His breathing was light and raspy, bringing bubble-infused saliva to his lips.

Nothing came to mind about how to address their various wounds. Kipner needed more tools or the knowledge to safely remove them. He wondered if anyone in St. Louis was prepared other than perhaps extensive surgery.

Daring a peek outside, the humming chattering of Upolios returned and began roaming near their door as if knowing their prey was just inside. The marshal couldn't leave his friend in darkness and explore deeper into the mound. Flying Hawk would take time before he could walk on his own.

Not many options were left for the Wraith as he sat there contemplating. Until Flying Hawk regained consciousness, they were stuck no matter what. Kipner tried tending to his friend, fed him a few sips of water, and made him more comfortable than propped against the tunnel wall. The harsh, labored breathing was stabilizing, and he appeared to rest calmly.

Some noise came from further in the mound. Someone had pushed something heavy and metallic across a hard surface that screeched as it struggled to be moved. Shuffling footsteps lined with muffled voices echoed down the chamber halls. Whatever they were doing was laborious as they grunted for several minutes. This repeated several times before the same heavy grating sound returned, then was cut with silence.

Kipner leaned against the wall, sighed, and released the hammer from his gun. Somewhere in these mounds were passages that gave access outside elsewhere. Nothing else would survive down here unless it was unnatural, but whatever they just did would be unheard of by supernatural things. Kipner had a suspicion of who they were.

The flame from his lantern was dying out, and he needed more kerosene. He tried cracking the door open a sliver to bring some ambient light inside, but the Upolios only allowed a hairline of a gap which didn't help.

A few hours had passed and left them in total darkness. Kipner lit his last cigar and drew air through the tobacco, and sent his face into a dull amber illumination.

"Well, partner," Kipner said, glancing toward his friend. "You could have stayed back at the hotel if you wanted to sleep through all the fun."

"I thought it was break time," groaned an awakening man. The native slowly opened his eyes and squinted into the dark. "What did I miss?"

Kipner brought him up to speed and explained their situation. It didn't spark a positive emotion out of the native. Instead, he grumbled and peeked outside the door. Several Upolios surged toward the gap, spiking their tongue-like appendage into the tunnel. They were relentless and showed no sign of giving up against their trapped prey. Their only enticing idea was investigating where the scraping metal sound occurred deep inside the mound. Perhaps it led outside elsewhere.

Dusk came to them before Flying Hawk regained enough strength to get back on his feet. He struggled when one barb would scrape another nerve or muscle fiber. The two still made their way down the dark path, using the wall as a guide.

It extended fifty feet before diverting sharply ninety degrees to the left, then immediately turning to the right. Kipner thought of getting lost in tunnels like this for hours or days. However, each turn led them on a more profound linear path into the mound.

The grate Kipner had heard earlier was in the middle of the floor once they had made several turns in darkness. Kipner's sensitive eyes gave just enough notice and the sudden change in flooring material to identify the metal grate flush with the smoothly cut stone. Like the granite that comprised all sides of the tunnel, the metal grate was polished smooth and laid proudly with a minimal gap between the two. If not for a sensitive footing from the marshal, they might have walked passed it in the dark.

It was meant to be only lifted from underneath. There was no nook for a crowbar or lever to hoist it up. The crack surrounding the grate was too narrow for fingers to grasp. Only a fine-bladed sword might wedge itself between but then likely break from the weight of the metal plug.

Should anyone lower the grate back into its resting spot in the tunnel above, they would be blocked from returning below. Yet another obstruction in his plan.

If they had a proper light source and weren't relying on Kipner's talent in sight they could inspect the area more thoroughly, but for the moment they couldn't progress downward so they ventured further into the tunnel.

When the deceased was brought in, their chambers were sealed to be undisturbed. The actual room containing those laid to rest was behind a double door adorned with beads and stones that might have once been polished. A stone slab painted in blue blocked their way and held no means of opening.

Someone had created a large hole in the center of the slab, sending a scattering of rocks and debris onto the floor of the inner room. Numerous large cracks splintered outward in every direction, indicating an explosion or a mighty sledgehammer. Its weakened state gave the idea it would fall with one good shove.

With some discomfort, the two men managed to wedge through the opening to find two old torches on either side of the door. It took great effort to get one of them barely lit. They had only a few minutes of dim illumination in the room.

One glance and it was clear the room had been the victim of tomb raiding. Wicker baskets were toppled over and empty. Two stone low-sitting tables had broken debris from a past long forgotten. In the center was a pile of marine-shell beads arranged in the depiction of a falcon. At one time, someone had been laid to rest on the mound. Their indention still remained to tell the tale of their crime.

"This is such a terrible tragedy," Flying Hawk spoke softly as he held back his emotions. He carefully ran his fingertips across the contour of the body's former resting place. His fingers balled into a fist and shook momentarily as he controlled his anger.

Over by the door, the Wraith inspected the opening. It was easier to tell with the semi-lit torch there were remnants of black powder along the hole. A single stick of dynamite would have removed considerably more of the slab. Still, only a tiny portion of black powder was used to create the hole.

"I know, my friend," Kipner said, dusting off black powder from his hands and standing back up.

"This hole is strange. Dynamite would have made this slab disappear, but they used black powder instead. That makes me think of an older time.

"Someone accessed this mound's interior for an unknown reason. I heard the metal plug move aside while you were recovering. Unless the Upolios give up outside and let us escape, I see no other avenue than waiting for whomever to return through it."

What was left of the torch went out and replaced them with darkness again. The two sat silently for several minutes as they considered their situation.

"It might be longer than we want to stick around here," Kipner said. "Those things out there should head back underground at some point. They'll be alerted as soon as we get back out there. From what I learned, they are susceptible to ground vibrations. The only question is if we can navigate those cracks quickly enough to get outside their nesting range."

Flying Hawk remained silent in the dark, slowly shuffling along the wall following the marshal leading to the exit. Checking again outside, the Upolios stayed active and dashed towards the door the second it cracked open.

The two friends lowered themselves to the floor with their backs against the wall. A few pieces of dried meat were split between them, and Kipner offered his flask to the native, who politely declined. Despite their circumstance, they enjoyed the moment of solitude for them. They were often chasing after someone or avoiding something they had waken that was far beyond their weapons' limit.

"Never seems to be getting any easier, does it?" Kipner asked after finishing his flask. He could make out his friend in the darkness and thought he spotted a sympathetic smile cross Flying Hawk's face.

"Much of how it once was remained," Flying Hawk said. "I fear nature has grown sick and will continue to worsen. Each time our paths cross, you search for answers to more questions."

Kipner felt disheartened at the accurate statement. All his life, he had witnessed time and again countless horrific experiences that seemed to be unending.

The map from McMannon came to mind, and he pulled it back out to inspect it. It was odd to see the various locations of interest he had across the country. None of them made sense. They should have been more focused on major cities or famous landmarks. Only when the largest circle fixed around each dot was taken into consideration did the entire country become threatened. Yet to Kipner, the country was already riddled enough everywhere he traveled.

"It seems that way, doesn't it?" he asked. "Sent out to figure out what brought on this madness and where have I gotten? All I find is more trouble. Each town I pass through has its own problem, usually driven by a power beyond my fathom. Nothing seems to lead me to the beginning..."

"You are the beginning, warm flesh."

The voice jolted the marshal, hearing it just behind his ear. For a moment, his mind flashed a vision of an empty train station with several benches lining the building. It had a familiarity, yet he couldn't recall ever seeing it. It disappeared as fast as it appeared, only a flash of a memory in his mind triggered by the voice.

Through the darkness, the Wraith's extraordinary sight revealed little. Only his friend sat before him, rising slightly from the floor, equally startled but for different reasons.

"Something wrong?" he asked the marshal. He struggled to see what Kipner was doing.

The wall behind Kipner was barren. He couldn't find any hidden niche or loose stone that might give access to a chamber beyond. It was as if the voice came from within his mind.

"I'm not sure. I thought I heard a voice."

His native friend rose and gently felt his way to the other side of the tunnel where Kipner stood. He, too, felt only a solid wall.

"What did it say?"

Kipner brushed off the question, but Flying Hawk insisted.

"Spirits speak to us in times of need even if we are not aware of that need. It is important to listen with caution."

"It said I was the beginning," Kipner answered, continuing to probe the wall to no avail. "It sparked some sort of vision, but I wasn't sure where it was."

"Any idea what it meant? Have you heard of it before?"

The station was extensive, with a boardwalk stretching out to the nearby tracks. A sign hung above the exterior ticket counter, but the angle in his image was too sharp to read. He did his best to recall the sight and hear the voice again.

How did the message mean anything? Kipner was the beginning. He had been contemplating the Harrow's origin, something he had thought about numerous times before. Yet up to that point he had a volume of Harrow encounters, a map from a lunatic, and a few stones.

"Remember finding these?" Kipner withdrew the pouch containing the three stones he had found along the way. He struck a match to give Flying Hawk some light to inspect them.

The stones were smooth to the touch like exceptionally round river rocks. There were no imperfections save for several markings that someone had scratched deeply into the surface. To Kipner they didn't ring any bell, but the patterns looked to be of purpose and not incidental. Each one had been discovered in remote, often tricky or hidden locations. Kipner and Flying Hawk had found two of them while traveling together years ago. Both had been challenging to acquire.

They had been deep in the Rocky Mountains, hoping to find a small, isolated settlement. A few trappers crossing through Snake River Pass brought stories of a group of mountain folk summoning and controlling unholy beasts to perform unspeakable mating acts.

Kipner investigated the story to see if something more powerful influenced the poor folks. Flying Hawk had crossed his path a few weeks prior on his way to establish better trade with another tribe.

The two had barely escaped with their lives as the deranged people channeled dark powers to fuel twisted otherwordly creatures. Before they got free, however, the trail of rituals led them to a strange, ominous hole surrounded by large stones. Being near the cavity brought terrors to their minds. The longer they remained, the deeper the trance they fell into, unable to resist staring into the unnatural hole. Thin wisps of dark smoke curled out from within and tried pulling them deep into the abyss. They couldn't resist. The power was overwhelming and the smoke took them into the darkness below.

What they experienced that night was not discussed by either ever since.

An entity of vast proportions no rational mind could understand slept in a cavern of immense size. It stretched endlessly in all directions for miles. The walls surrounding the beast were carved in terrifying and confusing shapes depicting wondrous oddities no human was meant to see. Inhuman bodies, still moving their appendages to and fro, were partially fused to the walls to complete the arrangement of the pictorial nightmare.

The two helpless victims were held suspended in midair and slowly spun before the monstrosity. The creature consumed most of the great cavity they were in, which bore deep into the earth's surface as well as towered above them to the peak of the mountains.

It was as if the vast mountain range of North America was indeed a hidden colossal of monumental proportions, stretching some three thousand miles in length.

One enormous bulbous eye fixed close before them. From under the lid swirled the great eye in deep dreaming slumber. No mouth was present, but the two humans felt the immense vibration of a voice resonate in their heads, warning them of the inevitability of an ancient, unfathomable race soon awakening throughout the earth. It would result in utter oblivion, and nothing known to mankind presently or in the distant future was capable of resisting.

The terror shattered their minds, and both had fled only after being released and brought back to the surface. In their possession, a single round stone with scratches across its surface that meant nothing to them at the time appeared.

Kipner had considered turning in his badge after witnessing the great one. It took months of medical help before either were capable of rational thought. Even with their sanity returning, they never could shake the memory from them.

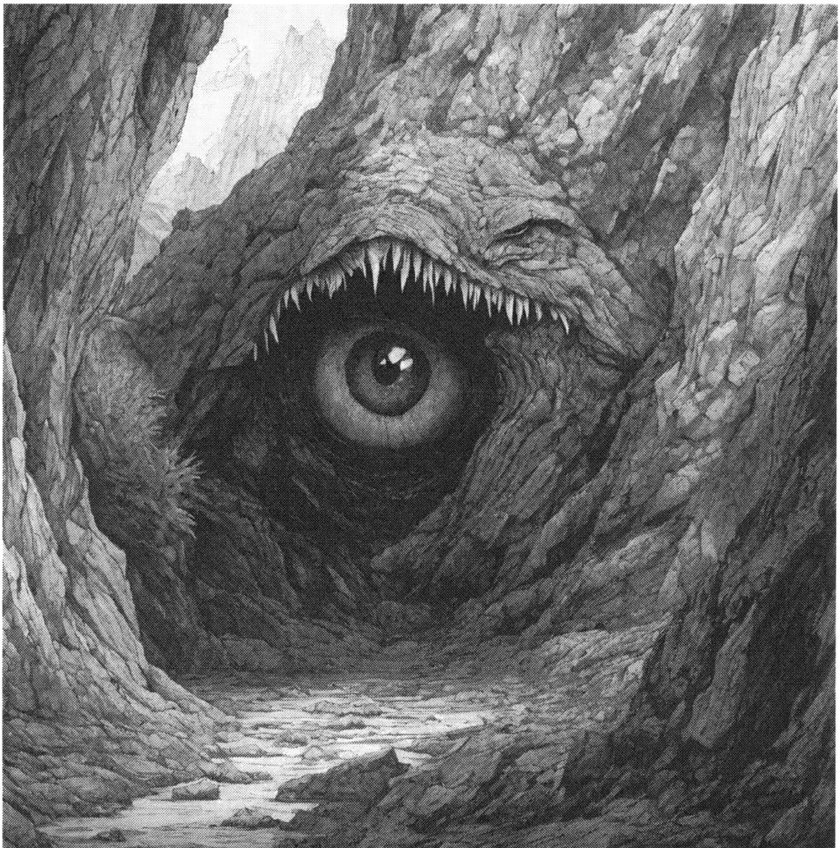

"How can I forget?" Flying Hawk said while holding the four stones in his hand under the match light. His eyes moved to the new ones Kipner had acquired. "Two more?"

The marshal nodded and lit another match. "Came from south of here. We keep finding these near sources of the Harrow. Found it inside some dried up fetish fueling a wraith. I had thought after all these years perhaps you learned something I hadn't."

Flying Hawk carefully replaced the stones back into the leather pouch and returned it to Kipner. "I've tried not to think of them. They brought us nothing but unthinkable terrors that I still fight sometimes in my nightmares. Why do you have them?"

The dark tunnel flashed alight for a moment to another match held close to the tip of Kipner's cigar, and he puffed a few times to relight it. He savored another toke and let it out slowly.

"The price I paid before they came into my possession was too great to toss them aside. Besides, whatever they may be, I'd rather have them than some tyrannical maniac."

Flying Hawk joined his friend in a smoke, using a small carved reed he had crafted when he first became chief of his tribe. Along its surface were four animal heads representing his four most vital assets. The turtle was for his resistance, the elk, his wisdom. For his diligence the beaver and temperament the hawk who waits patiently for the right moment.

"It's been a long time, Wraith," the young native said. "But I hope she can shed some light for you. She is wise to the ancient tongues."

Kipner forced himself not to wince. It had indeed been a long time since he last saw Lucy, and with each closing day upon seeing her again, he wondered if he was making a mistake. He had hurt her and altered her life. Something like that would be remembered. She might not even talk to him let alone help.

The pouch vibrated rapidly that caused a low tone hum. The two glanced at each other curiously as Kipner unloaded the spheres onto his hand.

Their movements were so quick they were a blur to the eye. Each of the markings was pulsing with light as they shook in unison. Removing one caused it to stop gyrating leaving the remaining three to continue but at a much reduced rate.

They weren't sure why they hadn't shown this kind of action before. Altogether they buzzed lively along one side of Kipner's hand, then motioned across his palm to the other. Coincidentally or not, the path followed the direction of the tunnel leading back in. Once they had traversed across his hand, they defied gravity and leaned over the edge of his fingers as if drawn magnetically. Whichever way he moved his hand, the spheres remained locked in that direction.

The humming ceased, but the vibration continued. As the two friends sat in silence, the grating of the metal plug slid to one side, and the ominously loud slapping of feet filled the air and approached with purpose from the depths of the darkness.

Nightmares seldom contained such an unspeakable sight of terror. It was a digitigrade bipdel that walked much like a bird with backwards knees.

Much of its body was covered in a satin sheen of rubbery substance that was not quite stretched properly over its internal structure causing wrinkles throughout. It had three appendages resembling arms but with numerous branching tendrils at each end. The tendrils narrowed with each split and ended with tiny holes that breathed like mouths, puckering repeatedly. Where its head would be expected, a worm-like gaping maw filled with numerous circular rows of holes burrowing into pink gum-like flesh.

Frozen in terror and caught off guard, the two mortals sat for their fate to be sealed, knowing a fight was mute against such a being. Still the spheroids vibrated on Kipner's hand. What caused humming a moment earlier almost sucked the air into a vacuum and forced no sound to appear.

They sat in utter silence as the stuff of nightmares clearly attempted to locate their position despite being a few feet away. It used the numerous narrow tendrils at the end of its arm to catch scent like a snake's tongue, but somehow they remained undetected.

Soon it gave up searching for them in that location and shuffled back down the hall. Strangely enough it did not make a direct retreat to the metal plug and forced a panel to shift and reveal another corridor to which it shambled on down.

The vibrating spheres ceased their motion when it was out of earshot. Kipner kept them in his hand for the time being.

Neither had to discuss where they wanted to go. Both knew heading back outside was death from the Upolios, and following such an abomination that was lingering in the halls would almost certainly prove fatal if it should find them. It might be entirely coincidental, but it appeared the spheres saved them from discovery.

As carefully as they could move without creating too much noise, they hustled down the hall.

Kipner tried to control the rapid beating of his heart and heavy breathing but noticed he made no sound despite the fact.

At the plug, the opening below was a short drop to another tunnel that went perpendicular to their tunnel.

Not far off, the slapping of broad, flat feet approached, sending them down the hole without caution and sealing the plug behind them. They weren't sure if the creature could lift it, but they wasted no time finding out.

There was no clear direction for this newly discovered tunnel, so they set off what they believed to be west. Their tunnel came to a juncture, which soon was met by another, creating a grid-like maze with no angles. There were additional plugs they passed along the way that they chose not to attempt lifting.

With each turn, they heard the wide slapping of another similar monstrous creature hunting for them.

The spheres continued to vibrate, which kept their detection impossible. Of the numerous times he had encountered strange Harrow entities recently, Kipner could not understand why they were behaving this way only now.

The tunnel system angled down steeply as they continued making their way what they hoped was back toward St. Louis. The further they went, the lower they descended until the tunnel ahead was partially filled with water. The temperature reduced significantly, too, sending goosebumps across their skin from the chill air.

Kipner tried asking Flying Hawk if he wanted to risk hyperthermia traversing through cold water, but his voice was silent. No matter how loudly he attempted to speak, only his lips moved. The stones eliminated all sound from the two.

He tried pantomiming the look of being cold, and the native seemed to understand and nodded then took the lead into the frigid waters. The temperature immediately shocked the first few steps, and Kipner began hyperventilating until he could control his breathing again.

What started at ankle deep went to their waist within a few steps, and in the darkness, Kipner's sight could just make out the tunnel's ceiling barely breached the surface ahead.

It became entirely submerged shortly after that.

The spheroids went back into the pouch, but they vibrated violently. They quickly became a blessing and a curse preventing them from discussing their circumstance.

Flying Hawk reached out in the darkness and found his companion, putting his hands over the marshal's eyes to remind him in case he forgot not everyone could see as well as Kipner in the dark. Underwater, it could become disorienting for both of them and quickly turn to fatal.

They weren't prepared to take this kind of risk.

Grabbing Flying Hawk, Kipner led him back to the previous juncture and turned down another hall only to find more flooded tunnels. In fact, all of them beyond their current position were inundated with water.

Whenever they approached the water, the spheres became more agitated, however, but as to why or what was their cause was unknown.

Even with Kipner's vision, their progress could have been faster. He could see well within a few feet, but there was nothing to see that helped guide him.

The tunnels were all the same with no landmarks or even imperfections to recall a previous turn.

Only the tunnels along the western part of the grid contained water, which made sense with the proximity of the river. Beyond the water, the tunnels maintained their grid pattern and frequently had metal plugs in the ceiling and floor.

Once, they tried lifting the plug overhead to find a different burial mound identical to the one they originally entered.

They increased their pace to as fast as Kipner could guide his friend through the dark, but all they found were dead ends and more burial mound entrances. The longer they delayed, the more nervous they became. The vibration slowly began to lessen in intensity, and they only wondered if their protection was about to run out.

The horrific masses stumbled up and down hallways, pausing before them to attempt to sniff the two, then continuing on their endless, mindless journey. With each turn, Kipner's fear grew as his mind returned to the flooded corridors. What he needed to understand was what their purpose down here was. What were they doing down here?

Flying Hawk abruptly stopped Kipner and gently patted the wall to what seemed like yet another identical corridor. Flying Hawk had run the palm of his hand down the walls while Kipner could see well enough to walk normally. The marshal had concentrated more on navigating and overlooked what the native had noticed.

The walls were made of concrete, clearly manmade, but Flying Hawk had come across a fault in the texture where it had cracked. The marshal nodded and tried to move on, but the native grabbed his arm. He reached out in the darkness, touched Kipner's ear, and then felt the cracks.

Something was chiseling from the other side. It wasn't by a tool and had the movements of some animal trying to slowly burrow without hurrying.

Again, Flying Hawk touched Kipner's ear and pointed to the wall, knowing he could see his motions.

So he pressed his ear to the wall and could just make out the familiar humming sound of dozens of Upolios on the other side.

The Wraith recoiled in horror from the wall and looked at his friend. Flying Hawk waved his hands in front of him, pointed down the hall, and made a wave motion. Kipner had been avoiding the inevitable too long, aimlessly wandering the halls underground, desperately wishing to find another way out.

After a few quick sprints, they returned to the still surface of the black water and paused to boost their courage. This was suicide, they knew, but they had been overwhelmed by Upolios outside, and once the wall behind them fell, the entire nest would swarm them. Which death was better?

Through the darkness, they took one more look at each other, swallowed all the air their lungs could handle, and dove in.

CHAPTER IX

Missouri, 1875

He floated some fifteen feet above the ground, taking in a monstrosity carved in stone. The full scale was difficult to judge as it rested in a deep cavity in the floor of an immense cavern, chiseled finely to a smooth finish. Besides a fatal leap to death in the vast hole, the only visible exit was a long corridor channeling warm, fresh air in from outside.

He wasn't alone. Below was a collapsed man struggling from some horrendous pain he endured. Nearby was a gentleman adorned in an all-white suit inspecting a vast column of stone covered in carvings of various etchings and glyphs the observer could not comprehend.

As the observer watched the two, the man in white slowly walked the circumference of the structure, finally settling on one of the markings in particular. Something snapped in the mind of the person taking in the scene, and the selected symbol became familiar to him. He had seen such a marking before, but he knew not where.

However, it burned in his mind, and he knew he would remember.

Meanwhile, the man in pain writhed in agony as he was assaulted by the suited man. He opened a secret compartment in the stone pillar and removed a device that fit onto his hand or wrist; the observer could not quite make it out from his distance. With it equipped, the man in white thrust his hand into the chest cavity of the captured man and proceeded to torture him.

Time passed quickly and faded into another scene for the observer. He was in the same room, but now the two other men were gone. Before him was a strange doorway that was not secure to a frame or wall. It freely stood and revealed another location on the other side that did not match his room. It was as if a painting was displayed before him that moved with life. In fact, it was so lifelike the observer was sure if he stepped forward, he would pass through and into the painting.

He spoke without consciously empowering himself. The sensation was of hearing his voice echoing within his head as if he were speaking freely, yet he didn't feel his lips move.

"When and where it all began," was all he said. The vision in front of him rapidly whirled in a blur. It halted to a scene that reminded him of America's southeast region. Like the one before, it, too, moved in a lifelike motion with a series of covered wagons and natives on horseback making their way across a vast open area.

The observer stepped closer to inspect the detail of the moving painting better. Although they were set some distance away in perspective, he could make out they were a native tribe.

Water splashed over his face repeatedly though he stood in a dry chamber. Over and over, the sensation of cold water poured over his face, chilling him to the bone.

Against his stomach was an intricate, sharp item that gave him considerable discomfort. It pressed against his stomach, and his hand instinctively swept across the area only to find no resistance. When the pain became too unbearable, Kipner felt his eyes open, and his sight dramatically changed.

He stared at three men dressed in military uniforms, each carrying a rifle and bayonet, pointing them down at him. One of the three sharp metal pieces was repeatedly jammed into his gut.

None of the three men were smiling.

Like a vacuum suddenly allowing air to flow in, their screaming voices came into focus.

Kipner heard them all yelling for him to get on his feet.

The marshal was frozen to the bone and dripping wet with cold, frigid dampness. He had to spit out the water that rippled down the side of his cheek before he could turn over on his stomach and push himself up on his feet.

The soldiers did not give him any more time to rise despite the noticeable soreness and disorientation Kipner was suffering from. They hoisted him to his feet and suspended him until he found his footing and stood alone.

Finally upright, Kipner took in his surroundings. They were in a cavernous tunnel that ended at one side with a steel door while the other descended into a pool of water. Two other soldiers held an arm of Flying Hawk, who was awake but hung helplessly. The native's eyes grew large with excitement. Still, when he tried to acknowledge his companion, he was struck in the face with a tightened fist from a soldier. Flying Hawk went back limp.

One soldier had more ribbons on his uniform than the others and addressed Kipner with doubt and disdain.

"Want to tell me how you two managed to get here through there?" the commanding officer's voice was surprisingly high pitched, almost squeaky. Kipner wondered what his subordinates said behind his back.

The Wraith stood groggily before the officer, now seeing he ranked as the first sergeant. Most of his weight shifted left then right into his adjacent soldiers, who took turns shoving him upright.

The sergeant grew annoyed at the delay, strode up to the marshal, grabbed his jaw with one hand, and squeezed controlling.

"I say again, how did you make it through the tunnel?" the sergeant spoke through gritted teeth.

"A family secret, my father was a sturgeon," Kipner said, spitting out more distastefully muddy water he had swallowed on the swim.

His arrogance caused him a vicious backhand from the sergeant across the face and sent the officer into a rage. His short fuse was a perfect fit for his ranking, Kipner thought as he was violently dragged faster than he could walk through the iron door and up a flight of stairs to open air.

Although it was night, Kipner could easily recognize the old fort he once was stationed at during the War.

A large courtyard within the walls of Jefferson Barracks was suitable for cavalry and infantry.

Several smaller buildings had been constructed since he had last visited, one of which he was being involuntarily taken to.

Not until he had made it inside did he notice the absence of weight at his hips where his holsters usually rested. One soldier took them over to a cabinet by one of the windows and placed it on top.

They had brought him into a brig. Its design was identical to a typical jailhouse of the time, with three cells on either side of a walkway with a desk up front for whoever was in charge that day.

Kipner's eyes immediately fell on the lieutenant sitting at the desk with his arms on either side of a stack of documents. He glared up with the annoyance of being interrupted.

"Lieutenant Ketchum?" Kipner inquired of the man, unmistakable from the large gash in his face that separated a thick, prominent mustache on the right side. Kipner already anticipated the man before him was always very salty. He had been an enlisted Sergeant Major when Kipner was stationed there. In all that time, some twenty years, he had only reached Second Lieutenant.

Ketchum's face darkened from confusion as he stared more closely at Kipner.

"Am I supposed to know you...Marshal...Kipner?" the officer asked while someone handed him his badge.

"Sir, I was stationed here after the War. First Lieutenant Robert Kipner, Sir." the marshal gave a crisp, experienced salute.

The remaining soldiers in the room were thrown off guard at the reveal. They instinctively returned the salute, knowing they were lower ranking than the officer. They were met with a scolding look from Ketchum.

"Uh huh," Ketchum said. "Under what Battalion?"

"Third Battalion, 13th Infantry, Sir," Kipner replied. He knew he outranked Ketchum but thought buttering him up would feed his obviously bruised ego. After all these years, Ketchum should have been a significantly higher-ranking officer than a Second Lieutenant.

The officer remained unimpressed with Kipner and folded his arms with a glare. The marshal caught a brief moment in Ketchum's eyes, leading him to believe he was pretending not to remember him. Judging by the almost subservient behavior of the present soldiers, Ketchum led with egotism.

"I don't recall a Lieutenant Kipner ever stationed here," Ketchum said. At his desk were a few stacked books Kipner was confident one probably contained a record of stationed staff. The man made no indication of checking anything to confirm Kipner's dubious remark. He had dealt with zealous officers before, and usually, they were a waste of energy to convince. Reporting them elsewhere was also fruitless due to their posting being given through favors. Ketchum was probably the nephew of some general.

"I do recall, however, reports of numerous civil disturbances across the river that has led to a fearful group of Cahokia citizens," Ketchum continued.

"Reports of vandals barbarically attacking innocent civilians, biting and swiping their fingernails at them. This has led to an uprising in spreading diseases, which St. Louis would prefer not to fall victim to if such conditions were to spread across the river.

"The City Hospital is already overrun by a few dozen sick individuals who were the victim of those attacks.

"That's why I had decided to investigate," Kipner said. He had to butt into Ketchum's rant while the officer breathed.

"Several folks from Cahokia had settled into the same hotel as myself and my friend...who I would like to know of his whereabouts if anyone here spotted him. He was just behind me. Those folks practically begged me to look at the reports of attacks. We found ourselves trapped in one of the mounds after being ambushed by Upolios.

"Our only way out was a flooded tunnel we came across. I guess I passed out while attempting to find the end of the tunnel."

Eyes darted from Kipner to Ketchum as the two stared at each other, giving no ground. Kipner looked a few years older than the officer, but Ketchum's vain had aged him more.

"Well, Marshal Kipner, First Lieutenant," Ketchum said with solemn mockery in his voice, "as an agent of the United States government, I would assume you knew before entering the burial mounds that they were highly protected and against the law to breach them?"

The officer had time to concoct whatever story he felt would keep Kipner at a disadvantage. The marshal knew his jurisdiction and areas where he could operate above the law, especially when his life was at stake.

Ketchum was hiding something. It wouldn't matter to the officer before him. He was already a prisoner. Somehow the disturbance citizens from Cahokia had experienced were tied to Ketchum and his troop, Kipner could deduce. Usually, no military operation would be so authoritative and police-like for the situation.

Kipner cleared his throat.

"Lieutenant, as a U. S. Marshal, I am authorized by Attorney General Pierrepont to investigate any and all Sightings potentially relating to the Harrow. During my search, I encountered a species called Upolia, which is directly associated. The situation rapidly became a life or death moment while we were overwhelmed, and my decision to seek safety within a mound falls well within my rights."

The marshal stood at attention when he spoke as if reporting to his commanding officer. He knew he would rub the lieutenant the wrong way, contradicting him. He was already in a dicey situation that he preferred not to be in. Just like in Coffeyville, there were places his badge meant little.

Ketchum launched himself from the chair and slammed both fists on the table. Immediately the soldiers around him backed away from apparent past experiences with his behavior. He snarled at the marshal like some animal baring his teeth. When he shouted, he splattered saliva everywhere, and his mouth foamed at the corners.

"Your jurisdiction means nothing here! You meddled where you didn't belong and should have stayed trapped in the tunnels.

"I'll make the rest of the few hours of your life on this earth far more painful. Knowing too much can be deadly, First Lieutenant," Ketchum screamed and exaggerated the rank. "Slophouse. Now!"

There was a brief moment before the soldiers reacted to the order, having distanced themselves from fear of the officer's unorthodox outburst. He became so violently enraged over such petty reasoning it was highly unnatural.

Kipner looked at the soldiers, in turn daring them to apprehend him. It took another round of blood-curdling commands before they went into action.

Suddenly both of Kipner's pistols were hovering mid-air and pointed directly at two soldiers.

As each time before, Kipner had nothing to do with their behavior. It was as if they had a life of their own.

They froze the men in their tracks as they stared horrified at the floating guns. Unlike before, there was a soft purplish glow that emanated around them.

A click came from the officer, who quickly drew and cocked his pistols, pointing both directly at Kipner.

"I would love to put two holes into your chest right now, Kipner," Ketchum said through gritted teeth. "Your witchcraft, Harrow charade, gives me the authorization to drop you dead right here and now. It's well within my right." Ketchum spoke mockingly at the last statement.

The Wraith stared squarely at the officer, returning the look with a deadly stare. "Do it. They will tear you all to shreds even when I'm dead. I don't know what kind of operation you are running here or your connection to the mounds but put me down, and you will see why they call me Wraith. I am a harbinger of terror to scum like you."

Suddenly Kipner's eyes became inflamed with a similar purplish color. His voice echoed and amplified as he spoke that bellowed and shook the building they were in.

None of the performance was in his control. Something else awakened within him as if to channel through like a beacon. Its surge was overpowering, and Kipner could not resist.

It sent the soldiers bolting out of the building, but Ketchum's rage locked him in. Neither of the Wraith's pistols fired at the fleeing men and instead spun around to create a standoff with the officer.

Ketchum unleashed his anger, and his body shed to the floor. In his place from within, his cocoon flesh spread a toad-shaped figure, its face covered with writhing tentacles. Two eyes bulged bulbously on either side with frog-like pupils. As it enlarged, more eyes formed across its surface, and wings emerged from its back.

Within his state, the Wraith had no train of thought or logical reasoning for what he was witnessing.

He was a passenger on a mental train to which he could only look out the window. His voice became deafening and pushed the structure's integrity to its limits.

"I am the voice of eternal terror and damnation. That which cannot die. Return to your slumber, for we have grown tired of your intrusion. You have no domain here, Mnoyunfel."

The creature grew before Kipner, and the building's roof creaked with agony before tearing free of its supports. The wooden boards toppled over one another, but the Wraith's controlling figure easily dodged out of the way. All four pistols went off, and Kipner felt one of the bullets lodge into his shin as his body flipped backward.

The marshal lay on the ground just beyond the collapsed building as his phantom eyes stared at the colossal beast before him.

Both pistols of his smoothly flew up at either side of it, now pathetically dwarfed by the sheer size of the monster. All around him, soldiers were sprinting for their lives out of the barracks. Along the way, they dropped whatever they had in hand and scattered dozens of weapons across the ground.

The pain in his leg was nonexistent, but his mobility was limited to a growing stiffness. Still, without control of his actions, Kipner gazed at the creature as he backed slowly away. One of his hands had reached within a satchel hung over his shoulder, and it found one of the round stones with strange markings.

By now, the creature had reached its final size, some two hundred feet in height. This was a complex form of the Harrow. It was an unfathomable size for any living creature, far more extensive than anything Kipner had experienced. Its presence shook Kipner's mind despite protection from the power that controlled him. He stood before a god.

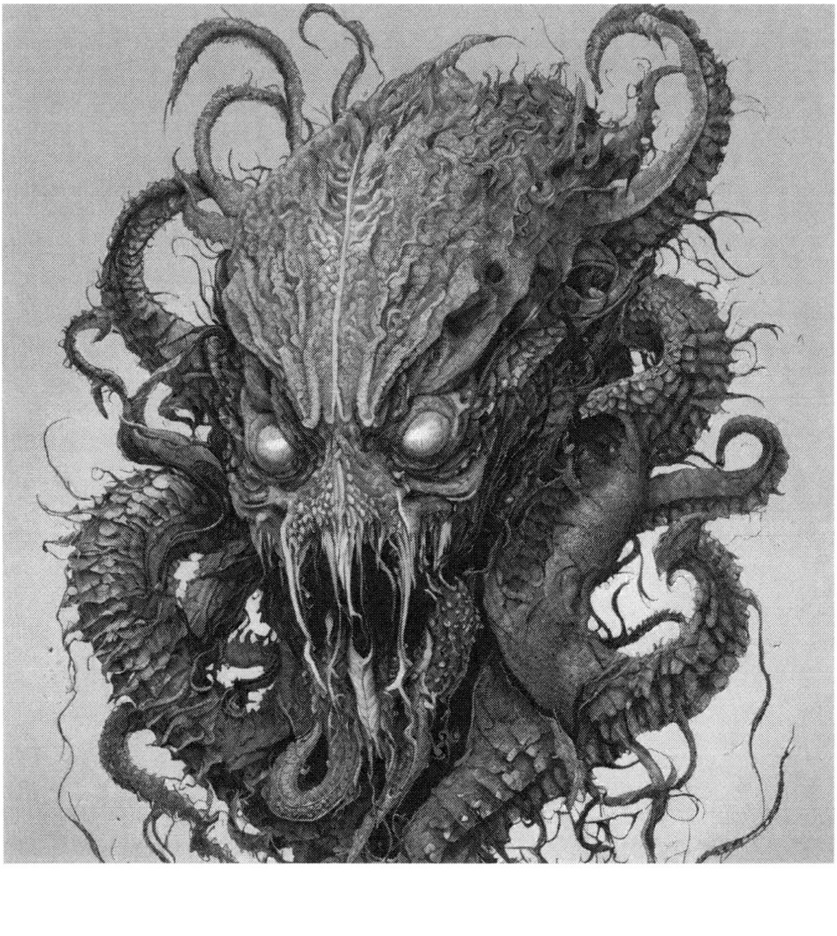

Much like years before when he discovered the vast god that lay hidden within the mountains of the Rockies, his vulnerable mind could not withstand the incredible presence of an entity that fell well beyond the comprehension of any human. This was a being that spoiled many laws of science and passed the scope of reasoning. He knew nothing mankind possessed could kill it.

The Wraith stood firm, however, unphased by the creature's presence. Whatever was driving his body like a vessel was as influential as or believed it was. It held out the round stone, and the Wraith began to speak in a language so alien to him he couldn't make out a single word.

Mnoyunfel surged with unnatural speed, extending several tentacles from its face down upon Kipner.

Each one was as thick as a human's waist, and he was quickly grappled and constricted.

Still, Kipner was void of the pain he knew would otherwise be excruciating. Instead, he was numb from head to toe and couldn't even feel the contact.

Yet his body was horribly squeezed by the creature, and he sensed his body quickly breaking down.

His eyes bulged out, and his inner ear became exposed. Without the protection of whatever controlled him, he indeed would have succumbed to the trauma.

His grip was tight around the sphere, but with the tentacles around his head, he could not continue the encantation he had started. The constriction became so tight around his hand, Kipner experienced the odd sensation of the stone slowly burrowing through his flesh and out the back of his hand.

With the stone freed, it disappeared within the numerous tentacles. Kipner's body was drawn to a maw hidden in the middle of the swarming appendages. The opening was vertical and lined with countless stiff, flesh spikes that circled the void inside. Several rows followed behind and disappeared down the dark throat of the beast.

Something caused Mnoyunfel to halt and turn its attention elsewhere. Kipner was utterly blind but only felt him swing around to one side of the beast. The grip around him loosened, and the Wraith took advantage. His body exploded with a fiery burst that pushed the loosened grip far enough to let him fall to the ground below. It was a tremendous fall, several hundreds of feet, and he heard the cracks of his legs as they shattered against the hard dirt. They lay motionless and sickeningly bent in odd directions. He hoped the numbness would hold on longer.

Towards the back of the opened courtyard of the barracks where the chaos ensued swarmed a large group of natives encircling one of their own as protection. Each held beads and charms in their hands instead of weapons.

The center individual was garbed in decorative attire with both arms raised in a V while shouting in her native tongue. She was anciently old but stood with a fierceness that defied her age.

A chorus of screams in different pitches erupted from Mnoyunfel. Each rang with a shrill that jarred Kipner's head like he stood within a giant tolling bell. Still, the chanting of the woman rode on.

The great beast quickly swiped down along the ground and easily sent a dozen native warriors flying like ants into the air, landing well outside the barrack walls. Still, the chanting of the woman rode on.

Immobile, the Wraith twisted his torso to free the satchel underneath him that contained the three other stones with markings. Kipner watched the madness unfold before him as the natives stood boldly against an immortal entity. Another stone found Kipner's hand, and he began speaking in a tongue like before.

His mouth and tongue moved in an odd pattern that was a strange sensation. It was unlike speaking another language and more like dextrous movements that otherwise would be awkward to reproduce.

The words caught the creature's attention. It swung momentarily back to gaze intensely down at Kipner with hundreds of eyes that blinked over its body. It gestured with one arm, and a cellar door that laid flat upon the ground near Kipner opened from within and poured dozens of shambling walking corpses of wet flesh towards the Wraith. They reeked from the stench of rot and mildew from the dead fish and decomposed plants wrapped around and infused in their bodies.

Kipner hopelessly crawled inches at a time in an attempt to gain ground. Still, the creatures of the dead quickly overcame him, baring down on his flesh and tearing pieces away.

The presence of his powerful guardian felt fleeting. The searing pain of his torn body started returning, sending Kipner in screaming torture. There were too many to all have access to his vulnerable body, but the few who did waste no time sampling the human skin.

The rapid firing of large caliber rounds came from nearby. Though the pain didn't cease for the marshal, the sensation of being eaten alive stopped. Above him flew his double pistols, unloading round after round at each undead creature and sending them to the ground. As before, the guns had a limitless supply of ammunition as body upon body fell motionless.

Kipner writhed in pain and could not breathe. His body shook violently as he went into shock. He heard the orchestra from hell in screams from the beast, chanting from the natives, and another familiar voice.

Something gripped him under his arms, and he was dragged. He tried opening his eyes, but the pain was too great. The voice felt comforting through his agony, and he felt his mouth return to mumbling the strange sounds he had started before, still clutching the round stone.

Before his mind slipped into darkness, his lips finished, and he rested.

*

"Bobby, you really did it this time," came a voice from nearby. Kipner's vision was black and disorienting. He felt his back against something firm.

"I told you I can only help so far. Now, look what you went and did." The voice was aristocratic and full of bravado though not without deep concern.

Each word had a spring of confidence and optimism, like cheerful sarcasm.

Kipner's eyes slowly opened.

The strange presence he felt before was gone, and he was again in control. The feeling had returned throughout his body, yet he was at ease. Bandages had been wrapped in numerous locations around him, each one soaked in cold water.

A large, rotund man with an ornately trimmed beard stood at his side and garbed in a black doctor's coat.

He wiggled his fingers in the excitement that complimented the wide, jovial grin he wore on his face. The genuine happiness he held could not be penetrated by pessimism.

To Kipner, the man struck a vague memory he could not grab entirely. His voice didn't match, however. Dr. Sales was who he heard come from the mouth of the large man, but it was definitely not Amos.

"I've seen you before," Kipner said with a befuddled mind. "You're not Amos, though. Have we met?"

With a rumbling of laughter, the man said, "Oh, Mr. Kipner, my friend, I'm no expert, but I believe you have suffered from serious trauma."

Kipner partially sat up with the man's help and felt support from behind him as the bed he lay on was adjusted. He was in a room identical to the familiar office of his friend and long-time doctor, Amos, but a vague stranger stood in his place. The man's sharply pointed van dyke beard struck a memory, along with hearing him claim to not be an expert. Kipner struggled to remember where it came from.

"You'll live, Robert, but not without some nasty scars this time. I couldn't fix you completely. Flying Hawk hasn't said anything since he hauled your sorry body here. You're just lucky I was in the neighborhood."

Kipner was given a glass of water and ordered to drink all of it. When he was finished, another glass was filled, and he was also requested to drink it. Each gulp felt incredible against his otherwise dry throat. Somehow it was almost frigid in temperature.

"Refrigeration," said the man at the confused look from Kipner. "I figured you could be spoiled a bit after what you apparently went through. You still look terrible. What in God's green earth did you poke at and rile up this time?"

Visions returned to Kipner of the encounter with Mnoyunfel. He remembered nothing of the specifics of his mouth moving to perform the ritual that apparently accompanied the stone he possessed. Still, he knew its purpose was some form of attack upon the creature.

Relating the story to his bedside friend, the rotund man remained excited. He asked for more detail with enthusiastic questions and was riveted by each response. The more he told of what he remembered, oddly a lot, the more he recognized the man.

Glimpses of the past became more vivid, and he soon found himself melding his encounter with tales of another.

"It caught me off guard while on the train," Kipner said. "I guess it followed me from London and..."

"London? Robert, what are you talking about?" the man said, suddenly missing the sharp beard he had a moment before. Now facial features appeared differently to Kipner.

He was bewildered about who truly stood before him or what nasty tricks his mind was playing on him. Amos Sales, his old friend and the doctor, was before him now.

A slight headache throbbed behind his eyes, and Kipner rubbed the bridge of his nose. It lingered for a moment just before it became nauseating.

"Nothing, never mind, Amos. Just a weird experience after getting beaten to an inch of my life."

The doctor grunted and handed him a few pills to take. He stood there studying Kipner like he was reading his mind. The appreciative fatherly expression of concern and care eased Kipner's mind. At least someone gave two beans about him.

"No, I've seen that look before, Robert. You've had visions again. They have become more frequent in recent years, too. I would pass those off due to your field of work, but I'm beginning to wonder if it's something else. You thought I was someone else. Did you recognize them?"

Kipner shook his head, "No, he was some large man I..." The marshal trailed off for a moment into silence as he stared intently at the floor in deep thought.

"Archibald," Kipner said. "Someone named Archibald. He had something to do with a train, but I can't quite place it."

"And London," Amos added. "Something about you being from London. I don't know what to make of it, Robert. It's so specific and peculiar I can't convince myself to suggest you see a psychiatrist either."

The bandages were numerous across Kipner's torn-up body. They were sore but didn't hurt. The doctor revealed he had given him something special but didn't admit anything specific. He only assured the marshal it would wear off, and he'd have to grind through some of the pain at the end of the healing process. Whatever he did to Kipner was something of mysticism, according to Kipner.

After the monstrosity was repelled, Flying Hawk brought him to the City Hospital in St. Louis.

The rituals the native woman had conducted were somehow empowered by Kipner's words and the odd spheres he possessed. Mnoyenfel stooped back into the bottom of the Mississippi River and burrowed underground. No one knew how long it would remain down there, but what was left of the native tribe after being nearly wiped out by the beast constructed a temporary settlement near the bank and periodically performed similar prayer-like rituals. They assured Flying Hawk it would not return soon.

It was not surprising to the young native that Kipner's medical friend was operating in the town they happened to pass through, but for the marshal, it was. It had been several months since he needed his help in the Dakotas. While Dr. Sales often traveled where he was needed most, it perplexed Kipner how coincidental the occurrence was.

"It is a strange story," Amos had explained when asked. "Sometime after you left, a letter arrived from an old colleague of mine from many years ago. We had started our careers working together until we had made enough to go our own ways.

"I hadn't heard from him for ten years or so when our roads had crossed down in Georgia. He had set up practice in Alpharetta for several years by then. Seemed to be happy there. Married. A few kids. Then this letter arrived in my office in South Dakota, where I had been for just a month or so. He said he had come across something highly odd from a body the local police had brought in for him to analyze. Said it was too unsettling, too alarming to put to words."

The doctor spoke with a great concern relating the tale to Kipner. Finishing was troubling for him, and he paused to swallow numerous times to push himself further.

"Of course, I made my way there post haste, but that is where the story takes a disturbing turn.

"When I arrived, one of the staff informed me of Clark's passing. He had been found hanging from the roof's iron cresting, pierced through one hand. God bless his soul."

Amos had to gather himself to go on, choked up at the memory still fresh in his mind. He stared off as he fought to find the words.

With trembling hands, Amos gave Kipner the letter. "He was found before the letter was sent. I'm not sure how that could have occurred, Robert. Perhaps it was sent posthumously after someone discovered it." He shook his head at the thought. "How would they know where to send it? How could he have known where I was?"

Kipner reviewed the handwritten letter addressed to Amos in Stonewall, Dakota Territory. It spoke of a strange oddity.

Changing the subject to focus on what Clark discussed brought Amos' thoughts back to the present. Clark's office had been cleaned for another physician's arrival. All his belongings were still stored in Amos' room until his next of kin could be contacted.

The late doctor left his professional papers describing a partially decomposed body arriving at the hospital early one morning. Police had not identified the victim and had hoped Clark could shed some light on the mystery. It had been discovered securely strapped to dead wood far below the surface of the Mississippi by an unlucky fisherman. The police were baffled at the unusual position the poor deceased man had been arranged.

With Amos' help, Kipner went through what Clark had left, uncovering another small stone sphere with a similar marking as the previous ones. According to the notes, it had been deeply lodged grotesquely into the victim's lungs with no sign of a laceration in his chest. The esophagus was enlarged considerably, and his front teeth had been shattered to the likeness of its diameter.

The doctor shivered as Kipner read the notes out loud. The position of the body strapped to the log mimicked the shape of the marking on the stone.

Kipner had seen his fair share of dark rituals and sacrifices tied to the Harrowing. Still, most of them were fruitless attempts using frivolous past occultic literature. Had he not witnessed the godlike beast emerge from Ketchum's body, he might have passed the connection off as another senseless waste of time.

He held the small stone in his palm, joining the others he had, and twirled them in circles.

"These keep showing up whenever I encounter something far more sinister and powerful than I can handle or fathom. It would appear a few out there are learning the proper methods to awaken these colossal gods that have been asleep and out of sight for who knows how long."

Kipner pondered back to the night of Mnomyunfel. Seemingly out of nowhere, a tribe appeared and risked their lives to repel the creature, but from the reports he was given later, not until his uncanny words were spoken did the effects genuinely take effect. Their ritual required a combination or some enhancement from the stones. He just needed to figure out how to replicate his side of the help.

When everything Clark had left behind was analyzed thrice over, Kipner bid his old friend farewell and sought Flying Hawk. While Kipner had been interrogated, Flying Hawk had been tossed in the brig cells below.

He had escaped when the onslaught of dead walkers stumbled passed and shoved his guard into the cell door. He quickly grabbed the keys and slipped out behind them, dragging Kipner's unconscious body out of harm's way.

While Kipner recovered, Flying Hawk had spent hours in silence among the mysterious native tribe. Their numbers had been small, deemed harmless to the surrounding towns, and left alone. They were the remnants of a Creek tribe from Tennessee once led by Red Sticks before being murdered to near extinction by Andrew Jackson's army at the Battle of Horseshoe Bend. Only two had escaped with their lives that day, and the elderly priest who led the ritual against Mnomyunfel was the daughter of one of them.

Now they were only a few.

"They were already dying," the native spoke in hushed tones near a campfire the night Kipner rejoined him. "Many of them are tormented by diseases from being forced to trade with towns to survive. They owed nothing yet sacrificed much."

Flying Hawk blinked from staring into the fire and looked up at Kipner for the first time since he had arrived and wiped his eyes from moisture.

"I thanked them when I could for saving my life. There was little I could do..." Kipner began.

"They didn't intervene to save your life," Flying Hawk said with friction in his voice. "It was only to delay the inevitable ending of us all. Menawa's daughter, Katee Ann, told me of her grandfather's stories of great sleeping demons under the earth."

The elderly woman known as Menawa to her tribe slowly approached the two seated and offered them water. With great effort, she sat beside them, aided by two young men. She closed her eyes for a moment and regained her breath before speaking.

"My father had great wisdom," she began with her soft, frail voice. It was motherly comforting and gentle, like a calm, warm night.

She spoke with purpose and care without ever wasting a word.

"He warned my people of the dangers that lurked where our eyes could not see. A world within our world that bridged only in our darkest dreams. These tales came from across the land and from other tribes long ago. He learned one person, much wiser than he, recorded the stories, but much was lost as their great civilization was killed by men from ships to the east. What little was kept told us that our songs, prayers, and ceremonies were essential to keep us safe.

Her voice cracked as she began to cry. Her face was sorrowful, and tears trailed through the deep creases of the skin.

"We remain no longer. Home has vanished, and we reside in unfamiliar lands brought by cruel men. Our songs and prayers are now weak, and the demons begin to stir from their slumber."

She said no more to them and was aided in returning to her tipi and leaving the two men to dwell on what she said.

The marshal was in deep thought as he slowly pieced a puzzle together that had plagued him for years.

"The tribes have been pushed aside for years," he said. "Forcefully removed..."

Something in his memory, long forgotten, snapped to his attention. It was such a powerful thought he had no choice but to stare at it squarely. It was the vision of him standing amid the same great statue he had seen before with the moving painting frame in front of it.

Different this time was the awareness of who he was and why he stood there. It was for an important reason. He was there to learn of the secret to the Harrow's origin, just like he was now but for his own cause. He felt the anguish, the mental pain, and fear within him, brought on by the torture of knowing these gods of chaos exist. He had lived a life of anguish and suffering that he did not deserve, which had been mysteriously hidden from his consciousness until now. Only snippets of strange visions had clouded his mind, leading him to this moment.

No, it was not a painting. He had found a portal of immense power with the help of others who had been good companions. By stepping through it, the marshal had hoped to find the truth.

"Renaldo Archibald III," Kipner said aloud. Flying Hawk raised an eyebrow at the name, but Kipner dismissed him.

"They were all removed. Jackson's law. It started everything. Menawa was right, my friend," the marshal concluded.

The native's face dawned as he took in the marshal's epiphany and slowly nodded. "I know of that law well. But tribes were assaulted for years before."

"Yes, but never to the extent that he proclaimed. What's left of Menawa's tribe is proof. No tribe remains where they once called home. Their beliefs were all their own, but that knowledge of protection spread long ago from whatever civilization she was referring to," Kipner pointed out.

It struck the marshal with such a bolt he braced himself on the fallen log he sat on. He had lived much of his life with the clue he had sought for years. His existence was tied to it.

"1830," he said. "May 28th, 1830. The day of my birth fell precisely on the day he passed that act. That was no coincidence, but why must I have been born when I already lived?"

Flying Hawk showed no surprise and sat poised with a solemn expression. "Many tribes, my own as well, believe one may be born more than once. Some few possess even memories of their past life. You have such memories?"

His friend nodded and told what he knew of his past, and the more he spoke, the more came to light.

By the time he had finished, he had nearly a vivid recollection of where he had come from. The sensation, however, overwhelmed him, and he grew dizzy.

Flying Hawk brought out Kipner's flask and placed it in his hand. A few deep swigs later, Kipner regained his senses.

The vision of his father beside the strange wagon. A Model T that he once owned. Thinking his decision to step through the portal had devastating consequences was sickening. He altered his family's existence, and it crushed him.

There was a snap somewhere deep within his psyche, and his mind tumbled apart from the blunt truth he was being fed. The sheer weight was too much for a human brain to withstand. It made him chuckle out loud, like suddenly remembering an old joke.

Flying Hawk watched his friend's eyes flicker and twitch briefly, then return to normal. When asked if he was okay, Kipner took another swig and nodded.

"I've handled worse," he lied. "At least now I have a clearer vision of my task."

"What's done is done, Wraith," Flying Hawk said. "You can't expect to reincarnate again and again."

"You're right. I can't. That caused too much harm. I paid a horrible price for it. But I know now the truth of what I was sent to do. With that, I can form a plan to finish what I initially set out to achieve."

"What was that?"

"Stop the Dreamlands from awakening."

CHAPTER X

Illinois, 1876

In the spring of 1876, U. S. Marshal Robert Kipner rode slowly into Chicago's city limits accompanied by his friends Flying Hawk and Roy. Trying to save time and avoid further delays on the open road, they boarded Chicago, Pekin, and Southwestern Railroad, better known as the CP&SW, with a nice stock car for Roy. The stubborn horse initially refused to step into any stall in the car until Kipner arranged for a small opening to be cut out of the car's wall so he could look outside during the journey. Afterward, Roy complied.

Chicago was a resilient city rapidly growing after the quick recovery from the 1871 fire that destroyed much of the town and killed 300 people. A valiant effort to reduce the poor sewage treatment was in full effect by raising much of the city to give room for below-ground pipes. Stone buildings were covered in scaffolding as the visitors strolled through the streets.

With each passing block, immigrants from Central and Eastern Europe shuffled to health-threatening conditions in numerous industrial factories like the meatpacking firm of Armour & Company. Some folks were protesting the working conditions or unfair business practices like the mail-order company, Montgomery Ward, over on North Clark Street.

Flying Hawk shook his head at the endless number of people crowding the streets. Cities were multiplying he feared even the land his tribe now called home would soon be owned property by expanding towns. If Kipner's theory was correct and the tribes were responsible for keeping What Slumbers Beneath away, he doubted there was any hope for a future for humankind.

It had been years since Kipner had last heard of Lucy's whereabouts. She had initially landed a job with the Smithsonian Institute in Washington, D. C. , shortly after Kipner left her. For whatever reason, she soon left the company, bound for Chicago, where she found work at the Academy of Sciences on LaSalle Street just east of the tunnel below the Chicago River.

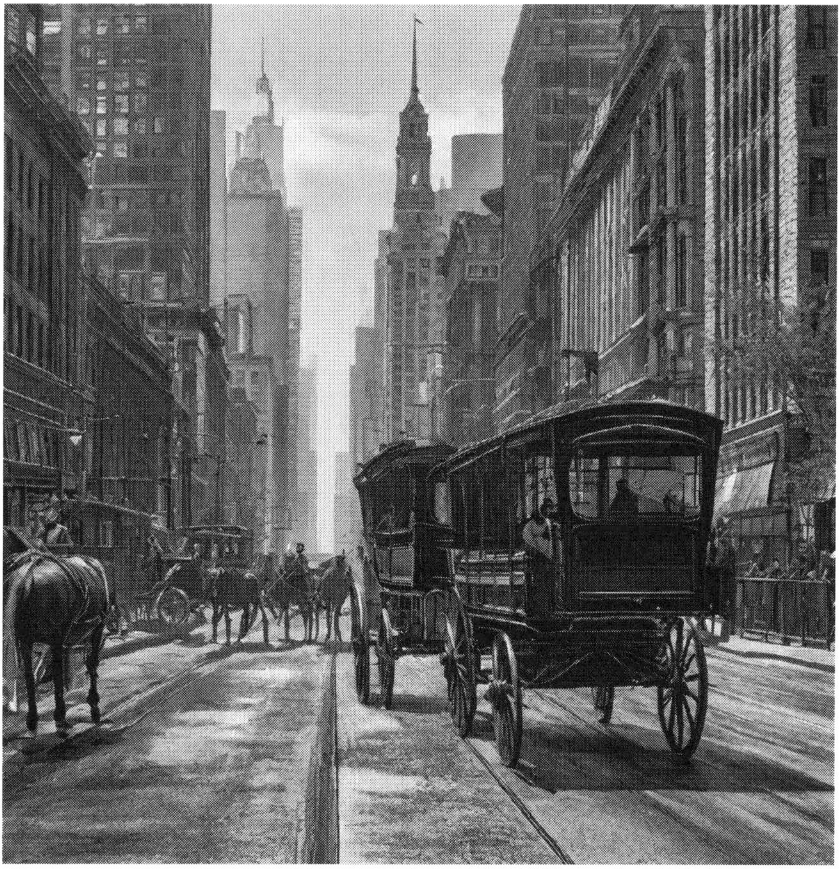

Word of her moving to Chicago was news to him after telegraphing the Smithsonian to confirm she maintained employment. However, the return message needed to shed more light on where she worked in Chicago. It took a lengthy search through the city's census bureau to pinpoint her last employer. It had been six years since the census had been taken, so they hoped she still worked there.

Kipner felt it best to see her in a public environment rather than her residence first. An impending fear and anxiety developed in Kipner's chest the closer they got to the facility that he didn't enjoy.

Enough years had separated their romance, but it didn't erase the memories or the feelings. Kipner had been a younger man, eager to pursue the beginning of his career and impress those of high authority. Yet his heart wasn't stone. What he had felt years ago was genuine. The numerous letters he wrote to her showed that well enough, but her absence gave him plenty of doubt she would not be thrilled to see him.

Fears and doubt pushed aside, Kipner led his friend inside the building and to the front desk, where a young lady greeted them cheerfully.

"Good Morning, dear," Kipner began with his hidden smile tucked neatly behind his prominent mustache. His wide-brim hat was held in his hands to avoid the heavy shadow it cast on his face.

Before arriving, he had stopped to bathe and don a fresh set of clothes, neatly cleaned, capped off with his long, black duster. His boots were polished, and his spurs jingled lightly with each step.

Flying Hawk was familiar with city life, having traveled with Kipner frequently in his younger years and traded with merchants in the surrounding towns. While Chicago was sprawling with immigrants, they were mostly white Europeans. He knew where he stood in society despite the advancing city. While Kipner cleaned up, Flying Hawk found a lovely navy three-piece suit and a flat-brimmed hat that concealed his native face.

"Good morning, Sir," the cheerful lady replied. "How may I help you?" She spoke with a German accent and had hypnotically large, striking brown eyes. She had set her blonde hair in a bun atop her head with a needlework pin slid through.

"I hope to speak to a woman who works here named Lucy. Lucy Lovejoy. I believe she is with the archaeology department," Kipner said as he struggled not to trip over his words. It was as if he was courting a lady for the first time. On numerous occasions leading up to this moment, he had been strongly tempted to consume a few swigs from his flask to gain courage. Still, the last thing he wanted was her smelling alcohol on his breath.

The young secretary's smile slowly faded, and she fiddled with a small box of index cards. Kipner watched her fingers flip through them, skipping large sections and finishing her search without stopping to read any of them more clearly.

"I'm sorry, Sir," she said without a hint of concern. "There doesn't appear to be one of that name employed here."

The marshal glanced around at the few people entering the building and heading down a hall to an elevator. No one else was waiting behind them for her help, so he pursued the matter further.

"Thank you kindly, Ma'am. I do believe she worked here at one time. Perhaps she has since found other employment. Perhaps you know of past records, payment ledgers, or tax forms?"

Shaking her head, she said, "I'm sorry, Sir. No one of that name has ever worked here. There may be other companies in the area you might have mistaken for ours."

Kipner stood upright and sighed heavily as he took another nervous glance around. Flying Hawk gently touched his shoulder and nodded to the corner of the lobby, where two armed men stared directly at them. They hadn't been there a moment before.

"Not again," Kipner mumbled to himself. He felt he had one more shot before he drew the guards over. The marshal motioned for his friend to step outside to tend to Roy.

"I sincerely appreciate your efforts to help me, Ma'am. I do not wish to waste any more of your time today, but is there anyone with the name Lucy here or of recent history? The thought had just come to mind she may no longer use her maiden name."

That recognition jolted Kipner in the heart. She was deeply caring and thoughtful, brilliant and sincerely beautiful. It hadn't occurred to him after all these years she might have married, but a woman like Lucy wouldn't live a solitary life for long. She would have more trouble keeping men away in a city as large as Chicago than finding one to settle down with.

In response, the secretary looked at the two armed guards walking towards them.

She said, "I'm sorry," and kept her head down.

He knew that was his cue, and he turned to exit the building, but the two men cut him off. One had his pistol drawn, and the other firmly gripped Kipner's upper arm.

"We hope you enjoyed your visit, Sir," the man who held him said in a low voice, leaning in closely to Kipner. "It is in your best interest to refrain from revisiting again. Good day, Sir."

The Wraith narrowed his eyes at the man. The brute was clean-shaven and wearing a pinstripe suit accented with a derby.

From the structure of his broad jaw and tight-fitting clothes, he was in perfect condition for a winning brawl that Kipner had no interest in partaking in. Instead, the marshal stared him down and slid out his badge tucked away in his breast pocket, letting the outside sunlight reflect off its surface and into his eyes.

"You best take care, Son," Kipner growled in an equally low voice. "A Marshal's business rides higher than museum guards."

His grip loosened enough for Kipner to slide free, and the marshal tipped his cap after placing it back on his head and bidding them a good day. The two guards were left in frustration.

"Something's not right, Chief," Kipner said as he strode down the front marble steps to the street where Flying Hawk was brushing Roy's neck while the horse winked at passing fillies. "It may have been a few years, but she worked there. That I have no doubt. I don't like how that young lady passed through names like she knew of her and didn't want to admit it."

Flying Hawk untethered Kipner's horse and handed him the reigns as the marshal led Roy down the stone street to a nearby restaurant.

"For a place of science," the native said, "they aren't welcoming. It wasn't me who drew attention this time."

"No," Kipner said as he squinted in the midday light at a tether post and lazily tossed the reigns around it. They stepped inside and found a seat to order lunch. "No, it wasn't you, my friend. Something about her caused the commotion. What puzzles me is how they quickly jumped on recognizing her name.

It was as if she had a significant impact, good or bad, on the place."

"She wouldn't have done something wrong," Flying Hawk said. "From everything you have told me about her, I always envisioned good character."

The marshal didn't respond and stared off in deep thought of her again. She had always lived with a golden heart. To find her in ill standings with anyone was unheard of.

The two enjoyed a quiet meal together. Kipner ordered a late breakfast of ham and eggs with wheat toast lightly covered in raspberry jam. His companion chose a small bowl of fruit and tried the restaurant's house salad, which he politely disagreed with.

During the idle conversation of past adventures together, Kipner's observant eye caught sight of an old man who had hobbled into the restaurant and sat by the front window. He had picked a chair that faced inward and, to the best of Kipner's awareness, had glanced numerous times in their direction. Toward the end of their meal, the old man worked hard to stand up and shuffled over to their table when they were about to leave.

His voice was raspy like a whisper, and it took him to repeat himself before they could understand what he had said. "You were right, Good Sir. About her."

Kipner perked up when he finally heard him clearly, then nodded for the old man to sit down, who did so obligingly. Kipner and his friend extended a hand to aid the man into the chair. He was devoid of any muscle and felt as frail as glass. His eyes were deeply recessed into their sockets, and his bushy, unkept eyebrows cast a deep shadow over them. His clothes were old and heavily patched, and his skin was veinous and riddled with liver spots.

"Thank you, Gentlemen," he spoke, trying to get above a whisper so he wasn't asked to repeat himself. He held a napkin to his lips and coughed violently into it, soaking it quickly.

"Are you alright, Sir?" Kipner asked with a concerned look and was answered with a nod.

"I'm fine, just getting close to my time, is all," he said as his eyes drifted into some faraway land. There was a sadness in his soft face that gave pity to the two younger men in his company. It was tough to tell precisely, but he had lived far beyond most expectations.

Another round of coughs concluded, and he finally said, "I overheard your inquiry at the academy. Only her name would have sparked my attention. I'm sure the others around me took notice, too, but they know better than to pretend they don't know her."

Kipner and Flying Hawk exchanged puzzled glances. "Pretend they don't know her?" the marshal asked. "What happened to her that led to that kind of treatment?"

With a shaking hand, the old man signaled the waitress for a cup of black coffee. "She was a fine lady. Bright. Inquisitive. Held her own against the men who had power there and was welcomed for a while.

"She arrived with a thesis that didn't fit right with the board, however. Her theories were heavily pointed to the Harrow, which is frowned upon at the academy.

"I know many have seen Sightings, although I have not, it's become a widely spread phenomenon. It just needs to be more widespread to become common knowledge to be tested.

"Your girl didn't last very long. She insisted on field research in hopes of bringing back evidence, but the board wanted no part of it and released her."

With his coffee on the table, he tried pouring a little into the saucer below the cup, but his trembling hands sent the dark liquid onto the table. He cursed his hands and reluctantly allowed Kipner to pour, which he sipped directly from the saucer.

"It's a might cooler to drink this way," he said with a pleasant sigh.

"You have been accommodating, Mr. ?"

"Stimpson. William Stimpson. I was the director there several years ago when Lucy was employed. Guess I got too old one day." There was a faint smile that cracked across his thin lips. His sad eyes never wavered and remained staring longingly at whatever memory had come to mind.

"Mr. Stimpson, this has been enlightening. I don't suppose you remember her saying where she was headed when she left there?" Kipner asked, pouring more coffee into the old man's saucer.

He was barely able to shake his head. Each moment he was there, it was as if he was slipping away and holding on to help the marshal. The few sips of coffee were as far as he got before giving up on it altogether.

"I'm sorry, Son," he whispered. "That's all I know." He momentarily turned to one side, searching for a train of thought.

There he stared for a few seconds before being satisfied he was sure what he wanted to say. "She isn't Lovejoy anymore. Hodgins."

Kipner's heart sank.

So it was true - she had married.

The bolt hit him again like earlier that day, and he slouched in his chair. He wasn't sure why he was so disheartened to hear the news. He was still married to his career and wanted her to be happy. Assuming her husband treated her right, he should feel delighted for her. Yet something inside stung that he feared was more than just old romance.

William didn't feel like leaving with them, and the two bid him farewell and thanked him again.

"I haven't seen someone that old since my grandfather," Flying Hawk said as they wound past the tables to the front door. "I hope to see as much as he did in my...Kipner!"

The native stopped dead in his tracks and pointed behind them. The marshal followed his finger. The table was empty. No coffee was resting on it, and no man was sitting in the chair. As difficult as it was for the man to sit down, he had not enough time to get up and leave, not to mention there was only one exit. He was nowhere in sight.

"What in the world?" Kipner said as he scanned the room.

"You don't suppose he...?" Flying Hawk asked, looking at Kipner.

Giving up on the place, Kipner shrugged and stepped outside. "Who knows anymore? For all we know, he was just a phantom."

*

William Stimpson was a prominent zoologist specializing in invertebrates with the Smithsonian Institute. In 1853, he embarked on an expedition to the North Pacific, searching for new species to document. He was highly successful in the three-year stint.

Once he returned, he was appointed director at the Chicago Academy of Sciences. He worked beside Lucy until he died in 1872.

Kipner felt goosebumps trickling down his neck when he learned of the man's demise three years prior.

They had endeavored to investigate past records of Stimpson at Chicago's census bureau while searching for any evidence on Lucy Hodgins. Now knowing her current name, she was relatively easy to track down with her latest occupation at the Chicago Public Library beginning a year after Stimpson's death.

Chicago's only public library was inside an abandoned water tower. The lower half of the building was a rectangular brick layout with a central cylindrical basin resting above. Inside, the walls were equally cylindrical all the way to the floor and were lined with thousands of books donated by England after the Great Fire laid waste to much of the city. Among those who offered a portion of their private collection were Queen Victoria and Prime Minister Benjamin Disraeli.

It was a busy Thursday morning in April when Kipner and Flying Hawk entered the library.

Numerous people hung around the outer walls in search of their desired books. In contrast, young and old people read or studied among the countless wooden tables scattered in the center.

Kipner would have spotted Lucy in seconds. She sat behind a curved desk along the back wall with numerous books stacked across the counter. There could have been hundreds of people in the room, cluttering the view towards the back where the help desk was found.

Lucy had not changed at all in her beauty like a painting, as Kipner remembered. Her blonde hair was bundled up in a sloppy bun and accompanied her soft blue eyes that always eased him when frustrated or angry. Her white blouse was properly neat and buttoned to her neck, as she preferred, with a brown skirt that stopped just high enough to show off a pair of matching heels.

Several people were hovering around her, inquiring or attempting to borrow various books. Still, no one hovered over her as dramatically and commanding as the tall gentleman wearing similar attire to Kipner.

The figure was slightly taller than the marshal, with mutton chops that nearly touched the chin.

For a U. S. marshal, he was overly protective of himself, Kipner thought as he strode up to the desk with suspicious eyes. He wore a shiny badge upon his lapel, and a derby hat Kipner guessed still covered a receding hairline. In an unconventional method, he leaned from one side to the other while studying Lucy as if observing some specimen. Here and there, his duster would wave open and briefly reveal a hog leg strapped to his leg. It was positioned just below the holster of his pistol, which had a twin of its kind on the other side of his hip.

Marshal Hodgins spotted Kipner before he got halfway across the room and moved to intercept him.

Kipner switched his eyes from Lucy to him but never caught her attention.

Until he had seen Ward in the library, Kipner hadn't connected the dots of Lucy's new last name to him. The thought of him married to Lucy disgusted him.

"Marshal Hodgins," Kipner acknowledged when he drew himself near.

"Kipner, I'm not even going to give you a warning," Hodgins said with a voice as dangerous as sharp glass. "Get out. Now. I don't want to ever see you around her again. Do I make myself...very...clear?"

Hard metal rapped firmly against the bone of Kipner's knee that, nearly toppled him to the ground.

The short end of Hodgins' shotgun quickly returned beneath his coat. The pain shot up Kipner's leg, buckling momentarily before he regained his balance.

"Still upset you're left off of my Christmas card list?" Kipner asked mockingly, this time avoiding another belt from the shotgun barrel. "Ah, I'll send you a special one this year."

Hodgins tried grabbing Kipner's coat, but the seasoned marshal powerfully swung his wrist out and deflected it. A few people nearby caught the gesture and took their leave elsewhere.

They stared each other down in a feat of will while Flying Hawk could only stand by and watch. The native caught sight of Lucy, who made a double take at Hodgins' absence beside her, then scanned the room. Her mouth dropped open in shock as she stared.

Flying Hawk politely waved, but her eyes were on Kipner.

The Wraith stepped closer to Hodgins to clarify his point and avoid being smacked again with the shotgun. Nearly nose to nose, neither backing down, Kipner spoke through a clenched jaw.

"You feel like shooting me, Boy? Go on. Throwdown. There's no other way you are keeping me from talking to her."

Like a flash of lightning, the cold metal of a pistol's barrel was jammed under Kipner's chin.

Hodgins looked like a deranged lunatic, his cold, hateful eyes replaced with rabid, wild intensity.

His expression recalled a memory of Kipner's. He was holding a gun to his chin while sitting alone in the darkness of an office.

The smell of alcohol was thick, and his mind was uncertain. Swirling amid the intoxication was the vision of a monstrosity of black and covered with nightmarish mouths that puckered and beckoned to come closer.

Although a foreign and faded memory to him, the gun brought forth the idea of his pain and suffering that propelled him into a life of heavy drinking and harsh living.

When his memory ended, Kipner's hand now held Hodgins' Colt revolver and had jammed it underneath Hodgins' chin. Ward looked terrified and confused.

"That's...not possible. You don't deserve to have that kind of pow..." he began to say.

"Bobby! What are you doing?!" came a yell from nearby.

Lucy was rapidly approaching, sifting through the tables. She still looked breathtaking even while enraged at him.

The marshal dropped his arm down and subdued the hammer, spinning it quickly in reverse to hand Hodgins the handle of his own pistol, which he returned to the holster in disbelief. From his vantage point, his gun suddenly left his hand and appeared in Kipner's without any movement. It was just there.

Sheepishly, Kipner stepped back from Hodgins and looked apologetically at Lucy. "Hello, Lucy..."

"Don't 'Hello, Lucy' me. What were you doing pointing a gun at my husband? No, never mind that. What on earth are you even doing here?" she said, lowering her voice quickly to a hurried whisper. Most of the room had fallen silent, staring at the confrontation in the center.

"I'm not here for what you might believe, Lucy. I could use your help with something I found," Kipner said, watching her face relax again. She composed herself quickly, seeing the guns safely stowed away.

"Bobby, I'm swamped right now. Can this wait?"

He glanced at Flying Hawk, who shrugged. "We aren't exactly in a rush, per se, but we need your help as soon as you are available."

Hodgins recovered from his shock and moved deliberately between Lucy and Kipner to block the marshal's sight.

"I'm sorry, marshal, but I am afraid her job just doesn't provide any means to accommodate...whatever you may be inquiring. It would be best if you sought help elsewhere."

Whenever Kipner tried to move around him, Ward, like a child, sidestepped smoothly to cut him off.

It was amusing to him; that was clear from his smirk. Kipner wanted more than anything to pistol whip the smile right off his face but kept calm.

"Lucy, I can come back anytime you would like," Kipner said, speaking directly into Hodgins' body.

She made no motion to move Hodgins. From behind, she said, "No, he's right, Bobby. I am really busy with work, and I doubt I will have free time to assist with...whatever you may be inquiring."

The tone in her voice had changed dramatically. She didn't sound like herself to Kipner. It sounded like she was reading a written note.

"Now...Bobby," Ward said, emphasizing his name sarcastically. "You have talked to her. Now you can leave, or I will escort you out myself."

The afternoon sun was beginning to settle behind the tall buildings that made up downtown. Shadows crept across the floor and hid books in plain sight as the cascading window light drew to a gray. Long visiting by-standards sought elsewhere for dinner, and the rest looked to shuffle out before nightfall.

"Fine," Kipner said. "Alright, alright, I'll be on my way, but first, I need to find something that might help me with some ancient language. My friend and I will tend to ourselves without bothering Lucy. I just need to be pointed in the right direction."

Ward began to object, but Lucy's voice urged it was allowed as long as he kept his distance from her.

She pointed him toward the foreign language section and returned to her desk. Hodgins now hovered over Kipner as he made his way to the section.

Flying Hawk saw the pain and anguish Kipner was trying to hold back. Being treated so coldly after all these years was hard, he was sure.

While he never had met her, from the endless stories Kipner told him, her reaction was out of character, even under the circumstances when they parted years ago. There was something odd about Hodgins that rubbed the native wrong.

Watching the gun switch hands was baffling, but he had seen Kipner do extraordinary feats.

It was as if he stopped time and removed the gun from Ward.

"What is that supposed to be, some book of silly magic spells?" Hodgins poked over Kipner's shoulder and peered at the odd writing in McMannon's book.

"Do you mind?" Kipner said as he turned to face the other marshal. "You're in my way."

In response, Hodgins barely took a step back, slightly chuckling. His presence could still be felt when Kipner turned his back to him again.

None of the books were helpful. They each listed known languages that never came close to what Kipner had. Even the first languages of civilization were completely different. What he needed was a linguist like Lucy.

The library was approaching closing time, and the four were all that remained. She slowly walked up to the group with a sigh.

"You've been staring at the same small section for hours, Bobby," she said. "It's bothering me. What exactly do you have..."

"Lucy, don't worry about his problems," Hodgins interrupted. "He told me he could not find what he was looking for and needed to depart. Correct, Marshal?"

All eyes turned to Kipner.

He returned the look with daggers.

Ever since Kipner had been granted this position as a U. S. Marshal, Hodgins had made it clear he wanted him out for the pettiest reason. But his gut told him that Hodgins had a secret he was eager to unveil at the next opportunity.

You know we only awaken once, Kipner remembered hearing the marshal say back in D. C. , nine years earlier.

Now seeing him married to Lucy, his blood had gone cold, wondering what he had done to her. Several people who were easily tempted had made pacts with the Old Ones. These mighty entities were slowly stirring over the past few decades and giving out boons to dedicated followers. They were well beyond the comprehension of humans. Even the brief experience Kipner had in Kansas with What Laid Beneath shook his psyche, and the encounter under the Rocky Mountains with the colossal Old One took months to recover from the brink of insanity.

"Actually, it looks like I'll have to return tomorrow," Kipner said, glancing around the empty library. "I'm struggling to find a translation to a book I found. I'm sure it's here if I look long enough."

He turned around and pretended to search book by book from the top shelf. Behind him, the sound of teeth-gritting from Hodgins made him smile.

Someone stepped directly behind him, and Kipner felt the cold steel of a gun pressed against him once more. Lucy didn't interject and remained silent.

Warm breath swept across the back of Kipner's ear. An unusual odor permeated the air that stung Kipner's nostrils like ammonia.

Ether. The marshal's breath reeked of the foul vaporous stench that gagged Kipner. There had been necromantic encounters during Kipner's career involving the liquid for preservation, much like Formaldehyde. Still, ether was also used for entering trances to communicate with the Old Ones.

"Back off, Kipner, slowly. We're through with this charade. If I ever see you back here again, you can bet Grant will be looking for a replacement. Now move!" Hodgins hissed into his ear and shoved the pistol tighter against his left kidney. It was just enough pressure to give him discomfort, and he obliged the marshal. They made their way to the front door, but Lucy called out.

"Wait. Ward."

The marshal kept urging Kipner out of the building, but Lucy ran up to them and blocked their way.

"I said wait, Ward," she said more firmly. The familiar tone in her voice had returned. It rang like a silver bell and wasn't the deadpan attitude she had greeted him with earlier. It sounded like the Lucy he remembered.

Hodgins stopped and glared at her with fire in his eyes. There was a brief dilation of his pupil, and, at that moment, Lucy's eyes glazed over.

"Fight it, Lucy," Kipner tried to whisper, but he wasn't quiet enough.

The pistol behind him was shoved harder into his back. "Shut up, Kipner! She is mine now."

Lucy's eyes darted and shook away the spellbinding attempt. They glared back at Hodgins in defiance. "Stop it, both of you. I don't know what has gotten into you two, but this is a library, for God's sake."

For a moment, it didn't seem Hodgins was going to back off, but he relaxed the pistol.

Kipner stepped away though the gun was still pointed at him. Behind them, Flying Hawk was poised and ready to attack Ward if Kipner gave the signal, but he shook his head.

"There," she said with a long sigh. "That's better. Now, what is this book you're going on about?"

Kipner's eyes were still narrowed at Hodgins. The last person he wanted to reveal McMannon's book to was holding the gun.

"Perhaps without your husband here..."

Ward lifted his gun a bit higher and gritted his teeth. "Out of the question, Kipner. You're lucky I'm even letting you talk with her."

Yes, I wonder exactly what he was scheming, Kipner thought. Lucy appeared to be a victim of a controlling power, but it didn't always work on her. If Kipner had to take a guess, it was her strong will. He didn't know how long she could last until the power regained control.

Turning his eyes away from his enemy, Kipner's face softened at the sight of Lucy again. Even when distraught, she looked at him with caring eyes.

Somewhere deep inside them was a flicker of feelings she once had. But surrounding it all were years of sorrow and disappointment brought on by a man who chose his career over her love, which led her down a different path than she wished.

"I came across an old book filled with odd markings that don't match any glyphs or pictographs I can find. You were always the master of linguistics. I came all the way from Kansas for just a little help," Kipner said.

He handed the book to Lucy.

Out of the corner of his eyes, he caught Hodgins' eyes widening with excitement. The marshal from Washington recognized the book somehow.

Lucy took it and flipped carefully through the pages. She paused every so often, but they all contained similar markings. One page was the same as the next.

"Where did you say you got this exactly?" she asked while returning to the book.

"Again, I would rather not discuss the details in front of your husband, Lucy."

"Again," Lucy said, looking up at him without lifting her head from the book, "stop worrying about Ward. He's not hurting anything and doesn't care about a book anyway."

She liked to mimic him when there was any kind of disagreement. Kipner always remarked she was the brighter of the two, and her arguments nearly always won because she was right.

He wasn't going to win this battle either. "Some crackpot worshiping the Harrow down in Kansas," he answered.

She stopped thumbing through and stared off in thought for a moment. "That strange man..." she trailed off.

"Lucy? What strange man?" he asked her.

Flying Hawk had deftly slid behind Hodgins and quietly pressed the blade of his hunting knife against his back, whispering something in his ear that Kipner couldn't hear.

Whatever was said helped as Hodgins lowered his pistol and stood still. The wild fiery stare was now subdued to heavy, sleepy eyes while listing side to side.

Lucy immediately snapped out of her thought and looked up at Kipner. "We had a visitor come in the other day wanting to donate a wooden chest of books. The man said they were almost a set, save one missing volume."

She paused and looked uneasy, running her fingers through her hair. Her voice lowered, and she drew in closer to Kipner. "He knew we had a private collection downstairs that was off-limits to the public. There was no way he could have known."

"Books of value?" Kipner asked as she began leading him across the room to her desk.

"More like occult books of immorality," she said. "Books written by horrible people long ago that somehow survived the years and wound up here. They aren't meant for the public eye, and their presence is kept a secret."

One of the bookcases concealed a doorway leading down a tight spiral staircase that she revealed with a hidden latch. She gently touched Kipner's chest to stop him before he stepped inside. He remembered a woman's gentle hand on his shoulder from some time before that had interrupted Kipner's observation and resulted in snapping at her. It had been just as delicate as Lucy's.

"No, Bobby. It doesn't matter who you are to me. You are not going down there. Even with your...background. Wait here, I'll bring them up, and you can see what I'm talking about."

With my background, Kipner thought. What was really down there? Lucy swallowed hard, took a deep breath, lit a candelabra, and, after looking once more at Kipner with what could have been interpreted as longing, disappeared into the darkness below.

"You will never have her again, Kipner," Hodgins said after she was out of sight.

"She is too far gone and within my power for any hope from you."

The sleepy expression remained on Ward, but he began to move as if strung like a puppet and manipulated by an invisible hand. Like a lifeless body, it danced and dangled across the room, almost playfully, with its arms spread outward.

Kipner gauged the puppet closely. "Who are you?"

"Ahhhhhh," it spoke delightfully. "Who am I, indeed? We have not met yet, but I enjoyed gazing at your adventures. Carrots dangling in front of your eyes that led you here will not go on much longer, and then you'll be lost and aimless."

It spun in a pirouette and chuckled maniacally. Hovering before Kipner, it leaned in, bending at the waist.

"I'm not so sure I need any more carrots. I'm confident I've discovered what I was sent out to find," Kipner said while trying to strain his ear to Lucy downstairs.

"And what might that be, Wraith?" the voice rang out, drawing out the name in a long syllable.

"You've been watching up to this point. I would hate to spoil the surprise. Wait, and you'll find out soon enough."

Kipner turned his back to the puppet, which responded with a frustrated yell and then swung over in front of Kipner.

"You are too inferior in wisdom to learn anything the Great Ones possess. You're too late. They are already awakening, quicker with my help, and soon the world will witness a power beyond nightmares."

From downstairs came a shriek of terror that was suddenly cut short. With a start, Kipner shoved the puppet to one side and dashed down the stairs, letting his eyes of night guide him. He missed what Flying Hawk yelled out from behind. All of his focus was on Lucy.

The basement was the same shape and size as above. The only difference was the bookshelves lined across the floor instead of along the circumference. Only the light from Lucy's candelabra, now quickly burning out on the floor, illuminated the room.

Kipner leaped over the staircase railing to a grizzly sight that plagued his memory for weeks.

Hunched over a half-eaten corpse was a goat-like bipedal figure. Its head was covered in black fur with two bulging eyes on either side and elongated ivory horns that extended several feet. Its hands were like a bear, wide and clawed, and they had made an enormous cavity into the chest of Lucy where its face was buried with dire hunger.

The Wraith sprung to life with both pistols drawn, each erupting in purple flame. Two quick shots exploded out of the gun barrels with such speed the beast had no time to react and took both bullets to the head.

The sheer force of the special guns launched the beast back ten feet and off Lucy's body. Still, it recovered quickly, showing no signs of injury.

It was no ordinary beast.

The two had crossed paths years before deep in Washington Territory. It had spoken to Kipner then, revealing itself to be of the Old Ones, its name Xcthol to the mortal tongue. It had attempted to constrain the marshal's mind then, but the Wraith barely managed to escape with deep wounds that took all Dr. Sales' abilities to save him.

Encountering Xcthol a second time made Kipner's blood run cold, but he could only react to the creature's quick speed.

A blare of devilish sound came from deep in its lungs before it burst forth down the aisle with inhuman speed. It was too much for the marshal to handle, and he took the full blunt force of the diving spear into his gut, shattering him against the brick wall behind. Within him, each bone ripped and shredded from the power, and he could only stare from sheer agony.

The beast let Kipner crumble to the floor. As it raised its enormous clawed hand to strike him open, a flash of light surrounded Kipner, lifting him off the ground by an invisible force. Shrouded in purple light, he was no longer in control of himself, and his pain instantly vanished.

Like before, he succumbed to whatever force beckoned his body, unaware of the consequences or price he might pay later.

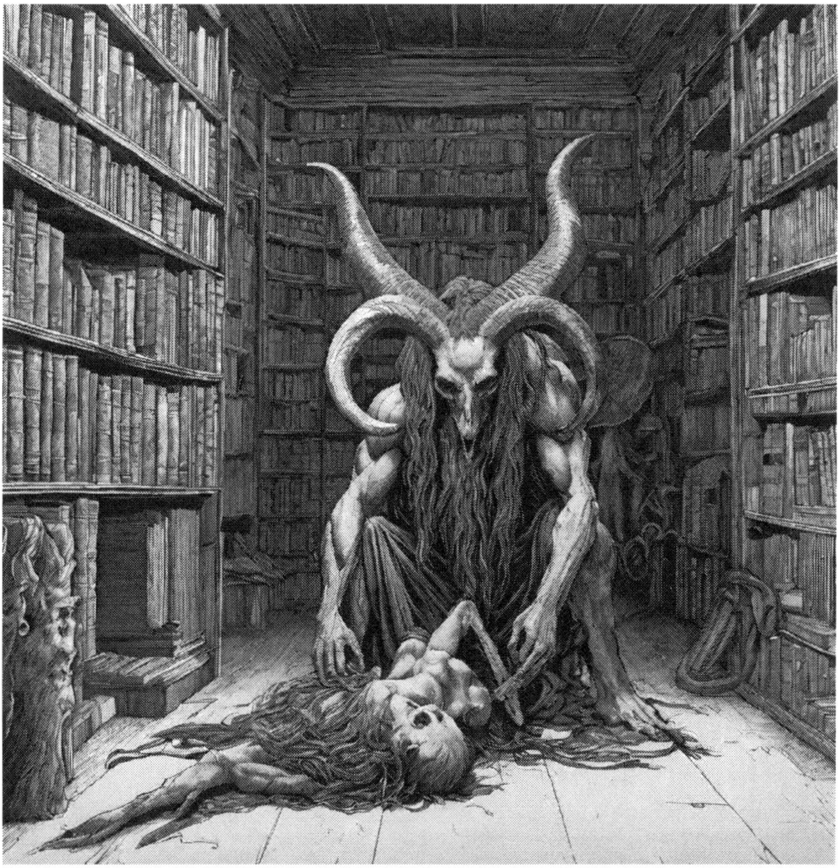

With the movement of a god, Kipner dodged the blow of the beast and returned four more shots into its back, forming holes large enough to drive a fist through.

Raging in furious anger, it spun around. It tried mentally empowering the marshal like their first encounter, but he now was the Wraith, truly by all means, and few things of the earth could stop him.

From the stairs stood Flying Hawk as he crouched helplessly in the wonder of the sight. Two Tomahawks were gripped tightly in each hand, but he knew they were useless. Only the gifts from the gods that Kipner wielded now could help.

The Wraith, despite his strange new powers, was caught off guard by a sly move from the creature, and he was launched with Xcthol into one of the shelves, toppling it over and a few more behind. He placed the ends of both barrels against the foe from a resting position as it lay on top of him and fired a few more rounds. The wounds were deep and, with the previous several, formed a gap through its torso large enough for separation with a good kick. Xcthol is laid in two pieces, separated entirely across the torso.

The power of the Wraith subsided quickly. From the fight, Kipner had numerous slashes from the beast's claws. One particularly nasty cut went straight down his chest and looked like it was festering. He laid there momentarily, gasping at the exhaustion and pain that shot through his body. Strange as it was, he wished he knew more about what was behind his transformation but, more importantly, what he paid for to receive such a boon.

His friend came down the stairs, but Hodgins was nowhere to be seen. The native explained how Hodgins collapsed into a pile of lifeless flesh as soon as they ran downstairs. The skin had turned molten and then cooled into a conical shape.

The few ointments Flying Hawk carried, medicinal herbs his tribe often would use, were not effective against the supernatural wounds.

After a minute, Kipner was able to rise slowly to his feet with a bit of help and made his way to what remained of Lucy.

Against Flying Hawk's wishes to see a doctor, Kipner remained in the library until the early morning. He had covered Lucy's body with some shipping tarp and laid her gently on a makeshift bed of a few books. There he sat beside her and tried to replace the last memory of her with thoughts of the past. Nothing made him feel any better. He couldn't help but take some of the responsibility that she was gone. Her life would have been so different had he chosen to remain with her. Perhaps she would still be alive if he had followed her sooner down the stairs.

In silence, he mourned with his friend, who sat quietly beside him, his hand resting on Kipner's back.

The native didn't know Lucy personally, but Kipner had told enough stories about her he felt like he did.

When their paths had crossed, Kipner spoke of finally tracking her down and turning in the badge for good. A lot of good it had done. Still, the conversation always ended with his duty taking priority because it would ultimately keep her safe if he succeeded in his task.

When the dry tears were over, Kipner gathered himself and spent the rest of the morning investigating the basement to find what Lucy was after. He found the small chest beside one of the few bookshelves still standing from the fight. Inside were four books similar to McMannon's, but the trunk was missing a fifth book.

As Kipner reached for one of the books to pull it out, searing pain shot up from his fingertips to his shoulder. Some invisible protection kept him from taking out a book, but it allowed him to add the fifth book without pain.

Once all five books were nested in the chest, black vein-like branches surged up from under the books, wrapped themselves around each spine, and interlocked across the volumes.

"Someone just came in and donated these to the library?" Kipner asked rhetorically as they studied them.

"These are unholy tomes," Flying Hawk said. "Perhaps they wanted to get rid of them."

"Then set fire to them. They brought them into a place of distribution. Someone wanted them to be used or found. You're right, though. They can't be for good, but I need to know how they tie in with the Harrow. Something tells me they hold all the secrets from the past about them."

Flying Hawk looked worried.

"Don't read them, Wraith. Even if you learn how. Don't read them. I feel pure evil rising from them. They cast an aura that is cold and dark. We have forbidden scripts that only those learned in shamanic practice can safely read."

Some presence surrounded the chest and books. Kipner could feel it, too. It was a different form of evil he had fought for years as a marshal. At no time did he encounter the Harrow tied to religion. There had been no demons or angels to fight, only powerful entities that were very real in form and not from this world. He may call them god-like occasionally, but the Harrow was an invasion of a species, not of holy or unholy grounds.

At least, that is what Kipner hoped.

Nevertheless, he took the precautionary words of his friend to heart. He knew he shouldn't crack open any other books, but they needed to be understood somehow. With the native's help, they carried the chest upstairs and rested it beside the fleshy remains of Hodgins.

Kipner was curious about who delivered such a gift to a public library. As the earliest rays of the morning sun began to peek over the tops of Chicago's buildings, the marshal searched through the past records of charitable donations. One, in particular, stood out to him - Thomas Foley.

"He's the Bishop here in Chicago," Kipner explained when Flying Hawk was unfamiliar with the name. "Came in a few months ago, dropped off the chest. Sounds to me like Foley felt the same things we're feeling. Let's go pay him a visit."

"You need to tend to those gashes across your body first," the native said. Each slash had a light green hue that was sickly.

"The only one who could help is still in St. Louis," Kipner pointed out. "I doubt too many doctors practicing traditional medicine could do much with these. I'll be fine." When Flying Hawk was unconvinced, he added, "If it gets any worse, I'll go straight to the hospital."

The Wraith was very tolerant of pain, which resulted in being stubborn - a terrible combination.

Many of the scars and odd markings he carried with him on his body could have been prevented had he taken heed.

The truth was he didn't trust anyone other than Dr. Sales. Amos was the only one who could heal the way he could. If there ever was such a thing as angels, Kipner silently thanked God he found Amos. Sometimes he wondered if Amos found him instead.

Lifting the chest with one man was tolerable but cumbersome, so the two found a convenient store that offered wagons for rent. It was far too big for the small size of the chest, but it allowed them to hide it well.

Its presence among the streets still had a strange effect, however. People would look towards the wagon as if they knew the books were under the cover, then divert their route dramatically to distance themselves. A few fist fights spontaneously broke out immediately around the wagon for little or no reason. Throughout the short trip, heated arguments would erupt in several places that would escalate until the wagon and its cargo were out of sight.

There was more than an evil aura cast about the books. There was a manipulation.

Quickly as they could ride, the two drove the wagon to State Street and paused momentarily to reflect the Holy Name Cathedral's beauty. It was asymmetrical, with a single spire rising up along the right. A dominating rose window hung above the front entrance.

Bishop Foley had given the dedication to the newly reconstructed cathedral in 1875 after having been a victim of the Great Fire four years earlier. It took considerable donations from across the country to rebuild.

Kipner and Flying Hawk enjoyed the brief history lesson one of the deacons insisted on giving when they stepped inside.

None of the clergymen knew what was inside the chest, but they all were deeply frightened by its presence and forbade it from entering the building. Something told Kipner no one would be able to steal it if left unattended, but Flying Hawk chose to remain outside and tend to Roy while Kipner went to find Foley.

According to the deacons, the bishop had been secluded for several months. After the dedication and reopening of the Holy Name, he briefly mentioned receiving an unusual package but refused to reveal it. It had been delivered late at night, and only he had seen it arrive. For the following few weeks, he refused to come out of his quarters until one morning, a few choir boys claimed to have seen him quickly leave the cathedral awkwardly carrying a chest-sized package wrapped in brown paper. When he returned sometime later, he locked himself back in his studies and had not come out since. The clergy only knew he was still alive by the meals they left at his door returned empty.

Kipner took in the odd story he was told and made his way into the back rooms of the cathedral where Bishop Foley's quarters were located. His door was of heavy wood grain and reinforced with two ironwork plates.

A few raps on the door brought no answer. While there was a keyhole, no one at the church possessed a copy of the key Foley held, and little could be seen peering through it.

"Mr. Foley, I know you once had the chest of books that are now at the library," Kipner began while leaning against the door. "I know it has horrible effects on people. We witnessed it bringing it here. It even attracted some diabolical creature that murdered my...a friend." He paused momentarily to catch the lump in his throat at the thought of Lucy. They had never been more than a couple. By now, he didn't know how to refer to her.

"It pains me to ask you for help because it's clear you won't have any part of it, but I desperately need your assistance. I'm on the verge of discovering a means to end what is tormenting the country, and you can greatly enlighten me if you can answer a few questions. Please."

The room was eerily silent beyond the door.

"Don't let the love of my life die in vain, Bishop," Kipner said quietly with both hands resting on the door. "I don't want to live my life knowing she died needlessly."

After waiting several minutes, the marshal grew impatient and began to work on the lock. Given the church's young age, he suspected it would be intricate and complex, but it soon surrendered to his tools.

The room was empty and contained no other doors. A fireplace smoldered in dark coals along one side while a made bed lay across from it. There were clearly vacant areas along the wall and across the mantle where holy trinkets and symbols were once present. Dust settlement showed depictions of crosses and statues, all now missing. There were no signs of religion in the room.

The marshal went about the room, studying every detail closely. A few meals had been eaten and left in a stack of soiled dishes in one corner, which had begun to grow mold. Near the bishop's bed was a series of wide wood beams fitted in intervals along the stone wall. Kipner could not recollect seeing such large pieces anywhere else in the church from his tour earlier, which drew him in for a closer look.

He ran his hand over each piece, perfectly flush with the surrounding stone, until he reached the beam near the corner. Against his weight, it was loose, but he couldn't get his fingers around it to remove it from the wall. Instead, he tried pressing firmly onto its heavy weight. Begrudgingly, it pivoted like a pendulum, suspended by a metal rod above, and revealed an uncomfortably tight vertical shaft leading down and lined with rusted iron rungs.

"It couldn't be," Kipner said out loud in surprise. He had heard of priest holes being popular in Europe when Catholicism was outlawed in the 16th Century, but they were not needed in America. Men of the cloth often created cleverly hidden rooms to avoid persecution. Why this church's designer felt it needed one was beyond Kipner. He intended to find out as he wedged through the claustrophobic opening.

A man of Kipner's age with full, thick brown hair and a clean-shaven face sat in a simple, wooden chair that took up much of a cramped, moldy room. His eyes were profoundly bloodshot and puffy from significant crying. He stared with a hollow look as the marshal descended the ladder.

"You must believe me," the bishop said. "I had no other choice but to get rid of it. Those books are not of this world, nor are they diabolical. There are no known means how to destroy them. Do not bring them to me."

"Please, why must you torture me?" Foley pleaded. "I have suffered enough."

"It sounds to me you have a great burden still weighing you down, Bishop," Kipner said. "Why don't you explain how you came into their possession and what you know of their history?"

The bishop fought to continue, but a part of him needed to confess. "I have lost contact with God," he began, staring into the fire as he gathered his thoughts. "I no longer feel his presence each morning when I rise or pray. What drives my faith in him is the growing presence of demons. They have spoken to me. They are...afraid. Afraid that this new presence of utter terror, of a new definition of evil, is inevitable."

In the short moment Kipner had been there, Foley had consumed two glasses of wine in quick gulps. He spoke like he was out of breath from running.

When he wasn't holding the wine goblet, he fidgeted obsessively with the folds of his robes with repeated patterns.

"Their presence has always been here but warded off to our awareness and shielded by the Trinity with immense powers that rival..." Foley said, trailing off.

"God?" Kipner guessed. Foley nervously nodded.

"With heaven in silence, we men of the cloth have no choice but to strengthen our faith and form alliances against our code. God, forgive me, but we are at war with a new threat. Something mankind is unable to fathom even through faith and religion because they are indeed among us.

"Several years ago, long before the fire, a large man visited the parish and spoke to me after mass of his studies concerning the Harrow. I never caught his name in the conversation. Still, he knew a considerable amount, including a theory on reversing the path unfolding worldwide.

"At the time, I was aware the threat was at our doorstep, but I leaned on my faith to protect me. As the presence of God faded, I became more scared and turned my attention to what he had told me."

A knock came above, followed by an inquisitive voice. To the visitor's joy, Foley answered that all was well and to return later.

"Do you remember what this man looked like?" Kipner asked as the sound of the visitor's footsteps faded away.

"Nothing that stood out to me other than his size. He was slightly taller than you but equally as broad-chested. His hands were relatively large for being so dexterous with a pen. He wore a derby that wasn't quite big enough and noticeable mutton chops."

Kipner nodded without surprise at Hodgins' description. He had sure done his sworn duty as a U. S. marshal, alright.

"Several documents had been written by my visitor that day, to which he went over them one by one.

They covered his broad studies over the past several years that resulted in his discovery of a hierarchy among the Old Ones, as he called them, for he thought they could be millions of years old, if not older. This hierarchy was set by power, and the Greater Old Ones, the most powerful of them all, were slowly beginning to awaken over the last several decades for whatever reason."

"Native tribal relocation," Kipner said to a confused look from the bishop. The marshal shrugged and urged Foley to continue.

"Our lengthy conversation ended with his emphatic insistence on delivering a collection of books, four in all, to me that I might further study and help translate. He deeply believed they held the means to either return them to their slumber or eradicate them from existence altogether."

Judging from the experience Kipner witnessed while delivering the books back to Foley that afternoon, he highly doubted they would be helpful in a good way. He was on holy grounds and still felt the horrific aura from the wagon outside. It made him shiver.

"Were you able to decipher any of the books?" Kipner asked.

With alarm, Foley stared at Kipner. "You would take me for a madman if I did, wouldn't you?"

"At this point, I don't think anyone can be called a madman when dealing with what we're faced with."

The bishop acted like he didn't hear Kipner's words. "Not at first, no. They were only strange markings to me. I spent days scouring documents, books, and pamphlets. Anything I could get my hands on. When I had exhausted the known ancient languages, I turned to lesser favored texts and went against the Church's support. That's when...That's when darker shades approached me.

"I knew then I faced something far different than what fell into my religion. With nothing celestial to turn to, I sided with the things I tell the parish to veer away from in mass. I know I am forever destined now for Hell for my actions, but there was no other way. I needed help beyond mortal powers."

"I was given new sight to understand the books, granted to me in exchange, I'm sure, for my doomed soul. And for what? All I learned was that I had been betrayed and fooled. Reading thoroughly through all five god-forsaken tomes in order will spawn and disturb all that slumbers and awaits. Immediately. No more waiting. They are not for the benefit of mankind but for total annihilation! Do not bring them before me and leave me be!"

Foley began crying again and turned away from Kipner to his thoughts. A dark cloud hovered over the bishop that frightened him. The holy man had made unspeakable decisions that were unnatural to be so quickly chosen. Something had driven him to dishonor his faith and embrace sinister methods, all to understand the books.

They were never meant to be read in the first place. Not to anyone of good intentions, Kipner thought. These fundamental elements could bring mankind's downfall by accelerating the awakening. Whoever made them desired to aid the Harrow.

"I have the fifth in the set," Kipner told the bishop, who refused to look at him.

"If they are meant for what you say, they're a danger to us if supporters of the Harrow acquire them."

The marshal sighed and leaned back in his chair. "That doesn't get me anywhere closer, and now I have a target pinned on my back to those who know I have them. I'm getting nowhere."

It had been a long and tiring journey since he first was in D. C. among the country's leaders. There had been pieces he had uncovered, clues that had led him further down the path. But with each turn he came to, he saw the road narrowing until it ended here.

"You miss the piece that I possess," came a voice Kipner had heard many times before.

Something or someone that empowered him in extreme danger of becoming the true Wraith. Someone that put life into his pistols. Someone he felt should not be trusted.

"We grow weary of the Old Ones. We can help you. You need only ask."

"Are you the same who tricked Foley?" Kipner asked out loud. The bishop immediately stopped sobbing and snapped his attention to the marshal.

"They're speaking to you now, aren't they? Don't listen to them!" Foley desperately shouted. "They only seek their benefit, not yours!"

"Trickery was never given," the voice continued echoing in Kipner's mind. "The fool asked for the wrong, missing piece. You, however, know what is needed. Ask, and we shall aid you to finally be at peace. Lucy still longs for you."

"Lucy! What have you done to her? She doesn't deserve to be tormented by demons!" Kipner shouted and rose out of his chair with fists clenched.

"Easy, Marshal," the voice spoke slowly and soothingly. "We do not have her yet, but therein lies your missing piece. She knows what is to be done. But she, too, misses pieces to the unworldly puzzle. Pieces you acquired. Pity the two are so far apart."

So far apart, Kipner wondered. Looking back, he remembered Judge McMannon's reveal that he had bargained with an Old One to create a doppelganger to be in two places at once.

"Yes, Marshal," the voice acknowledged as it read his mind. "She left clues behind. Crumbs to follow. Start at the beginning. She's waiting for you at the end."

The voice trailed off and left him to himself. Foley stared blankly at him, hoping to hear the marshal had heeded his words.

"There's only one place to start following her trail," the marshal said as he left the bishop, begging him not to pursue any further with demons. "Don't worry, bishop. I've already paid the price."

CHAPTER XI

Illinois & Arizona, 1876

Lucy lived on the second floor of a stick-style apartment a few blocks north of Van Burren Street. Its tall windows gave way to plentiful ambient sunlight that filled each room with warmth and comfort. Thin wooden floors spread from room to room and creaked in protest. From the small, street-facing living room to the even tinier bedroom in the back, Lucy had decorated her apartment with stacks of research papers, published archaeological and historical books, rolled-up maps, pieces of rock with embedded fossils, chipped off portions of ancient pottery, and dozens of miniature teapot sets.

"She loved collecting them," Kipner explained to Flying Hawk as he carefully lifted one off a shelf to examine it closer. It was made of pure porcelain and delicately painted with flowers and a Cardinal across one side. Another resting beside it was clear glass and etched with holly.

"When she was a little girl, she told me her father gave her a dollhouse that fell victim to a fire that destroyed most of their home. A miniature tea set in it somehow survived, and she collected them as a remembrance."

He pointed out the one, which was a simple glazed clay set.

The two had spent the better part of a day exploring her house after Kipner skillfully picked the lock of her front door. He knew if there was indeed a copy of her somewhere in the world, she would not be near her other self. She was always wanting to cover vast areas in her field. He didn't expect her home anytime soon.

Something peculiar about her career had not struck Kipner until he had been in St. Louis and spoken with the Creek tribe. She had always loved archaeology, which he often thought he should have pursued with her instead of wearing a badge. Now that the strange past life he had once lived had surfaced in his memories, he realized the connection. There was an inner desire that fascinated him while sifting through the endless research papers she had written. A yearning desire.

Another strange occurrence had happened when he saw Lucy in the library that hadn't rung a bell until he had time to contemplate the notion later. Her radiant blue eyes sparkled when they laid eyes on him. For years, he had thought of her beauty in his heart, never forgetting every detail of her face and hair follicle. Still, now a memory made the vision more familiar to him than he realized.

He had once had a secretary. She had a different name, but her face was so similar to Lucy's that the two could have been sisters. Perhaps even identical twins. Maybe she was the same person. The memory was there, but Lucy's memory interfered with the focus.

The farther along he went down the rabbit hole of his mission, the more he questioned himself. This past life he once lived was becoming more parallel with his current life. From Lucy having a striking appearance to...her name was...Natasha to mistaking his friend Amos for Renaldo, and he wondered if there was mischief at play.

He had stepped through a doorway of immense power that demanded payment to be activated. The cost was far more than resurrection.

"Kipner, you should see this," Flying Hawk said in the other room, snapping the marshal's thoughts.

He stepped into a second bedroom, which had been made into a study. However, much of her apartment could be considered her study.

Lucy had hauled a roll top desk into the room that accompanied a few narrow cabinets and a wilting potted plant in the corner. Attempting to close the rolltop would prove impossible from the enormous pile of papers on the desk. Much of the floor was covered with additional documents, although these had been half-heartedly placed in cardboard boxes.

What drew Flying Hawk's attention was in the cabinet, however. A false back was inserted into the piece that could be removed to reveal a hidden series of shelves, each filled with leather-bound books.

They each took a few books and began scanning through them. They all were handwritten journals from Lucy, specifically about her research on the Harrow. Why they were hidden was anyone's guess. Her details hinted that she was being pursued or watched by unseen beings and concealed people hiding just out of sight where ever she went. She questioned herself of paranoia since she could not witness any of these stalkers. Still, her fear kept her awake at night and constantly looking over her shoulder.

Accompanying her worries and fears, her journal was filled with theories and hypotheses on her studies. Numerous entries had been struck through as she would find evidence against the idea. Still, towards the end of the journals, which read like a chronological series, she posed the idea Kipner had learned about removing native tribes from their homelands.

With dramatically heavy, dark lines, she had circled one of the ancient civilizations in present-day Mexico or Central America, having significant knowledge of the Harrow long before it was known to the world.

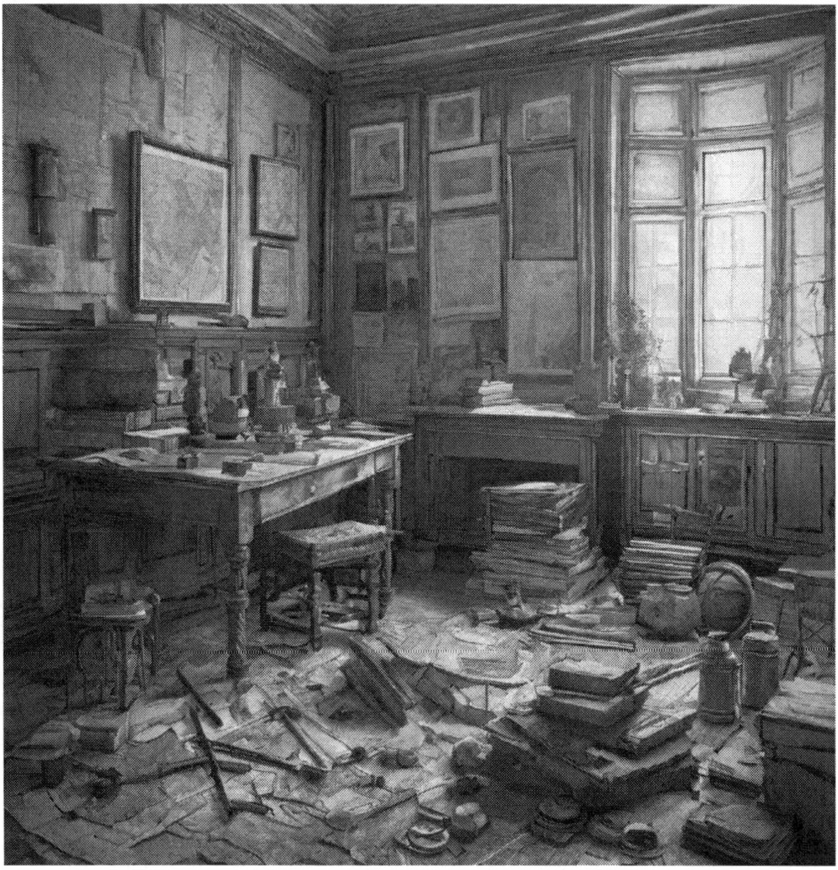

"I thought she worked for women's rights or native tribes," Flying Hawk said as he returned his books to the shelf. "Everything here is about the Harrow."

The marshal thought about it momentarily, reflecting back to her again. Suddenly being around remnants after a decade of separation brought out solid memories and feelings. It pained him to see she gave up her passion for Washington. Despite the lack of his presence, he had hoped she would keep pursuing the promotion of voting for women or improving the quality of life for native tribes. It was clear from her apartment she had given it all up to follow precisely what Kipner had been doing all this time. It broke his heart to wonder why the two hadn't stayed together and worked as a team, but he knew why. She had picked it up to spite him. She could throw that in his face to prove he had been foolish to leave her for his career if she could learn what he couldn't.

He turned his back to Flying Hawk, pretending to inspect the desk but secretly shielding his tearing eyes.

"Her passion spread everywhere," he said after gathering himself to speak.

"Archaeology was her love, though. She found a connection to the Harrow's origin through it."

Some of her books were of ancient Mexican history, long before it became a country. Among them was a high concentration of Aztec lore. She had done extensive research on their civilization. Nothing among the publications did it speak of the Harrow or anything similar. She had written hundreds of papers describing their culture. She believed in a race that came from the stars and lived on Earth for thousands of years before the Aztec's ascension. These entities were considered powerful gods that could give boons at a high cost to mortals or wipe out their civilization with little effort.

The Aztecs feared them greatly, Lucy wrote. Whenever they experienced a meteor shower, for example, they would heighten their concentration on maintaining the god's slumber. They recognized these great gods slept for hundreds or thousands of years and only awakened under specific circumstances. Among these were deadly rituals, powerful artifacts, or significant natural catastrophes.

Among the last pieces of information she had gathered was that the Aztec people were wise to understand such god-like entities were most likely present across Earth, which to them was in the shape of a giant disk and not just in their immediate vicinity. To this, Lucy believed they fashioned some large-scale device that would aid them in keeping all the gods asleep indefinitely.

Both men had not eaten since arriving at Lucy's apartment, so they concluded their search to find a restaurant and return to their hotel for the night. On the way out the door, Kipner stopped in his tracks.

Along the wall beside the door was the mantle of a fireplace, now filled with concrete. It was made from plaster and ornately designed with intricate Gothic trim. The apartment's theme revolved around loose papers stacked upon one another, so the nearly bare mantle was peculiar. Only a single envelope rested on it with "Bobby" written in Lucy's handwriting.

The marshal's hands trembled like a night of heavy drinking as he gingerly took and opened the envelope to read the letter.

After a few lines reading to himself, he gave way to revealing what Lucy had written to his native friend, who politely gave him space.

"I have no doubt you will someday find where I live and stand here to read this. You may have chosen your career over mine, but I understand your decision. Somewhere down your road, you'll cross my path again because no matter how I turned on me, I saw your past trail. My love for you was all I thought about for years, accompanied by the pain you gave me. However, having a better understanding now, I see the importance of your decision. I now pursue it myself, and I have made great strides that would make you proud of me.

"Despite this, I made a decision that will disappoint you upon hearing. I made a pact to finance my trip, and now I am forever paying the cost. I regret my decision too much to confess to whom I struck the deal, but heed my words - it knows you will try to find me and is waiting. Trying to convince you to follow me is useless, so I will leave you with these parting words - I look forward to seeing your brown eyes again."

A gentle hand from Flying Hawk came to rest on Kipner's shoulder as he finished reading the note with a choked voice. In all his travels with his friend, the marshal was rough around the edges and showed little of his feelings. He had to remain rigid and fearless among the enemies he faced daily. There was no room to show vulnerability, or he might wind up dead. As he grew older, however, the native noticed Kipner's thoughts were of a loving life devoid of monsters and sinister people and with the one person who could turn the Wraith into the soft-smiling Bobby Kipner.

The receipt for a one-way ticket on the Illinois Central Railroad to New Orleans was tucked inside Lucy's envelope. Written on the back was the name "Oxtlipa."

With Lucy's immense wealth of information in her apartment, it took them longer than expected to pin down a map old enough to list former cities and villages of the Aztecs. Her letter had sparked something in Kipner that caused his body to forget he hadn't eaten for hours, and Flying Hawk knew to politely keep silent. At the same time, his friend got the satisfactory answer he sought.

Without spending days scouring through the hundreds of thousands of papers throughout her apartment, finding much information on the ancient city was virtually impossible. Still, they were able to identify where it once stood. San Luis Potosi, they learned, was the current name of the state in Mexico that once included a portion of the vast empire of the Aztecs.

It wasn't until dark that the two finally left Lucy's apartment and sought food. They were limited to a few bars that could put a simple plate together at that hour. Over beers, they discussed what direction to take.

"I've been away from my tribe for too long," Flying Hawk said. "I can't go with you that far. We can't be sure when you will return."

The marshal took a long draw from his mug and wiped the foam from his thick mustache. "It's been good traveling with you again, old friend. This has been my job from the start, and I should finish it as it was given to me. I'm grateful for all your help, not just these past few months but all those that came before."

Smiling, the native nodded and toasted his mug to his friend. "It has been an adventure that I will miss. Until the next life."

The last words made Kipner wince inside. He couldn't imagine having to recall yet another lifetime of memories. He hoped wherever this road ended would be the last for him.

The following morning, Flying Hawk set out west before the sun, leaving Kipner to slowly rise alone and contemplate the final leg of his journey. The hotel coffee warmed his blood and gave him a new vision for a better purpose. For once, he felt he was not chasing phantoms and weak leads but solid evidence that could end with his mission complete and see Lucy again.

He would follow in her footsteps and take the same rail she had down to New Orleans, then find a ship that would take him the remainder of the way. There was a brief sense of doubt upon contemplating a ship's voyage as if he had a phobia or an awful experience before being aboard. He shrugged off the notion and wondered what to do once he reached where the ancient town of Oxtlipa once stood. He just hoped Lucy's blonde hair and blue eyes would make asking the locals easy.

A man working at Kipner's hotel approached him with a telegram, and the marshal accepted with a tip. A brief telegraph had been sent to President Grant the night before of his intentions to travel to Mexico.

"Denied," it read. "Remain in States. America's threat top priority."

"That's odd," Kipner said out loud as he finished breakfast and dabbed his mustache with a napkin. "I don't recall asking your permission."

A second telegram arrived after he had checked out of the hotel while preparing Roy for the ride to the rail yard.

Annoyed, Kipner took the paper briskly from the clerk and bid him off without a tip. He didn't have time to linger around waiting for further instructions from a man he didn't entirely trust. Grant may have sided with him against the cabinet members, but Kipner knew the President would do whatever was necessary to gain more favor from the American people. This included considering Kipner an expendable.

"Inquire rail Baron Ties, Arizona. Potential Harrow connection. Report findings."

For the love of...Kipner exclaimed privately to himself in frustration. He was unsure why Grant was suddenly calling the shots. The marshal had free reign until that point to make any decision without interference. In fact, Kipner seldom bothered sending any report in except an occasional "Pursuing lead." Since he was always on the move, no one could send him any inquiries.

Tracking down Lucy was going to take a significant amount of time to venture down to Mexico and back, and he had decided to give notice to Grant. In a roundabout way, he had hoped the news might lead to some form of assistance in traveling. The effort turned out to be a waste of his time. At the end of the day, he knew they didn't care what he was doing until something was discovered worth reporting.

Baron Ties was unfamiliar to him, but it was probably one of the numerous companies Washington had hired to stretch rails across the country to help with industry. For the life of him, he couldn't guess how Grant and his band of disenchanted misfits could associate some railroad company with the Harrow. Should they fail and the Old Ones awaken, the railway would be the least of America's problems.

Arizona was significantly out of his way, too. There were railroads present out west that could get him there eventually. Still, it would mean delaying his venture to Lucy by several months. Something ate at him, however, as he thought of the telegram.

The rarity of such an order given to him nagged his curiosity. There was something behind this request that was deemed significant enough Grant wished for him to drop everything and investigate.

Those in D. C. hadn't known his whereabouts for several months, not since the Dakota Territory. There was no telling how long they had wished him to look into the matter. By now, the opportunity had passed.

Cursing under his breath at his dilemma, he walked Roy through the streets of Chicago down to Union Station.

The air was thick with harsh coal smoke and burned Kipner's nostrils. People politely pushed and shoved their way through the dense crowds to make their train on time. The marshal subconsciously kept both hands on his belongings to discourage curious hands from snatching anything.

"Last I heard, BT already runs into California," said the teller when Kipner inquired about railways heading west. The man behind the station screen spat tobacco into a can at his feet and shook his head. "Can't for the life of me know how he does it. He must have made a deal with the Devil himself to get his crew to work that fast."

One of the unique features Baron Ties offered was an open invitation to use any portion of the rail system they had laid. Instead of working from either end like Central and Union Pacific, Baron Ties had chosen to begin their rail system at one end in New Orleans and then make their way west. So far, mile for mile, they were nearly ten times further along than the other companies. A few curious reporters for newspapers had ventured to catch up to the construction site, which was a feat in and of itself due to their development speed. The stories were just a large workforce allowed for around-the-clock work.

Roy was carefully boarded into a cage car and given enough oats and sweets to keep him from becoming too grumpy. Lessons had been learned in the past when Roy had broken out of his stall and made his way, car to car, to Kipner's cabin, using his teeth to unlatch the doors as he went.

Against his better judgment, Kipner arranged transportation to Pheonix and then to the site via a handcar.

If he was lucky, he would catch a ride with a supply wagon.

With multiple stops along the way, he knew to expect more than three days to arrive at his destination.

Although his plans would be delayed, he accepted a few days wouldn't negatively impact the grand scheme. If the world was doomed by the end of the week, a few days wouldn't matter.

*

Beginning at a specific part of the afternoon, a corner of the train station grew darker than the others at any given point of the year. Hundreds passed by this particular corner, unaware of what could be lying in wait, studying passengers' faces in silence. Should anyone dare look in that direction, a sudden, unimaginable desire to look elsewhere would overcome them. Yet profound from within, a portentous presence manifested from obsessive desire and forsaken sacrifice. Drawn to the connective powers across the land, it shifted through the station's shadows. It formed in a dark corner of a sleeping cabin inhabited by the Wraith. Its existence on Earth began the chain reaction to oblivion now on borrowed time.

*

Kipner woke to a silent, motionless train. The silence was deafening, and he could hear his own blood pump in his ears, rising from his bed and putting on a shirt. Night had fallen and darkened his room to near pitch black that even his sharp eyesight struggled against.

Outside, the hallway was void of people, though expected at that hour, whatever hour it was. The rhythm of the train was gone. He clearly could tell it had stopped and was shut off. Something had gone wrong while he had slept.

Each car was empty as he slowly worked up to the engine. Everything was set up for morning passengers when they rose, but there were no signs of overnight activities. In between cars was frigid with a ghostly wind that froze Kipner and covered his skin with goosebumps. Any look to the area outside the train was empty, endless flat fields.

A thought came to mind while navigating the second car's tables. One of the pistols was in Kipner's hand as his suspicion escalated. The experience was familiar, and he wondered if it had been another past life event. One of the Old Ones had hunted him since leaving his hometown in London. Somewhere in Africa, it had caught up to him while latching itself to the caboose of Kipner's train.

He paused before he came to the door of the dining car. No, he thought, that wasn't correct. He had only imagined it to be some monstrous abomination, but he had murdered a crew member. Had he committed such a vile act in his past life? What kind of a man had he been? No, he gave second thought. It was someone else. Renaldo. Right?

Drawing up to the dining car door, he saw movement from within. He let his eyesight refocus through the dense night and made out the figure of a man sitting at a table with his feet resting on top. Garbed in black from head to toe, his hat resembled Kipner's, smothered in thick cigar smoke as the figure puffed quietly.

Beautiful white tablecloths had been laid over each table. They were garnished with a small assortment of flowers and white porcelain plates. Two delicate chandeliers hung down the center crest of the barrel ceiling, and candle sconces lined both walls in between the windows. Nothing was illuminated and put an unusual strain on Kipner's remarkable eyesight.

"End of the line, Wraith," came the dark figure. It looked up at him from under the brim of his hat with two pinprick glowing red dots.

A thick, dominating mustache covered much of his face that gave a stark resemblance to Kipner.

The marshal kept calm. "That would mean I'm in the presence of the owner of Baron Ties."

"What makes you so sure?" the voice asked. It spoke with such smoothness and a profound, rich boldness. There was no hint of urgency.

Kipner sighed with annoyance. Again with riddles and philosophical discussions, he thought. He wished for one Harrow encounter to be simple and straightforward. They discuss fishing, then move on to the gunfight.

"Quite frankly, I don't care at this point. I'm not interested in games or riddles. The sooner I can talk to whoever runs Baron Ties, the happier I will be. Let's cut to the chase and get this over with."

It humored the figure to hear Kipner's sarcasm, giving off a soft chuckle in the night. Its facial features were distinguishable, yet no smile crossed the face as it laughed. Only its beady red lights for eyes peered menacingly up at the marshal.

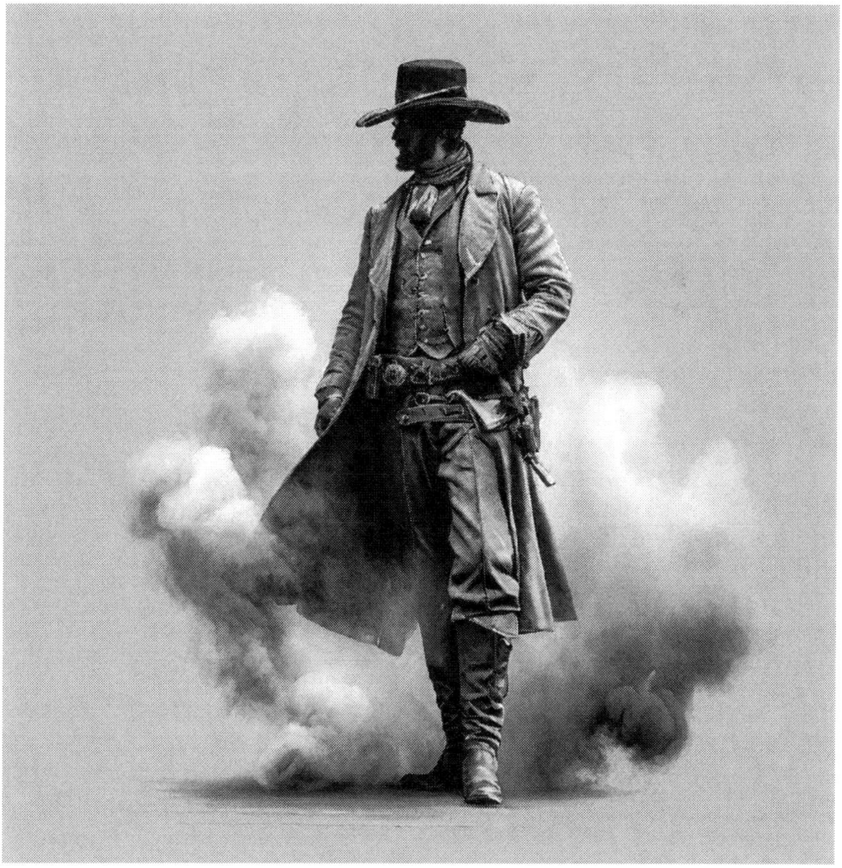

"As you wish, Marshal," the figure said, withdrew its feet from the table, and stood up to face him better.

"What is it then you want of me?"

At full height, the figure was a beast of a man and towered over Kipner. While taller than the marshal, it bore an eerie resemblance to him. It had a translucent appearance, primarily made of smoke, shifting slightly against a nonexistent breeze. Standing now, it was armed with the familiar long barrel Colts similar to the choice of Kipner's weapon.

"Whom am I speaking to?" Kipner asked.

The figure tilted its head to one side.

"Why that who runs the Baron Ties, as you so wished. I thought you wanted to avoid silly questions."

Kipner studied the figure closely.

There was concern that he was in the presence of something far superior in intellect, which always worried him.

While countless entities in the world were entirely immune to all physical attacks, nothing frightened Kipner more than the level of brilliant comprehension and planning many of them possessed. They could develop plans and ideas that could only be easily countered with excessive contemplation.

"What common name do you go by?" the marshal asked.

"What does it matter to you? We are just another phantom in your eyes. A nuisance, a threat to your humble world."

It was right to think that way. To Kipner, these were all the same to him. It mattered little what it was or its intentions. They all threatened their livelihood, and if it weren't for them, he would probably be married to Lucy and living a comfortable life.

"It would just make this easier," Kipner explained. "But I don't care either way. Your company has seen a lot of success. I'm here to inquire about the origin of your success."

The figure stood like a stone statue with wisps of ash and smoke drifting off its body in an endless air stream.

The direction subtly changed course and began making its way toward Kipner. The first traces of the odor it produced was of burning flesh that singed Kipner's nose.

"The origin? A company is prosperous, and you question the integrity?" the voice asked.

"When the success is abnormal, that is exactly what we do. We call that suspicious. Nothing will come about the company if there is nothing to hide. Now I ask to see your operation to make my own observation and report."

He could feel the first tendrils of smoke brush over his skin. Like thousands of tiny hair-like needles, it poked and stuck Kipner's skin and immediately caused irritation. He waved his arm away, but the punctured area remained attached, then expanded its contact area. Rage was quickly growing into pain.

"The operation accelerates," the voice spoke more coldly and pointed. "Completion will propel the country into a prosperous new era of fortune. It will provide aid for months if not years, before other companies fulfill their promises of a railroad. It would be best to leave us be as we are nearly finished."

Kipner gritted his teeth at the pain that now nearly engulfed him. No matter how hard he struggled, the wisps of smoke latched onto his flesh tightly. Although his knees buckled, the tendrils kept him upright like a puppet.

Mockingly they moved about, bringing his arms and legs along with them, creating an odd, mechanical motion. His body moved helplessly and swung about the room like a dancer to music.

It reminded him of Lucy's so-called husband when Hodgins was overcome by some powerful force. His body had flowed similarly and spoke with the same dark voice that addressed Kipner now.

"At what...price did we...pay though?" Kipner growled through the pain. He felt within him the familiar emergence of the true Wraith.

Whatever triggered it before seemed to be returning.

However, the festering remnants of his last encounter with an Old One in the library lingered down his chest and across his body, none of which had healed. Feeding off the injuries, the tendrils slid down the trenches of his wounds, plunging thousands of needles deep inside.

His yell boomed with death and tore throughout the cabin. It sent Kipner shrieking with excruciating pain. His clothes shredded along with his flesh while he hung in naked humiliation before the creature.

While screams of agony cried out from the marshal, the creature shouted equally as loud in triumphant rage.

"At what price? What price! At the cost of your benevolence! Your insignificant species' selfish, cruel, blindsided actions fueled it all! You brought this on yourselves, and I only usher the inevitability into a new era in honor of whom I serve. Connection across the country will see to it. Like a electric conductor, it will accelerate and expand our gods influence to great lengths."

To his relief, the Wraith took control of Kipner's body, but the pain did not vanish like before. He could feel the power within the fight to erupt and consume him, but the tendrils were found to be failing. They wrapped his body like a cocoon and enveloped him completely. The Colts in his holsters desperately fought to free themselves, but the Wraith had met a genuinely superior creature.

Kipner's body was torn apart. The moment he felt his body begin to separate, he screamed out for the one that had been with him for the entire journey - through this life and the one before. Just before his life ended, his final scream went against all that was holy in life. Throughout his years, while he held no devotion to religion, he sought a life of righteousness to protect those who suffered. He gave in ultimately, knowing it was probably in vain, but if it wasn't, then it would be a decision that would doom him for eternity.

The body of U. S. Marshal Robert Kipner was rendered into a fleshy mass and became lifeless.

The demon, Wraith, came alive. In the coming century, historical catastrophes in great wars and fearsome violence grew from its influence.

CHAPTER XII

Mexico, 1875

For the second time in the day, Lucy had been hunted by a jaguar. The first encounter should have resulted in her death. The well-concealed door leading into a subterranean teocalli had saved her life.

However, she didn't expect the Aztec temple to have an additional entrance, this one in the form of a collapsed ceiling. Her second encounter with the jaguar came immediately after the first when it quickly entered through it.

Luckily, the cat was confused, trying to pick up the unusual scent Lucy brought with her mixed in with the old musty temple full of floating mold spores, hampering its sense of smell. It deftly stepped over the broken stone pillars and leaped up to higher ledges to peer around the vast room, searching for its prey.

Desperately trying to control her panic, Lucy lay wedged in a burial loculus high overhead, which had already been occupied by the skeletal remains of an Aztec warrior. To find safety from the predator, she had climbed the ladder-like stack of burial niches until she felt she was safely out of reach of the jaguar. That feat was almost too much for her ability, and she slipped more than once during her ascent.

It took hours before the great cat gave up on its prey and made an exit, but at last, she could precariously make her way back down to the room's floor once again.

Now that she could focus more on the environment, she noticed telltale signs of other visitors. Along the walls were new torches that were all burning brightly.

She had been too scared at the time to notice the lights were what allowed her to scale the wall, but knowing now she was not alone made her skin crawl.

Years of research and questioning scholars had finally paid off for Lucy. She had been sure the location of Teonachata was here and that she could find its entrance if she had time to explore the area. She should have been the first to step inside in hundreds of years. Yet the true discovery had come moments before by an unknown person or persons.

Now she prayed her luck held up, and what she hunted for was hidden in the temple away from whoever was there.

She liberated one of the torches from its sconce and carried it over her head. There was no layout map, so she aimlessly made her way down one of the several corridors.

Past underground aqueducts, vividly designed pottery, and anthropomorphic statues of sneering beasts, Lucy made her way deeper underground. She wisely had packed chalk to help mark her chosen path, which came in handy as the underground temple held numerous dead ends.

She was not as young as she once was on her father's farm, climbing trees and swinging on ropes, but she found her way up the backside of a nearby statue and pressed herself to the wall for support. Her ears suddenly picked up voices, and she instinctively hunched down and stepped into the shadows. One person was speaking to another, and the sound was coming her way.

Around the corner ahead, the light from several torches grew as they approached. When they appeared, five in all, she didn't recognize any of the men.

One man was leading the way and dressed well for being in the sweltering jungle. He gave orders to follow the directions the great stone tablets had passed and to follow everything. From the sound of the conversation, they had come across exactly what she was seeking, so she peered closely.

Her arms were screaming from holding herself up so long, suspended several dozen feet in the air. When she shifted to relieve her arms, the movement dislodged a few tiny specks of the statue. The pebbles fell loudly to the floor below, and everyone suddenly halted into silence.

The group leader wandered over to the statue and slowly studied it upward to the top. He didn't notice anything unusual, so he departed with the group.

Lucy breathed a sigh of relief and thanked her blessings as she shimmied down from a great height for the second time that day. She was beginning to tire of the interruptions and athletic demands just to see ancient directions that would change the world if the legends were true.

A stone slab covered in Nahuatl script rested within a small chamber devoid of decorations. On all four sides, from top to bottom, ideographic letters combined with phonetic logograms and syllabic signs made up precise directions to a hidden structure. What precisely the form was, however, could be anyone's guess. It was believed by Lucy and, apparently, now others, to have been used by the Aztecs for amplification.

She stepped out of the temple by the same path as the jaguar, just as the men took to their horses and disappeared westward. Here the jungles of Mexico were light enough to transcend the confines on horseback. Still, Lucy decided against it to be less conspicuous knowing stealth would be her strength if she came across anyone.

The presence of the men disturbed Lucy.

She was in a wildly remote region of Mexico at the location of a submerged temple that had never been discovered. Not only had they found it before her, but it was also only by a handful of minutes. The coincidence didn't have much validity. What were the odds of an expedition coming across the same day and time as her?

While contemplating the chances, she reviewed the etching she had sketched onto paper. For straightforward directions, they were dramatically complicated and overwritten. They reminded her of old written documents by pirates, lengthy and wordy to conceal any secrets.

Following the direction the men ventured, she, too, went west, trudging across ant-covered soil and pushing aside leaves that could be hiding a viper ready to strike her hand. It had been her first time in an environment as harsh as this, and she had been lucky up to this point she wasn't dead.

The movement was slow following the directions, and she wondered how the men were moving so much quicker. Each line read like a riddle that needed solving before the order was revealed. While fluent in Nahuatl, she wasn't firm in solving puzzles. That was Bobby's strong side.

Suddenly he came to mind out of the blue. It had been years since she had last heard from him. He once wrote all the time until she moved to Chicago. She would have loved to write back if she ever could learn where he was located at any given time of the year. Yet nothing ever changed with him. At first, the Post Office had tried to forward his letters, but they soon gave up and let them disappear. His job took him all over the country, but hers did too.

The difference was hers was less often and better controlled.

It took her a few hours to catch up to the five men, which had been reduced to three. The lead man and one other had split off from the group at some point, leaving the rest to seek the structure. The benefit of horseback had been reduced from speed to only comfort as the jungle's density grew the further they went. The remainder of their journey would be as slow as walking or perhaps less.

By morning, she got the upper hand and departed before the men to maintain an advantage for half the next day.

The forest was so dense in this region that little light reached the jungle floor, yet thick plants and long vines blocked her way. She began to regain hope of escaping the god-forsaken area when morning light penetrated from above once again, and her steps became easier.

She wasn't sure how much of a lead she had on the men, so she had to act quickly. She picked up her pace and pushed herself onward though she desperately wanted to stop and drink from her canteen.

Her gamble paid off as she finally broke free from the treeline and gasped at the vision she witnessed. In all her research and studies, nothing prepared her for the type of structure that spread out before her in a vast clearing.

Digging down immensely and stretching out a quarter of a mile was a large bowl. From what she could see from her vantage point, it was entirely made of orange-colored adobe. It was built in rings, each with odd markings and pictograph images. Each circular piece was so perfectly laid inside one another that only hairline cracks separated each one, giving the appearance of a solid surface. They reduced in diameter as they lined their way down to the center of the bowl some hundred feet below.

Nothing compared to the monstrous size and feat it took to build it except for the pyramids of Egypt. At least in Egypt, the land was flat, allowing large blocks to be transferred at great distances. Here, tons and tons of clay were brought through dense jungle, and massive amounts of soil had to be removed. As advanced as the Aztecs were, Lucy needed help comprehending the method that could have been used to complete the operation.

The bowl was so vast that it angled gently down to its center, allowing Lucy to descend. It was tough to make out from that distance, but something was at the nadir. She paused momentarily to hear if the men following were within earshot, knowing she would be vulnerable by stepping out into the bowl. Hearing nothing but the sounds of the forest, she quickly descended.

As she went, she glanced at the rings and their markings, which initially appeared repetitive. Further along, however, the markings, though highly similar, were unique. Directly in front of each marking was a perfectly hemispherical divot about two inches in diameter.

Judging from the size of the entire bowl, tens of thousands of individual symbols and shapes made up the language system. None of the markings made any sense to her. She guessed they had to be some form of a phonogram, but she needed clarification on whether they were whole words or a part of a complex alphabet.

If she were to find and select any specific marking, at the very least, it would take her days to find it among the chaos.

Midway down, the slope dramatically dropped to a steeper grade, and she slid several feet dangerously before regaining her footing. There had been no warning either. The bowl was so cleverly crafted it hid the change from the naked eye. Even now, Lucy searched vainly to find the exact spot it altered.

Each footstep now was more precarious than before. She walked with her feet pointed to one side and took small steps as she approached the center. Another change in the slope was fifty feet from the center. It dropped so steeply this time that Lucy knew she would have difficulty getting out. There were no footholds except for the markings, which were too narrowly cut for fingers.

Now that she was closer to the nadir of the bowl, she saw a short pedestal that rose six inches off the ground.

In the noonday sun, something brightly reflected the rays from atop it. It was so brilliantly bouncing light she had to shield her eyes.

High above at the rim came shouting from the men. They each had a rifle and started taking shots at Lucy with incredible accuracy.

Bullets ricocheted off the clay floor around her, forcing her to leap down the steep slope to the bottom.

The pedestal was not large enough to provide shelter, but she crouched behind it. Their aim was not as precise at this distance, and the bullets bounced wildly around her.

A gem was the source of the intense reflection on the pedestal, and it rested in a marble cup that had been sunk into the platform. Several rods extruded from holes on the side that allowed for the cup to be angled.

When she had been up at the edge of the bowl, Lucy never saw the reflection despite its brightness, which had been puzzling to her at the time. Reflecting light could be seen from dozens of miles away if without obstructions. Mirrors were a common item to signal ships at sea. Yet the gem's shining light never left the diameter of the bowl.

She could not experiment with the strange device while being shot at, but suddenly the firing ceased.

It was unsure if they were out of ammunition or another means.

Timidly she gazed up at the rim, squinting her eyes at the sky's brightness. No one was there anymore. No one was to be seen around the edge in every direction.

It appeared safe for the moment, so she turned her attention back to the pedestal. The marble cup holding the gem could be rotated up to nearly ninety degrees in any direction. It could shine a highly intense beam of sunlight to any point in the bowl.

"Some kind of code?" Lucy muttered to herself as she spun the cup around and pointed the light beam at various rings. She wouldn't get very far without some kind of cipher to translate the meaning of each marking.

She leaned against the pedestal, took a few swigs from her canteen, and wondered about her next move.

Her excitement of the discovery felt short-lived. Rather than being the first to find the bowl, she felt more like a track runner, having narrowly crossed the finish line before the rest. The only achievement left was to find a way to crack the code, but this was entirely new, uncharted territory for her. She only had searched for the strange apparatus. It never occurred to her that it would be covered in strange symbols that had no meaning.

Thinking the instructions leading her there would shed some light, she spent a few hours reading and re-reading the etching, but nothing seemed to make any sense to her. It gave no hint as to what the device was intended for other than a means to intensify certain practices. She only assumed they pertained to Topan, the thirteen levels of what the Nahua people thought of as heaven.

High above in the blue sky, the sun bore down on her. She had been soaked with sweat since she arrived in Mexico and couldn't solve her constant thirst no matter how much she drank. Each minute had been miserable, but her drive had kept her moving forward.

Now that she was stumped, the sun's burning heat wore her quickly down.

She sighed in frustration and went to the steep slope hoping her nimble fingers could fit in the narrow grooves.

They did, but they were highly discomforting. The harsh surface tore against her skin, drawing them raw. Her progress was halfway up before the pain went too far, and she slid back down. Again she tried after cooling her fingers down with a few drops of water, but she couldn't manage to get to the middle slope.

Her eagerness for her work had always been a dramatic flaw. When she was a little girl, working at her father's farm, she would devise clever ways to cut corners and get her chores done to give her more free time to climb trees and dig up rocks looking for fossils. Most schemes she concocted were short-sighted and left unfinished work or poor quality. Later when she was much older, her eagerness pushed her to act first and think second. She did her research well, but she only thought of the discovery and not the consequences or obstacles that might come up. It often led to predicaments like she was in now.

She was used to it, however. It took more than being trapped to make her panic, and she gauged her surroundings while giving them more thought.

She lacked any climbing equipment, but she had brought a few archaeological tools, which would appear to be standard gardening tools, to the untrained. Among them was a hand cultivator that resembled three claws and was used to gently loosen hard soil.

Using it as an extension of her arm, she jammed it into the markings, letting the metal prongs take the brunt of the surface, and pulled herself up. With this method, she was able to quickly scale the steep slope. She smiled proudly to herself for clever thinking and returned to the bowl's rim.

Although the sun was still drifting across the sky, she knew nightfall would come sooner than expected with the dense vegetation and decided to set up camp. A large tree to the north of the bowl, a few hundred feet, was hollowed out at the base and provided shelter. With some gathered elephant ear plants, she soon secured the opening to dissuade all but the most curious forest animals from entering.

That night's dinner for Lucy was dried beef. The trip had been planned to be short; she hadn't prepared to spend more than a few days before needing to return to America. There had been rumblings of thunder hinting at the chance of rain, so she had left her canteen outside, hoping to replenish what was becoming a dangerously low amount.

Funding for the trip had fallen through with the Science Academy, and she had been forced to pay her own expenses.

Most of the academics thought she was a fraud in her studies. They were all delusional towards the Harrow, each with their scientific explanation of why Sightings were tricks on "simple minds." When she began to find evidence to date the Harrow as far back as the Aztecs, they bluntly kicked her out. She had to find work at the city library to save for the trip, but bad luck continued to favor her when her employer denied her a leave of absence.

During her studies late one evening at the library, a tall gentleman bearing a U.S. Marshal's badge rapped at the front door.

He introduced himself as Ward Hodgins from D.C. and said that he had been tasked by those in Washington to shed more light on the Harrow. His investigation had led him to her as a leading expert on the subject, and he hoped she could help.

Over the next few weeks, Hodgins stayed in Chicago to work with her, showing deep interest in her wealth of knowledge. Still, Lucy could sense he had other motives that he wouldn't reveal to her.

She couldn't tell if they were business or pleasure.

Once all of the information could be transferred to Hodgins, he suggested she investigate her theories firsthand. To counter her financial problem, he offered her a special deal that she found unreasonable and unthinkable initially. It directly related to the very entities that dwelt just out of sight across the globe and haunted people's dreams. She believed in the Harrow but wasn't aware of the potential offerings to those willing to listen to the Old Ones' whispers.

It was suggested that if she appeared to continue working at the library, she would be free to go wherever she desired. Two Lucy's in the world. Her income would remain while she pursued a life in the field. When asked what the catch was, Hodgins coolly explained there was none and that the gesture was merely a token of appreciation from a misunderstood foreign species.

Over time her willpower was whittled down to the point only her eagerness for adventure remained. The pact was made, and part of her left for Mexico while the other remained.

But there really had been a catch. The original's mind was divided into two equal halves to make two Lucy's. Now each Lucy's thoughts weren't quite as sharp as they once were, their memories failed to recall from time to time, and their emotions got the best of them frequently.

She was only half there and was no longer smart enough to realize the difference.

As the sky darkened over the Lacandon Jungle, Lucy could only come up with the idea to return to Teonachata and scour from top to bottom for any missed clues to unlock the bowl's mystery.

She wasn't too excited about the plan because it was extremely time-consuming. Her supplies would run out, and she would have to return to the coast.

It had taken her months to save for this trip and would require as much to return. By then, those who had come before her would undoubtedly solve the puzzle.

Trying to go to sleep that night was challenging with her frustration. She knew something was off with her but didn't know what. Her cognitive skills worsened each year more acceleratedly than natural aging. Her regret of listening to Hodgins hung heavy with her every day.

If only life had gone the way she had dreamed of, but that would have taken a different decision from a man in love with something greater than her. Even so, she closed her eyes and hoped to dream of what could have been.

In the next life, things would be better for her.

*

Someone grabbed her ankles and violently pulled her out of the hollow tree. She sprung awake, but her vision was blurry, and she could only make out outlines of figures gathered around her. One had her pinned down to the jungle floor while the others gawked.

There was no need to struggle. The man over her was vastly stronger. She lay there helpless and breathing heavily, feeling panic explode through her veins. Overhead another man approached her with a long burlap sack which he began shoving her inside.

Others gave him a hand; she counted four, including the one holding her down. Just before her head was shoved into the sack, her vision cleared enough to recognize the men from the temple.

Someone hoisted her on his shoulders and carried her upside down through the thick forest. No one among them spoke a word. Each of their steps crunching against the forest floor was the only sound they made.

Soon she was dropped heavily to the ground, her head smacking against the soil and ringing her ear. She could just make out movement through the burlap netting of them seated around.

Were they native savages, she wondered, kidnapping her to eat her? No, she reminded herself they were not local and were here for the same reason she was.

She worked to control her overactive imagination.

At the spark of her thought, she heard the voice of the well-dressed leader. They informed him she had been found in the beacon, as they called it, and asked what to do with her. He paused, then ordered them to seal her in the calpulli and return to searching for Florentine.

With equal care as before, she was lifted off the ground and carried roughly into a stone-carved room, trapped inside by a heavy block covering the door. She wiggled herself out of the bag when their footsteps faded to total darkness.

Feeling about the room, it was small and empty. She had nothing but the solid, wet floor to sleep. She momentarily propped herself against a wall and thought about what she had just heard.

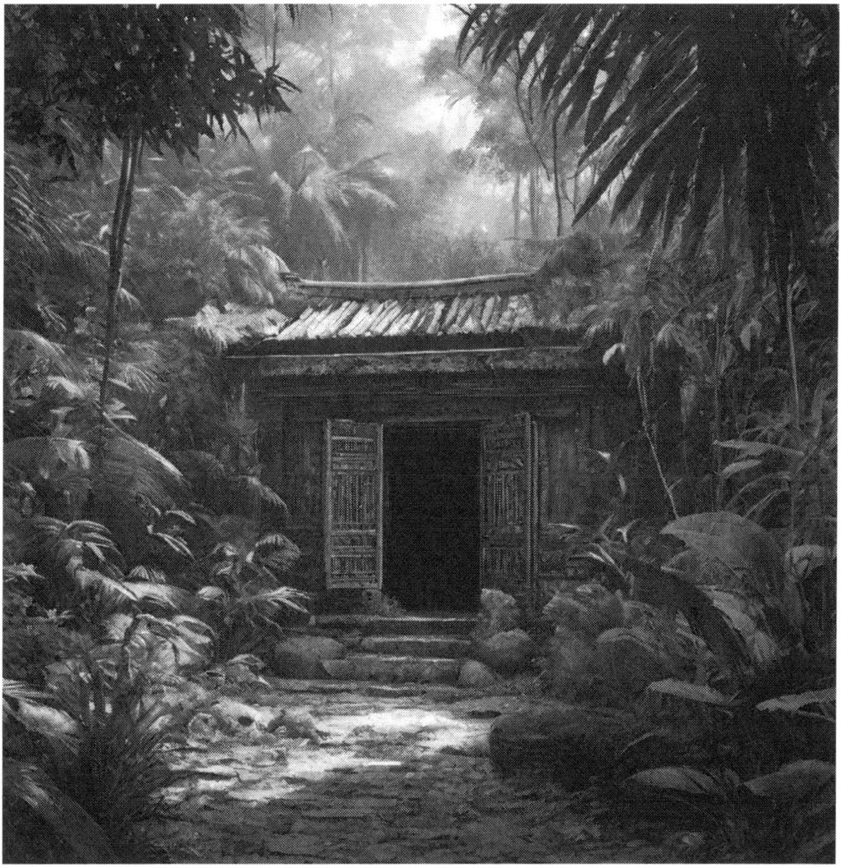

Florentine. Something about the name rang a bell, but she had to strain to focus. Finally, her mind snapped into gear, and she was enlightened by the word.

He might have been referencing the Florentine Codex, a series of books by the Spanish friar Bernardino de Sahagun. They had been an essential recording of the Nahua peoples that chronicled the culture and history of the Aztecs. Sahagun had crossed translations between Nahuatl and Spanish that helped bridge the modern world to their past. As to the importance to her captors, it was anyone's guess. From her recollection of the books, twelve total in the set, none depicted anything remotely close to the symbols found in the beacon.

Calling it a beacon was peculiar to her, too. She knew it was meant to amplify, but it hadn't crossed her mind that it might be a means of sending messages. Its sheer size could reach the other side of the world...

Her restricted half-mind pushed itself to its limits as a thought slowly grew. Or elsewhere. If the Aztecs had known the Harrow's existence, and the modern natives practiced traditions to keep them at rest, then that would mean they had practiced similar traditions back then, too. She had heard firsthand accounts that some native ancestors came from the jungles of Mexico. Indeed those beliefs would have been passed down from generation to generation.

Now that Lucy understood what was at stake, finding a proper cipher was critical. She didn't think she could trust the men who had kidnapped and imprisoned her, which sounded odd for some reason, so she could only assume they wanted it for ill motives. Kipner had warned her of those striking deals with the Old Ones in exchange for powers, but she had succumbed to the temptation from the same type of people he warned her about.

She now had the missing piece she had been looking for all these years - a potential means to set the Harrow back to its catatonic state and rid the world of its fear. What good was it to her, though, while she was imprisoned?

Hours drifted by as she sat in pitch-black darkness without anyone bringing her food or water. She had been forced to designate a corner as the bathroom, but her thirst was becoming devastating. With the great slab leaning against the opening, she heard no sounds from the forest outside. She feared her air supply might also be limited and attempted to slow her breathing and control her panic attacks. She could only wait and hope, but if they had abandoned her, she was as good as dead.

CHAPTER XIII

Mexico, 1876

He dreaded the knock at his door though he knew it was coming. Beyond anything, he had wished things would have turned out differently for the man. He had liked him from the first moment they had met. Through his brash, emotionally suppressed attitude, he slowly found his true self. And that made his friend proud to see. For years he had watched his friend grow past the hindrances and burdens of habit he had acquired from the fear and stress of his occupation. Sometimes the booze still overcame him, but the daily battles with the drink were long gone.

It was always wonderful to see Kipner, but this visit would be his last. The doctor's face was melancholy, but he found the means to bring a warm smile to it. The sarcastic bravado he brought into Amos' office always made him chuckle. After seeing so many sad patients that were past hope, it lifted his spirits to know the man.

"Hi, Bobby," Amos said with a bit too much sadness than he had intended. "Come on in." Kipner nodded and stepped through the wooden doorway with a frosted glass window.

Amos led him through the small, quaint office painted green with white tile flooring. A dentist's chair with green embroidery gave way to an examining bed in the center of the room just below a bright hanging light fixture. The doctor helped the man lie down on it and relax.

"I would say you look like hell, Robert, but I think you've outdone yourself. This is too much. What were you thinking?" the doctor said while following the typical checkup routine. In Kipner's current condition, it was pointless to check his vitals. He was, without a doubt, dead. Still, Amos liked using his instruments whenever he felt like a doctor.

The marshal closed his eyes mostly to shield them from the intense light bearing down on him. While he didn't feel bad, he didn't feel anything. He was numb all over. He knew though he had met his match, his confidence caused him to approach his adversary without the respect the Baron deserved.

"I thought he would be friendlier," Kipner said, wincing out of instinct and not from pain. "Usually, someone of that power likes to talk more than get right to murdering. I was wrong."

Amos shook his head in disappointment. "You were warned going in that something odd didn't add up with the Baron's success. I know you weren't giving him much thought since your mind focused on someone else. Am I wrong?"

"Well..."

"Am I wrong?"

"Well, no. You're not wrong."

"She misses you, Bobby. You know that, don't you?"

"I wouldn't know. Lucy never wrote back after all those years. Thought she had moved on when I saw her twin with that two-bit marshal."

For the first time during the visit, Amos genuinely smiled with happiness. He lifted Kipner's right leg, bracing it on the doctor's shoulder, and stretched his hamstring. Amos loved making Kipner stretch as if it made any difference during his visits. He switched over to Kipner's left and repeated. It was fun to him when he replicated general medical practice. Still, with his powers, a mere snap of his fingers and Kipner would return to his feet.

In fact, Amos didn't even need to snap.

"Nonsense," he said while he checked a dead man's pulse, which read zero, to which Amos nodded expectantly.

"You were always off gallivanting around the country in search of something she could have helped you find.

It was you who couldn't be reached.

You never would sit still for one minute and just...breathe."

While Kipner lay there reflecting on what he said, Amos added softly, "Same for her other life, but you just treated her as a secretary."

That confused Kipner at first, but soon dawned on him what Amos was implying. Natasha had a striking resemblance according to his memory of her.

Having a second identity and only recalling it through faded memories was still strange.

"This time will be the last, Doc," Kipner said as he was gently lifted off the bed and into a chair. "I know approximately where she is, and I've been told I have what she needs. We can finish this thing together as it was meant to be."

Resting his hand on Kipner's shoulder, he looked down at him through fatherly eyes. The marshal didn't know how long Amos had kept him safe through the years.

Even before Kipner stepped foot in his office, he had never been too far away, watching his back and offering his aid when he faced any dilemma. Even if doppelgangers of would-be friends attempted to backstab Kipner outside the dark, hidden temples, he remained a protector of Robert, rifle in hand and ready to keep him safe.

That's what guardian angels did.

"Yes, it will be the last for you, my good friend," Amos said, holding back his eyes from watering at the thought of never seeing Kipner again. "I'm no expert, but that is how it works. You will be alone on your final leg of the journey to the end."

Somehow Kipner understood what the doctor meant. He had always been grateful for Amos' help. Too many times was he found buried in the mud on the street riddled with alcohol. Too many times was he dragged in after a fight against something he had no business facing. For the years he lived in this life or that, he had to cope with the hopeless fear of inevitable forces that posed no solution to stop. The realization plagued him too much, and nothing in the world could alleviate the pain without creating new complications.

The visits would be over after he left Amos' office. There would be no do-overs this time. He had leaned upon the brilliant powers of his excellent friend long enough. If he couldn't face the final step with the assurance of recovery, it would force him to approach it cautiously and logically. Perhaps he would survive this time.

"It's been a wonderful ride, Bobby. Whatever happens here on out, you've been a good friend, and I wish you the best of luck," Amos said, having finished his mock exam to a now fully recovered, living Robert Kipner. The wounds were now scars, but he could function as he always had before - with vigor.

They embraced one last time, and Amos felt his eyes well up. He could watch from a distance, but his interference was now forbidden. The Old Ones might cheat whenever they can, manipulating and twisting fate to their chaotic whim. Still, others of Higher Power existed with rules and order. It had been so since the dawn of man, so heavenly bodies could help nudge humans here and there without handholding. However, with the presence of the Old Ones, sometimes the nudges were closer to shoves.

Kipner stepped out of the doctor's office, and Amos closed the door gently behind him, leaving the marshal in the dense forests of Mexico.

In his satchel, he had a compass, map, and past possessions, including the collection of books.

"Sometimes the shoves are stronger than others," Amos said to himself with a smile as he waited for his next patient to arrive.

*

A compass and map would only help Kipner when he got his bearings, though. He was grateful for Amos's gifts and remained spellbound by what he had learned. It had always felt like an extraordinary coincidence to Kipner running into the roaming Dr. Amos Sales practically wherever he needed him most. Still, it had never occurred to him Amos was more than just his savior when injured. His healing ability was magic to Kipner, and now he understood why.

Kipner tried scaling one of the large hills that overlooked a relatively broad valley to figure out where he had been dropped off. The forest was dense with vegetation, bringing up the notion of how crowded life was than he had thought when he was just a child. Back then, his father would try teaching him the ways of faith, but the concept of a Higher Power was too much for the young mind to believe. Kipner knew it disappointed his father, who was a man of the cloth, so he had been convincing enough whenever Sunday school would come around to put a satisfied smile on his face.

Now that he had been exposed so deeply to three separate forms of Higher Power, each with their own motives and rules, he couldn't help but wonder if the world could handle such a monumental fact. The world discovered what he knew was a scary thought. His mind was strong, yet he succumbed to drugs to take the pressure off reality.

After an hour of gaining elevation and being able to compare the area to his map, he pinpointed his location. Lucy had left plenty of bread crumbs for him to pick up and follow, making it easy to track down the same entrance to Teonachata. However, something much more apparent from his vantage point caught his eye.

Over several rolling hills thick with vegetation, past a snake-winding river, rose a ziggurat. Plumes of smoke drifted up into the air around its pyramidal shape. It was several miles through the jungles of Mexico, which struck a chord somewhere in him at the idea of a grand adventure.

The familiar memory of pushing through the thick bush of Africa came to mind as he descended into a valley. Much like now, he had embarked into the unknown without a guide or companions, which thrilled him.

As he went, his thoughts kept him company. He once had traveled like this in his past life. He recalled that it was to seek secret fortunes hidden around the world, much like Lucy endeavored to do. He chuckled at how so many of these strange past memories of another life he barely remembered paralleled with his.

At one point, he shared the same passion with Lucy though he knew not where it came from. He wasn't sure whether it was influenced by his care and love for her or a more profound desire sparked from a past memory. However, he had found it oddly coincidental how the notion became so intense whenever he had learned of her background.

The marshal marched on like his days as a soldier during the War, stopping infrequently and eating even less. Although years were ahead of him, the dark years behind tried to slow him down. The excessive drinking and the constant lighting of a cigar to ease his nerves haunted his health. Some days it took the mental strength of a past soldier to ignore it. On other days it was much more difficult.

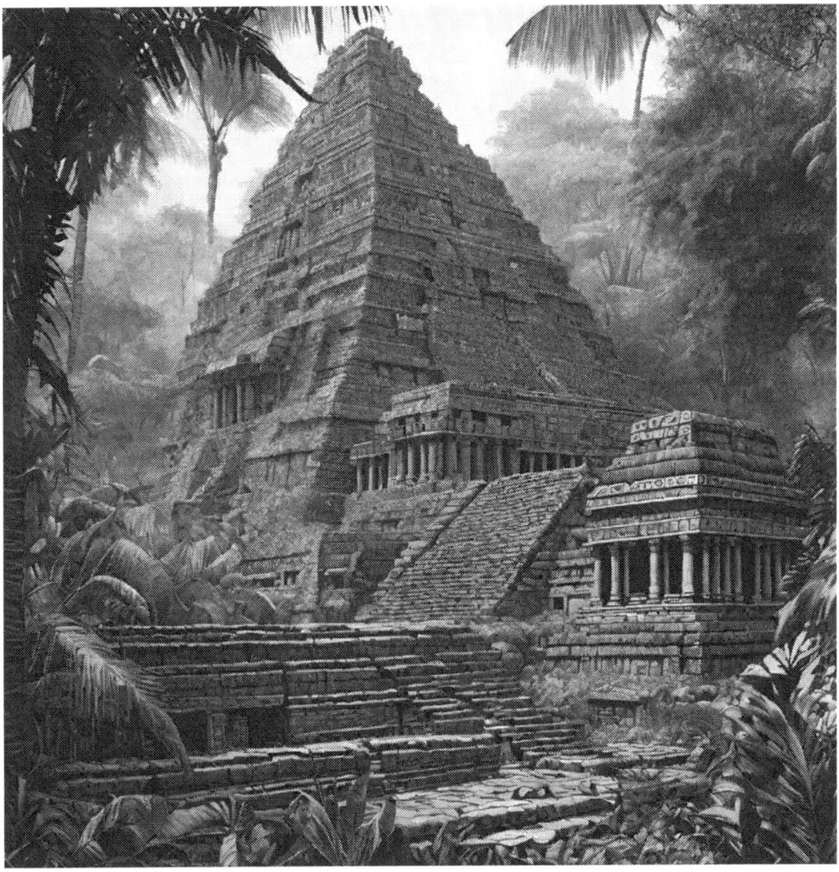

He suspected Lucy had already discovered the underground temple she had clearly illustrated in her journal. Still, she said nothing about a ziggurat being within sight of it. The fact that smoke rose from it cautioned him that something was wrong. These were ancient, forgotten areas of an extinct civilization. While there might be a few scattered natives roaming the region, he doubted they would utilize these forgotten relic structures. He guessed an uninvited guest had recently moved in.

He paused when he reached the winding river close to his target destination before wading through. The water was opaque with mud and sediment, which gave no warning of anything lurking below the surface. He always feared deep water growing up, though he never knew why.

No lakes were near his hometown, and his parents never took him to the ocean. Yet a distant, vague memory lingering in the back of his mind made him mindful of colossal beasts with great tusks lurking just below the surface.

Upriver within eyesight was a narrowing that he felt could be traversed. Several juvenile Ceiba trees leaned heavily over the water from both sides, crisscrossing closely to form bridges. The arch they made was low enough that he would be in no danger of falling into the water should he lose his grip.

The first portion of the crossing was simple as he shimmied his way up the trunk of a particularly stout Ceiba. As he rose, however, he switched to dangling beneath, sending hand over hand, to reach the midpoint.

Something splashed in the water, only two or three feet below his shoes. The first time it occurred was simple and small. He dismissed it as a fish snatching at the millions of insects that annoyed everything in the area. When the third splash sounded more like a giant stone being cast into the water, he took a moment to glance down and hold his position for a moment.

The delay cost him. A great caiman, as large as saltwater crocodiles often reached, was launching itself out of the water into the air to grab Kipner's feet, then plummeting back into the murky waters. Its mouth snapped wildly with each leap and only missed him by a few inches.

Instinctively Kipner lifted his legs up to separate the caiman from him more, but he knew he wouldn't be able to climb across that way.

The beast's size was abnormal. As Kipner got closer, he realized it was another creature affected by the dangers of the Old Ones, much like the wild cat he battled in the Dakotas. Its back was blanketed with thin, needle-sharp spines that gave it the appearance of fur. They waved like wind over prairie grass. When its mouth gaped open, Kipner could easily make out two parasite-like insects attached to its throat that wiggled desperately up with squeezing pincers.

Holding himself now with one hand, Kipner tried pulling out one of his pistols and taking a shot down the beast's throat. He wondered for a split second where his phantom pistols were, but then he realized the demon was free after the fight on the train, now roaming the world all because of Kipner.

His stomach screamed at him for raising his legs for so long, although they had been for a few seconds, and his hand shook as he took aim and fired down upon the beast's gullet. It was enough to send the creature back underwater, giving Kipner enough time to continue his trip across the river. However, more splashing came down below as other caimans, the size of wagons, tried to snap at Kipner's feet.

Progress was agonizingly slow. Every few feet, he gritted his teeth while pushing his muscles to lift his legs and took a shot upside down, but the five bullets were quickly gone, and there was still more river to cross.

He had made it as far as the other tree at least, and his legs, though painful, could wrap around and aid him while keeping just above the peak of the caimans' jump.

To his bad luck, however, the tree needed to be rooted better and was in loose soil beside the water's edge. His massive weight pulled the trunk down, and he quickly drooped to where his back shaved the water's surface.

Panic struck the marshal, and he desperately surged ahead, causing the water below to splash wildly. Suddenly he felt the support on his back while a caiman lifted him high above and then dropped with him in its jaws below the surface.

Immediately he was disoriented and nauseous from being twisted abruptly around and clouding his vision. The powerful jaws held him tightly, making several puncture marks from the tiny teeth.

The wind was taken out of his lungs from the blow to the back, and he felt the stinging pain from a lack of air. The water swirled around him like a vortex mixed with thousands of bubbles as the caiman slashed about.

Another had grabbed his legs, which ironically saved his life.

The first caiman, sensing its prey being stolen, let go of its grip to lash out at the second. The two engaged in a brief ferocious battle, two titans of armor and needles slamming against one another that surged the river's water over its banks.

Kipner pulled himself towards the brighter-colored water and burst out into the air, gasping. He quickly spun around to see he was only a few leaps to the edge and kicked with all his might.

More caiman was beside him, giving way to the fighting beasts and trying to sneak off with the meal. Kipner's hands were free, and he savagely beat the incoming snouts with his bare hand. Their hard-plated skin ripped into his flesh, bringing the scent of blood to their nostrils. The smell drove them wild, and they each plunged viciously at Kipner.

A mere foot away from the edge of the river, as he reached out with all his might to grab anything, to pull him free from death, he felt the returning grips of terror on his ankle that crunched at his bone. He screamed in agony as loud as he could, which surged his body with desperate strength. With the fury of a caged animal, he kicked brutally at the caiman, which began rolling him dizzyingly. Still, he kicked over and over, then sent the heel of his boot down upon the nostrils, his sharp spurs cutting through the thick skin and into its flesh.

It released him for a moment; that was all he needed to scramble out of the water.

Though the silent caiman quickly swam after, Kipner hobbled quicker on land and made his escape.

He bled from several wounds across his torso and ankle, forcing him to stop and attend to them. No medical kit was in his possession, but his years accompanying his old friend, Flying Hawk, had taught him what to look for in the wild. The difference was he was nowhere near the region Flying Hawk had been familiar with, and none of the plants he knew were present.

His backpack contained a few books from Lucy's personal collection. He rummaged through to find the one he had spotted holding Aztec traditions and culture. It was a type of codex, from what Kipner could deduce, written by a Spanish friar that detailed some Aztec medicinal interests. It wasn't much to go by, the illustrations were vague but in color, but he soon found some plants that matched those in the book and did his best to dress his wounds. They would have to do as his knowledge was limited of the area until he could find Lucy.

Knowing he shouldn't push himself more than the rest of the day, he groaned as he made a makeshift camp for the night. He knew he would be sore tomorrow and needed as much strength as possible for whatever lay in store.

A few growls from jungle animals came throughout the night, but they all kept their distance from him. It didn't provide him with any better sleep - his wounds and biting insects did their jobs to keep him restless.

Before the sun illuminated the jungle, he gave up trying to pretend to sleep. He headed the duration of his hike to the ziggurat. It had been considerably closer than he realized the night before, needing only half an hour to reach his campsite.

Whoever was staying there could easily have found him had there been patrols.

Kipner wasn't sure if he was relieved or more worried when he finally caught sight of a small troop of armed guards milling about the pyramid.

Each had rifles hung on their backs and wore solid green uniforms. Adding to their presence were numerous wooden crates, some open, containing a variety of supplies. More rifles were the dominating item.

The guns were peculiar to the marshal. A narrow metal box that stuck out several inches was mounted near the triggers on the underside. He couldn't spot any bolt handle on them to open the chamber above for a cartridge. It was as if the ammunition was stored within the boxes.

A memory from before brought to the attention of a more modern weapon.

At one point, he was somehow a prisoner with guards wielding similar rifles. He remembered while digging away at rocks on a blistering hot day, they could fire their weapons repeatedly without reloading.

He had not heard of any invention with such a rifle, yet these men acted as though they were familiar. That memory didn't add up to what he saw, however. How were these weapons available now if his memories were from a more modern era?

All of them were positioned around the front of the ziggurat.

None of them were alert or patrolling.

They didn't seem to be concerned about any outside interference. Any natives in the area would be severely inferior and pose no threat to them. It also showed Kipner that no one knew he existed.

He planned on keeping it that way for now.

Towards the back of the ziggurat, Kipner crept quietly through the cover of the jungle. A small entrance burrowed downward at the base of the pyramid that he decided to take. No torches were lit along the way, which Kipner took as a good sign while his eyes came alive to the darkness.

Downward he slowly made his way, trying to dampen the echoing of his footsteps on the hard clay steps. They took him twenty feet below ground and ended at a solid wall.

It had no latch or obvious mechanism to open it, but with a steady, forceful shove, the door begrudgingly rotated open to an empty chamber with a dais in the center. Resting without support on the dais was a door frame with no door. It quietly rested on the raised platform without an apparent reason. He could walk through it without it revealing any truth behind it.

Two doors besides the one he used led him to other areas. Through the silent halls underground, he saw evidence everywhere of modern inhabitation.

Whatever group stationed outside had called the place home for quite a while, by the looks of things.

Room after room, someone had converted it into a domicile of sorts or eating area.

Strangely no one was down there, and he heard nothing but the occasional condensation drip into small pools of water. It was fortunate for him to have picked such a good time, but he knew someone would need to wander back down there at some point, so he picked up his pace.

Wandering the halls eventually brought him to a door that was locked. It was unlike any previous dozen doors he passed through with a modern lock. It was obvious to Kipner it had been installed deliberately for better security. Still, his curiosity was getting the best of him what could be so critical.

Despite the door's modern style, it was no challenge for the marshal. His lockpicks swept into the gap and brought a satisfying click seconds after.

He opened this door with more caution though it was locked.

There was no light inside, but his devilish eyes picked up a series of metal bars that made up a row of prison cages.

Each was lined with dead leaves and contained a large pale. The smell of rot, foul bodily waste, and mold overwhelmed his sense, and he grabbed his nose and mouth to prevent coughing.

Into the room, he softly stepped, immediately spotting motionless bodies in the first two cages. No one was guarding them, but judging from the smell, they weren't escaping anytime soon.

The cage in the back had another naked body lying against the wall. Its hair had grown exceptionally long, nearly the length of its body, and was ratted with crusty dirt. The excessive hair appeared like fur and concealed much of its frail body. Kipner just made out the gentle rise and fall of breathing.

"Hey," Kipner whispered in the darkness. "Hey, who are you? Why do they have you down here?"

The body stirred with a shake, bordering epilepsy, then turned over weakly. Kipner couldn't determine whether it was a man or a woman; they were skinny. In the dark, they peered up at him trying to see him more clearly.

When they spoke, Kipner's knees nearly gave out from under him.

The voice, though soft and pallid, was indistinguishable from the marshal. Excitedly, he grabbed the bars tightly with both hands and pressed his face against the cage.

"Lucy!" he shouted a bit louder, realizing too late he shouldn't have, but he was too happy to see her, though appalled at the shape she was in.

Suddenly her vivid blue eyes widened, and a weak smile appeared. Her energy was so low she talked as though half-conscious in a dream.

"Bobby?" she asked, trying to lift herself up. Her arms shook from the lack of muscle, and she slumped back to the plant-covered floor. She whimpered at the pain when she landed.

The iron cage posed no threat to an eager marshal, and he was quickly at her side. Gingerly he cradled her nearly lifeless body in his arms and brushed the caked hair from her face. Past the matted hair and dirt-stricken, frail body shined the two most brilliant blue eyes Kipner had ever seen. Whatever pain they had caused her for however long she had been down there, nothing could take away the beautiful hue. He could do nothing for the moment but quietly weep at them.

She whispered his name again, and Kipner went to work. He removed his shirt to gently slide over Lucy's torso, which was just long enough to cover her decently. She didn't speak again and silently sat beside him while he prepared her to carry her out.

There his luck ran out on him. Footsteps approached from down the hall, and he wondered if his excitement hadn't clouded his alertness to pick the sound up sooner. He didn't have much time to react, so instinctively, he quickly kissed her dry, chapped lips and closed the door behind him. There was only time to step to one side to remain out of sight.

Hidden in the dark, Kipner crouched with his pistols ready and raging bloodlust in his eyes.

Just before they entered, the footsteps stopped. Through the closed door came a muffled sound of someone muttering in a monotone voice. Suddenly, the room was illuminated without a light source.

The door swung open without being pushed, and a man confidently strode in with his head swiveled toward Kipner's hiding spot as if he knew all along.

Wonderfully dressed, the man wore an elaborately tailored three-piece suit accented with a matching fedora and a cane with the head of a golden serpent. He was relatively older than Kipner, judging by the wrinkles. Still, as he walked into the room, an aura of energy warned him not to underestimate him.

With the alluring smile of a snake oil salesman, he broadly grinned down at Kipner, who realized his pistols were no longer in his grasp.

They were nowhere to be found.

"My...My...My," the man said, dramatically taking his time to express how surprised he was. "Never in a thousand years would I have made a guess that I would see you again, my dear friend. How the times have changed."

Behind him were several armed guards that pointed their rifles at Kipner. Out of the corner of his eye, he saw Lucy shielding her eyes from the sudden brightness of the room and trying to see what was going on.

He knew this man, Kipner thought quickly. It was from a memory he knew before, but this one was far more vivid and striking than the others. The name rang in his mind, and he remembered the past. Like a thunderbolt, a wave of thoughts struck through his mind of the horrible deeds this man had done to him. How he had ruined his life, and how he had tried to murder him.

"Delven," he said. "I know you."

It delighted Montgomery to hear this, and he laughed heartily to his guards. "He knows me. What a relief. And here I was expecting an embrace from a long-lost friend."

Montgomery extended both arms with the invitation, but Kipner remained poised on the ground. Disappointed, he lowered his arms.

"No? I suppose I was too ambitious. Your memory still is cloudy, it would seem. No matter, it will return as I trigger them with a walk down memory lane. Come," Montgomery said as he strode as confidently out as he did in. After Kipner hesitated to follow, his condescending tone invited the guards to help show him the way. He was seized by two, with a third trailing behind.

Through the hallways, they went until Montgomery stopped in the room with the single doorframe.

How was this all possible, Kipner thought to himself as he was held firmly by the two men. The last encounter he had with Montgomery came to focus. He remembered holding a relic in his hand. A mirror. It entrapped Delven, who was torn to shreds by some monster of the Old Ones. Afterward, it was given to his old friend Renaldo for safekeeping.

Just as Delven dramatically spread his arms in preparation to begin a grand speech, Kipner interrupted and asked how he escaped the mirror. It soured Delven's moment, which wiped the smile from his face.

"Ah, is that what is most puzzling to you? Not why I am here in the past, how I got here, or what marvels I have uncovered since my arrival. No, of course not. Your concern is solely focused on an irrelevant fact. It's a pity. I had hoped your unique upbringing in this life would have shed more intelligence upon your doltish mind. Very well, simpleton Kipner."

Sighing, he lowered his arms and leaned heavily on his cane.

"Your eagerness and short-sidedness to step through the door, similar to the one behind me, cost you far more than you will ever know. You should have waited and learned how to use it entirely instead of blindly eradicating me.

"I spent decades learning powers few mortals possessed. They were simply given to you freely without agreeing to deals. Yet, you wielded them like Christmas toys, tearing them open only to break them through ignorance.

"Among the numerous setbacks suffered, I, like you, was given back the life you so graciously removed from me. Time and space, two subjects your dull whit never comprehended, were erased, rewritten, and warped by gods so powerful your sanity would fail at the thought. Does that satisfy you, Mr. Kipner?"

It wasn't surprising to him to hear how his actions stepping through the door caused far more damage than he initially realized. Until recently, he felt the only price he paid was his rebirth and shifting of his parents' existence back a century. Although detrimental to his family, he hadn't considered the more significant ramifications until he pieced together the puzzle that connected this life to the previous one and how many were affected.

Kipner nodded sarcastically. Montgomery looked at him, sighed, then turned back to the door frame.

"Then you should need no explanation as to what this magnificent device is," Delven said, returning to his elegant demeanor. "I will admit I was aware of your arrival long before you devised the plan to visit me. I have kept close ties with the Great Ones, anxious to awaken first among them.

"I was granted the foresight of you coming and have prepared for what you will do for me."

Gesturing to the door frame, it came alive. It swirled in a blur for a moment before arriving within the focus of a large chamber dominated by an enormous statue. Pillars stood to either side and were adorned with various markings and symbols all foreign to Kipner, yet he knew immediately where it was.

"Familiar to you," Montgomery said mockingly to help Kipner recall the sketch of the nightmarish creature he had hunted into Africa.

"Then you recall there was a gem. A red ruby that fit perfectly into a bracelet which those possessing it could manipulate many wondrous things."

Delven turned away from the portal and came up within nose length of Kipner. The older man's eyes were each replaced with mouths synchronizing in unison but at different pitches to give an eerily harmonized sound.

"They gave me the power of the portal, now able to travel as I wish without the great price you paid, but I seek the ruby for other means. My Great One has challenged me by cleverly hiding it in a different location than where you put it. You may be dimwitted, but that demon you bargained with gave you the insight to find it again."

Kipner drew his best poker face to hide his reaction.

Montgomery didn't know he had released Wraith into the world and no longer possessed the powers it granted.

If he should discover Kipner was useless to him, he was sure Delven would kill him.

Something briefly drew his attention from Montgomery out of the corner of his eye. Whatever, it was moved too quickly for him to get a good look, but he thought there was a pair. Something skittered out from the portal and disappeared through the concealed door leading to the surface.

"You will enter with me, and we shall see what your benevolent gift can find," Montgomery said. He boldly walked through the portal, signaling the guards to drag Kipner. They seemed not to be intimidated or fear the power of the doorway and roughly brought Kipner on through.

He remembered the place well now. The marshal craned his neck to look down the main hallway, hoping to see his old friend Renaldo charging to his rescue, but it was deserted.

Before the colossal statue, Montgomery fell to his knees. He spoke in a strange tongue, then kissed the feet of the monstrosity. Unlike Kipner's memory, the figure did not stir.

"Now, Mr. Kipner, save me the trouble of torturing you to death and show me where the bracelet is first," Delven said.

Kipner stood still. The guards threw him onto the ground roughly and seized him up again.

He groaned with pain as his head bounced off the hard surface.

After a moment of waiting, Montgomery sighed. "Mr. Kipner. Bobby. I have kept Lucy here in horrible conditions for almost a year. Just enough food and water to keep her alive until the day you arrived. I have granted freedom among my guards with her as they wish."

He allowed a long pause in hopes the thought would spark anger in Kipner. The marshal kept his poker face steady.

"I knew I would never be able to convince you otherwise, so I was relieved she came into my possession when she did. It was fortuitous, perhaps, but I know my Great One. His gift to me was her, so you would finish my task."

A soft whimper came behind them as Lucy was carried like a sack through the portal. Kipner could not hold back at the sight of her and began to furiously fight against the two strong oxen Montgomery had brought for guards. He wasn't getting out of their grasp.

"I will begin with harming her just enough that she doesn't die but suffers greatly. It won't be the first time, either. I know her threshold precisely," Montgomery said as he snickered and approached Lucy.

Writhing in fury, Kipner shouted with saliva foaming at the corners of his mouth. "You lay a finger on her, Monty, and I will personally deliver you to Hell."

It had been a long time since Delven had been called out by his nickname, and he shivered at the disdain from hearing it. Slowly turning to face Kipner, he said, "Hell will be a paradise to hide after the Great One awakens."

He returned to Lucy, withdrew a wickedly curved knife from inside his coat, and gently traced its sharp tip down Lucy's cheek, allowing a trickle of blood to flow.

"No!" Kipner shouted, furiously fighting in vain to free himself. "Fine, Puppet! You'll just be discarded like the rest of us after they are done with you."

He calmed down and looked toward the pillars. With a nod, he was escorted near it, and he placed the palm of his hand on one of the symbols. He had no idea how he had settled on that one in particular. It was entirely random.

Montgomery was no fool and looked at him with doubt as he inspected the spot he had touched. Gingerly Delven reached out with his fingers as if scared it might bring him harm. The surface became liquid, and his fingers passed through.

To the astonished looks of everyone, Montgomery slowly pulled out the same bracelet from before. His greedy eyes jubilantly lit up, and he savored the moment he slipped it on.

Ignoring Kipner and the guards, he slowly approached where the red ruby was embedded and touched it just as lightly with the bracelet hand. It practically fell out of its socket and into his hand.

Eagerly he placed it into the cavity that bore the same diameter, and it locked into place.

"For far too long, I have waited for this moment to repeat itself," he said slowly, gaping wildly at the bracelet. "I have followed your instructions so closely all the while. I am humbled by the gift you graciously granted me today. Thank you."

Montgomery slowly walked toward the portal in a trance, still staring longingly at the gem. The guards looked at each other, and one questioned what to do with the prisoners.

"They matter not to me now," he answered, stepping through the portal. Do as you would enjoy, but I am closing the door..."

Realizing the impact of Montgomery's words, they dashed toward the opening, dragging Kipner like a doll behind. The fourth guard, trailing behind the other three with prisoners, came just short of entirely passing through and left a portion of himself in both locations.

With Montgomery gone, the guards dragged the prisoners outside and tossed them to the ground. The rest of the guards, twenty in all, gathered around to argue who would get the honor of shooting them.

All Kipner could do was hold Lucy in his arms, feeling her weak heartbeat below her thin skin. All she could whisper was "Bobby" over and over. She tried to follow it with something, but her voice failed each time.

The arguing finally ended with the decision to fire upon them simultaneously. They formed a line and loaded their bullets into the chamber.

Kipner's hopeless mind was breaking. He had faced countless creatures, dealt with Old Ones, and lived two separate lives. Yet all that had come tragically to an abrupt end to simple mercenaries and one conniving monster who struck a deal to become a puppet. In one fleeting moment of thought, it felt like a long journey to be wasted instantly.

More than twenty rifles were raised as laughter ended, and they all took aim.

Lucy whispered from under filthy hair, held in his arms, "You came back to me."

All around them, gunfire boomed and shattered the jungle's noise. Bullets rattled quickly in succession like the loud chattering of shivering teeth.

Screams rang out but not from Kipner or Lucy. Behind them, the guards shouted and were quickly silenced in seconds. As soon as the burst of firearms began, silence returned.

Waiting a second in fear, Kipner slowly lifted his head from the ground to see a line of bodies riddled with bullet holes before them.

Each one still held their rifles in their hands, but none moved.

Chitter came from the edge of the clearing where the vegetation grew thick. Two dark faces, no more than a few feet off the ground, poked through the plants and stared at Kipner. Two Pygmies, one holding a tin can and the other a strange metallic knife emerged and approached the two prisoners. Despite their short height, they squatted closer to Kipner, still lying on the jungle floor, and got their faces affectionately close. One reached out with both hands, gently patted Kipner's cheeks, and lightly squeezed them. Both laughed at each other and chittered more.

Finally coming to his senses and realizing he wouldn't die, he gathered himself and gently lifted Lucy off the ground. The Pygmies, seeing the frail Lucy resting in his arms, went to work. One held out the can for the other to open it with the metallic device. It smelled of tuna, slightly pungent but not intolerable. They offered it to Lucy.

Kipner's eyes filled with tears as he gently fed a few pieces to her. He now fondly remembered of his two lost friends. He owed them his life from before and had wished he had the chance to thank them. Now it was twice.

"I can't offer enough of my thanks to you both," he said with a broken voice. "How did you get here..."

He trailed off in astonishment as he felt Lucy begin to stir.

Where she was near death a moment earlier, she gradually became more alive in his arms. Although still frail, her expression was herself again, and she smiled broadly.

"Bobby! Oh, I can't believe you came for me!" she began to cry and threw her arms around his shoulders, holding him as best as her strength allowed.

The Pygmies nodded in agreement, smiled at the two, then headed back inside.

Kipner was so overwhelmed by the change in Lucy he didn't notice them vanish around the corner. After several kisses and a long, caring hug, he finally looked around to see his little companions gone.

I hope you find your way back, my friends, Kipner thought as he lowered Lucy to her feet and braced her. At least he was lucky enough to thank them after all these years. Still, he wondered who they really were.

Perhaps he had more guardian angels looking after him than he realized.

There was no straightforward answer to how the guards died when Kipner and Lucy inspected them. All of their weapons had been fully discharged. Somehow they had fired upon each other instead. It would remain a mystery to him just how the two fellows pulled it off, but he knew there were more secrets to this world than he would ever know. He was partially grateful for that fact, too.

High overhead, dark clouds began to rapidly gather in an unnatural pattern. They swirled into a central focal point and slowly descended into a funnel.

"Monty," Kipner said. "What is he doing?" With his aid, Lucy could walk, but not very briskly.

"Oh no, Bobby," she said, trying desperately to walk faster than her malnourished legs would allow. "He's using the beacon!"

They hobbled toward the chaos with Kipner's bandaged ankle keeping them equally slow.

As she gasped to catch her breath, not used to exerting that much effort, she told him how Montgomery had been looking for the artifact to evoke the beacon. She had learned while overhearing them for the past year it was used by the Aztecs centuries ago to amplify their rituals used to keep the Old Ones from waking. Something would be placed before specific markers, and the sun's beam would reflect onto each in order. She'd never seen the markings before and needed a cipher to translate. Montgomery knew the beacon would boost powers and planned to unleash the gem. Reversely to the Aztec's intentions, it would accelerate the awakening of one of the Old Ones.

"You were the missing piece to my puzzle," Kipner said almost to himself as he remembered the Wraith's clue. "And I was your missing piece."

Lucy looked up at him with questioning eyes. The blue radiance still glowed brightly against the overcast sky.

"I found five books with strange markings that match a collection of stones that I brought," he said as they reached the rim of the beacon.

Far below, Montgomery stood alone at the pedestal, arms raised in a V and the gem lying on top.

"You're a genius, Bobby," Lucy said while continuing to find the strength to return to her. The peculiar food fed to her by the Pygmies had a wonderfully positive effect on her, but there was no time to ponder.

"Give me the stones and the books. I'll see if I can figure them out. I can't deal with him. That's the Wraith's job," she said with confidence. She winked at Kipner and accepted the stones and books he had, then took off as fast as she could walk down into the beacon.

Kipner could now see the thousands of markings that lined the rings within the bowl and wondered how she would find them all in a lifetime.

He limped down the curve with his injured ankle, slipping midway at the hidden degree change. Montgomery was in a trance as he cast whatever power he had and didn't notice Kipner's proximity. Kipner wasn't aware of the second slope change and toppled his way down into the basin, sending pain shooting through his wounds.

"It has already begun, Mr. Kipner," came the voice of Montgomery from all around. The bowl enhanced the decibels, and he spoke like an actor in an amphitheater. "Your broken ankle and brittle girlfriend are far too late. Try as you wish, though."

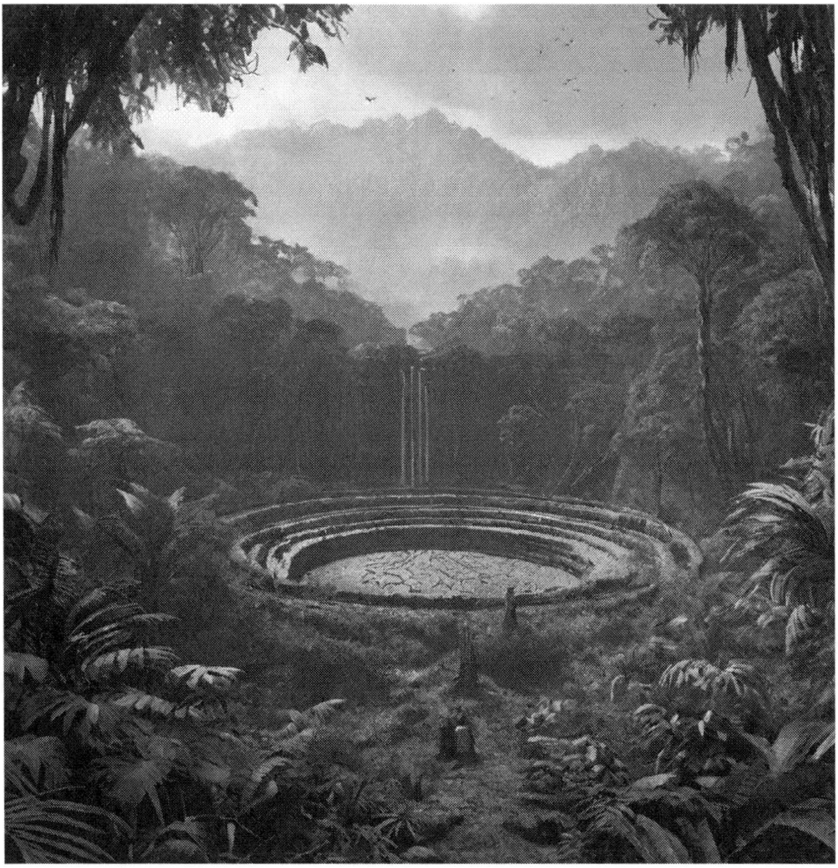

In the darkness of the rings, Lucy began to find the order she was after. Her bargains made before did not help her now, and she was forced to strike new ones with untold forces. She could feel her eyes water as she went from book to book in the order she now knew to perform. The pattern burned in her brain with fire, driving her to the ground in pain as she clawed at her face. Like no other headache, she felt her brain throb within her skull, causing the bone to crack and give way to the increased size. She tore her hands away, covered in blood from what she thought was water dripping from her eyes, and forced herself to take one step at a time to each placement, where a matching stone was set into the divot in front.

Kipner got up from his feet, wincing in pain as he tried to tackle Montgomery having no guns. Some force around his adversary blocked his way, and he slammed into it. He placed his hands on the invisible shield and tried desperately to find a way past it.

High overhead, the funnel grew long, extending toward the ruby gem that brightly glowed, casting them all in a sea of red light.

Kipner's mind sought any information he knew from his past life, and it suddenly hit him. He had control, but it had never been because of the Wraith. Powers granted to him were dramatically enhanced by the demon within. Still, he remembered his feats and the desire that drove them. He didn't need the monster.

He was the Wraith. His eyes darkened as he turned to Montgomery. Out from the beacon's rings emerged the horror that started it all. Numerous long tendrils, black as pitch and covered with sucking lesions, pulled their way out from the Dreamlands and into the world. Kipner willed it forward, allowing it to grab ahead of the marshal's body to move across the base toward Delven. Its tendrils wrapped harmlessly around Kipner, a sight he once feared and dreaded, launching itself into the shield. The force that kept Kipner away was nothing to the creature from Elsewhere.

The sight broke Montgomery's concentration as he turned to face the creature again. However, he was better prepared and empowered this time, engulfing the creature with bright, white light. The brilliance of the illumination chewed away at the black ooze that made up its membrane, and it was gone.

"It took you too long to perform at the level I knew you could," Montgomery bellowed. "It's a shame your slow-minded thinking couldn't have ...oof!"

Blocking the fiery pain in his ankle one last time, Kipner launched himself into Montgomery with an incredible gamble the summoned creature had eradicated the invisible field. His luck stayed with him, and he sent Montgomery to the ground.

Without a loss of breath, Delven began laughing once he was pinned by the arms. The maniacal laughter rippled through Kipner's core, awakening past visions of countless times he had caused pain, anguish, frustration, and sadness. The cruel man used him as a puppet for so long, Kipner's very existence was crippled.

The anger inside him overwhelmed him, and Kipner grabbed Montgomery's throat with both hands and squeezed. With clenched teeth, the marshal shouted, "I've craved to do this all my life! You ruined me, and I want to ensure I don't have to do this..."

Kipner's grip went limp, and his face was covered in painful shock.

The continued laughter of Montgomery turned to child-like giggling as a third arm, jutting out from his chest, retracted a wicked blade from Kipner's chest. The wound struck deep and true to his heart, and he fell back, leaning on the pedestal as he clutched his chest.

Circling madly above, the funnel bore down upon the gem. Lucy laid the final stone down its rightful spot and stared in horror at the last instruction.

"Oh no," she muttered while, unaware, far below, Kipner struggled for his life. She felt the blood cascade down her cheeks as she finalized the ritual, knowing her blood would suffice and appease the power she invoked.

She turned and ran down the bowl, suddenly seeing Kipner dying before Mongtomery. Holding the blade in his hand, Delven loomed over the body, and Lucy screamed out, knowing she would not make it in time.

Like a bolt from a god, the crackling boom of a high-powered rifle exploded and echoed violently across the beacon. Its deadly and accurate bullet pierced Delven Montgomery and sent him to the ground headless.

Too wounded to look, Kipner bled upon the pedestal as Lucy reached him, screaming in fear as she cradled her love. The marshal lay with silent, staring eyes at the body of Montgomery, and he slowly exhaled his final breath.

The giant funnel receded to the sky, forcing the clouds to dissipate and return to blue.

High along the edge of the beacon, the silhouette of a rotund figure stood in silent mourning in remembrance of a friend from another time.

"I finally shot the monster, my dear friend." He wiped the tears from his eyes. "I'm sorry, my boy. Your destiny was written." A gentle, warm breeze swept across green leaves, and the figure was gone.

The beacon shuddered as the blood of Kipner seeped onto the pedestal, the final step Lucy had dreaded to read. It had said only the blood of someone awakened could keep others asleep. To be awakened meant far more than slumber, Lucy knew from years of studies. It meant possessing a quality stronger than his foes, including his inner demons. It would drive a person through turmoil, fear, and doubt, so if life became hopeless, that one quality would push them through it all. She knew Kipner had the one thing that resisted the endless attacks. It was one thing that made her love him through the years.

His heart.

EPILOGUE

Kipner woke in his study in London. He was sore from a night with his head on his desk but otherwise well rested. The late night had been consumed by skimming over a few volumes of books he had received from Renaldo covering what little was known of Gobekli Tepe, a religious neolithic site in southeast Turkey. He wiped the accumulated moisture from the edge of his mouth and blinked awake.

Natasha, with beautiful blond hair and deep, piercing blue eyes, looked upon him with concern from across the desk.

"Mr. Kipner, did you sleep here? That's unlike you. Are you feeling okay?" she asked, leaning over the desk and gently brushing the tangled hair from his face.

He did feel okay. In fact, he felt better than he had in years – perhaps all his life. No headaches, no paranoia, no sight of booze or smokes in sight. His mind was clear and focused.

"I feel terrific, Lu... Natasha," he said, barely catching himself. He looked at her with a genuinely warm smile. She bore a striking resemblance to someone he thought he remembered before. Still, the name was a fleeting glimpse of a thought then vanished forever.

She returned the smile with relief and excitement dancing in her eyes.

"Well, you still need to pack for the Gobekli Expedition, Mr. Kipner. The archaeologists are anxious to finally meet the great Robert Kipner!"

He felt odd to hear her say such flattering words, but somehow he knew the words were true. He was an archaeologist, though it always felt like he nearly missed his chance in another life. Sometimes he wondered if he really was one or only dreaming. Either way, no one stood in his way now or could thwart his dream. He was in control.

A thought crossed his mind as he studied the beauty of the sweet smile of his secretary. There was more to her than he knew, something mysterious and intelligent about her that he had always wanted to find out but was always caught up in unpleasantness.

"Would you like to have dinner with me tonight?" he asked her confidently. It was as if he was meant to ask her all this time but never realized it until now.

Like a schoolgirl being kissed for the first time, her face lit up joyfully.

"Why, Mr. Kipner! What a surprise! I always wanted... yes, I'd love to!"

Kipner took his neatly folded jacket off the back of the chair, and Natasha helped him put it on. Subconsciously he reached into one pocket though he didn't know what drove him to do so. Like always, his fingers traced the matchbook given by the cleaners whenever Natasha picks up his suit. He smiled at her and turned off the light to the study.

After locking the door that read "Robert Kipner, Ph.D. - Archaeology" across the frosted glass, he offered his arm to the lovely lady.

He winked and said," Call me Bobby."

Made in the USA
Columbia, SC
19 November 2023

e597c4fd-f556-442e-839e-1f397d455558R01